RH
Hold

St. Helens Libraries

Please return / renew this item by the last date shown. Items
may be renewed by phone and internet.

Telephone: (01744) 676954 or 677822
Email: libraries@sthelens.gov.uk
Online: sthelens.gov.uk/librarycatalogue

Nov

1 7 NOV 2020

- 4 JUN 2022

STHLibraries   sthlibrariesandarts   STHLibraries

ST HELENS LIBRARIES

Published by Darlington Press Australia

ISBN: 978-0-6483691-0-3

MICHAEL

BOOK THREE OF THE TRIPTYCH CHRONICLE

Darlington PRESS

AUSTRALIA

Characters

Michael Sarapion – Byzantine. A merchant working for Saul ben Simon and Guy of Gisborne. Married to Jehanne de Clochard of Lyon

Dana – also known as Jehanne de Clochard. Worked as an embroiderer and tailoress in Constantinople and as an *espie* for Gisborne

Tobias Celho – famed minstrel and troubadour. Friend of Blondel and singer of songs for the courts of Europe

Tomas Celho – deceased twin brother of Tobias and enemy of the Byzantine Empire

Ariella ben Simon – only child of Saul, accomplished merchant and friend to the Gisborne and de Clochard houses. Betrothed to Guillaume de Gisborne

Guillaume de Gisborne – Deceased betrothed of Ariella. Half-brother of Guy, formerly an Angevin archer in the Third Crusade. Lately a merchant

Ahmed – Gisborne's trader, sailing the Middle Sea, Adriatico, Sea of Marmara

Faisal – Ahmed's second

Yusuf Al Fayyad – spice merchant of Gallipolis

Father Nicholas – a priest from the Church of Saint Stephen near Agathopolis

Father Symeon – a priest from Sancta Sophia

Father Giorgios – a monk in charge of the church on Limnos

Christophorus – also known as Christo. Notary for Gisborne-ben Simon in Constantinople. Manager of the merchant house in Basilike Street

Ephigenia – housekeeper at Basilike Street and related to Christo and Phocus

Phocus – former galley slave and now guard at Basilike Street

Bonus – a former galley slave, friend of Phocus and now guard at Basilike Street

Julius – from Cyprus. A former mercenary from the Balkan front and now a guard at Basilike Street

Hilarius – a Chaldian from Trabzon. Served as a mercenary in the Balkans with Julius, and Leo. Now a guard at Basilike Street

Leo – from Khorasan. Ex-Byzantine mercenary from the Balkan front and now a guard at Basilike Street

Pietro Vigia – a Genovese merchant who met his end after he had denounced Tobias' brother, Tommaso, to the Byzantine authorities

Branco Izzo – a Genovese merchant

Pieta Izzo (formerly Vigia) – Branco's wife and a member of the Genovese trading family, the Vigia. Sister to the deceased Pietro Vigia

Anwar al Din – Arab physician to the nobility in Constantinople. Brother to Mehmet, physician to the house of Gisborne in Venezia

Fatima – a female Arab physician

Ignatios Trafines – master jeweller to Gisborne-ben Simon

Nāsir – an Arab *peirate*

Giacomo Contarini – member of the powerful Contarini family of Venice

*Tommaso Viadro – famed Venetian explorer and trader

*Isaac II Angelus – former Emperor of Byzantium

*Alexios III Angelus – Emperor of Byzantium

*George II Xipphillinus – Patriarch of the Byzantine Christian Church

*'I left Sistan with merchants of fine robes.
The robe I bore was spun within my heart.
And woven from my soul.'*

Farrukhi Sistani 11th century

αρχή
(BEGINNING)

×

The canvas gave an almighty crack, the sound harsh – like a whip cracking or a thighbone snapping. The trading galley fell off the wave and Michael Sarapion glanced up, then turned quickly to examine the sea behind. At first, the following sail showed like a wavelet, the sea lumpy on the horizon. But the vessel gained on them as their own craft, loaded with salt, wine and grain from Sozopolis, sat low in the water. Michael Sarapion thought nothing of it until a nervous hum began to vibrate across the decks from the men. The shipmaster ordered them to the oars, his voice strained as he yelled. 'Your lives depend on it! Pull!' He yanked on the sail ropes, calling on Allah for speed and for their lives...

Michael's wife, Helena, chewed on her lip, and his daughter, Ioulia, searched her papa's face for reassurance. He asked them to sit beneath the canopy and then quizzed the shipmaster.

'What is it, think you?' He indicated the approaching *dromon* which lifted on the tailwind, cutting through the wave at a frightening pace. It was narrow and light and had ten oars either side. She would catch them soon enough.

'*Peirate,*' spat the shipmaster. 'We can't outrun her, we have too much weight. Arm yourself.'

'You would fight them?'

'To survive, yes. For you, I think of your women...'

It was unnecessary to say more. The slave trade for females of suitable age was flourishing. Michael's heart began to pound.

1

His hand slipped to his *paramerion,* bought from an Arab trader. His wife had laughed when he buckled it on before they had departed, but he merely replied, 'I have to get it to Constantinople somehow…'

'It makes you look fierce,' said his daughter. 'None would dare come near you if you waved it in their face!'

And now the blade held value.

He caught his wife studying him with concern as he unfastened his cloak and threw it over barrels of salt. He grimaced and clenched his fist, tapping his chest near his heart and her smile was small in response – an anxious expression but a smile nevertheless. She was a strong woman, had survived two stillborn children to bear Ioulia and he knew she could handle a knife as well as a man. After all, he had taught her.

The approaching *dromon* was within hailing distance and the shipmaster stood in the stern of his own to call a greeting. The *dromon*'s intimidating bow lifted over the swell, oars rolling in perfect unison in their locks, creaking above the sound of the hissing sea.

The reply, when it came, was definitive.

A barbed arrow whacked into the shipmaster's chest, driving deep and killing him in an instant. He flopped forward onto the wale and then toppled into the waves, the attacking vessel rolling over the top of him.

Ioulia shrieked and went to stand but Helena grabbed her hand and pulled her down, dragging her between rows of barrels.

The *peirate* ordered oars on the trading vessel to be shipped and the sail furled, the *dromon* drawing alongside, larboard oars also shipped, sail shortened. Hooks impaled the wales of the trader and the two vessels clung to each other like lovers. The only voices were loud shouts as a part of the attacking crew jumped aboard.

Michael grabbed his cloak and flung it across the gap in which his family hid and stood in front of the barrels, praying to God above to spare the women. Swarthy or bald, turbaned or capped, six seamen and their master stood with robes flapping around them. They were armed with daggers, swords and menace and Michael tried to anticipate the moment.

The crew of the trading vessel were quickly lined up, obeying without a murmur. The message had been given on the end of a barbed arrow – they would not dispute it. Michael watched them as much as he observed the attackers, seeing a cunning desperation as they stood taller, bulked out their arm muscles, showed they had value at the oar.

'You!' The lead *peirate* slapped the one closest – a vicious backhand that might have sent anyone else flying off their feet. This man however was taller than anyone on the boat, and dusky. Perhaps from the Maghreb – prodigious in physique, so that Michael wondered at the *peirate*'s idiocy in treating him so.

But the man remained docile in front of his fellow crew and in front of the *peirate*.

'Who of you is the shipmaster?' the *peirate* growled up into the sailor's face. He was middle aged, gnarled, whip-thin and angry, and his rat's tail hair hung from beneath a badly folded *keffiyeh*.

The giant answered in fractured Greek but his answer was easy enough to understand. 'He's dead. You killed him.'

Another crack across the face. 'Who is in command then?'

The sailor had bunched his Herculean fist but then let it hang loose and Michael breathed a sigh of relief. 'Me. I am his second,' the man's voice rumbled from deep within his cavernous chest.

Are you? I did not know. Or do you protect your fellows?

The *peirate* eyed him over, stepping back, gauging the fellow's value on ship and at the slave markets.

'Your cargo?'

'Salt, wine, some extra goods for Constantinople.'

The *peirate* gestured for one of his own to come forward with ropes and the man was tied hands and feet. Three others also whereupon they were urged to hobble to the wales to climb awkwardly onto the *dromon*. The big second managed it with no problem as the vessels rose and fell in the swell, the wood of larboard and starboard sides screeching. But as the second fellow, shorter and not as agile, swung his legs over the side, the ships dipped and he hung balancing for one moment too long. With hands tied, he scrabbled frantically at the wet wale and then fell between the vessels as they scraped side by side again. There was a punctuated scream and then nothing as the unearthly screech of wood against wood filled the gap.

Not a word was spoken from the trading vessel crew. Those left on the galley watched, the whites of their eyes showing and sweat staining their chemises, but they minded themselves in desperation.

The *peirate* turned then and Michael's heart rate lifted another notch as their eyes met. The man swaggered over, hand still holding his *kilij*. Michael gripped his own.

'And you,' his breath smelled of cloves which he chewed as he spoke. 'What are you?'

'A passenger. Travelling from Sozopolis to Constantinople.'

'Why?'

'I begin work there as a merchant.'

'Is this your cargo?'

'No.'

'Lucky for you. Move away from the barrels...'

The dilemma of it all flashed through Michael's mind. If he moved away, his family might be revealed. If he did not, something might happen to *him*...

'They are filled with salt,' he said.

'I would see for myself. Move!' The *peirate* pushed him aside and whipped Michael's cloak away. Helena and Ioulia crouched in the shadows, Helena's arm round her daughter.

God, safe in Your heaven, from this moment, You are dead to me!

'Salt? More likely something sweet, I think,' the *peirate* said, his own voice cloying. But then it hardened like honey left too long on a shelf. 'Out!'

Helena looked at Michael and all he could do was nod back. She squeezed past her daughter, coming out first, and holding her hand behind her back to Ioulia but standing protectively, shielding her as best she could.

'You are?'

'They are my wife and daughter. Leave them...'

The *peirate* laughed. 'Or what? You are a prisoner, *my* prisoner, and judging by your appearance, you will make coin for me at the slave markets. But not, I think, as much as these little things will.' He turned back to the women. 'Take off your cloaks and tunics.'

'No!' Michael stepped forward but the *peirate*'s *kilij* pointed at his belly.

'Do as I say,' the Arab warned as the point of the *kilij* pressed harder against Michael. 'Or else this man will be disembowelled.'

Helena's eyes never left Michael's as she took off her cloak, her veil, her damascened girdle and then pulled her tunic over her head. She stood in her skirt, bare skin showing to all who watched. Her gaze met the *peirate's* – no shame, only courage.

'You!' The *peirate* ordered Ioulia.

Helena whispered as the young woman stood frozen, 'Look at me, Ioulia. Do what he asks but look at me.'

Michael's heart cracked as his family stood half naked, inspected like goats in the marketplace. Tears slipped down Ioulia's face but she stood next to her mother, upright, the two holding each other's hands.

The *peirate* held Helena's face in his dirty palm and on the surface of the hand, Michael saw a tattoo of a half moon. The man squeezed his fingers into Helena's mouth, feeling her teeth and then running his hands over her body. He moved to Ioulia and she flinched as she was touched, crying as he squeezed and palmed her youthful breasts. 'What languages do you speak?'

'Latin and Greek,' Helena replied and as if sensing the doom approaching them with speed and wanting to secure the best outcome, she added, 'and we both write and count numbers and we can cook and stitch.'

Michael squeezed his eyes shut so that spots danced, shaping and reshaping into a tattoo of a half moon.

God, are You listening? You are nothing to me from this moment...

That morning, on the harbour wall at Sozopolis, the sky had been as clear as a *poûs* of blue silk – not a blemish. But the breeze from the northeast had been brisk and fractious waves smacked against the larboard bow of the merchant galley as she waited for the last of the cargo to be loaded and for her passengers to embark.

The Sarapion household were leaving Sozopolis for Constantinople. Michael was to work for the Venetian-based Jewish merchant, Saul ben Simon, and would be sourcing goods from across the Speris Zǧua – the Black Sea. His abiding interest, compatible with his Jewish friend, was silken cloth from beyond Trabzon, but he was not averse to scouring the trade routes for other valuable commodities.

The move from the Black Sea to the Bosphoros filled Michael with hope and energy. He had been unable to help the smile when the document had arrived from Venezia a month before. To be tied to a merchant house of the stature of ben Simon. He had met Saul once – at a market in Constantinople.

The two were of kindred minds – goods to be found and money to be made, but a deep respect for the artisans and craftsmen who made the goods.

Helena had never lived outside Sozopolis but Michael, born in Trabzon, filled her with his confidence and thus she grew to believe that only good fortune would come with the move. Twelve-year-old Ioulia looked toward Constantinople every day, for what eligible and attractive woman would not want to live in the pearl of Byzantium's crown?

And now their future was to be determined by their physicality and abilities – valued like a she-camel or a goat. How could such a day have changed so quickly? Hopes dashed on the break of a wave.

'Let them go. I will pay you…'

'You have coin?' The *peirate*'s eyes sparkled.

'Some…' Michael reached into the purse that hung from his belt. He tipped out four *hyperpirons*.

'And that is all?' the *peirate* said in disbelief. 'You think I could not double or triple that with the sale of these women?' He grabbed the coins from Michael's palm and thrust them into the folds of his sash, calling for more rope. Michael and the women were trussed but left to stay on the trading vessel as part of the *peirate*'s crew split to sit at the oars with what was left of the trading vessel's men.

Within moments, the vessels were unlashed, oars pushed out and they began to move through the water, the trading galley guarded at the starboard side, shepherded toward the Thracian coast, the sea even choppier and the wind beginning to keen through the shrouds.

'Michael?' Helena whispered.

He shook his head. 'I don't know…' He felt more impotent than a feeble grandfather. Trussed and disarmed. 'Have faith…'

Ioulia said nothing, but her trembling limbs betrayed her fear.

'Listen to me, both of you. You have told them you have value. You will not be hurt. Have courage.'

'And you?' Helena asked.

'I must show him I have value also.'

The ships continued across the uneven sea as the day slipped ever closer to dusk, the sky filled with birds wheeling on the rough updrafts. Michael thought land was close – he could not see between the cargo and over the wale but he thought they might find shelter soon. Ioulia slept, despite the damp journey, slumped on her mother's shoulder, and Helena whispered as low as she could.

'Michael, we will be separated…'

'Most like.'

Her breath sucked in with a dry sob.

'Courage, my heart,' he said. 'It is all I can offer you. Just remember – you and Ioulia are the loves of my life.'

And as the words left his mouth, a Black Sea night descended and they both sat with their daughter, unable to believe their life had disintegrated to almost nothing.

'Try to sleep,' he offered. He had nothing else, not even able to smooth her hair.

'I can't,' she replied and he liked that her voice held no tremor.

But she dozed anyway as about them, the sea rose further. As a larger wave slid toward them, both Ioulia and Helena woke with a start, Michael urging,

'Keep calm. It's alright. We'll be wet, that's all…'

But the rowers could barely dip their oars and the yelled order came to ship them. One jumped up, slithering and sliding to the stern where he helped the helmsman hold the rudder so that the ship could continue to run with the wind behind, sail shortened to almost nothing. Whilst the darkness gave Michael concealment, he worked feverishly at his bonds, wriggling and pulling and using his teeth. The ropes had softened in the storm and he made headway, loosening enough to pull one hand out. With speed, he unlooped the other, hearing a roar, a booming sound.

'*Petrómata! Petrómata!* Rocks! Rocks!' shrieked a crewman at the bow and the men at the helm pulled with everything they possessed, shouting as they heaved the boat slightly to larboard.

But she was heavy and slow and Michael ripped the last of the ropes from his feet and began pulling at Helena's.

'Ioulia!' she shouted above wave and wind. 'Free Ioulia!'

He shifted on his knees to his daughter, managing to get her hands free, leaving her to pull at her feet whilst he worked again at Helena's bonds. Just as he managed to get a knot free, a wave hit the three, almost dragging them to the wale. Ioulia slid to his side and began working on Helena's feet, struggling with the dark and the sea as it broached the vessel time and again.

And all the time, the ceaseless roar and crash of waves hitting rocks.

An almighty screech sounded, the bow climbed and the Sarapion family slid back, cargo breaking free and tumbling over and about them.

Shouting, yelling, shrieking from men all around them and bruising crashes as barrels rolled into them.

'Ioulia!' Michael grabbed her hand. 'Hold this!' He shoved her hand into a rope wrapped around a piece of fractured barrel. 'Hold it because it will float and save your life!

'Papa!' she cried.

'Do it! Helena, here, this one. Never let it go!' As he screamed at them above the maelstrom roar, another wave hit and the boat lurched to larboard, Ioulia and Helena tumbling with their hogsheads into the sea. Michael grabbed some debris closest to him as he too began to slide.

The ocean enfolded him in cold fingers and it tumbled and turned with him – a demonic fight he could never win, but he held tight to the rope round the timber, coughing, grabbing air and holding it in his chest. He began to kick away from the vessel as it broke around him, kicking with the fury and fear of someone who had been denied his dream but would not see it end in nightmare. He caught sight of Helena. 'Kick away, Helena. Kick as hard as you can! Ioulia! Ioulia!'

'Here, Papa!' his daughter coughed and yelled. 'Help me!'

'Kick away from the boat! Get away from the rocks!' he called back.

A wave smashed into his face as he yelled and he choked, gasping for air, kicking, always kicking. And when he could, calling to his wife and daughter. But a further wave lifted above him and crashed down with something in its foaming white paw, something heavy which knocked him senseless and he knew no more...

Life after death was a release.

He tried to lift his head, even an eyelid, but sank into blackness. By his ear an unrelenting seabird squawked, and he woke again, the sand cool beneath his cheek. His back was warm from the sun, his hands stiff, one still threaded through the ropes and timber lying next to him. He moved his arm a little but his hand stayed within the ropes. Hearing voices, he turned his head to face along the beach, staring into another next to him – puffy grey eyes unblinking, an expression of dismayed despair frozen into perpetuity. He recognised the man – the one who had tied up he and his family.

Ah, the Divine irony…

More barrels, more wood, more bodies.

'Dead!' a voice shouted. 'All drowned!'

'The cargo?' He recognized the *peirate*'s voice.

'Useless. All of it!'

Swearing drifted on the air, Michael glad the man had been frustrated, enjoying the colourful fury punctuating the seabirds' shrill calls. He lay as still as a corpse, desperate to search for his wife and daughter but knowing one move could spell the end for him.

The *peirate* ordered the crew back to the *dromon* which lay in the shallows. *Did they see me, touch me? Assume me dead?*

Sounds filled the air – of shouted orders, of oars dipping as the *dromon* reversed away from the shore, of the squeak of oars as the boat turned west, of the roll and flap as canvas was set. Of the *peirate*'s voice yelling about slave markets…

Michael waited, watching from the corner of his eye as the *dromon* headed westerly beyond the fateful sawtooth reef. In time, nothing sounded but seabirds and the most tentative wave and he released his hand from the rope grip, flexing the stiffness from it, hauling his gritty, bruised body up to gaze at the destruction along the small cove. The smashed cargo, boat wreckage floating back and forth and bodies loosely rolling as the incoming tide shifted them here and there.

Birds had settled on a corpse, fighting over eyes and glutinous tissue. Michael picked up a piece of timber and hurled it toward the scavengers. Anger at God, at the sea taking from him the two most valuable things in his life. Anger at his own folly for agreeing to work for ben Simon in Constantinople.

Drowned? Deep in the ocean?

He flung round and scoured the sea – checking the wreckage until he saw folds of turquoise and a limp figure toward the far end of the cove. He ran through the shallows, his heart racketing.

'Helena,' he grabbed the folds. 'Helena!'

She floated on her back, her hair wafting on the tide, her face tranquil, eyes closed. He thought how beautiful she looked – apart from the ugly blue bruise at her temple. But her pallor horrified him and he slipped his arms beneath her, whispering, 'Helena, my love. Wake up! See, we are safe…' But as he stood with her in his hopeless arms, her head lolled back.

'Helena,' he whispered, burying his head amongst her wet hair. 'I did not mean for this…'

For what? For she and Ioulia to die because of his ego; because of his desire to move upward in the trading game?

He carried her to the back of the beach where rocks lay at the base of cliff walls and laid her down with the tenderness of a man placing a child in its crib. As the sun moved toward dusk, he scooped a bed of gritty sand, covering her with a damp cloak from the shore and then placing small rocks on top, because he would not have sea-birds peck at her eyes and her decaying body.

At first, he could barely place one rock upon her and he walked away. But the seabirds shrieked and fought further down the beach and it was easier then, rock after rock. He offered prayers for her soul but inside a voice said, 'Hypocrite!' because he hated God. But he said the prayers anyway.

Finally, it was done and he kissed his fingers and touched the head of the rocky tomb, 'Helena, Ioulia is missing, my love. I…'

I what?

Will find her, he thought.

But as sure as Helena was now gone, in truth he knew his daughter was floating in the sea, rocked by the waves, and his heart set to stone. Somewhere, a Greek-speaking *peirate* with a *dromon* of God-forsaken slaves was looking to have a return on his assets. Michael would find him and recompense would be demanded.

An eye for an eye.

He lay down next to Helena's rocky tomb, pillowing his head on his arms and curling his legs into his belly like a newborn as the dusk shadows stretched down the beach. His head ached with a ferocious timbre, each heartbeat roughly measured. And as he felt himself slipping into the blackness of a faint again, he thought what a powerful drug was revenge. He might have been happy to die here and now, but he would find the *peirate* and he would kill him. If nothing else, as the black edges of unconsciousness claimed him, battle fever warmed his blood through.

'Ah,' a deep, gentle voice sounded from above him. 'You are awake.' Michael turned his head. The morning sun shone brightly and all he could see was a large black shape, with hairy sandalled toes half-buried in the sandy shingle. 'God has seen fit to return you to us, instead of taking you to His side.'

Michael pushed back the heavy cloak that covered him, feeling the roughness under his fingers, questions forming in his mind. But liverish, in pain and grief-stricken, he croaked, 'God is no friend of mine.'

He stood then, reaching to touch his pounding head, feeling congealed blood, and then a further warmth began to trickle down his neck.

I was hit on the head...

His losses hammered down upon him so that he could barely breathe, let alone move. He stumbled, and a strong hand held his elbow.

'You are injured and weak. You need care.'

Michael trembled – shock, illness and vestiges of the night cold, but the man held even more firmly as he bent and began to puke his guts away.

'You are ill. Come, we can help.'

Michael wiped his mouth and stood straighter, seeing the black robes of a priest, the cross swinging from his neck. 'No. My wife...' But his knees folded and the priest lowered him to the ground and sat beside him. Michael noticed men moving back and forth on the periphery, carrying bodies, disappearing up a track.

'I am Father Nicholas from the Church of Saint Stephen close by Agathopolis. When the storms hit, we always keep a close eye on the reef, but it is a long time,' he crossed himself, 'since we have seen such a thing.'

The priest had kind eyes which disappeared into the forest of his windblown hair and beard. He seemed wild, with none of the demeanour of the priests Michael had known in Sozopolis.

'We take the dead to bury in consecrated ground at the church. The cargo we leave for the sea to take back. You, my friend, are a lucky man to be alive. The reef rarely gives us survivors. But you need help – your head bleeds freely, you are thirsty and you shiver. I will help you...' He took Michael's arm.

'No! My wife! You don't understand.'

'I think I do,' Father Nicholas indicated the piles of rocks. 'You have buried her. But you need have no fear. We shall disinter her and carry her with the utmost respect to my church. She shall have a church burial under God's eyes.'

But Michael stood, unable to think.

'My son,' the priest's gentled voice seemed to drift in from faraway. 'You cannot think with clarity. Is it possible that you might just trust us to do what is right for your wife and thus for you?'

Michael tried to nod but once again pitched into black-as-death darkness.

Footsteps echoed on stone and Michael opened his eyes to a comfortable gloom. Around him he could see a wall of icons and yet he did not think he was in the church itself.

'Ah, good.' A mug was held to his lips and he sipped at clear, cool water.

'You have better colour,' Father Nicholas said.

'Thank you. The water is like nectar.' Michael's voice was husky, but he was nearer to living than the day before. Except…

'We have a small fall of fresh water when it rains. We make good use of it. We tire of wine.'

'Father Nicholas, my wife…'

'She has been washed and prepared by the women. They care for her.'

'Can I see her?'

'Yes…' Doubt hung in the air.

'I would say goodbye once more,' said Michael.

The priest sighed and stood. 'Do you feel strong enough to stand?'

Michael levered himself up, waited until his equilibrium returned and then followed Father Nicholas through a door.

Helena lay before the altar on a makeshift bier. She was wrapped in a linen shroud, her face clean, her hair pulled back. She smelled of rosemary and he laid his hand on her chest.

'The women do not have the skill to embalm but they have done their best by her. And I have a small space, a lovely place beneath an aged olive tree. The men have dug a grave for her there.'

No tears came. Michael just nodded his head and found the thread of revenge that he had lost. Whilst he ached with grief, he found he could go through the motions of a burial, the thread becoming a rope which anchored him to what he saw as a reality. After Helena had been interred beneath the shifting shade of the olive and when the women and men had scattered wild thyme upon the grave, and whilst dusk shadow moved once again across the sky, he turned to Father Nicholas.

'I thank you for your kindness, and whilst I am unable to repay you or the villagers, I will return one day. I swear.'

'There is no need. We merely do what is right,' the priest began to walk back to his living quarters, signalling Michael to follow. He closed the heavy wooden door behind them and poured wine into coarse mugs.

'A bad time, Michael Sarapion, but you must have faith that your life will turn.'

Michael grimaced. 'Not immediately, I think. I ache with my loss. It is more than anyone could imagine.'

'I know...'

'No, Father. You don't. I didn't just lose my wife.'

Father Nicholas took a swallow of his wine and sat on a stool. 'Go on,' he said.

Michael gulped his wine and sat on the other stool, facing the priest, placing the mug on the floor. He clasped his hands between his knees, his knuckles bleached white and shaking. 'I lost even more. You see, I had a daughter...'

CHAPTER ONE

×

1195AD

'The sea is all about give and take, Ariella.' Michael Sarapion stood with the Jewess at the prow of *Durrah*. Beneath them the water was as dark as midnight, as deep as an abyss, and waves creamed to form a hissing wash. Behind them, the sail cracked as the vessel slipped off course and then back on again.

'Then I shall give it a gift,' Ariella said, the breeze catching her dark veil and tossing it skyward. 'In the hope it takes nothing from me in the future.' Ariella's fiery hair had been concealed behind the dour cloth and in place of the coloured and embroidered *bliauts* of the past, she wore a dark tunic the shade of shadow. Her flamboyance had died with the love of her life, Guillaume de Gisborne, and Michael understood her grief. It sat with one forever, no matter if joy sat on the other side.

Michael watched her as she looked at the betrothal ring on her finger. He knew she had the strength of lions. It was the meaning of her name, after all. Ariella had fought for her life and those she loved often, and with a strength as strong as forged steel, but Guillaume de Gisborne's death had bent her, if not broken her.

She and Michael travelled to Constantinople to source goods for her father's trading house. It was perhaps Saul ben Simon's way of soothing his daughter's grief – to allow her to travel far, something she had craved but which he had

15

always forbade. Now he trusted Michael to guard her. They had been acquainted for long enough for trust to be a given. Besides, they were accompanied by Tobias, minstrel of fame throughout west and east and not unused to knife-wielding. She would have men of grace and courage to protect her.

Tobias had spent his life in disguise for Gisborne, ben Simon's partner. The minstrel was an ear in many courts, listening, catching messages between melodies, sending them back to Gisborne who then sold them on to the highest bidder. This sensitive visit to Constantinople however, required him to be himself. The officials knew him. He could not hide. As for Ariella, she was a merchant's daughter. She represented someone respected by the administration – a Venetian no less. Everyone knew the Venetians worked hard to have the ear of government.

It was a simple and straight forward voyage.

Almost…

Except for Michael.

He assumed the role of merchant. Of course he did.

But in fact, he travelled to the city to find a hog bristle needle in a pile of straw.

Ariella slipped off the sapphire ring.

It glistened in the white light of the Adriatico. It was a small, smooth midnight blue egg clasped by a circlet of twisted gold, Byzantine for sure, as Michael had told Guillaume when they found it deep in the *traboules* of Lyon.

She lifted it to her lips and kissed it, but just as she moved to hold it over the wale, Michael put his fist over hers.

'Think, Ariella. Once it is gone, you will have nothing of Guillaume.'

'Oh,' she replied, one hand lying at her waist. 'But I do. I have memories, and nothing can take those away. No, I give the sea my ring willingly in the hope it will take nothing from me ever. Indeed, in its own way, it may give me something back.'

He still compressed his hand over hers, wondering at her curious words, but then, observing pain so deep in her soul and sharing the experience with his own, he let her hand go. She kissed the ring again, held it out over the sea and it fell, taking a betrothal with it, lost in the sapphire tint of the wave.

'So tell me, Michael. What has the sea taken from you, or perhaps given back?'

'Taken.' He felt the familiar lash of loss across his chest and said, 'It is history and best left in the past.'

But in truth, it was why he was on *Durrah*. He had once paid a price for sailing away. A huge price. Lives lost at sea – dead, gone.

Or so he had thought.

Until a letter had arrived.

'The past *can* be murky,' Ariella said as she rubbed at her now naked finger. 'You are right in a manner of speaking. The only way is forward.' She wrapped her arms around herself and leaned back against the wale as Tobias joined them.

Michael liked the diminutive minstrel – witty and brave and quick on his feet. The two had survived against the odds the year before, in Constantinople. Toby's brother had not been so lucky.

'Ahmed says we are not far from the entry to the Hellespont, and for you, Ariella, to take a seat beneath the canopy where you will be safe. It is a challenge for *Durrah* on the tides.'

'Ahmed is an admiral in a *peirate*'s boots,' Ariella replied.

But she and the sharp-eyed Arab sea captain got on well. Michael was heartened by the group with whom he travelled. Human nature being what it was, it could have been very different. 'You will excuse me. I have had a thought about a trading contact and there are things I want to check in my ledger.'

In truth, he had the thought days ago – the one about a merchant in Gallipolis; it would serve to speak to him when they moored in the town and his comment had just been a ruse. No, what he really wanted was to read the letter again and in private and where better than concealed behind the wooden covers of his ledger.

Despite that he had read it so often – he knew every single word, every single inkspot – he needed to feel the parchment sheet beneath his fingers so that he knew it was real. To know *the words* were real.

To believe.

To hope.

He opened the ledger, the wooden covers creaking in protest at their leather bindings. And then he unfolded the parchment, already creased and broken with repeated openings and closings. It was written in close-scribed

Greek and uneven in its calligraphy, but from the man whose quill it had sprung, Michael knew it had legitimacy.

To Michael Sarapion from your friend in God, Nicholas of Saint Stephen, greetings.

I write to thank you for your continued charity. I have heard that you are far from us now and hope that God will see this through to your hands. I send it to an actuary I know in Constantinople. If you return to that city, I would suggest that, with God's blessing, you seek my brother in Christ, Symeon of Sancta Sophia. He knows of a cargo that was sold in Agathopolis some years ago. Perhaps when you lost your own.

I leave you, my son, with blessings from God in your endeavours. Σε ειρήνη. Se eiríni.

In peace indeed. Since that letter had arrived, he'd had barely a moment of peace, his heart lurching from a kind of latent euphoria to despair. Finally, his wife, Jehanne de Clochard, had urged him to return to Byzantium. 'You must see for yourself, Michael. It is the only way.'

When Michael had read Father Nicholas' words, his heart had leaped into his throat and he wondered if he would choke. The note was old; had travelled from Agathopolis to the mentioned actuary, thence to Venezia and then via courier to Lyon. Almost nine months had passed before it lay in Michael's hands, a creased and dirty roll with the wax seal almost entirely crumbled away. Someone had placed the Gisborne seal of three arrows over the top and tied the roll with a plait of red silk. *That* must have come from the hands of Lady Ysabel of Gisborne herself; he would bet his life upon it.

He found Father Nicholas' words ambiguous, maybe deliberately so, and wondered if the priest protected himself and his flock in case other eyes read the letter. Such a thing surely gave veracity to their meaning.

Lost cargo? Then sold?

Father Nicholas knew the cargo scattered around the cove had not been Michael's. He knew that Michael's cargo had been infinitely more precious, more valuable than the finest silks. He also knew that Michael's cargo would have been sold by an iniquitous man to the right buyer for more than the value of gems and dyes.

After all, Michael's *cargo* was young, nubile and skilled.

And beautiful. Just like her mother....

'Michael,' Ahmed called from behind him.

He shut the ledger with a snap and swung round to *Durrah*'s master.

'I wish to talk with you,' the Arab said, walking toward him, holding a fold of his robes which threatened to flap in the seawind. His bald head gleamed and he leaned against the mast. 'About Gallipolis. There is a...'

'Merchant. Yes. Many in Gallipolis. But the one of which you speak sells a fine line of frankincense resin.'

'Ah, my friend,' Ahmed laughed. It came from deep in the back of his throat. His voice too, a low register, slightly guttural, the kind that set women's loins tingling. His dark eyes glinted with ill-concealed avarice. 'We are the same, you and I. Cut from the same cloth, perhaps. So don't conceal what you truly want. It's not *olibanum.*'

For a moment, Michael held his breath. Was he so transparent that Ahmed could see he searched for his daughter? But no. Impossible. He smiled and placed his ledger in a bag containing the few belongings he carried to Constantinople – giving himself time. 'You are right. We are indeed similar. And because we understand each other, I will tell you. There is a rumour that quality alum has found its way from the Black Sea to Gallipolis and will be sold to the highest bidder. By our friend the spice merchant.'

'Alum! How did our friend procure it, think you? Because let us be honest and admit that he is a thief.'

'But there is honour amongst his ilk, is there not? And what does it matter how he procured it? I heard that it would be in Gallipolis...'

Ahmed's eyes sparkled. 'Think you there is enough to share?'

Michael laughed. 'I think your payment for its transport must surely be to share some of the supply...'

'Good.'

Ah, Ahmed was such a web of devious schemes beneath such an urbane exterior.

A peirate?

Michael thought so.

And such a thing must surely have value for later.

'But we need to keep it quiet,' Michael added.

Ahmed opened his eyes wide. 'And you think *I* would tell anyone? Me, the renowned trader?' He stepped forward and slapped Michael on the back. 'You don't make money,' he replied in quiet, convivial tones, 'by shouting secrets in the marketplace.'

'Exactly so,' Michael agreed. 'Shall we toast Gallipolis then? There is some pomegranate syrup under the canopy.'

Ahmed reached to the tray, the clink of pewter sounding as he poured from a stoppered flask. He grabbed a couple of plump dried dates, *tamr*, purchased on Chandax at their last stop. He smelled them and then threw them into his mouth. 'Ah, the lifeblood of wandering Arabs like myself. They last forever when dried, perfect on shipboard, and a date honey can be extracted when they are fresh – a good source of energy when there is precious little else at sea. Look at this…' He held a date up to the light and it glistened, almost transparent in the sun, a dark amber tint here and there. 'Plump and soft like a good woman.'

He passed it to Michael and Michael's mouth watered. Dates had sustained him when he was a thief, hiding from the Varangian Guard. There was little else to be had once his flatbread had been eaten.

'Here's to Gallipolis, my friend.' Ahmed downed his syrup in one gulp. 'There is more I wish to say but it will have to wait until we pass into the Sea of Marmara through the Hellespont. Can you feel the sea becoming fractious beneath us? I must take the helm.'

He moved away, calling for the sail to be furled and for men to take to the oars and Michael examined the approaching twin points of land through which the sea raced back and forth with each tide change. He lifted his mug to the approaching strait, offering a toast, but then changed his mind and walked to the wale, pouring the last of his syrup into the sea.

A libation. A request for blessings. Of course he could always ask God but he and God had not spoken for twelve years and he was not such a hypocrite as to plea-bargain now. He turned away and found Ariella sitting beneath the canopy and watching him.

'Another offering?' she asked.

'Perhaps…' he placed his mug on the tray and walked to the bow where Toby stood, watching the twin points approach with speed. By nightfall they would be moored at Gallipolis – he would be glad to find his landlegs again.

Tobias was deep in thought and Michael left him to his rumination, thinking on what he had told Ahmed.

Alum? He knew of no rumours lately about the valuable mordant but he had no doubt there would be rumours of something valuable in the marketplace. Traders had sharp noses and wits and could sniff out money and a sale with the ease of the true beast of prey. No, Michael had said the first thing that came into his head in order to divert Ahmed from his own personal purpose for this voyage. And for some odd reason, alum had been it.

Tobias still stared for'ard, but he leaned on the wale with his elbows, saying, 'I am not so sure I am doing the right thing.'

Michael was surprised. 'Truly?'

'Perhaps it is too soon…'

'And yet you are here, my friend. Something directed you to come.'

Tobias grunted. 'God? The Virgin Lady? I was hoping it was my affection for the lady Ariella and for Saul. For myself, the visit to the church of Saint Akyntos and my brother's grave may be a step too far.'

'But you told them differently, didn't you?'

Tobias sighed. 'Yes. Ariella was in so much pain after Guillaume's death and Saul only wanted what was best for her. To have you, Ahmed and myself with her calms Saul's spirits.'

'Shall you go to Saint Akyntos then?'

Toby bit his thumbnail, a sure sign he was distressed. 'Saul's house in the city has a view of Nerion Harbour and I'll bet the little basilica's roof will be staring at me day in day out. When we arrive, I would visit Sancta Sophia and talk with a friend there who did much for Tomas and myself, against the odds. He is a priest, Father Symeon, and I owe him.'

Michael's heart skipped in his chest. 'Father Symeon?'

Caution…

'He arranged for Tomas' body to be taken to the Venetian Quarter. I still, to this day, have no idea how he managed it. Tomas had been found guilty of a crime against the empire and by rights, his body should have…'

Hell's teeth! How Fate ties us all in knots.

Michael touched his arm. 'Leave it, Toby. Best not think. Just be glad of good priests in this world.'

The boat lurched to larboard and back again and the mugs and flask clattered as they fell onto the tray. *Durrah* latched onto the current flying through the Hellespont and the two men held hard to the wale.

'Perhaps we had better sit,' Tobias said. 'Out of the way and safe.' As they moved to join Ariella, grabbing at whatever was handy to steady their path, he added. ''Tis true, you know. I find the priests here so much kinder than those of the Roman church back there.' He gestured behind *Durrah* across the Adriatico toward the Middle Sea. 'There was another one – remember Father Giorgios on Limnos? He and Symeon – saints, both of them.'

They both lapsed into silence, the three from Venezia watching muscles roll as the oarsmen touched the water enough to keep *Durrah* on a steady path, Ahmed calling the stroke from the helm.

It seemed moments and then they burst through into the Sea of Marmara, the water swirling round them in small whirlpools, the crew rowing with ease. The sun had settled to the lower part of the sky and apricot and violet had begun to tint the shadows around *Durrah*. The smell of land imposed its earthy self upon the water and gulls swooped low over the galley.

Do you think we are another chance of food, Michael wondered, as the gulls dipped and dived? Another day, another chance at life? It was indeed how he felt. Another chance coming his way and this time he would seize every opportunity and wring it hard until blood ran.

Anything to retrieve his daughter, if she lived.

A platter of golden fried sardines lay on the trestle around which Michael, Tobias and Ahmed sat. The inn was filled with men, women safely behind doors in the dark night. Neither stars nor moon lit the sky and torches flickered and flared in the nightbreeze blowing from the east.

Michael breathed in, closing his eyes. Fish, fried sardines, the smell of nutmeg in his *konditon,* the subtler smell of dirt and dust behind Gallipolis. It aroused such memories – good days, bad days.

A former life.

He looked into the mug as if it would show him his past and future, but of course there was nothing...

Toby drank off the *konditon* and coughed. 'Not so bad,' he said. 'Not as bad as my first taste. It was Dana who... I mean Jehanne...' he grinned at Michael. 'She played her part to perfection. Who would have thought?'

'That she could play act?' Michael asked.

'That as well because she hovered on the edge of danger daily. The Byzantine court is like a snakepit and she was more than efficient in her time there, and I say that in admiration.'

'Admirable indeed. She saved my life.'

'And you married her. Tell me,' Toby said. 'I collect stories of valour and love.'

'Ah, little music-man.' Ahmed broke in. 'Perhaps he does not wish to tell. Your curiosity is oft misplaced, my friend, even if you mean well in your enthusiasm.' He raised a mug of lemon syrup to his lips and then produced a scrap of fabric which he unrolled. Crystals gleamed white and pure in the torchlight. He took a pinch and scattered them across the sardines in his hand.

'Salt,' he said. ''Tis the finishing touch.' He devoured the crispy fish quickly and with appetite.

Michael tapped a damp finger into the granules and then licked his finger. 'Good salt,' he remarked, salivating, taking a sardine, sprinkling the salt and chewing. The olive oil reminded him of ancient groves near Sozopolis where he and Helena would walk with their daughter. Guilt spread in a flush through his chest as he thought of Jehanne who had saved his life when he was wounded, running from the Varangian Guard. Jehanne had been called Dana then and a little of her spirit reminded him of Helena. But only a little because Helena had not been worldly and fierce. But she had gentle, wifely qualities and made him complete and he mourned her even now. Jehanne de Clochard knew this and being wise, accepted that the man would always mourn the mother of his child.

'Ariella misses something delectable I think,' said Tobias.

'She is safer on the boat and Faisal will make sure she eats well.'

'Good. I thought she would fade away in the early days after Guillaume had died. But lately she has acquired a bloom upon her cheeks, if not in her manner.'

'Grief takes an age to deal with, Toby.' Michael said.

'Indeed.' The diminutive minstrel drank off his spiced wine. 'But there is something else...'

Michael and Ahmed looked up from the platter.

'Have you noticed nothing else about her?' Tobias asked.

'No...' both men said.

Tobias raised his eyebrows. 'Then, methinks Gisborne must reassess your value as his *espies*. First rule…' Toby tapped the trestle firmly with his finger and then tapped the corner of his eye. 'Observe!'

'So, we have missed something,' Ahmed said, signalling to the innkeeper. 'Enlighten us.'

The innkeeper approached and Ahmed requested another tray of drinks, some fruit and bread, complimenting the man on his sardines whereupon the man informed them of his wife and what an excellent cook she was and that the reputation of the place was second to none in Gallipolis. Tobias looked at Michael, eyes opening wide as if to say, 'I *will* tell you … eventually.'

Finally, Ahmed had his lemon syrup, flatbread and some fresh dates. He tore off some bread and dipped it in pale green olive oil, then slid it through his salt. 'Go on,' he said between chews. 'We are waiting…'

'Really,' Tobias snarked back. 'As were we.' He leaned forward. 'Ariella is with child.'

Michael sat back. 'You say!' An exclamation, not a question, and Ahmed's bread hovered in mid-air, his mouth ajar.

'Ahmed, my seafaring friend, it seems you are destined to convey interesting women on *Durrah*.'

'Are you sure?' Michael asked.

'Indeed I am,' Toby said, reaching for some bread and dipping it in the oil.

'You have asked her?' Ahmed said. 'Else how can you be sure? History has proven you wrong a number of times before.'

'No, I have not asked her. I am hoping she will tell us in her own time. It was purely chance that I noticed her two days ago. She stood in the seawind and her cloak blew back. Her tunic was pressed hard against her form in the breeze and she looked down at a very obvious bulge. She ran her hand over it and then pulled her cloak back around. There was no question.'

Michael shook his head. 'I have noticed nothing. How far along, think you?'

Tobias pursed his lips. 'Maybe six months – even more. And if you think on it, Guillaume was still with us six months ago. The thing is how would we have noticed? We were entering winter, women wear voluminous layers and cloaks. And she is small…'

Ahmed ran a finger through a drop of syrup on the tray. 'Then her father is unaware. She has travelled on a secret.'

'Indeed,' said Tobias. 'There is much to consider here. Her reputation, that of her father. Her safety...'

Michael broke in. 'The health of she and any living child is not at issue. She will be cared for in Constantinople by Mehmet's brother, Anwar. But it is the trading house I am concerned for. We are here for a three month, returning to Venezia before winter. If what you say is true, Tobias, she will give birth here. And whilst women habitually travel everywhere with their infants, this will be Saul's grandchild – the future of his trading house. It will effectively be the most valuable cargo we will ever take back to him. The risks and responsibilities are enormous.'

Tobias secured his knife in his belt. 'But do we not get ahead of ourselves? In the first instance, we must protect her reputation. An unmarried Jewess with a child is cause enough for her Faith to cast her out. She risks the future of her father's trading name by casting aspersion upon him by association. One or other of us must talk with her.'

'I agree,' said Michael. 'Much hangs on the reputation of ben Simon. But it also concerns me that within the Venetian compound, someone may have heard that there has been no marriage in either Venezia or Lyon. This requires careful thought, Toby.'

Hell and damnation! Michael could have spat. This latest would surely colour his time here in Byzantium and he had wanted to be unfettered. To handle the trade as Gisborne and ben Simon wished and then begin his own search, bothering no one, keeping it secret.

Was he angry? Yes. This was a search for his own, for God's sake.

He looked away, catching sight of the harbour of Gallipolis in the distance and imagining Ariella on board *Durrah*. He had observed the bond between Guillaume and Ariella long since and he knew she must be cut in two with her loss. Knew also that this babe would be a lifeline to her memories. She had known the risks but had thought at the time she would be married within a short period. But Michael knew one couldn't count on any surety in this life. Least of all the continued existence of those one loved. Everything was precarious and Ariella should have taken care.

Should have, would have? But did not. And now they must back-paddle before arriving in the Golden Horn to take up residence in the Venetian Quarter.

Ahmed pushed the platter of fruit away, stood and folded up his slip of salt, pushing it in amongst the folds of his sash. 'I have no argument with anything you have said, but it is not my business to question her or to order her. May Allah bless you, my music-man. I do not envy you your task.' He laid some coins on the table almost too carefully. 'I would walk. *Ila-liqaa'.* He left them then, his robes swishing past Michael's arm, a lingering aroma of spices hanging on the air.

'He's angry,' said Toby.

Michael shrugged. 'Then that is something he must address. *Our* immediate problem is that Ariella must not be importuned in any way.'

'But she will be,' Toby said. 'Her most private secret…'

''Tis true. Except that what we say is for her own good. She will forgive us in time, I am sure.'

'Us?' Toby sat up straight. 'You and I?'

'Of course. Whilst you have known her longer than I, I would not have you do this alone.'

Toby sank back again, a dejected heap. 'Perhaps I should have said nothing and left it to Fate.'

Both men sat in silence, sipping the last of the drinks on the trestle, Michael thinking on women and children as the night drifted onward. The sky remained unlit by stars or moon and every now and then a puff of wind from the east stirred leaves and detritus in the streets.

'No,' he said eventually as he stood, opening the drawstrings of his purse and laying some *aspron* on top of Ahmed's pile. 'It is better, more honest to say we know, and in the process to expedite a plan.'

Tobias added coins to the pile and saluted his thanks to the innkeeper. 'If you say…'

'But?' Michael asked.

'But what?' Tobias replied.

'You prevaricate, and Toby, I know you enough to realise that prevarication is not something you do without due cause. If we are to work on this together, tell me what concerns you.'

The minstrel puffed out his cheeks, scrubbing a hand through his hair so that it hung awry. 'It is like this. All along, I thought it was dangerous for Ariella to come to Byzantium with us. I prayed that Saul would prevent her. But seeing her pain after Guillaume's death and knowing how much she has craved to be an active part of his business and having no sons, he allowed her to travel. He does not comprehend the danger or if he does, he has become blind like the doting father he is. The minute we pass into the Golden Horn, there may be people who wish us ill for any number of reasons. It might be deals Ahmed has conducted, it could be that I am related to my brother, the icon-stealer, and in your case? Well, only you know if there is danger at your shoulder. My point is, excluding Ariella, we all have histories here. She might be fair game by association. Add a babe, and she and the little one become commodities to be bartered over.'

'God's breath, Toby!' Michael said in amazement. 'The very scenario you paint is the worst…'

'Which is why I painted it in such detail. I am nothing if not an artist,' Toby replied with a grim smile.

They began to walk back to the docks, a rat watching them, hair standing on end at its neck. The vague smell of pine drifted from the low hills around the town.

'But perhaps a little bleaker picture than it need be,' Michael added.

'Perhaps. But it makes me stand on my mettle, Michael. I could get lazy and treat this voyage as a self-indulgent exploration of feelings for my brother. Instead I face the realities of the Byzantine empire with all its petty jealousies and insecurities and I would watch out for her amongst that. Whilst it is good for the Venetians to have the temporary ear of the Angelids and to be current trading favourites, Genova and Pisa are not far behind. The whole stinking atmosphere of the imperial court hangs on a knife edge and I don't want Ariella caught in any trouble. Apart from anything else, who knows how the Angelids view Jews from one day to the next?'

'Tobias! Settle, my friend,' Michael said. And then as they walked on, 'You are a good man.'

A doleful grin was all he received in return and he thought on what Tobias had said – 'a self-indulgent exploration'. Was that what this was to Michael? Surely a search for one's child wasn't a self-indulgence.

The streets were dark, wall becoming shadow and shadow masking rutted road. Here and there, bars of light bled from between shutters, but little broke the gloom. Few were about and those who were hurried along without eye contact, as if afraid to be caught out at this late hour. But most streets were deserted with only the odd leaf blowing in the night breeze that funnelled from land to water.

'Do you feel it too?' Toby asked so quietly it was but a murmur, as if he talked to himself.

'Yes,' Michael refused to turn around. Instead, he and Toby continued toward the waterfront.

'How many?' Toby asked.

'At least two. No more than three. They are softly shod, barely a sound…'

They pulled their knives with stealth, Michael wishing he had not left his *paramerion* aboard *Durrah*. He wondered if those who followed them wore soleless *balgha* slippers – soft leather from the Maghreb. It would account for the lack of sound. Ahead, he noticed a small arbor draped with old vines and cloth and he nudged Tobias into its shadows, pushing him further against the wall of the house, edging round the corner to a gap between two buildings. The rank smell of piss seeped from the walls and somewhere behind empty barrels an animal had died – probably a rat. Michael's sardines took a tumble in his belly and he swallowed on the acrid taste in his mouth.

He and Toby kept still, pressed hard against the walls. The barely-there footsteps stopped beyond the arbor, some indistinct whispering occurred and then the shuffle of two sets of feet running away.

So, one waits to see if we are hidden…

Michael tapped Toby on the shoulder, and when the minstrel turned, he shook his head and with a finger gesture against his lips, urged further quiet. They would wait this out.

Beyond the blind alley, a cat fight screeched and someone threw back a shutter and yelled. As further feline mewling continued, one of the cats jumped from the wall above their heads, springing past them and running away.

Toby let out a quick breath, brushing frantically at his clothes and lurching against Michael, but Michael kept his attention on the entrance to the alley. Nothing moved.

And still they stood – frozen in some odd tableau. He swapped his knife from one hand to the other, flexing fingers, feeling Toby shift from foot to foot. Behind the house wall, a nightly rut began. Michael would have caught Toby's eye and grinned but now was not the time. Instead, armed and poised.

In moments, footsteps ran back and Michael's heart leaped. This time there were audible Greek words.

'They were seen. Running up the next street. There was a fellow sitting on a step smoking. He saw them…'

'What were they like?' This one had a deeper voice, as ragged as a worn *djellaba*.

'One tall, one short.'

'Let's go…' the torn voice said and the feet pattered away.

'Two, three…' whispered Toby. 'All gone.' He heaved a relieved sigh.

'What was wrong with you?' Michael asked as they edged back the way they had come, sliding into the concealment of the vines.

'Scorpion. Hate them,' said Toby. 'Cat must have dislodged it from the wall.'

'You play hiding games now?' A laconic voice sounded from the other end of the shadowed canopy. 'No wonder you are not yet returned. Having too much fun, methinks.'

'Ahmed!' Toby's hand clutched at his chest. 'Christ above, you will kill me with shock creeping around in the dark.'

'How did you know we'd come this way?' Michael asked.

'This is close to the waterfront. Why wouldn't you? And you had company, I see.' He indicated their weapons which gleamed in the flaccid nightlight.

'Almost,' Tobias said. 'We were followed by three men. We managed to hide in the alley there. We fooled them…'

'Music-man, *you* may think so. But in truth, I diverted them.'

'Ha!' Toby laughed. 'The smoking man.' And then, 'I didn't know you smoked.'

'You don't know a lot about me, little minstrel. I am not averse to the quality *hashish* that one can find hidden around the coastlines here.'

'*Hashish?*' Toby said, scandalised. 'But it is bad for you!'

'The Sufis say differently, and I am my own man and draw my own conclusions. You heard them speaking?' he asked of Michael as they headed toward the galley.

'Greek. Like everyone else.'

'But you are disturbed,' Ahmed persisted as he swung himself across *Durrah*'s wale.

'In a way,' said Michael as he and Toby climbed across the wale, grasping at stays to prevent slipping. 'I have a history here and expect trouble.'

'Better to expect it, my friend, than to be caught napping.' Ahmed made to turn away but Michael grabbed his muscular forearm.

'Ahmed, was it circumstance, think you?'

Ahmed studied Michael in the light of Faisal's little brazier. It glowed softly next to Faisal as the ship's second sharpened a *kilij*. The movement was meditative and slow, a sound that was as much sigh as song and would have lulled the crew to sleep. The kind of sound that gave confidence to the concerned.

Ahmed twisted his lips with a grimace. He was a fine-looking man with strong planes on his face and the faintest upward tilt to his dark eyes. 'Maybe…'

'But maybe not,' Michael replied.

Tobias' head flipped from one to the other. 'But who would know we are here? And Michael, you look very different now to last year…'

'One would hope no one knew I was here,' Michael said. 'Saul contacted no one before we left. There wasn't time.'

'Then,' Ahmed said over his shoulder as he moved away to the helm where he slept in a salt-stained bedroll and cloaks, 'it was circumstance. Good night, my friends. We visit the spice man on the morrow and I need sleep so that my wits will be sharp.'

Michael and Toby stared at Ariella who lay stretched on her back, asleep to the world, a blanket and cloak draped to her chin. She slept on a cushioned roll with a pillow beneath her head and something about her comfort spoke of Faisal's care for her. Toby whispered as much.

'I remember he was like that with Lady Ysabel. He's a gentle giant of a man. But she should sleep in the sterncastle. It would be more comfortable.' He yawned and stretched. 'God's breath but I'm tired, Michael. I'll be glad when we are on land and in our villa. I haven't good sea-legs. May we sleep on our adventure till tomorrow?'

Michael nodded, following the minstrel's example and unfolding his bedroll and stretching out under the awning. He wadded his cloak for a pillow and lay there, knowing sleep wouldn't come. He was stretched as taut as a bowstring.

Maybe this journey was wrong. Maybe someone was hunting him. Maybe the Varangian Guard knew that the infamous thief of the imperial dye they called Tyrian Purple was back on Byzantine shores…

Or maybe he was merely self-indulgent to think thus.

His thoughts travelled in circles until eventually he dozed, the mild rocking of the galley and the repetitive song of the blade-sharpening quieting his mind. He rolled onto a hip at some point, cool air touching his exposed neck and shoulder where one of his cloaks had fallen away and he lay still, staring into the paling sky behind the roofs of Gallipolis. Clouds sat low – a moody light immediately quashing any hopes he had for a bright day.

He sat up, yawning and pulling the cloak around his shoulders, noting that Toby lay on his back, a snore bigger than the man emerging with excruciating regularity.

'One expects a smaller snore,' Ariella sat up, her swathe of rugs and cloaks falling away. 'Or at the very least, a harmonious sound. He *is* a renowned troubadour after all. I wanted to grab my pillow and smother him through the night!'

'You lay awake all night?' Michael thought she looked as fresh as the morning dew that rolled off the canopy and dripped onto the deck. 'You should have slept in the sterncastle.'

'Perhaps. But I like the fresh air. In any case, I have not been awake all night, no. I have slept. But…'

'Yes?' Curiosity has benefits, he thought.

Ariella flipped her plaited hair back and placed a veil over her head. Her rebelliousness had been like a candle flame on Guillaume's death, snuffed out, never to burn again. Except that Michael thought taking up the merchant's mantle for her father might be a slight mitigation of her grief. 'I was cold. I remember my father talking of the biting cold of the almost-dawn hours here in the almost-east. Once awake of course, I heard Toby and that was that.'

Nothing more was forthcoming as Tobias gave a stellar snort worthy of a hefty sow and woke. He met the morning like a well-fed and contented infant – on the right side of life, as if possibilities were always to the good. He smiled, his eyes bright, with no sign of having hidden from shadows during the night.

'My lady Ariella, good day to you. You too, Michael.' He looked around, stretching his diminutive arms above his head as surveyed the grey silk skies. 'I suspect it *might* burn away by the time we sail. But dull now.' He jumped up and flapped his arms round himself. 'And cold! God's toenails,' he said, dancing on the spot, 'I need to… oh, begging your pardon, Ariella.'

'Oh Toby,' Ariella said, grinning. 'Be gone and do what you must. And bring back some food!'

Michael was sure Toby would have just pissed over the wale if Ariella had not been close. After all, they all had on the voyage. Landfall wasn't always available and the perils of a woman aboard had been dealt with.

Toby returned a short while later, his face damp and black hair slicked back. As neat as a courtly troubadour should be. He tipped his cloak up on the deck in front of them and fresh flatbread fell out, still warm, along with some plump dates and two leather costrels.

'The costrels are filled with *konditon*. It was that or syrup and it's a bit early in the day for syrup for me. It's so very – syrupy! I apologise for the repetitive supplies.'

'It's food,' said Ariella, tearing hungrily at the bread.

'It is good to see you so well, Ariella,' Toby ventured as he divided a segment of bread into regular pieces.

Here it comes…

Ariella looked up questioningly.

'It is merely that early on, you were not eating and you were pale…'

'Yes,' said Ariella, not backing away at all.

'I put it down to grief,' said Tobias with the manners of a courtier. 'But I was wrong, was I not?'

'Were you?' It was said with a certain wistful tone.

'Yes. I think you will give birth whilst we are here.'

CHAPTER TWO

×

Silence reverberated and then,

'Yes,' said Ariella.

'Your father?' Toby continued.

'He is unaware.'

'I see,' Michael took up the conversation as Toby looked to him for help.

'You see *what*, do you think, Michael?' Ariella's tone lifted a notch.

He chose simple words in reply. 'I see an unwed Jewish mother...'

Ariella slammed her palm on the deck. 'If Guillaume had lived...'

Tobias touched her, a gentle gesture. 'But he didn't, my dear. And he above all others would want your future and that of his child secured.'

'Meaning?' Ariella pressed the knuckles of one hand against her chin. But of course, she knew. She was an intelligent woman.

'Meaning, Ariella,' Michael replied. 'That for the sake of the house of ben Simon, you must appear wedded. I think your father will understand when he hears.'

She huffed out a sigh. 'Indeed, you are right. And I have thought exactly that, all the way here from Venezia. I just needed someone to tell me. It has been difficult...'

'You told no one? You managed to keep it a secret?' Toby asked.

Ariella flared momentarily but it subsided and she sighed. 'I felt no sign. And in any case, everyone assumed I grieved. Which I did. I wanted time to indulge myself. If I had told my father, I simply would not be here.

By not telling him I was with child, he was more likely to indulge me over Guillaume's death. Sadly, I neglected to think wider – what might happen if I am seen to be an unwed mother. At worst a whore…'

'Ariella,' said Toby, patting her hand. 'Leave it to Michael and myself. We will contact your father swiftly through Gisborne's men, using our codes, and we will also spread a subtle rumour about the widow of Guillaume de Gisborne. The Venetian Quarter will cosset you – Jew and gentile alike.'

Her eyes sparkled with unshed tears. 'My child and I are in your debt.'

'Not at all,' said Michael. 'We are all family in the trading house. You know this. Toby, will you seek Ahmed and brief him… yes, Ariella, he knows you carry a child… and then we must visit our spice merchant. Shall you come with us?'

She thought for a heartbeat. 'I will. Best start as I mean to continue.'

'Michael, before I go to Ahmed,' said Tobias. 'What did he mean about wits needing to be sharp. Are we in for trouble?'

'Not trouble exactly, but perhaps Ahmed might not get what he wants.'

'Which is?'

'Alum.'

'Alum?'

'Yes. It's my fault. I mentioned a rumour. There's probably nothing in it, but if there isn't a truth, I think our shipmaster may be a trifle angry.'

'He doesn't do trifles, Michael,' Toby sighed. 'He vents like the winds from the Maghreb!'

'Oh, I think he will settle down. Alum or *olibanum*, silks and silver, Ahmed will always want a deal.' Michael rubbed his thumb and forefinger together. 'Money, money, money.'

Tobias gave a rueful laugh. 'There is a famous saying from thousands of years ago. Have you heard of Publilius Syrus? He was a freed Syrian slave and had rather a clever mind. He said *Honesta fama melior pecunia est. A good reputation is more valuable than money.* Do you think we should tell Ahmed?'

'No,' said Ariella. 'I think what you say is more apt for me just now, given that I could bring shame upon all of us.'

'Not at all. All will be well.' Toby manufactured a little *carole*. 'I will go talk to him and then we shall do our business!'

He walked away, humming a melody to match his footsteps and Ariella and Michael watched him go.

'I do love him, you know,' Ariella said. 'He picks up on nuance swiftly. No doubt his life as a troubadour has taught him to assess emotion and to act accordingly. It's the art of the performer, isn't it? To gauge one's audience and smooth their feathers?' She began to lever herself from the bedroll and Michael helped her. 'I need a wedding ring of sorts, Michael. I have brought no jewellery....'

'I am sure Ahmed will have something. Is there anything else you need?'

'I would like to wash and to change my clothes before we visit the merchant. If I must playact, I must playact as if I mean it.' She pulled herself over the wale and pointed at a well against a wall. 'I will be a moment only.'

'I'll come too. I need to freshen *my* wits if I am to be of any use.'

They walked across the dusty square together and took turns to wash, Ariella using her veil to wipe herself dry. On their return to the vessel, she went to the little sterncastle that stored her chest and some of the more precious goods needing protection from seaweather. Michael left her and joined Ahmed and Tobias at the stern wale, running his fingers through his hair, attempting to neaten it before their meeting with the merchant.

'She changes her clothes,' he said as Ahmed looked up enquiringly. The Arab played with something silver in his palm.

'I have a ring for her,' he said. 'Music-man thought it might be a good idea.'

Toby sat astride the wale like a child on a horse. 'Apparently she threw her betrothal ring into the sea as a libation as we left the Adriatico,' he said.

Ahmed nodded. 'Then she is wise. The sea takes if it is not granted offerings.'

I gave it my life and the lives of my loved ones. It need take no more from me, surely.

Michael turned and smiled at Ariella as she joined them, her hair pulled under a neat veil, her linen gown a deep blue redolent of the sapphire of her former betrothal ring. Her feet were clad in slippers with bronze embroideries from the market they had visited at Chandos.

'Ariella, this is for you,' Ahmed said. 'It shall be your wedding ring.'

She took it from him without looking at him and slipped it on her finger, keeping her gaze lowered as she said, 'I thank you.'

Michael thought it must have been like wrapping her finger in thorns, so painful would be the loss in her heart and he thought of his wife, Jehanne. Despite that this voyage had raised memories of the dead and of a former marriage built on love, his partner was now one who had seen him through a dark time in Byzantium when he had been in fear for his life. And like this present journey, that adventure had begun with a message. Whispered in his ear at an inn near the harbour of Theodocius by someone looking for a man by the name of Gabriel. Michael whispered back that he knew Gabriel and would pass the message on.

Portus Theodosiacus. Third moorings from the west. He would never forget it. It seemed to him as if every part of his life had been built on messages and he often wondered what would have happened if he had not accepted that any of the messages had merit.

Dawn had painted soft peach stripes from the eastern horizon to the heavens and the Theodosian harbour walls were the colour of porphyry. The sun lit the lacy machicolations; galleys, dromons *and other vessels all floated at their moorings within the protective arms of the seawall.*

Michael had come to the harbour from the western end, close by the Forum of Arcadius, showing his merchant papers at one of the gates. The green-clad harbour official didn't even look at him, just noted his name on a wax tablet and waved him on.

His stomach writhed because he was about to become a thief. Till that moment, all his trading had been honest, easily documented, and his standing as a merchant well recognised. But then he heard of the dye, Tyrian purple.

Highly protected by the Byzantines, the dye was the true indicator of imperial power. Imperial families were 'born to the purple'. The idea that the dye could be traded in the marketplace would be laughable if it wasn't treasonous.

But there were some who made the dye, extracting it from shellfish, who knew they could make exceptional money in an illegal market — if they could find a buyer prepared to take the risk.

As a man called Gabriel, Michael was prepared to take *that risk.*

He almost looked back at the harbour official, convinced the man's eyes burned into his back, but instead he walked on, dropping his shoulders and whistling because it loosened his tense jaw. He was under no illusion that if he was found stealing Tyrian purple, he would forfeit his hands first, for such was the punishment for a common thief. But his head would soon follow for treasonous crimes against the empire.

One, two, three…

The third wooden moorings projected into the still waters of the Theodocian harbour. On the starboard side, a dilapidated kaiki creaked against its hemp ropes as two men unloaded baskets of anchovies onto a handcart – the kind of activity being repeated a dozen or more times over in each of Constantinople's protected harbours.

The older man looked up as the boards of the moorings creaked under Michael's weight, nodding. He ordered his apprentice to take the handcart to shore and asked Michael aboard. He stepped in, holding onto the rigging of the short mast, and sat down on the deck planks which were greyed and smooth with weathering. Looking back at the seawalls, the sun had risen enough for them to be embellished with gold, and so impressive that there was little chance to forget they had been built by a superior and powerful civilisation.

'You are Gabriel?' the fisherman asked, shifting a twig that he chewed to the other side of his mouth.

Michael nodded. Better to be Gabriel than Michael Sarapion…

'You want the dye?' the man whispered.

Michael nodded again.

'We will talk money.'

'We may be watched…'

The man made a pretence of looking at the sky and pointing at clouds on the horizon. 'You pay now,' he said.

'No. I will pay what you want later. No haggling. I will come to your village.'

'The passing of one moon. After that, I sell to someone else.' He shoved a stoppered flask of squid ink into Michael's hands. 'This is what you bought from me today, should the official ask.'

Michael passed over two gold hyperpirons, well beyond the value of the rancid liquid in the jar. But he knew a good disguise when he saw it.

At that gate leading from the harbour, the same official stood in the shade of the mighty walls, stylus and tablet on a small folding stool, a guard armed with a glistening spathion next to him.

'You got what you came for, Master Sarapion?'

'I did, thank you, sir.' He uncorked the bottle and the foul odour of old squid *ink rushed out, the official stepping back quickly, hand over nose.*

'You will sell that?'

'It's for an experiment to see if dye can be rendered for cloth that I have.'

'But the smell…'

'I hope it will disappear.'

The official pulled his chin back into his neck with disbelief. 'Merchant Sarapion, your Venetian customers will only need to use their noses to know what you have done. I suspect this is a venture that might fail.'

'Who knows?' Michael smiled. 'Good day to you and God keep you.' He passed beneath the arch and chose a wending and alternate path to his lodgings, in case of being followed. At a small and empty square, he lobbed the flask behind some bushes and within hours had begun to execute his plan.

Michael Sarapion, merchant, was leaving for Venezia – ostensibly to manage the Venetian ben Simon house for the aging owner. He held a dinner at his home near the Nerion Harbour, inviting his friends to thank them for their support and to say farewell. And because it was almost the end of winter and the sea-roads were slow, he left Constantinople by horse, passing through the Gate of Saint Aemilianus – the Porta Tou Hagiou – it being the gate and near to the Church of Saint Mary of Rhabdos, where he worshipped.

It had been merely worship for show, though – to round out his persona. He had liked the inconsequential nature of the building and the fact that it was farther away from the hub of the Byzantine Church of Sancta Sophia and the Patriarchal Palace. His relationship with God died with his wife and daughter. But then of course, no one who knew him in Constantinople had any idea he had been married and lost what he valued most, or that he spent part of every day, looking for a peirate *whom he intended to kill.*

To those who knew him, after the farewells had been said, he vanished.

To Venezia they believed, but in truth to become a fisherman, a thief and enemy of the Byzantine empire.

He puked as if the devil festered inside him. Until poisonous yellow froth spouted from his mouth and his belly contracted for the sake of it. He groaned, rubbing a hand over his sweaty forehead and into his hair which had become matted and uncouth.

Of the former merchant, agent for the houses of Gisborne and ben Simon, there was nothing left. Of Gabriel, the fisherman he pretended to be, there were possibilities. But of the dyemaker rendering the putrid shellfish for the sanctified Tyrian purple, there was no hope.

His partner-in-crime laughed. Sabbas, the fisherman from the third moorings in the harbour of Theodosius, gave a mocking hoot as Michael's stomach rolled again.

'Gabriel, keep to the boats and diving. You will never be a dyemaker.'

'The smell...' Michael rasped.

'What smell? You belly-ache too much. The guards'll work you out in no time when they come.'

'When?' His belly flipped over and he belched.

'Once in every moon. They bring the officials who check their records against our quota and account for every little snail we catch.'

'Soon?'

'Two days. Unlucky for you that the weather is bad, else you could be diving offshore for the rest of my quota whilst they are here. As it is...' Sabbas shrugged and left Michael to his misery.

Michael paid for his supplies the next day as the coast was beset with ferocious thunder and needle-sharp rain. Sabbas packed the money and a small cache of possessions on his back, leaving in the dark of a wet night to travel to the edges of the Black Sea where he could disappear.

Michael pushed on into the coastal hills to a place above the River Lycus where he could vaguely hear religious voices in a convent close by. There amongst rocks, cypress and juniper, he hid the small bags of the powdered dye in dry, safe clefts. He waited then, his hair becoming entangled and his beard matted, foraging for food and killing the occasional hare until he found a man from his city past – Petrus, whom Michael had known as a Varangian.

Between them they spent days dropping the bags into jars of olibanum *resin, heating the tops and smoothing the waxy resin over to plug the hole. The smell of the holy resin was indelible, sinking into the weave of his clothes and the creases of his palms and Michael hated it. The jars were then stored in crates, waiting for the right time for delivery to a Venetian galley in Constantinople.*

'You need to watch your back,' Petrus said as the last stopper was moulded and he washed his sticky hands in heated water, scraping a knife over them under the watery surface.

'Self-evident, my friend,' Michael replied. 'You need to watch yours as well. The Varangians don't take kindly to absconders.'

'Petrus is bored and does not want to fight another country's wars. Let my

fellows fight for the Byzantines. I have an idea to travel.'

Michael looked at the giant northerner, noting his huge hands and the slave mark on his arm. There was so much to ask Petrus but the man invited no enquiry. Instead, 'Where to?'

'Northwest… Lyon.' Petrus' voice rumbled like a trebuchet being rolled out for war.

'Lyon! Why?'

Lyon and Petrus? Iisoús Christós, Petrus would be bored in a moment.

'I like the name.' Petrus cleaned his dagger and slipped it into a tooled leather scabbard at his side. Standing, he strapped on a sword, its length and breadth matching his Herculean size and then shook the effeminate purse at his belt which jingled with the sounds of coins. 'Money to be made. For Petrus, more than here with less risk.'

The man towered over Michael, his long blonde hair cascading in a plait down his back. 'But Petrus, everything about you is obvious and remarkable. How will you leave?'

'The same way you must, Michael. In secret. Petrus will help. And one day, perhaps you will pay Petrus for the service because Petrus always demands payment.' The northerner held out his hand and took Michael's in a bone-crushing grip that could snap every bone like a twig.

'Done,' Michael said, wincing, and rubbed his fingers. 'When shall you leave?'

'Today. As will you. I have talked with a friend. He will transport you by sea into the city where you will wait for your Venetian galley.

'You sail with us?'

'No. I sail to the Adriatico and then to Marseille.'

'How will I find you?'

'Petrus will find you one day, Michael Sarapion, because Petrus always finds those who owe him.'

Later, Petrus' voice broke through the sound of seabird and ship-song.

'I go now. By summer, I shall be in Lyon. You go now and by summer's end, you should be in Venezia if you play the game. One thing – a woman called Dana is watching out for you in Constantinople.'

Michael entered the city – just a sailor, one of many who disembarked with crates on shoulders. Sailors talk though, and the gossip running along the edges of the harbour like seaweed was rank. Tyrian purple had been stolen and the thief, a fisherman called Sabbas, had been caught, interrogated, and executed. He had an accomplice, they said, but he was on the run.

So Michael shaved his head to a shining baldness, watching the black lengths fall to the floor and unable to stop the image of his head following. His hand shook a little as he clipped his beard tightly so that with his olive skin, a cultivated accent and the ankle length thawb and cloak of the desert men, he might have been from the Maghreb or from beyond the Euphrates. Sometimes he wore the leggings and tunic of the Varangians and those from the north Balkans, because the secret to survival was surely to adapt and change.

One day, he chatted to a Venetian sailor as they sat at the edge of the Prosphorion Harbour, watching the ships pass into the Golden Horn after the chains were lifted – idle chat leading nowhere and everywhere.

'Durrah will be here from Venezia soon. The houses of Gisborne and ben Simon use it for transporting merchandise back to the west. You are a trader you say. You should come back with your goods. What do you trade?'

Michael talked of silk, of olibanum and of lapis lazuli from Khorasan, but admitted he was only a small trader – good quality but small supplies. He was glib with his lies.

'Quality is the marker for success, they say. You ought to come back when Durrah and the Arab, Ahmed, will be here.'

Michael knew Ahmed well. Had he not been trading with him for most of the years since he'd buried his wife and lost his daughter? But the irony of Ahmed's name being dropped into a casual conversation was not lost on him. He could be surrounded by Gisborne men and never know.

His lodging was in an alley near the Church of Saint George, far from the Nerion Harbour. It was easy to lose anybody who might track him by weaving back and forth until he arrived at Sixth Hill. Once, he had come across a quadrum of Varangians quizzing a man with long black hair and the stink of the fish market upon him. The fellow had no papers and the northerners showed no mercy as they pried answers from him along with teeth.

Michael swallowed on bile. He needed papers. But how to get them? The wait for Durrah was tortuous and began to wear him thin – and in such tension lay danger. He remembered Petrus saying: – a woman called Dana is watching out for you in Constantinople.

41

Dana lived not far from the imperial palace where she was an embroiderer and needlewoman to the court ladies and therefore privy to gossip at high levels. The women liked her, talked freely with her and she replied with bland acknowledgement as she made alterations and embellishment to their clothing. They had no idea she was not a city native, not even a sniff of a clue that this woman was no artisan and that she collected secrets.

'I can get word to Saul for you. But papers can be more difficult.'

'Papers to show I am a trader from Khorasan...'

'I will try, but a forgery is always just that.' She turned from him, her dark hair tumbling as her veil slipped and fell across her shoulders. She was as narrow and pliant as a sapling.

'When?' He sounded needy, but it seemed to him that he had been waiting to ship the dye all of his life and that the Byzantines breathed death down his neck.

She swung back, a small fire lit in her eyes. 'When I can.'

'Dana, I am living on a sword-edge...'

'Then you must use your balance, my friend,' she touched his arm and this time, her smile met her eyes. 'Some things can't be hurried. Meet me at Sancta Sophia in three days.'

'Three days!'

But she didn't answer, just showed him the door to her neat little house and shut it quietly behind him.

He had passed Sancta Sophia a hundred times but had never ventured inside. It had been enough in his time to attend the Church of Saint Mary Rhabdos over on Sixth Hill. And even then, the back row near the door had always been where he stood. For he would not sit in God's house.

He climbed the steps to the south gates, counting each one, anything to take his mind away from the hurt he felt at God's betrayal of Helena and Ioulia ... of him. He wanted to look back to the Propontis, to see the glitter of water and hear the sound of seabirds but he had to be content that all would be there when he left the basilica. The narthex *seemed to stretch for leagues and as he walked, he was unable to help staring up at the dome which floated in God's light above him. All was gold – light, leaf, icons and olibanum-filled* thymiateria.

And then he froze, aware the fresh sea air had lost its hold upon his back. He wanted to turn and hurry away, but the crush of people pushed at him and so he looked up, the face of the Theotokis staring back. Such compassion, and he should have felt safe, but the place began to close in as if the walls would smother him. Olibanum fragrance and burning beeswax candles filled the air and he began to sweat with the sickliness of it.

The noise of a hundred footsteps clamoured in his ears and far away, he could hear the monks – a sound as beautifully harmonious as anyone could want to hear, except to him the whisper of prayer sounded like the hiss of coiled snakes.

He frowned and spun away, knocking hard into a plainly dressed and veiled woman.

'You leave before you have what you want?'

'Dana!' he whispered.

''Tis I.'

He pulled the fraying edges of his composure together. 'I hate porphyry and I hate olibanum even more. Can we walk outside?'

They left the basilica together, walking down the steps facing the Great Palace and the Column of Justinian. Finding a stone bench, they sat under a Judas tree that provided shade.

'Dine with me,' she said. 'You, the trader from Khorasan, will like our Byzantine food. We are gentle and subtle with our spices. You must take the experience back to your wives and children. How many wives do you have, Hussein?'

I am Hussein?

He had forgotten for an instant that he was a nomadic trader from Khorasan. A tribesman with wives and children, and in the spirit of her mood, he answered. 'Five, I think. Or is it six? I have been away for a long while.'

'Yes…'

'I think my papers say. I lose count of days.' He grinned. 'My wives will expect stories and gifts.'

She smiled. Her face lit up like the sun and he found he wanted to talk more with her, to look at her…

'They say you trade in ancient essences and lapis,' she said.

'It is true…' And in case they were watched, he dropped a rolled parchment at the foot of her tunic which draped over the ground. They both bent at the same time – she slipped the forged papers into his hand and then pushed the blank paper into the side of her kid slippers. It was such a smooth exchange, as if they were dance partners who had practiced the move many times over.

43

He tapped the air with the forged papers. 'It is what my papers say.'

'In truth then, tell me about your lapis. I have a deep affection for the blue of it.'

And as they walked away to the food stalls, he found he liked her. Her quiet nature, her evident courage, her lack of artifice. For the first time in many months, he felt happy.

Somewhere a church bell rang and Michael thought on the daily offices that had once meant much to Helena. Sixth Hour for him meant food and rest. For Helena, it had been praying for Christ on the Cross. She was committed to her God and he joined her by association. But the prayers were a mere lip-service whilst he secured their future. To her it was lifeblood. For the little good it did her.

And so it was Sixth Hour by the time Ahmed had shouted at his men to reconfigure the lading of the galley and Faisal had settled him to a state of calm. Starving hungry, the four walked to the merchant's house along a broad road that ran along the eastern edge of Gallipolis toward the town gates. Foot traffic, horses and donkeys passed back and forth and one man looked at Michael. His head was swathed in a worn *keffiyeh* and he had a band of dust around the bottom of his robes. His skin was the colour of leather and yet his eyes were as blue as the sky in summer, the corners weather-creased. A nomad, Michael thought. One of the *'Badiyah* dwellers'. He'd bought goods from them in the past – rugs, animal skins tanned to perfection, soft slippers made of goatskin.

Would the *badu* who stared have recognised Michael? Michael's hair was much shorter now and had begun the final turn to grey, a seasonal shift like the trees along the edge of the Saône that suggested the autumn of life – the Saône, where lived his wife and her mother…

'Michael?' Ahmed's voice broke into his thoughts.

'Yes…'

'You think he has sold the alum?'

'I have no idea. If so, what does it matter? His spices are the best, Ahmed. You ought to know. You have dealt with him for many years.'

They could smell the house of spice before seeing it, Tobias stopping, closing his eyes and inhaling deeply so that his chest puffed out like a pigeon's. Then he let go with a satisfied 'Aah… this is a pleasant memory of Byzantium. The smell of spice drifts on the winds and the whole empire seems to float on a cloud.'

'This man, Yusuf al-Fayadd, is the best,' agreed Michael. 'I remember him from my time here. His name means Yusuf the Generous…'

Ahmed snorted and Michael frowned, continuing, 'Yusuf was spoken of with admiration when I traded in Byzantium. Try as we might, none of us could equal his quality. And we tried hard. We travelled far and wide but always, he managed to secure the best before us. He thought with latitude as well – I remember he set up this small tavern with excellent food and it was a way of proving to spice customers what could be achieved with his commodities.'

''Tis true,' said Ahmed grudgingly. 'Although I would hardly call him generous. Wily, clever, all of that, but whatever he is called, the imperial court sails here on occasion to taste of his food. They demanded he give them his cooks but he replied that it is his spices which tantalise and so they buy those from him instead. He is either brave or stupid to be so offhand with the Angelids who are all mad. But then he *is* immensely wealthy and can do what he likes.'

'Hush, you fool,' said Tobias. 'Walls have ears. And money isn't everything!'

'Oh yes, it is,' Ahmed gave an acid laugh. 'Besides, we are in the open, little music-man. No walls, unless you count that row of Judas trees.'

They continued on to the tavern and took a seat around an outdoor trestle pressed hard against a wall. Beyond, artisans hurried along with baskets filled with knives, soft leather boots, belts and more. A donkey stepped delicately, its hooves pattering on the stone and dust, its back loaded with tanned goat-hides. A man walked past with the air of an acrobat, a board balanced on an embroidered cap upon his head, fresh flatbread piled to the skies. Little children ran and yelled, screaming with high-pitched delight as the donkey defaecated further up the street.

'They remind me of William of Gisborne,' Toby said. 'Children are so innocently amused with such small and smelly things.'

They ordered some bread that arrived warm and flavoured with anise and fennel seed and which they tasted with a shared platter of *barridah* – a cucumber and chicken dish with cumin and cinnamon, fresh tarragon, thyme and mint. As he sipped a mug of syrup, Toby muttered to no one and everyone, 'My palate sings…'

'Then write a song,' said Ahmed.

'I might. A homage to taste.'

They finished with *keftedes*, small meatballs flavoured with cinnamon and more of the piquant mint.

Ariella sat back, nursing her bulge. 'With my babe, I have no room for anything else.'

'Not even stuffed dates?' Toby asked.

'No,' Ariella laughed.

'You like my food, madame…' The voice that rumbled from behind, as if from a deep abyss, resonated on the air and for a moment all else was silence, as though people listened just for the sake of it.

Ariella and Michael turned. The man was tall and corpulent, a sense of presence as his silk tunic fell in damask folds to the top of his feet, belted with a plaited leather girdle. His head was girded in a red and white folded *keffiyeh* and it sat atop, balancing there by the grace of God. He mixed Byzantine and Arab dress with eccentric surety.

'Yusuf!' Ahmed stood and bowed. '*Salaam Alaykum.*'

'*Alaykum as salaam,* my friend. Are you come to fleece me and then run far?'

'Me? You jest, of course. No, we are here to buy spices and perhaps other things. As usual.'

'We?'

'These are my friends from Venezia, from the house of Gisborne-ben Simon. This is Madame Ariella de Gisborne, daughter of Saul ben Simon with whom you do regular business.'

'*Salaam Alaykum,* Madame. I respect your father greatly.'

'*Alaykum as salaam,* Yusuf al Fayadd. My father speaks highly of your merchandise.'

'Madame, did I hear that you are also a part of the excellent Gisborne house? How is this?'

Ariella sat very still and Michael wondered if he should intervene, but then,

'Yes. My husband is… *was* Guillaume de Gisborne, Sir Guy of Gisborne's half-brother. Sadly, my husband passed away not long since…' Her hand crept to her belly and Yusuf's eyes followed. His fingers flipped his forehead and chest, a move of sadness and recognition of hurt.

'My humble apologies for my impolite questions. Please accept my deep condolences.'

She said nothing, just dipped her head and Ahmed jumped in. 'And this is Tobias Celho, from Liguria. My other friend is Michael Sarapion, once from Sozopolis but now a Venetian for four years since.'

'Huh,' Yusuf studied Michael's face. 'Sozopolis. Then I can see why Venezia might entice you to its shores.'

Michael's hackles rose as Yusuf continued. 'So, Master Sarapion. What do you do in Venezia? Count money? Dance to the Doge's tune?'

Toby clapped his hands, drawing attention to himself. 'As a troubadour of some note,' he said. '*I* pluck the Doge's tunes on my *vielle* and I can tell you, Michael, hasn't danced to any of those lately.'

Yusuf laughed, a reverberation that wobbled his belly. 'Ah yes. The minstrel. I remember you from last time and besides, people talk. It seems you are a memorable man. *Salaam Alaykum.*'

'*Alaykum as salaam,*' said Toby. 'And it's *Messire* Celho, if you please.'

Yusuf chuckled, but not to be deflected he turned back to Michael. 'And you, sir, you the mystery. What place do you hold with these who are my friends?' He seemed puzzled. 'I feel as if…' But he shook his head and stood taller, towering over their table, *keffiyeh* folds falling over his shoulders. 'Come. You wish to see spices? We will go to see spices.'

As they walked across the road from the tavern to a walled compound, Michael decided that to pretend was pointless. Yusuf was sharp – a merchant used to assessing and surmising. Even as they walked he would be sifting through his recall…

'In answer to your question, Yusuf, it must be obvious what I am. You observe my clothing, my dagger hilt, even my belt and boots and you put a price on them. All merchants are the same. I assess the value of your damask, of your own belt. So yes, I am a merchant and you would be familiar with me because I sourced goods from you and from others for the house of ben Simon until I left Byzantium a year or so ago, to work in Venezia for Ariella and her father.'

'Ah,' Yusuf clicked meaty fingers. 'I remember. You lived near the Nerion Harbour, close by the Venetian Quarter. I sent messages to your house.'

'You did. Did you not hear that I was leaving?'

'Most likely, but I deal with many people, Michael, and a month is a long time in business, let alone a year or more. I had forgotten. But you see, at least your face remained familiar to me. It is good to do business with you again. So you have just returned to Byzantium?'

'Yes. I met the lady who was to become my wife in Venezia, and after our marriage, we moved to Lyon to help her mother manage the Lyonnais wing of the house of Gisborne-ben Simon.'

'Two houses functioning as one… you are forces with which to be reckoned, I think.' Yusuf pushed open a gate and they entered a sweet-smelling garden of citrus, oleander and olives.

The sound of women singing wound through the greenery, accompanied by pots clattering and the soft chitter and splash of an unseen fountain. They followed the big man as he wove amongst tubs and reached another door which he unlocked and pushed, the timbers grating across a layer of grit and dust, and then everything faded into an aromatic oblivion as the fragrance of the chamber's contents floated out.

Above them all, Michael smelled cinnamon but there were undertones – cumin, anise, fennel, nutmeg, pepper and more. The rough linen bags stood in rows – scarlet, beige, bright yellow, brown and vermilion. To Michael it was like a painting. He had no doubt that to Tobias, it would be inspiration for words and music. And to Ahmed? The smell of money. Nothing else.

'Yusuf, the Angelids are facing rebellion in the Balkans and I've heard more than one person say that the court is foetid with jealousies and that the Komemnoi bide their time. How does such instability affect all this?' He waved an arm to encompass the multi-coloured room.

'Huh, it doesn't. The world will still want its salt and pepper, cumin and cinnamon…' He picked up a cinnamon stick and broke it in half, 'spikenard, *olibanum* and alum. It may be harder to get during times of strife, but it will still come and I shall still sell. Perhaps for a little bit more to ameliorate the difficulties I might face.' He sniffed the cinnamon and then placed the two halves delicately back upon the pile. 'In any case, once a demand is created, it would be a stupid merchant who ignored that demand. One can expect a certain amount of give and take in the marketplace but you would know that it is also impatient and fickle. One does what one can…'

'Indeed,' Michael replied.

Ahmed, who had remained unusually quiet, said, 'You mentioned alum.'

'Alum?'

'You have quality alum they say.'

Yusuf shrugged, shaking his head. 'I don't know who *they* might be, but I do not have alum. May Allah bless me and instead of copious sons, send me a consignment, then I would be a happy man. But it is what it is. *Insh'Allah.*'

The look that Ahmed threw Michael's way was one of contempt and Michael's eyebrows rose. Toby's words hammered in his ears. *He vents like the winds from the Maghreb!*

'It is my fault, I think, Yusuf. I heard a rumour of alum at the docks...' Michael said.

'The docks? Rumours are like gull-shit there, plentiful and rancid. I wish it were true, but no alum has come to me for more than a year. *Olibanum* however...'

'We have *olibanum* suppliers,' Ahmed replied with a cool snap. 'We do not need any more. We came because we thought you would have something unique to offer Gisborne-ben Simon. If you have not, we will maintain our existing orders for spices and leave you.' He stood.

'Yusuf,' Ariella's quiet voice filled the gap that had begun to bristle between the two Arabs. 'You must forgive my father's shipmaster. He seeks only to source special merchandise to increase our standing in trading circles in the west. We are no different to anyone-else in wanting to be leaders, but we mean no disrespect.'

'My dear madame, there is none taken. Ahmed and I have known each other long. He thinks I am a thief, I see him as a *peirate*, but we have always, always been good for each other, have we not, Ahmed?'

Ahmed's expression had the heat of Greek fire, but he nodded. Michael knew he was biding his time in this game and that he intended the winning score to come their way. He wondered how much he needed the shipmaster on his side – his apparent volatility was surely cause for concern. On the other hand, how he admired Ariella's manner. For sure, if it had been his Jehanne, she may not have been quite so diplomatic. '*Mea culpa*, Ariella and Yusuf. I told Ahmed there may be alum here and with his customary business acumen, he thought to procure it. I apologise.'

'Meh,' said Yusuf. 'You all make a fuss of nothing.' He clapped Ahmed on the back. 'You want something not readily available? Then I have some dye...'

Michael's heart crashed, and he was sure everyone would see his face paling to chalk.

'Well, not exactly dye – in time and with preparation, it will be a pigment. I have a red one, cinnabar.' He held up a bag of small blocks. 'From faraway mines and very poisonous. As you can see, it is very pure. It is hard to procure and worth as much as gold leaf, did you know that? Don't snort, Ahmed. Listen to me, you Christians, your church monks will want this. Think of the illuminated scripts…'

He left them to examine the cinnabar whilst he searched for another bag. 'And then there is this – lapis lazuli.' He opened the bag and heaven sat in his palms, shot through with gold like the rays of the rising sun. 'Again, your artist-monks crave it. It grinds to a perfect blue.'

Michael knew they had stumbled across a supply that could add greatly to their business – church scribes would beggar their churches for the purity of these colours.

'These are very expensive…' Yusuf began.

'How expensive?' Ahmed asked.

'Tell us its provenance,' Ariella broke in, moderating the air with skill. 'Both the cinnabar and the lapis.'

'From Khorasan. Conveyed with difficulty from barren terrain and often under threat of attack from the nomads.'

'How expensive?' Ahmed repeated.

'Our church scribes will want it, Ahmed,' Ariella said. 'If we can meet Yusuf with an acceptable price to us all, then I believe we should take it. Michael, what think you?'

Michael nodded. 'Without doubt. I have not seen such pigment for years and it is a new market for us to canvas. What of the stability of the supply, Yusuf?'

'It is slow, it is hard, and it costs accordingly.'

'So you say. But if we find a market, can we rely on you to supply us and *only us,* with regularity.'

'But of course. *Insh'Allah.*'

They began to haggle, Ahmed dismissing Yusuf's original price out of hand, figures traded back and forth in Arabic. Tobias watched, patently soaking up the atmosphere of a deal in progress. At one point Ahmed stood, walked to the door, calling the others to follow, but Yusuf pulled him back with a middle figure.

Michael managed to grab Ariella's attention with a quick nod so she took Ahmed's arm and he bent to her as she whispered.

He called out a last figure and Yusuf spat on his palm, holding out his hand. Ahmed shook it and Michael removed five gold *hyperpirons* from his purse, passing them over.

'A small token in lieu of full payment, Yusuf. Tally what we owe and send the invoice to Ahmed's galley. We will pay half before we sail on to Constantinople and the remaining half when we sail back in three months. Can you hold our stock till then?'

'Of course. It will be safe in my warehouse. I am pleased to be supplying you with the best minerals on the market, Michael Sarapion.'

They walked into the garden with the spice merchant as two fat doves flick-flacked their wings, landing close by. 'Ah, my little feathered friends…' He pulled some grain from a small bag that he held. 'These are my birds – Hercules and Helena. Do you like them?'

A pain shot across Michael's chest at the sound of his deceased wife's name, but he was able to smile as the doves cooed and pecked around their feet. The sound was at once genteel and soothing and they left with compliments and good wishes flying back and forth – *Safe journey. May Allah give you a smooth sea and wind to fill your sails. May you have long and happy health. May you find what you seek in the city…*

May I find what I seek, thought Michael. God and Allah willing.

CHAPTER THREE

×

The gate swung shut behind the four and they headed back toward the docks.

'Our business venture has begun.' There was a quiet confidence to Ariella's voice.

Michael smiled. 'I think your journey has just begun too, Ariella. A new identity, a new role…'

'In truth, Michael, it began some time ago.' She ran her hand over her belly and her lips twisted. 'Let's be honest.'

'That lapis!' Tobias piped up from behind them. 'The blue is un-nerving. It was like looking at the purest sky. Imagine the illumination, a triptych…'

'You found it so, did you, little minstrel?' Ahmed's tone was dismissive of Toby and Michael began to tire of the lazy sarcasm that had been part of the conversation that day. He wondered why the Arab was in such a mood. He was given to arrogance, but never so frequently as this day.

'Me,' Ahmed continued, 'I prefer the gem. Polished so the gold radiates from a smooth blue surface. To crush it for pigment seems a sin.'

'Each to their own, Ahmed. It is why you are a trader and shipmaster and I am an aesthete.' Toby danced away from the cuff that came his way, laughing over his shoulder and Michael was grateful for the minstrel's manner of manipulating Ahmed's mood. Tobias walked backward, speaking to his friends. 'In any case, the blue has value and we make money accordingly.'

'It is a good start,' Ahmed agreed grudgingly. 'I am moderately content. But it would have been better with alum.'

53

Michael cursed himself for even bringing the thought of alum to the proceedings, even if he had been seeking a way to divert Ahmed from other things at the time. A bump in a private journey that promised to be filled with ruts and holes. He wished he could enlighten the others, include them in his self-imposed task. But something always drew him back. And he second-guessed his thought about including Ahmed.

If Ioulia was indeed alive, he had no doubts at all about any kind of life she may have led. He sometimes thought that finding out about that would be worse than not finding her at all.

They reached *Durrah* and as Toby and Ariella sought refreshment from a nearby seller of syrups, Ahmed said quietly to Michael, 'Like I say, a good day's buying, but it would have been better with alum.'

'I have already said I am sorry I misled you, my friend.'

Ahmed's gaze stripped layers off Michael's skin. 'You did. I dropped my guard.'

Michael slapped him on the back, laughing. To which Ahmed continued scathingly, 'But I won't do it again, Michael Sarapion.' He began to walk away.

Fury filled Michael. Fuelled by hate of another *peirate*, fuelled by horror at what was and what might be, fuelled by fear, anxiety, grief, impatience – all of those.

'You arrogant piece of gull-shit,' he called after Ahmed. Around the galley, the heads of the crew flew up from their chores. Faisal straightened and took a step forward.

Ahmed turned. 'What did you say?'

'You heard.'

The Arab approached Michael with a defined step, his shoulders broadening and his expression tightening like a slingshot. Anyone less than Michael would fear what might fly his way. 'Men have died for saying less.'

'You think I'm afraid? *Iisoús Christós*, I've been through more than you can ever know and if you think to scare me then I suggest you come closer, look me in the eye and try harder!' Michael knew that every word he uttered would be like salt in a bloody wound to the shipmaster to whom no one except Tobias, ever answered back.

'May Allah protect you with His mercy, because you are a very unwise man, Michael Sarapion.'

'May Allah protect *you* from your opinion of yourself, Ahmed.'

Ahmed's fists could curl no tighter and he stood so close, Michael could smell his clove-scented breath. A memory flew through his mind of another sea captain whose breath had smelled of cloves and who had promise to slit him end to end with a *paramerion*.

The two men eyed each other like snarling dogs and then Ahmed laughed, punching Michael's arm.

'You are a fool, Michael Sarapion. It is as well I like you.'

'It takes a fool to recognise another fool, Ahmed. You have been as sour as a lemon all day. You deserve the lash of your own tongue sometimes.'

'*Ya kalb!* We all have days when we should have stayed in our bedroll. This is one such. Enough now!'

He held out an arm and Michael grasped it, squeezing. Around them the crew and Faisal subsided like a weak seabreeze, and Michael knew at some point, this was a man he would have by his side.

Constantinople sparkled like the imperial crown that it was, Sancta Sophia's cupolas basking in the sunlight. After a week of glowering sea skies, this day of *Durrah*'s arrival was a gift from God.

'You see,' said Tobias. 'The angels have painted the sky with lapis.'

Ahmed bunched up his cloak and threw it at the minstrel. 'Do you ever see life in anything other than poetry?'

'Not if I can help it,' Toby replied blithely, picking up the cloak off the deck and folding it. 'Life is generally a basket of pig-shit, so why not gild the edges a little?'

Ahmed rolled his eyes and turned his back on Toby, walking to the helm where Faisal stood calling the stroke as the crew bent to the oar. The galley glistened in its own sea-wracked way, Ahmed had made sure, and a new Venetian pennant flew from the masthead. The furled sail was a fresh one, un-faded by an ocean sun and the crew had been trimmed and shaved, dressed in presentable tunics and chemises. New folds of linen flowed around Ahmed and Faisal and together with the comely if quiet costume of the passengers, *Durrah* was the epitome of a successful Venetian galley arriving from its home base.

Michael leaned on the port wale, surveying the hills that had been his home for twelve years. In the distance, Sixth Hill had been his most recent home – the secret one, the one that had hidden him. But when he had arrived in the city twelve years before that and after the *peirate*'s attack upon his family, he had lived close to the Nerion Harbour so that he could watch boats come and go.

Above his head, gulls, the ever-present pirates of the skies, swooped and glided but there was evident calm in their graceful manner. Nothing disturbed them as they circled the city and its waters and Michael took comfort from the fact – as if their relaxed flight presaged smoother times ahead for himself.

Durrah journeyed past the Theodosian sea walls, past the Hippodrome, the Augusteion, Justinian's Column and the Patriarchal Palace where no doubt Father Symeon hovered under the aegis of George II Xipphillinus. Past Sancta Sophia which dominated Michael's view. From the sea, it was indeed the jewel in the imperial diadem – the larger building buttressed with smaller chapels with no less dramatic cupolas. Like a copper-coloured *skoufos,* Michael thought. To deny the beauty was surely to deny God, the hitherto unfamiliar Father Symeon would say. But surely it was possible to appreciate it and still deny God? He sometimes felt such a tide of anger at God that he thought he could scream, throw rocks – kill someone. He squeezed his eyes tight until white flashed across his vision, anything to make him think clearly, not to succumb to vengeful thoughts – not yet.

'It's like the Mask of Janus,' he said to Toby. 'So perfectly crafted, seemingly ordered and benevolent – the smile of the benign. But the other side is rotten. Malevolent emperors who maim to protect their position. Brother blinding brother or mutilating a son so that the imperial throne is kept for the Divinely perfect. And then there are the guards…'

'You don't like the Byzantines, then?' Tobias asked.

'I *am* one, Toby. Lest you forget. But the imperial court has always disgusted me. It's barbaric.'

'Barbarism rules the world, Michael. Always has, always will.'

'A depressing thought.'

Around them, the oars squeaked as they rolled, Faisal's voice still calling the rhythmic stroke, *Durrah* pulling neatly through the waters of the Bosphoros as the vessel approached its turn into the Golden Horn.

'Michael, if you feel as you do, why did you return?' Tobias asked.

The question was like a bolt of *naphtha*, lighting the surrounds with truths, untruths, revelations and secrets and as Michael went to reply, a horn sounded to the larboard stern, a slick galley beginning to pull past them – glossy and oiled like a dark slave from the Maghreb.

'Genovese pig-shit!' Toby said, glancing at the pennant and the fancily-robed shipmaster and his companions standing in the stern.

In truth, Michael thought, less like pig-shit, more like manna from heaven, giving him time to divert Toby from the question. 'You don't like the Genovese?' he asked.

'Pisans and Genovese – I hate them. Florentines not so much. But, they are all the same. They pick the eyes out of Constantinople like crows at a carcass.'

'Rather like us then,' Michael replied. 'And not much different to the emperors who pull the eyes from *their* competition.'

Durrah turned smoothly to larboard and entered the Golden Horn, the anchor points for the great chains that kept the harbours secure glistening in the light. Even though other harbours across the Adriatico had sea-chains, they never had quite the impact of the ones in the Golden Horn.

The Nerion Harbour approached. The Genovese galley began to swing into the Prosphorion Harbour which the Genovese shared with the Pisans and they took comfort knowing the Venetians had their own harbour, their privileged status apparently still recognised.

Ahmed saluted the Genovese shipmaster as they glided past, and Michael would swear the salute ended in one finger, that signal not so polite.

'May Allah give them boils on their arses and fleas in their ears,' they heard him say.

He was no real diplomat.

He now called for the delicate feather stroke and dip that would manoeuvre *Durrah* to her moorings. They laced with care through the vessels in the harbour, Michael and Tobias in awe of the crew as they turned on a knife-point, knowing Ahmed was determined to display the skill of the boat from Venezia. But even so, Michael found himself dwelling on Helena and Ioulia. It was all so fresh, despite it being twelve years and another life before today; seeing the city spread out before him was like a key unlocking the way to abysmal places.

He'd never realised that he had functioned as two different people after his family's demise. He had been the merchant trader travelling round the Sea of Marmara and the Black Sea; the merchant who closed remarkable deals of high value which illuminated the name ben Simon within trader communities. He made friends and enemies as he elevated the Jewish house higher up the ladder. And he was aware of how others viewed him at the time – urbane, insightful, a man with a fiscal understanding that impressed even the wealthiest of Jewish businessmen. The women thought him a young and eminently available man because no one knew he was widowed and daughterless and had no interest in marriage.

He kept the secret, the dark side hidden – the side that so infected his soul with such vengeful grief that sometimes he thought he might just split apart like a pus-filled wound. In those twelve years before he became a thief, he had only heard of an Arab slave trader once and the man too far away, off the coast of the Maghreb, to suffer. He knew it was he for whom he searched – there was the tattoo. But if he prayed at all, he prayed the scabrous murderer would sail into Constantinople and let him have his one chance at revenge.

'Ariella is still asleep?' he asked of Tobias.

'Yes, but I think I shall wake her. I think she's more at ease, now that her secret is known. A secret is a heavy thing to carry, is it not, my friend?'

Michael kept his gaze upon the Nerion Harbour, not daring to look at Toby for fear his soul would be peeled open like the skin from a peach. 'Indeed. Better for her to have all of us looking out for her than Ariella carrying the weight alone. Go wake her. She may appreciate time to prepare, to make herself look like the daughter of the successful ben Simon house. It's all in the playact, Toby, isn't it? Impressions and opinions? We get off this vessel looking like quiet success is our best friend, and it is quite likely that quiet success is what we shall have.'

From the helm, Ahmed shouted a command as they glided into the moorings.

'Then,' said Tobias with a wry laugh. 'Shall you tell Ahmed we need to sound quietly successful, or shall I? And you are right, Michael,' he tapped the side of his nose. 'It's all in the playact.' He hurried to the sterncastle where Ariella lay sleeping.

The mooring lines cracked as they were pulled tight and a small crowd of interested onlookers had gathered – shore workers, whores and merchants –

all assessing the newly arrived galley. There was smart precision in the way the crew snapped to – oars stowed, ropes coiled, gangway laid out.

Ariella joined her companions dressed in a grey textured silkweave, a textile Michael recognised from Damascus. They had received *ells* of it in Lyon and it had sold well – it had a subtle elegance about it that appealed to wealthy merchants and their wives. Ariella's had been embroidered along the hem in silver, attractive work that had the touch of the east. Michael knew she would be well-judged by those merchants and their matrons who walked the docks. Her veil had folded creases from its time in her travel chest, but it was sparkling white linen and held in place at her hairline with two silver pins. Her eyes danced as she looked about her and Michael recognised the look. It was the kind of excitement that had soared around his body as he left Sozopolis so long ago with his family. Excitement born of anticipation and hope.

'I almost feel,' she said to no one in particular, 'that I can bear Guillaume's passing after all.'

'It is a magical place...' Michael replied.

'I have wanted to come here all my life. I would record our merchandise in the ledgers and I would feel silk weaves in my hands and I would just crave to see them arrive in Constantinople from the silk routes. There was a raw story there that I needed to hear and see for myself.'

'I understand, but you see only *this* part of the story, Ariella. The real story is on a camel's back so far away that your child would be two years of age before you reached the end of the journey.'

'But this is surely better than sitting in Venezia waiting for a shipment. This way, I get to *choose* the shipment. It is something Father never understood. I was a housekeeper and an excellent embroiderer in his mind, not someone who could take her place by his side as a merchant. I didn't want to be *just* the merchant's daughter.'

'He was watching for your safety, Ariella.'

'Indeed. But one day he will be gone. This,' she nodded toward the shore where Ahmed's crew had carried their chests and loaded them onto a cart, 'is my inheritance and I want to carry it on. Should I have been born a man, the better to be accepted by society and do my father's work? Probably. But I wasn't and so I must make my mark in whichever way I can. With you here, it will be easier. But I will succeed, Michael, babe or not.'

'Ariella, I have no doubt. And there is much in your attitude that reminds me of Jehanne, and of Ysabel of Gisborne. You are strong women, all of you. Shall we disembark?'

Toby had already gone ashore and was observing everything around him. Ahmed called to them that he would follow on after he had cleared the ship's papers which made Michael think of their own.

'You have your papers? The Byzantines will want to note them as we leave the docks. They are officiously bureaucratic.'

'Yes, in my purse…' She indicated the worn leather that hung from her silk girdle. 'How shall we find our way to the villa?'

'I know where it is. It's been the ben Simon quarters here since even before you left England. Your father had great foresight. In any case, see that man running along the dockside, the one in black? That is the ben Simon notary, Christophorus…'

'Christophorus? Oh! He has been but a name for so long. I shortened it to Christo for ease…'

'He is a good man, and since I left, has kept this side of the enterprise organised. But it is time we introduced new lines into our merchandise and it will be good for us to be here. We can establish new contacts and know that when we leave, Christophorus will handle it with his customary skill.'

Michael waved to the man as he skidded to a halt, breathing heavily.

'Master Sarapion! I did not know… Someone said they saw a ship with a Venetian pennant… Someone else said it was Ahmed. I have received no warning…'

'Christophorus!' Michael helped Ariella step down and then he grasped the man's arm and squeezed it. 'It is so very good to see you again. You look well…'

'I am, I thank you. But why are you…? Have I…?'

'You have done nothing wrong. As always, the business runs as smooth as the silk that we buy. Our journey was organised in rather a hurry and we will explain. But perhaps not here? Perhaps at the house? In the meantime, may I introduce Madame Ariella de Gisborne.'

'Madame.' Christophorus took Ariella's hand and bent over it. 'I am so honoured. I know you are Master Saul's daughter…' There was a note of curiosity drifting between them.

Michael took Ariella by the arm. 'And we will talk more in private. We are a group of four, Christo.' He winked at Ariella. 'There is Tobias Celho, a close friend of the family and of course there will be myself and Ahmed. Have you room for us all?'

'Of course. The house is always ready. I insist upon it. It is the ben Simon house after all, *and* Venetian; there are standards. Follow me, I have a cart waiting…'

He hurried ahead and they followed, Michael grabbing Tobias by the arm because he seemed lost in a dream, staring at the slope ahead and the cupola of Saint Akyntos gleaming between a leaf canopy. He said nothing when he joined them, just walked quietly and Michael chose not to invade his private thoughts.

'Christo?' Ariella whispered.

Michael chuckled. 'We all call him Christo. He is used to it. His full name is too much of a mouthful. As you discovered…'

They followed Christo at pace, their meagre luggage behind, pushed on a squeaking cart by a well-muscled man. At the gates to the harbour, their papers were checked, and they passed into the city with ease. The official was neither curious nor objecting and when Michael glanced over his shoulder and saw a line of merchants, monks, fishermen and sailors all with papers to be noted and he thanked the Saints for a busy day.

Not that there was anything wrong with any of their documents – the travellers hid nothing. Even Tobias, who had a sensitive history. Nevertheless, Michael found his chest relaxing, as if until then, he had been holding his breath, afraid to let it go.

Tobias jogged to keep up with Christo, having pushed his introspective mood aside to chat amiably, but Michael and Ariella walked more slowly in deference to the warmth of a Byzantine spring day and to Ariella's burgeoning load.

'I won't be sorry to live on land,' she said. 'To have steady ground under one's feet will be a Godsend and to sleep on a bed, even to have a bath after so long at sea. It is some time since Cyprus.' She referred to her stay in Famagusta and the last bath afforded her.

'They call it a villa, but it is not what you might expect. Nothing at all like your home or Gisborne's.'

'How do you know what I expect?' she chided him, puffing a little as they headed up the euphemistically named Little Mese toward Basilike Street on Third Hill.

He grinned. 'It is perhaps more like de Clochard's Lyonnais house – in height if nothing else. I have no idea of its interior as I lived further away. My business with Christo was invariably conducted in his office on the ground floor of Basilike Street – barely more than an alcove – or at my own quarters.'

'Rue Ducanivet in Lyon is a home to be proud of.' Ariella stopped for a moment and looked back toward the harbour, shielding her eyes against the sun, but a haunted memory flitted across her face.

'It has a familial warmth,' she continued. 'And despite everything, I do have good memories. It is where Guillaume's and my child was conceived and it is where I learned that I can survive, no matter the outcome. All that from a quaint house set high above the Saône. To be honest, I think having the water close by was balm. Since living in Venezia, I find I crave a proximity to water – it calms me. Does Basilike Street see the water?'

Christo stood on the steps of the house on the corner of the street, pulling at heavy, grand gates that Michael didn't recognise. The notary turned and scanned the way, looking for the remainder of the party.

'You will see. There it is. See for yourself…'

The stone blocks of the house had been laid in an orderly fashion, the colour of faded porphyry, continuing in stripes to a further stone level. The roof was shallow pitched with terracotta tiles, and two balconied windows hung suspended over both Basilike Street and the Little Mese. The windows had wooden shutters swung wide and they had been glassed – another Venetian innovation, along with the imposing gates, so that an air of prosperity abounded. The house sat detached, with a row of Holy Oak trees buffering it from its neighbours.

'It's bigger than I imagined, grander. Father never said…'

'Saul ben Simon is successful, and this house says so. It's all part of the posturing and playacting that I mentioned. Look along Basilike Street – the buildings are all quite similar except that yours, for it *is* indeed yours, commands premium position at the corner. I imagine from the balconied window that hangs over the Little Mese, you will see the water quite easily.'

Michael noted the gates were big and as solid as a fortress, that the ground floor had not a single window and the balconies were higher even than a man standing on another's shoulders. It gave one the sense of being well protected.

Good...

Christo waved and they hurried toward him, beginning to cross the Little Mese to Basilike Street. A large mob of men walked down the slope of Third Hill, filled with banter, swallowing Toby and Ariella into their rowdy midst. Michael called loudly, telling them to mind his friends, but they leered at him, Ariella yelling as they tugged her backward. A flash of fear crossed her face and Michael pulled out his dagger, shoving and pushing. This was no ordinary crowd – there was planned malice here and Tobias shouted, getting below the levels of girdles and belts and punching at groins and knees as a cry of pain echoed along the street. As quickly as the crowd had arrived so they melted away, leaving Ariella on her knees, her veil lying beside her, her *misericorde* in her hand. Blood tipped the end of it and she looked up at Michael and Toby, grinning.

'Women who have children within their wombs fight like lions it seems,' she said as they helped her up.

'So do minstrels called to account for their size. Where do you hurt?' Toby brushed at the dirt on her gown.

'Only my knees from the street. Tobias, cease fussing! I gave as good as I got. Someone has a deep wound from a *misericorde* somewhere on their body.' She dragged the blade across her veil leaving a carmine line, and then slid it into the dainty leather scabbard at her girdle. 'Michael, if that was mere happenstance, I will eat this veil. Are we targets?'

Tobias and Michael looked at each other and then at Christo as he ran into their midst, telling them to come immediately to safety.

'The city always has an edge to it, but not like this!' he apologised, and shooed them, like a peasant woman hustling her chickens. Eventually the heavy gates of the Basilike Street residence were swung behind them, a wooden bar placed across so that the monastic quiet of the property gave them time to get their breath, to calm, to take stock.

The house was built around an open square and shaded with old Judas trees, their pale violet blossom announcing spring. Tubs of thyme and rosemary guarded the entrance to the kitchens and filled the air with delicate promise. A loggia ran around the sides of the forecourt and the grapevine that graced the heavy uprights and horizontals was filled with green shoots and small bursts of leaves all over. The ground floor space, kitchens, store rooms, a small stable – all had heavy doors that could be shut if security or the weather required it. To the side of the gates, a narrower door stood wide and a sheet of parchment had fluttered from a scribe's desk to lie on the ground under the loggia. Christo's space was indeed little more than an alcove.

'That was no accident. Ariella is right,' Toby's small stature puffed up with indignation. 'Who is to blame? No one knows Ariella. It has to be because of you or I, Michael. But so quickly? It's…'

'Tobias! Stop!' Michael's voice rose a little over Toby's concern. 'This *must* come later *and* with Christo, after we have informed him of why we are here. Christo, can you show us to our chambers? We can refresh, maybe eat? And then, and only then, we shall sit and digest things.'

'Indeed, Master Sarapion…' A hefty knock sounded on the entrance doors and Christo turned. 'Excuse me, that will be Phocus with the handcart.' He lifted the bars and the burnished leather man pushed the cart in. 'Phocus is our guard, indeed our everything. Phocus, this is Master Sarapion, Master Celho and Madame de Gisborne. They will be with us for…' He looked at Michael, enquiry and curiosity in his expression.

'A three month at least. Phocus, thank you for your help. Would you join us shortly? If you are the guard here, you must be included in our discussions.'

The tall Byzantine bowed, and in a voice to rival Ahmed's deeply velvet tones, replied, 'Indeed, Master Sarapion. It would be my pleasure.'

As he walked away, Michael saw Tobias' eyebrows rise. *Such manners in a man who looks like a wrestler? Interesting…* Sometimes one could see straight through Toby.

Michael's chamber was plain. But he had the balcony that looked over Basilike Street and he gravitated straight to the thickly glassed window which was pushed wide. Leaning over a cushioned settle, he examined the buildings opposite, watching people walk back and forth, seeing the washed-blue sky above the terracotta roofs. The gulls were ever present but there were other birds as well, waterbirds of strident voice and he delighted in the white heron which stood on the roof ridge opposite, head turned toward the Nerion Harbour. In moments, it had stretched its wings and pushed off and with graceful flaps had flown in a half-circle to move out of view.

He unpacked his sparse clothing into a chest and sat on the bed which was big enough for two, running his hands over the bedding – fine weave blankets, a soft Persian silk quilt. The pillows were filled with goose-down, so much better than the thin bedroll and hard deck of *Durrah*, the ever-present dampness and the chills of night, no matter how tightly one wrapped one's cloaks. He looked around – *this* would be comfortable. Even better, he could allow a breeze from the water to enter through the opened windows, a God-send as summer days approached. The sheer domesticity of it all was a welcome reprieve from the tension that lay in his gut like fermenting wine.

There was a soft tap at the door and he opened it to a tiny woman standing with a bowl and a full pitcher of water, some linen squares draped across her shoulder. Maybe sixty years of life had etched the fine lines across her face and when she smiled, gaps were revealed in her teeth. As she spoke, her gold earrings winked in the spring light.

'I am Ephigenia,' she said in Greek. 'You speak Greek? Good. Welcome, Master Sarapion. Some water and linen for you to wash?' She pushed by him to place the items on the chest, shoving the cushions aside with her elbows. He smelled citrus as she passed, as though she had been peeling lemons. 'Do you wish for food or wine in your chamber?'

'No, thank you – but perhaps we can have something under the loggia? And can you take water and towels to madame, please? She is tired and has not been well.'

'It is done. I have given her a fresh lemon syrup and some dates and fresh bread. She must look after two, not just one.' Ephigenia laid her finger by the side of her nose. 'I can see she will need to be reminded. She is tough.'

He grinned back at the little Byzantine woman. 'You are right, and I think you are just the one to keep her under control. I thank you, Ephigenia.'

'Ah, it is what I enjoy. I knew her father and it is my pleasure to care for his daughter. I haven't had guests to care for since...' she stopped and then smiled her gap-toothed smile. 'Since I can't remember! Ha! Now, I will make sure a platter or two are placed under the loggia for you. This is madame's home after all and you are all her family I think. Are you not?'

She left, leaving an echo of clicking kneecaps and the fragrance of fresh citrus behind and Michael began to feel that Basilike Street was the haven they all needed as he dipped a linen square in the water and began to wash his face and neck. He glanced at the cloth, noting the dirty marks and thought perhaps he, Toby and Ahmed should find a *thermae,* leaving Ariella in the tender care of Ephigenia. He found his wooden comb in the bottom of his sac and began to tease the knots out of his hair one by one, until it lay smooth, if not salt-free, and as he stood, comb in hand, contemplating the view from the window again, Toby pushed the door open.

'I have the most delightful chamber – it looks out onto the forecourt and is so quiet. After *Durrah,* I shall feel I have entered heaven.' He looked around. 'God's teeth, Michael. Look at yours – *and* you have a glassed window! Christo has done well for Saul.'

'It's a spacious chamber – even a small scribe's desk. I have a feeling that this may be Saul's space, should he ever visit. Have you been to Ariella?'

'Not yet. Her chamber has the other balcony…'

'Good. She wanted to see the water, it calms her.'

'Then I hope it's doing its job right now. That was no fun, Michael.'

'Indeed. We need to pick it apart, but I wonder if we should wait and include Ahmed. He is part of this… what? Companionship? Delegation? Family?'

'I would call it family,' Toby said. 'Mind you, I remember Gisborne saying once that one is at liberty to select one's friends with care but that the same liberty does not apply to family. Perhaps we have built a family out of circumstance.'

'Family then.'

'And stronger for the circumstance which has built it, I would say.' Toby added.

'Indeed. Shall we fetch her to come to the loggia? It is time we talked.'

Time indeed, but Michael kept such rumination to himself. How much do I tell them about my dilemma? Is *this* the time? Still he shrank from involving others in his private affairs and yet it seemed wrong, as if by excluding them, he might be putting them in danger. There was a babe to consider – an even greater risk. As he and Toby walked to Ariella's door, he came to a decision.

He would tell them everything.

But not till he had visited Father Symeon at Sancta Sophia. Once he had talked to the monk, then he would have information on which to base a plan.

The sun trickled through the loggia to lie like scattered gold coins on the trestle and ground. Amongst the treasure lay large wooden platters of bread, spicy *keftedes* and dried dates stuffed with ground almonds, cinnamon and nutmeg.

''Tis an advantage living on a trade route and within a trading hub,' Toby remarked as he chewed a plump date. 'Although the venal side is a concern.'

''Tis so,' agreed Ariella. 'That was deliberate.'

'Why do you think so?' Michael asked.

'I felt it. One of them snarled in quite plain Greek, *Devil spawn die.*'

Michael sat straight, a complicit glance thrown Toby's way. 'Truly?'

She nodded.

'Do they refer to me the oddity or you the Jew?' Toby asked.

Michael sought to ameliorate the moment. 'Ariella, do you think they attacked you personally or the ben Simon house?'

'I *am* the ben Simon house, Michael.'

'As I am.' Toby wiped his fingers fastidiously on a linen square. 'But maybe they attack Gisborne indirectly. Who knows how many he may have offended.'

'My father or Gisborne or myself – we are indivisible. Personally, I think someone has a set against our trading house. My question is why?'

Toby sat back and blew out his cheeks whilst Michael made a pyramid of his fingers. 'What surprises me is how early this has happened. We have just arrived. Even Christo was unaware that we were coming. So how did *they* know?'

'Who are *they?*' asked Toby.

'Therein lies the problem… Ah, Christo! Phocus! Please join us. We talk of what happened earlier.'

Christo nodded, 'I have told Phocus.'

'Good. And we will talk of it anon but let me tell you why we are come here and without notice. Saul wished for new stock, something remarkable to be sourced and which would set the Venetian markets on fire. *Kyría* Ariella needed time to heal from the unfortunate passing of *Kýrie* Guillaume. So she and *Kýrie* Saul thought for her to step into Saul's shoes. It seemed right given that she will inherit his share of the company when the time comes. *Kyría* Ariella wished to depart as soon as was practicable and so once the sea lanes had opened again, we sailed on Ahmed's ship. I have come to escort Ariella because

I head the Lyonnais branch of the business, as you know, and am a close friend of the family. Tobias is also a friend but has private business to conclude whilst he is here. And whilst *Kyría* Ariella should perhaps have had a woman to escort her, there wasn't time to employ a companion, and to be honest, having met Ephigenia, I suspect *Kyría* Ariella is thinking she will suit eminently.'

'If she wishes to, I would be very happy,' Ariella added.

Christo smiled. 'I know Ephigenia well enough to know she'd be delighted.'

'Then that is settled,' Michael continued. 'Ahmed, Ariella and myself are here to find the unfindable. With your help.'

'I see…' Christo pursed his lips.

'We have already secured exceptional minerals for the pigments our church scribes use. The commodities will be devoured when we return.'

'May I ask where you purchased these?' Christo had been rapidly scratching notes on a wax tablet.

'From Yusuf Al Fayaad in Gallipolis. We collect the goods in a three month, when we sail back to Venezia. They are very pure minerals, Christo. The purest I have seen. Almost too good to be ground down for pigment.'

'I don't doubt their quality, *Kýrie* Michael, but I worry on the price.'

'An excellent price. Ariella has her father's skill and besides, Ahmed assisted, and you know Ahmed…'

'Only too well,' Christo replied dryly. 'And I am glad you have closed a deal with satisfaction. But may I say how concerned I am with what happened earlier. The city has its moments, without doubt, but that was something distinctly different. I believe it was premeditated.'

'We agree,' said Toby. 'They taunted us – *devil spawn* – a reference to something, but we are unsure what. Perhaps me. I don't know.'

Phocus looked at Christo, who shrugged. 'I am at a loss…' the notary replied.

Michael shifted his position to avoid the glare of a small sunbeam burning his eye. 'As are we. And because you have rather confirmed what we feared, I believe we need more guards. Phocus?'

'Of course, *Kýrie* Michael. Five, including myself?'

'Good – and with us to bolster the numbers.'

Phocus glanced at Toby who bridled.

'I know I am small – alright, very small – but I shall tell you plainly that this…' his stumpy fingers pulled his knife from its scabbard, '…this knife has wounded a number of men and even killed one. I can protect anyone's back.' He spoke without rancour. Others would be less equable. No doubt defending his imp status for years had honed a certain manner.

'I will vouch for Tobias,' Michael said.

'Forgive me,' Phocus touched his chest. 'I meant no disrespect, *Kýrie* Tobias.'

'None taken, Phocus.' Toby thumped him on the arm. 'And as we're all family here, call me Toby or Tobias. Everyone else does.'

To which Christo added, 'Indeed, Tobias.' He dipped his head as he said Toby's name. 'You are quite correct because Ephigenia is Phocus' mother and my aunt. Phocus is my cousin, and family is everything. *Kýrie* Saul always said so.'

Ariella's eyes sparkled momentarily but she blinked and it was gone. Michael could never imagine her revealing a gap in her defences. But that she felt the loss of what might have been her family was undeniable. And he knew what *that* felt like. For the moment, though, he was content. He had always trusted Christo, and Phocus was of the same ilk. He would find guards and they would be as trustworthy as those in Lyon. Big, solid, seasoned and discreet men – probably from an extended family somewhere in the city or just outside the walls.

'I am sorry that this should happen upon your arrival,' said Christo. 'This house has always been secure and on the periphery of issues, be they economic or political. A normal trading house existing amongst normal traders…' he looked round and shrugged his shoulders.

Michael felt he should ameliorate the man's concerns, but in truth, he was as astonished as anyone that tension should emerge so soon. He had always thought perhaps Tobias might have precipitated notice due to his past history. Or maybe even himself. But so quickly?

Ephigenia walked through the door to the loggia, pushing her son aside and reaching for the empty platters, reminding them as she bustled, that Ariella needed to rest. Phocus excused himself, promising to return with men, and Toby, blessed Toby, lightened the mood by asking Christo if there were baths nearby.

It served to break the meal neatly with Ephigenia and Ariella departing – a mother hen hustling her chick to the nest. As they left, Christo gave Tobias directions to the old public baths in *Thermae* Street.

CHAPTER FOUR

×

Later, stripped naked and in a pool with other men, curvaceous women walking along the periphery with linen towels in their arms and seduction trailing behind, Michael and Tobias surveyed the cracked walls and the worn floors and the few remaining statues that graced the humid space. Behind the shadows of the statues, faded paintings depicted alternating scenes of bucolic havens and Bacchanalian feasts.

They lazed in the water of the *tepidarium*. Neither particularly wanted to step into the scald of the *caldarium*, nor suffer the freeze of the *frigidarium*, so they lingered.

'Baths have that grand Roman logic, don't they?' said Toby. 'Affectation, cleanliness and a subtle invitation to licentiousness.' He watched a woman walk past in folds that left nothing to be imagined and then lay back, the fine black hairs on his chest wafting like a baby's down in the water. He scrubbed at a stubborn mark on his wrist and then let his small, muscled body float.

Michael sat in the corner of the baths, arms looped over the edge of worn mosaic tesserae. 'This one is well past its prime, but it does the job.' He relished the tepid water, beginning to feel human again. 'Too much salt before…'

'But that is what happens at sea.' A familiar voice sounded behind them and they looked back. 'Salt, sun, weathering. 'Tis why we end up like a piece of tanned leather.' Ahmed slid his lean muscular frame in beside them, dunking his shaved head and allowing the water to stream off. The woman of the transparent robes smiled at him from the edge of the baths and he grinned back. 'That's better. I hate the *caldarium* and despise the *frigidarium* even more. The *frigidarium* reminds me of drowning.'

'And have you ever been so unfortunate?' Toby asked.

'I am alive am I not? Thus, I have never drowned.'

Toby flicked an arm across the water, sending a spray over Ahmed. 'You know what I mean.'

'All sailors have nearly drowned, little music-man. It is one of the perils.'

'Then tell me!' Toby said. 'You know I soak up stories like a sponge. It is what makes me and my music so good!'

'Your ego is too big, little man. And you are as annoying as the *cincelle* fly that all the crusaders whine about,' Ahmed growled. 'A boat I sailed hit a reef. It sank, I nearly drowned. A common story. You would call it a refrain, so often do the words lace through sailors' speech.'

The pain in Michael's chest sharpened. He wished he could sink beneath the water until Ahmed had finished, but Toby persisted.

'Where?' Then he said with a complicit grin at Michael who didn't want to grin at all. 'Tell. We are all family here.'

'Some things are better left fathoms deep, little man. Deeper than an abyss.' And with the lightning change in mood that was his manner, he turned to Michael and said, 'What do you think of Basilike Street?'

Michael dragged his attention back from the image of Ioulia drifting down through the deeps, away from his hand. 'Good. It is comfortable and central and will suit us.'

'And it seems we have enemies to repel.' Toby spoke quite calmly as if all he remarked upon was the weather. 'Let the games begin.'

Ahmed's brows bent. He had expressive brows, almost like a woman's – black and finely sculpted and as his eyebrows moved, so his dark eyes hardened to the unforgiving tint of obsidian. Wildness that was a warning.

Michael had often thought Ahmed was like a wolf. He moved softly with a vulpine awareness of all that went on around him. It radiated from him so that people took two steps back.

Except for Tobias.

The lengths he took with Ahmed astonished even those who had known the Arab for a lifetime. A partnership of differences.

The imp grinned and said, 'Barely disembarked and we had our first drama.'

'What say you?' Ahmed sat still and at his tone, the hopeful bath attendant walked away. She knew when business became more than pleasure.

'We had almost reached Basilike Street and a group surrounded Ariella and myself, separating us. They meant to cause damage but we gave as good as we got and they departed with a few scratches they won't forget.'

'Deliberate business?'

'Very deliberate,' said Toby. 'Or so I believe.'

Ahmed sat back in the pool. 'So…' he muttered under his breath. He rubbed his chest and then down his arms, scrubbing hard. Anger? Michael thought so.

'And what did you do about it,' the Arab eventually asked.

'Talked with Christo and Phocus. They have no clues as to why. But Phocus is getting extra men to guard the house. My question is if it was deliberately directed at us, how were people in the city aware we were coming? Even Christo did not know…'

'We were in Gallipolis. We were no doubt seen. Perhaps a vessel left well before us. Who would know?' Ahmed rubbed at his scarred hands as he spoke.

Michael wanted to shake Ahmed's self-possession. 'Is it an attack on the merchant house itself – Gisborne, Saul and Ariella are all part of one of the most successful trading houses between Venezia, Constantinople and Lyon. Or is it an attack on me? Does someone know me from a former life? Or is it an attack on Tobias, the brother of the stealer of icons?'

Cynical, amused, Ahmed merely asked, 'And what did you decide?'

'Nothing yet, because the other thought I have had is perhaps it might have been an attack upon you. Perhaps someone is jealous of your success, Ahmed.'

Ahmed tipped his head, a wry grimace. 'It is good to be recognised.'

Tobias slammed his fist on the water. 'You arrogant son of a bitch! They could have hurt Ariella and her babe. Did you think on that?'

The eyebrows set hard and the eyes darkened. But then, 'I apologise. I like the lady Ariella and would not wish her to be hurt. Apart from anything else, her father would kill me.'

'*I* would kill you!' said Toby, climbing out of the pool. He grabbed a linen towel, tied it round his hips and strode off toward the *frigidarium*.

'He will cool down in there,' said Ahmed.

'I am glad you find amusement at our expense, Ahmed. For myself, I find this serious enough to have urged Phocus to secure extra guards. I have not yet forgotten Lyon.' Michael referred to the attacks upon the household of de Clochard, his wife's family. An attack that was in fact focused on Guillaume de Gisborne, Guy of Gisborne's half-brother.

'Neither have I, Michael. But we live in a tough world. It may be a trading jealousy as you say…'

'Revenge?'

'For what? That one has surely paid out.'

'I don't know. The point is that it was a very focused attack on Toby and Ariella. Ariella, I might add proved herself eminently. Sadly for the attackers.'

'Good for Madame de Gisborne.' Ahmed sat forward, the water slapping against the side of the pool. 'I would say revenge, jealousy – they all have a place. The difficult thing is finding out who feels so strongly they would attack so early and so brazenly.'

'Indeed. But what about you? Do you think you are the safe one amongst us?'

Ahmed stood, the water streaming from his magnificent golden body. There were puckered strips, for he had not led a blameless life, but his muscled build was a sight to behold. 'Oh Michael, I am never safe. What sailor is? But I remain philosophical about it. And I am always ready.' He tied a linen towel around his slim hips. 'Do you go to the *frigidarium*?'

'No. I find I am done with the baths.' Michael stood and followed Ahmed to the dilapidated dressing room, where they both pulled on clothing. Michael towelled his hair and shook it back. 'Ahmed, I think this business is serious. Don't rile Tobias by making it less so. He carries wounds from his time here. It isn't easy to have one's brother's grave so close – especially a brother that was executed as a felon.'

'And what about you, Michael? Do you carry wounds?' Ahmed's tone was one of insouciance and suddenly Michael was livid. He turned on Ahmed.

'You are so arrogant. So patronising. Think on it, Arab. I shall see you anon.' He stormed into the light of a Byzantine spring day, breathing deep as he walked in no particular direction, but finding fountains and corners that he recognised. Just above the Prosphorion Harbour, he sat, watching the boats swing at anchor, observing the sleek Genovese galley that had slid by them early in the day.

'She's beautiful, isn't she?' A man's voice sounded by his side.

'She is indeed. Does she belong to a particular company?'

'Of course. The Vigia family lease her. Do you know of them?'

The Vigia family! Mother of God!

'No. Are they famous?'

'They will be.' The man sat by Michael's side. 'Good day to you. I am Branco Izzo, of the Vigia house…'

The man was as tall as Michael, swarthy, much younger and whip-thin. A hungry young man…

'You are a son perhaps?'

'A son by marriage. My wife, Pieta, is a Vigia. The son and heir, Pietro, died.'

'I see…' Michael's neck hair lifted.

Toby's likely enemy, here…

'And you are?' the Genovese asked.

Izzo's nasal tones grated on Michael, but he replied with feigned equanimity. 'My name is Michael Sarapion.'

'Sarapion. The name has a familiar sound. Are you a merchant?'

Honesty…

'I am.'

'From Venezia?'

'Indirectly. I am a Byzantine. Most recently I have been in Lyon.'

'Ah. Lyon. I have heard that there is a house there being eaten up by the infamous Gisborne-ben Simon house. De Clochard, is it not?'

'It is. I know the house well. They trade superb silks.'

'Pah. I spit on their silks. Ours will be the stuff for which kings fight wars.'

'Any silk from over the water there,' Michael nodded his head, 'is the kind kings fight for. From where do you hope to source yours?'

'*Messere* Michael,' Branco touched Michael's arm, 'may I be so familiar? You are a merchant, why would I tell you our secrets?'

Michael laughed. To him the sound rang so hollow it could have been a resounding tocsin, echoing back to the house in Basilike Street. 'Indeed. And you are quite right to keep your secrets close to your chest. It's the secrets that give one the edge.'

If only you knew…

'I find I like you, *Messere* Michael. Would you perhaps do my wife and I the honour of dining with us in the Genovese Quarter? We know few here in the city. Tell me where you live and I shall send a more proper invitation.'

'The corner of Little Mese and Basilike Street, *Messere* Branco. I fear you may not like it when you hear that I stay in the house of ben Simon and Gisborne.'

Branco Izzo sat back, his eyes intense upon Michael. Michael returned an amicable gaze.

'Then we are rightly competitors, *Messere* Michael.'

'Perhaps. Who knows? But there is no reason why we can't be friends.'

Except that if you knew the man who killed your wife's brother shared a house with me, I would be your worst enemy...

Branco sat so still, his slim, almost feminine body as straight as the blade of a *misericorde*. Michael waited not so patiently as the moments beat by.

'They say, do they not, to keep your competitors within your ambit...' Branco began.

'I think it is more that we are meant to keep our enemies close, *Messere* Branco, and I hope against all hope that I am not your enemy...'

There was just one breath too long, enough for Michael to know exactly where he stood.

'Of course not. I find I like your quiet wisdom, *Messere* Michael. Trust is not an easily sourced commodity in Constantinople and I hope you feel you can trust me the way I trust you.'

Now there is an ambiguous statement if ever I heard one...

'*Messere* Branco, I am a Byzantine. Whilst I live in Basilike Street, I believe I have friends across all trading quarters. Let us hope we can rise above the pathetic squabbles between the quarters and set an example.' He held out his hand and Branco took it.

'I am happy to have met you and I suspect my wife will be pleased to make the acquaintance of an urbane man such as yourself.'

But the words sounded shallow and Michael expected nothing less. The same as he no longer expected to be invited to dinner at the Vigia house. Perhaps a blessing.

Branco Izzo stood. 'I must go. As my wife is with child, I do not want to upset her. *Valete.*' He saluted, fingers flicking his temple, and with a narrow grin from his starved mouth, he hurried along the street, turning down toward the harbour.

Michael let go his breath, closing his eyes against calamity – Tobias, revenge, and the Vigia bride with child, just like Ariella within their own house. Fate was surely playing games. He set off for Basilike Street with purpose, not surprised to find that his hand gripped the pommel of his dagger.

He banged through the doors not long after, calling for Toby. But there was no answer from the diminutive minstrel and suddenly he was afraid for him…

'*Kÿrie* Michael! There is trouble?' Phocus came running.

'I don't know. Toby…'

'He is inside,' Phocus said as four men approached from behind him – big fellows, like the public wrestlers Michael often saw travelling the country.

'My friends,' Phocus said. 'I swear on my life and theirs that they can be trusted.'

'Of course,' Michael replied.

'This is Bonus…' Phocus indicated a man with long brown hair plaited at the nape and who leaned on a *kontarion* as sharp as a needle. With the weight of his bulk, it was a sheer wonder the spear didn't bend.

'Julius…' Slimmer but with rippling forearms and bunched calves. Under the worn leather *epilōrikion* would be more of the same. Julius had a scar above his lip and when he smiled, his lip twisted.

'Hilarius…' The same build as Julius, but handsomer, with rippling black hair that he tossed over his shoulder. A *spathion* hung by his side and his hand rested easily upon it.

'And Leo.' Leo was as bald as a baby and perhaps the oldest. But terrifying – tall and broad, with a plait of black hair hanging from the side of his head, a touch of the exotic.

'From Khorasan?' Michael asked.

Leo nodded.

'I thank you all for joining us. I am sure Phocus has told you how much we will be relying on you. Phocus, as soon as I have spoken to Tobias, I need to sit with all of you and inform you of what we may be up against. And please, from now on, I am just Michael. We are all equals. Toby is inside, you say?'

'I think he may be with the lady, playing music.'

Of course…

He ran through the door from the yard and on up the stair, turning to Ariella's room as Tobias pulled the door shut with care, Michael's footsteps echoing along the passage.

'Hush, she sleeps.'

'Toby, come to my chamber,' Michael whispered.

Slipping into the room, Michael closed the door and leaned back against it as Tobias walked to the chest, climbed on it and looked through the window.

'Ahmed is such an arrogant bastard. May Allah shrink his balls to raisins,' he said peaceably over his shoulder. 'But Christ's toenails, Michael, I find I like him such a lot and would have him at my back any day.'

'What?' Michael frowned and then remembered the exchange of heat between Tobias and Ahmed at the baths. 'Oh yes. Of course. But this isn't to do with Ahmed.'

Toby stayed turned from Michael, elbows propped on the wooden sill, watching Basilike Street live its life. 'Lovely heron on the roof opposite.'

'Toby, pay attention! The Genovese galley that you spat upon this morning as we sailed along the Horn…'

'I didn't spit,' Toby said, turning around. 'But I could have…'

'Toby, the name Vigia…'

Toby jumped off the chest. 'If I didn't respect your room and the chest, *now* I would spit!'

'The Vigia house is alive and apparently well.'

It was as if all the life-giving air inside Toby was being sucked away as he sagged. 'It's *impossible*. I killed him…'

'That's as may be. There appears to be a sister.'

'That lying piece of blood and bone! He told me he was the only offspring, the heir…' Toby begun to puff up again.

'A sister who is married and she and her husband are here to pick up the fortunes of the Vigia where Pietro left off.'

Toby began to pace. He tried to speak but nothing emerged as Michael watched him kill Pietro Vigia over and over again in his mind. He had paled – his evenly tanned face the colour of a dirty death shroud. 'It's me then, isn't it? They saw me in Gallipolis and organised a welcoming committee. Oh, my Christ.' He sketched a cross.

'Perhaps.' But to Michael it all seemed a little too easy – Toby being seen and recognised by the Vigia family so swiftly that a boat could be sent forthwith to Constantinople to organise a response.

'You are not convinced? I really need to hear that you are not.'

'I don't know. I'm not downplaying the danger you now face if they are of a mind for revenge. But there is more at play here.'

'Huh! Normally I would be intrigued but I find myself unable to think on aught else but their need for vengeance. If the rest of the family is as poisonous as Pietro, I stand little chance but to commit more murder to survive.'

'Yes.'

'Unambiguous and thus my day plummets to the depths. This voyage was difficult enough – confronting my demons. Now I find those demons are flesh and blood. And of course, there is Ariella whom I make so vulnerable by my presence. I should leave. Find a galley returning to Venezia and sail forthwith.'

'Ariella would be devastated if you left and perhaps feel even more vulnerable. We must trust that the guards Phocus has employed will do their job. They are built like brick privies and have enormous scars of provenance with stories to tell. Toby, we can't deny that you are easily identified. It is what it is and you are what you are. We must just guard ourselves and you accordingly.'

They talked around in circles until Michael called an end to it. They had made no headway and he felt they needed time to pass to see if a pattern developed. But as they prepared to leave the room, a memory pulled him up short.

'Toby – remember Gallipolis? That moment as we walked back to *Durrah*? Someone does indeed know us. We need to talk to Phocus and the guards. Come.'

They sat round a table, Tobias dwarfed between Phocus and Leo but he seemed unperturbed, as if they provided security in what had been a breach in the walls of his life. Michael explained the detail – of Gallipolis, of the event earlier in the day, stressing the lack of pattern but saying he felt the house may be targeted.

'How so?' asked Leo of Khorasan. He had been toying with his side plait, a movement that gave him the quaint air of a young girl and utterly incongruous.

Michael wondered how much to divulge. Always cautious but how much was *too* cautious? 'We all…'

But Toby jumped in. 'It's because of me.' The big men all turned to the diminutive minstrel, Bonus' face alight with a sceptical grin. 'Don't judge me by my size, Big Man,' Toby added, pointing at him. 'You see, *I* killed a man. A man from a Genovese merchant family. And when I killed him, I thought the family would die with him and I did not care, but I was wrong. Not about killing him, mark you. I was glad about that!'

The men sat back. In awe? Perhaps, thought Michael, as Toby relayed the vengeful saga of he and Pietro Vigia. Toby's voice trembled with anger and his fists clenched and at one point he hit the table hard with both hands.

'My brother lies not far from here. Would he have died if Pietro Vigia had not sold him to the Byzantines? I say no. Others might think differently.' He looked Michael right in the eye and Michael shook his head.

'So,' said Phocus. 'You killed this man out of vengeance.'

'Yes.' Toby snapped.

'Tobias,' Phocus touched Toby's arm. 'I make no judgement. But if Pieta and Branco Izzo find out you killed a loved family member, do you not think they will feel they have the right to seek redress?'

'Of course. And I must be ready for them. My only concern is that none here are hurt because of me.'

'It is why we are here,' said Leo. 'We guard. Sometimes we fight and kill. It is what we do and we are good at it.'

Aware that blood was beginning to rise and weapons to rattle, Michael spoke quietly. 'We belong to a successful Venetian trading hose, Leo. One that has imported many exceptional goods to the west. There are no doubt business jealousies.'

'You have debts?' Bonus asked.

'None.'

Toby's eyes slitted and Michael willed him to say nothing yet of his own past, of the theft of the Tyrian purple. But Toby was ever forthright. 'Michael, you must tell them…'

Five heads turned in unison – puppets, thought Michael inconsequentially. He sat forward and clasped his hands together on the table. 'In a moment. Firstly, I want to hear *your* backgrounds. Phocus?'

Phocus frowned and then cleared his throat. 'I am Christo's cousin. I…'

'I know that. What did you do before coming here?'

'Christo employed me when I returned from the Maghreb.'

'Yes…' Michael encouraged.

'Bonus and I were galley slaves. You can see our chain scars if you do not believe...' They both stood and began to pull off their boots to reveal ankles purpled with scars.

'It is unnecessary,' Michael said. '*Peirates?*'

Phocus nodded. 'We crewed a trading galley. We have no love for *peirates*. *Kindred then...*

Leo spoke into the short silence. 'Julius, Hilarius and I were in the army in the Balkans. We tired of it.'

'You absconded?' Toby asked with interest.

'We left.'

'Without notice, though? And came here?'

'The Balkans are far from here and no one knows us. Julius is from Trabzon in Chaldia. I am from Khorasan and now look very different. In the Balkans, I had hair and my size is not unique. There are a lot of big men from Khorasan who use their bulk to wrestle and fight. I am one of many. Many good ones, of course.' He half turned and slapped his neighbour on the back. 'And Hilarius, our handsome one, is from Cyprus.'

Michael looked at Hilarius' sculpted face – no scars, just smooth skin and rippling black hair – wondering why such a man would take to the fight.

Hilarius grinned. 'I have a sword. I like following the fight. When Richard of England passed through on his way to the crusade, I joined his army. It was a way to get out of Cyprus. I fought against the Saracens at Acre and Arsuf and then the *cincelles* and the noise drove me mad, so I deserted. It wasn't hard and I found my way to the Balkans. Signed on there and met my friends. But then, as Leo said, we became bored and thought to make money more easily elsewhere and maybe keep our skins.'

'*You* just want to keep your face!' Bonus chided.

Hilarius laughed. 'That too.'

'And so, *Kýrie* Michael,' said Phocus. 'Now you know...'

Outside, there was banging on the gates and through the door, Christo could be seen running across the yard. Bonus stood, his seat scraping on the stone floor, hand on hilt, but Phocus stayed him. They all turned and watched as Ahmed slipped through the gates like oily water, helping Christo to replace the bars before walking toward the house with an arm across the notary's shoulder, Christo laughing.

In moments, he was in the room, his presence large enough to make its mark. Michael sighed. Was this the way it would always be? Ahmed garnering attention by just breathing? He raised his eyes to the heavens, catching Toby's glance as Phocus introduced the Arab to the new house members.

Tobias, ever aware of the sea captain's ego and aware also that more ground must yet be covered, said. 'Ahmed, stop hogging the moment. We are having an important meeting.'

Ahmed stilled, assessing his little companion. Sometimes it was like watching weather change, wondering if thunder and lightning would emerge or whether it would merely rain.

'So,' the Arab said finally. 'Have I missed much?'

Later, after Michael had told the story of the Tyrian purple, and the men began to file out, Phocus turned back. 'Michael, what you and Tobias have told us today makes being a galley slave and a soldier suddenly appear mundane. We will enjoy guarding this house and rest assured we shall do it well.' He saluted and walked away.

'You told them everything?' said Ahmed.

Toby looked down at his clenched hands as Michael replied, 'They need to have faith in us.'

'Faith in a thief and a murderer?'

'They could do worse,' Toby muttered.

'Of course, my little friend,' Ahmed clapped Toby on the back. 'For myself though, I am just eager to get to the business of trade. It is why we are here after all.'

'Agreed,' Toby pushed back from the table and stood. 'If we baulk at every shadow, we might as well leave, I suppose. Now, if you excuse me, I am tired and longing to sleep on a real mattress,' he headed for the door, calling over his shoulder. 'With real pillows.'

'Sleep well,' Michael replied.

'Make music in your sleep, little man,' Ahmed's base tones followed the minstrel out the door and they heard his feet clip up the stairway.

'You like him, don't you?' Michael said.

'Perversely yes, despite that he sends me hairless, may Allah return the favour. He's honest and I trust him, and I would watch out for him because of that. But in respect of him being unrecognised?' He laughed, that rich belly sound. 'His size and manner raise interest wherever he treads, even if he went into his enchanted world of disguises. Many are aware of another little man who stole a blessed icon and was bled to death because of it. Allah be praised for *deuil*.'

It was an oblique reference to the poison that had saved Toby's brother from hideous pain as he was executed – a deathly concoction of hemlock, bryony, opium, henbane and more, artfully administered by a kind soul called Anwar al Din, a physician.

'Tobias knew it was a risk coming on this voyage, Ahmed. As we all do. You too, perhaps.'

'It's as well then that Phocus is a good man who does not employ liars and vagabonds to guard us all.'

The two men moved on up the stair to their chambers, both admitting to a desperate need for sleep. Michael heard Christo below the stair and called to him that he would see him on the morrow, that he needed to sleep to reclaim his landlegs.

'And Christo, thank you.'

Christo's voice echoed up the stair. ''Tis my honour, sir.'

Honour...

Michael laid his head on the soft, down-filled pillow.

What was honour, he wondered?

Was it a husband respecting his dead family's memory by promising to avenge them?

Was it acknowledging his present wife and her trading partners by being the epitome of a successful merchant?

Or was it standing by his friends in times of adversity?

For sure it wasn't honouring his homeland by stealing from it in a past life.

He sighed and rolled onto his side. The bed – a large marital bed – creaked as he laid his hand on the cold side next to him. Jehanne's image filled the empty space and his heart jumped.

Not Helena then...

It surprised him because there had been barely a moment since he departed Lyon for Venezia that he had not thought of his deceased wife and their daughter. But to be honest, it warmed his heart that Jehanne's face and body were what he saw as his fingers stroked the bedding. The linen and silk were so soft that if he closed his eyes, he could imagine it was Jehanne's fine skin beneath his palm as it slid down over the undulation of her hips.

He missed her sharp mind, her intensity and her provocative sensuality. The end of a three month would not come too soon. As his fingers slipped over an imaginary belly and further, he drifted into the first real sleep since leaving the waters of Venezia in *Durrah*.

He woke to the sound of a cock.

It was barely light and he cursed the arrogance of some feathered fiend that must announce dawn's imminent approach in such a strident way. He climbed from the nesting warmth of his bed, the pre-dawn nipping at his naked body as he flung the shutters open, then dived back under the covers. He stretched, the linen, wools and silk settling on chest, groin and thigh, and bird or no, his eyes closed. But as he began to slip away again, an image of Sancta Sophia emerged. Bold, beautiful, wisps of sea-fog draping over the cupolas, the seabirds wheeling toward the south gates. A harmony of men's voices filled the air, singing praise. Momentarily he thought the time for enlightenment was approaching, but then sleep claimed him, the mattress holding him in its folds like a lover and whispering that sea journeys, maybe even *all* sea journeys were just bad dreams.

A thump on the bed woke him, his eyes opening to golden light and Tobias jumping onto the covers like a child. 'So! You sleep whilst we are all arisen and about our business. Are you ill?'

'And if I was,' croaked Michael, the thick humors of sleep still on him, 'your voice and bed bouncing would make me worse, so no, I am not ill. I just make up for the decks of *Durrah*.'

Toby slid off the bed. 'I dare you to say that to mighty Ahmed.'

'Where is he?'

Toby shrugged. 'The phantom in our midst, here and then gone. He grabbed some fruit and left with not a word as to why or where. He may have told Christo, I know not. Ariella and I broke our fast under the loggia.' He leaned against the chest. 'I told her about the Vigia. It seemed right.'

'And?' Michael had washed his face from an ewer of cold water and was pulling on clean clothing. His shadowy green tunic was embellished with a hem of griffons below the knee and as he dragged on soft boots, Toby continued.

'She was concerned for me. Showed no concern for herself at all and appeared to have only minor interest in the fact that Pieta Izzo is with child like herself. She has such immense fortitude, that woman. Saul would be proud.'

'One cannot grow up as a Jewess in this world, Toby, with skin as thin as eggshells.'

'Too true. But the women in our family are astonishing, Michael. Jehanne, Ariella, and my lady Ysabel…' his voice softened as the name of his patron's wife rolled off his tongue.

'Do you miss she and William, Toby?'

'More than you could imagine. Lady Ysabel and I were kindred spirits from the moment we met. And William? I call him my godson.'

Michael looked up from strapping a sword belt around his waist.

'Well … no,' Toby admitted bashfully. 'I know he's not my real godson, but he is as dear to me.'

'Did you ever ask Lady Ysabel if you might be a godfather?'

'No. I am just a minstrel when all is said and done. He was baptised swiftly on his birth because of the danger in which Ysabel found herself and I understand that none were named as his protectors at the time.'

'Noble or not, Toby, you have done more for the child's safety than most and you and he are like family. You should ask Lady Ysabel. She is your close friend after all.'

'Aye. She is that...' Toby's voice slipped into a reminiscent quiet.

The soft sound of a weapon slipping into the length of a scabbard underlined the heavily pregnant moment and then Michael said, 'Apart from wanting to shave three months growth from my chin, I wish to get to business with Christo. What shall you do?'

'I will visit Anwar al Din. I wish to give him a letter from Mehmet, and tell him that we have a woman with child within the house. Besides, seeing him makes me less sick for my home and soothes my demons – he and Mehmet are so much alike in manner and voice.'

'Then you must take one of our guards.'

Toby gave Michael a look.

'Toby, we all have to do this. We can't afford to lay ourselves open to attack, ransom, or worse. Please agree with me.'

'If I must. Can I take Hilarius? He's such a handsome man and I suspect I will find many a maid giving him the eye. It's all food for such wonderful love ballads! I shall see you anon.'

He hurried out the door and Michael couldn't help the grin that followed him. Tobias was so vibrant, even in the face of danger, and he loved him for it. He straightened the scabbard by his side and followed the minstrel, the air flowing up the stair fresh and cool but with the smell of fresh-baked bread laced in it.

The store room door creaked as Christo pulled it wide, its cavernous dark at odds with the aroma of light and life that tickled the inside of Michael's nose. Christo struck a tinder and set lamps to light the space, placing them carefully away from the now-illuminated bolts of cloth.

'I always forget how strong is the smell of the east,' Michael said and breathed deeply. 'I am reminded of stone canyons, sand, villages and towns drifting on a spice cloud. And something else…' he took another smell then clicked his tongue. 'The smell of silk is indefinable – musty yet not, astringent and yet not, speaking of so many things. If I were blindfolded and you led me toward a pile of silk I would know.'

Christo agreed. 'Silk has the smell of the earth, I think, which is at such odds with the sensual cloth that it is.'

'The sensuality is what drives our sales.'

'Then I have something that will please you greatly, I think. Perhaps more than please you.'

'You excite and intrigue me, Christo.'

'Close your eyes. Or would you rather me blindfold you?'

Michael laughed and did as he was bid. Christo walked away, something was opened with a squeak from ancient hinges – perhaps a chest or an old *armarium*. Michael almost opened his eyes but Christo called out.

'Eyes closed. It will be worth it.'

A sound then– like birds rustling their wings – subtle, barely there. Then Christo's feet on the stone floor. A soft step cushioned by goatskin ankle boots with fine leather soles.

'Keep your eyes closed and hold out your hands.'

Michael held out flat palms, his stomach fluttering with anticipation.

Something so infinitesimally light was laid across – cool but as nebulous as a cloud. Something and nothing. His skin tingled and his heart raced.

'You may open your eyes.'

He blinked and looked at small folds of exquisite nothingness lying in his grasp. In the light of the lanterns, it glistened like the finest golden baby's hair.

'The hair of angels...' he whispered.

'I thought the same when I saw it,' Christo replied as he ran a finger over the weave. 'Have you seen anything like it before?'

'No. But let me guess what it is. It isn't mulberry silk nor the finest linen. This is something even rarer. Is it *byssus*?'

Christo's eyes opened wider. 'You know? *Kýrie* Michael, most do not...'

'I've never touched it nor seen it, but I've heard the mystery and legend surrounding it. *Iisoús Christós*,' Michael rarely blasphemed, rarely even referred to God, but this voyage and its revelations were drawing forth things buried deep in him. 'It's as rare as mountain air. And as light. Where did you find it?'

'Limnos. I had sailed to Crete because there is the best saffron there. In fact, I purchased rather a lot of saffron and it is stored at the back of the chamber. Good money, I think. To continue however, we stopped at Limnos on our return to re-provision and I wandered along the shore. Perhaps I had the look of someone seeking something to purchase because I was approached by an old woman. She was as burned and wrinkled as a dried-out olive – no teeth, lines like cobwebs over her face. She looked straight at me with black eyes that burned with some sort of secret and asked if I wanted to buy silk...

CHAPTER FIVE

×

'Always, honoured mother.'

'Then I have the best.' But I must have looked at her the wrong way, because she said, 'I will sell to someone else. You have doubt in your eyes.'

'Honoured mother, I apologise most deeply if I have offended you.' I reached for her arm, a bony thing covered in faded blue linen, but she shrank from me.

'You should not touch an elder, let alone one of the secret weavers, young man. Show respect.'

She was very serious. She had hooked me and she was aware of it. In the sack on her back was something interesting, and I needed to see it because I had a feeling…

'Mother, I would be privileged to view the silk you have and to hear the story of the secret weavers.'

'I will show you the silk, but whether I tell you any more depends on any number of things…'

What? I thought. Whether a breeze will blow? Whether birds will fly backward? There was something truly enchanted about her, as though she had come from years under the sea and would go back there.

She squatted on the dusty rocks on the edge of the harbour. We were secluded by an enormous chunk of stone. In the distance and silhouetted against the blue sky, I could see the white church of Myrina that the monks from Mount Athos had built. All one could hear was the sound of seabirds and a dulcet lap of water against the shore – as if the very world waited with anticipation. There was no breeze and I had cause to wonder if that was in my favour.

'May I offer you some pomegranate syrup?' I held a costrel out to her.

She took it, swigged and then spat something onto a rock. 'They left a seed in the syrup, imbeciles!'

She had the manner of a potentate and the look of a pauper and if the feeling of being on the edge of something great was not so strong, I would have laughed.

She pulled off the sack from her back and with tenderness, extracted a small package. It was wrapped in clean, new linen and she unfolded it with enormous care with hands that were smooth and which had long, pointed fingernails. She muttered something – a prayer, an invocation – and handled the package like God's gift. When she unwrapped it and the sun caught the gleam, I sucked in my breath.

'Angel's hair,' I whispered when I got my breath back and reached out to touch it.

She swung her hands, moving the cloth from me. 'Sea silk. Angel's hair. Byssus. Call it what you will. You know of it?'

'I know that women dive for the shell and harvest the tendrils that anchor it to rocks. I know that it is so rare, it has only ever been used for priestly cloaks and stoles or shrouds for kings.'

Her expression changed a little then. 'You know quite a lot…'

'I am interested in silk.'

'So they say.'

'Who says?'

'The sailors.'

'Do you live on Limnos, mother?'

'Sometimes. Sometimes I live close to wherever the shells call from.' She waved her hand out toward the sea – the Middle Sea and the Aegean, home to the weavers of this godly cloth.

'You dive?'

'I used to. Now I teach others the ancient rhythms. For ancient they are. Do you know of them?'

'Not so much. How do you weave it? What do you do to make it so fine?'

'Some things are in God's hands, young man. Do you know that it never fades?'

'No. I did not.'

'Do you know of the veil, the one the Roman Church call the Veronica?'

'I know it has vanished. Been secreted away.'

'So they say, but who knows? It has the image of Christ on it which makes it important to Believers.'

She referred to the cloth with which a woman had reputedly wiped Christ's tortured face as he walked to Calvary along the Via Dolorosa. Afterward, some would say Christ's image was embedded forever into the weave. It is considered a miracle because byssus cannot be painted upon.

'And this?'

Truly, my heart pounded. Did she have the miraculous cloth? Wars would be fought to possess this.

'This is not the veil of which they speak.'

A little of me subsided then. I wasn't sure if with disappointment or relief. But then she held it toward me.

'Touch it.'

And I did. I swear, it was like touching the heart of an angel. It was like nothing I have ever felt before. And I knew that we needed to buy this. That we would never lose on such spectacular silk.

'Mother, I am in awe. For so many reasons. In awe of the divers, of those who prepare the silk filament, of the weavers. This is perfection.'

'Yes,' she said quietly. 'Will you be judicious with what you say to people about the art of byssus?'

'Of course, but in truth you have told me little.'

She looked at me then. Really studied me and then she said, 'I will trust you. What is your name?'

'Christophorus.'

She gave a little laugh. 'How apt. Well, Christophorus, there is not too much more to tell. We gather the tendril filaments, we wash them with fresh water and dry them. We bathe them in the juice of lemon and cedar which enhances the gold. We dry the threads carefully then, away from the sun. We dye, card, spin and weave in a manner which will forever be secret. The secrets belong to we sea-silk women, never to men, and not to women who are not of our sisterhood. You may have the cloth.'

'How much?'

'What would you pay?'

'Oh honoured mother, I think it is up to the keeper of the secrets to name a price.'

'Then give me enough to keep my girls fed and for us to keep weaving. It is

God's wish.'

I was truly afraid then that if I didn't offer enough, I would lose this cloth and someone else would have the chance to make a fortune. And I felt enormous guilt for thinking thus. In truth, I should have been marvelling at the cloth, and not at the profit to be made.

'How many girls?' I asked, treading carefully.

'Six.'

'Only six?' I looked out to the sea.

'Only six under my care. But there are others across the sea.'

'I will give you enough to clothe and feed yourself and your women for this coming winter. Is that fair, think you?'

She looked at the cloth, then at the sea. 'It will do.'

Now I felt I had been less than fair, so I upped my offer. 'I will give you enough for this winter and the next. But honoured mother, you must tell me if such a price offends you. I would not mean to disrespect the artistry of you and the women who create this cloth.'

'You do not offend…'

'And that is how it happened,' said Christo. 'In fact, I gave her more than I have paid for any commodity ever. But I think that like the purple dye you sourced, we can recoup this with money overflowing. I am thinking any of the royal houses, the Roman Church. Even the Angelids…'

'But have we much left in the coffers?' Michael demurred.

'Ah.' Christo rubbed his long nose, his face creasing.

'I see.' Michael thanked the stars that Saul had given him notes of exchange to take to the Jewish moneylenders who were his friends. He was appalled and awed at once. Would he have had the courage to offer so much for the silk?

I almost offered my life for the purple…

'Too much, think you?' Christo almost begged.

'For the size of a veil, Christo?' Michael measured with his hands. 'A *skepe?*'

Christo began to unfold the cloth that lay across Michael's palm. First this way, then that, pushing corners into Michael's grasp.

'*Iisoús Christós!*' Michael whispered as the lamplight swooped on the weave. It had a pearly lustre that could only come from the sea. It was liquid amber, melted honey, brushed gold, as finally the length and breadth of two men hung between Christo's and Michael's hands. 'All that from a packet the size of a folded document...'

'They say it is so fine you can fold it ever smaller into a nutshell. I would not try. It is disrespectful.'

'We should not cut it,' Michael said. 'Its value is in the amount we have. But who should be our target? That is the question.'

'You are not angry?' Christo bit his lip.

'No. But I shall be honest. I was afraid until you unfolded it. Now?' He blew out a breath and shrugged, then grinned. 'I am confident.'

'Will you take it to the west?'

'I'm not sure. We must think on this. Have you told Ahmed?'

'No...'

'Then don't. Not yet. I would like to discuss this with Ariella first.'

They folded the cloth, its weave soft and pliable, almost transparent until it lay compliant across Christo's palm. He swaddled it in the linen and returned it to the *armarium*, locking the door from the key at his waist.

'I admire your courage, Christo.'

The notary looked uncomfortable, as if he were being praised beyond his earning. 'When the Theotokis places opportunities before Her children, they should be grateful and act upon the chance. I give thanks in prayers to Her every day.'

The two men sat on stools, light from outside bleeding across the doorway.

'So,' Michael said. 'Saffron. *Byssus*. What else? Any more surprises?'

'I have silks from as far east as one can walk without falling off the end of the world. They are very beautiful. And I have a small cache of raw ivory I picked up from a trader at a market here. But mostly silks.'

'Do you wish to send it all west or sell it here?'

'I will do whatever you wish, *Kýrie* Michael.'

'It's Michael and whilst I must speak to Ariella, I think she might agree with me when I say I think you may have earned the right to decide, Christo.'

Michael wondered if Saul ben Simon had any idea of the value of the man he employed as his manager in Constantinople. Christo had trade running through every vessel and vein in his body. He was worth more than his weight in gold.

'Then, please tell *Kyría* Ariella that I believe the *byssus*, the saffron, ivory and your pigments should go west. I think we should examine the other silks, put them to the market here and build our funds again. Whatever is left, and whatever you find between now and when you leave, I would add to the shipment for the west.'

To Michael it made sense. The west craved rarity and would pay through the nose for the consignment. Money would flood Gisborne-ben Simon's coffers when the goods reached Venezia, Paris and Lyon. The Byzantines saw many of these goods regularly and perhaps viewed them differently to their western counterparts. Besides, there were rumblings that the Empire stood on shrinking and shaky ground – perhaps its treasury was not as gold-rich as in the past. That was something he must find out. But traders from everywhere mingled in the city – it was like a Babel Tower of voices out there. Suddenly Phocus' brothers-in-arms had immense value. The house on the corner of Basilike Street and Little Mese was a treasury just waiting to be robbed.

'Christo, do Phocus and Ephigenia know of the cloth?'

'No.'

Michael nodded. When the time was right, he would include everyone in the detail. Perhaps this evening. But for now? It must stay between he and Christo.

Was he guilty of carrying too much to his chest too often?

Without doubt.

But it had become a way of survival, and trade was no different. Underhand, secret, cut-throat. Each merchant wanting to best his competitor by whatever means. When he had found the Tyrian purple, he knew he could make a fortune for ben Simon, but it could have cost him his own life and the lives of others.

And now the *byssus*. No different. Although not embargoed by an empire, it was so very rare and men could be killed for it. Momentarily, he glimpsed the thin face of Branco Izzo. The personification of obsessive moneymaking. Intent on building a dynasty – what his brother-in-law, Pietro Vigia, had failed to do.

But what about the letter? Ioulia…

Izzo's image faded and Michael's true purpose for being in this city of dreams reaffirmed itself.

'… I agree. Secret for the moment.' Christo's voice pierced his thoughts.

'Mm? Oh. Yes, but not for long. Christo, you have treasure here. Even if we sourced nothing else, you will have made the name of the house of Gisborne-ben Simon with a few hand widths of silk.'

Christo dropped his head, a bashful blush staining upward from his neck to his chin. Michael approved of his humility and his acumen.

'There are one or two markets worth sailing to whilst you are here, Michael.'

'Good. I will talk further with you and include Ahmed. We must also discuss politics. Sadly.' The two walked round the chamber, snuffing out the lamps and carrying them outside.

Christo locked the door. 'Then if you don't require my assistance immediately, I will get back to my papers.'

'Of course,' said Michael. And I will speak with Ariella…'

'*Byssus!* I have only ever heard of such things in legend. I thought it was part of the myth of sea people.' Ariella sat by the window at a small table, holding a goose quill.

'The ink is dripping,' Michael said.

'What? Oh…' She scattered some sand on the inkblot. 'I'm writing to Father. It's quite a long one.'

'Don't mention the *byssus*, or even other goods. If your note is intercepted, and we must believe that it might be, we need to keep our secrets close.'

'Of course.' She laid the quill on the table and blew the sand from her writing. 'The Greeks have many legends of the sea gods. They called them *Theoi Halioi*. In fact, there is one called Bythos, which means sea-depths. He and his brother Aphros, carried the goddess, Aphrodite, to shore after her birth. Aphros' name means sea-foam. And when you put the angel lightness of sea-foam with sea-depths, you could almost have something like *byssus*. Perhaps *byssus* is a corruption of the name Bythos. Who knows?'

'Where did you learn this?'

'My mother told me many stories when I was young. We were often alone because Father would be travelling, sourcing goods, and it comforted us both to become lost in story-telling.'

'How came you to live in England? Your father seemed so happy when he was here that I thought he would bring you back as a family.'

'I wish he had.' Ariella's eyes glistened as she spoke, and she stoppered the ink flask and rested it back on the table. 'Perhaps my mother would still be alive. Father sent she and I to York, to live close by some cousins because he was travelling and preferred the idea of us near family for safety. York seemed as good as any place...' She laughed softly, a sound filled with regret. 'He had just returned from Constantinople as you know. King Henry had died and Richard had ascended to the throne. You know the rest of that terrible time in York. I swear, it will go down in history.' She looked at the quill in front of her. No doubt seeing the Jews of York preferring death by their own hand in the tower, he thought, than to be slaughtered by a mad crowd. 'After my mother's death in the York Massacre, Father and I began a peripatetic journey to find solace. We ended in Venezia. I think Papa would have bought Mama and myself here to Constantinople ultimately, else why have such a place to house his eastern offices? But he fell in love with the canals and islands of Venezia and he and Gisborne set to building a bigger merchant house, so Venezia became our home. I can see that he is content there and it served to give him an anchor after my mother's death. He needed that at the time.'

'And you?'

She looked at her writing and ran her hand over the parchment. 'Lyon was my anchor. Now?' She looked directly at Michael. 'I don't know.'

He would love to have shared the feeling of aimlessness that had shrouded him in the early days of his own grief, but he needed to talk with the priest first, so he merely said, 'I understand...'

She turned to face him in an aureole of sunlight. Her hair was the red of wine and the brown of chestnuts, a tawny sheen that made one look twice. She had tanned in their time at sea and there were freckles across the bridge of her nose. He was gladdened to see that her eyes, despite the hint of tears, held a sparkle of anticipation. There was nothing of the stress and pallor of the journey about her.

'Being with child suits you.'

'I am tired, but I suspect the babe takes some of my energy. Ephigenia intends to build me up as my time approaches, she says. I think she likes the thought of mothering me and I don't mind at all. In any case, another day or so and I shall be ready to be my father's daughter.'

'That you are a ben Simon has already been noted, Ariella.'

'Think you? Good.' And then more seriously, 'I agree with Christo's suggestions. My only concern is that the rumour of confusion in the German States could affect our market. We must find the truth of it, Michael.'

'I mentioned to Christo that we must talk politics in the next day. But in any case, we have other markets – the Russias, France and the Roman Church. If Rome has the Blessed Veronica secreted away, I suspect they might wish to clothe their popes and bishops in similar gold cloth.'

Ariella nodded and they discussed commodities and markets. 'Of course, right now we need ready money, do we not? We can visit Father's friends with the credit notes.'

Michael agreed, saying that later would suit him if she did not mind. 'I have business on First Hill but I won't be long.'

'You do?' she asked with startled curiosity. 'At the Imperial Palace? The Patriarchal Palace?'

'Neither. I wish to visit Sancta Sophia. It was my…' he cleared his throat. 'I liked the deep and quiet interior of the place when I was living here. I have some ghosts to settle before I continue…'

'I understand. Like Toby and yourself, I have yet to lay my own ghosts and am unsure how to go about it. You must do what you must.' She stood and kissed his cheek as he left.

Ghosts.

Chasing a wisp of mist, a skein of memory.

He tried to remember the good times with Helena and Ioulia but inevitably they crashed down round his ears like the waves that had battered the galley twelve years before.

In those beleaguered moments, he wondered why he had ultimately found good fortune. After all, he had lived two lives, twisting round each other like a serpent – the respected merchant and everyone's friend, and the embittered man – black and curling at the edges with revenge. For ten of the twelve years, he had frequented the waterfront, as did most merchants, but he searched as much for a man as merchandise. The man was a scrawny Arab with a tattoo on his hand and for ten years he had seen nothing, his grief and bitterness increasing ten-fold.

He heard of the Tyrian purple through the underground of waterfront gossip. Even now, he was surprised that he had become a thief. But the chink in his armour was fear, for who does not fear death, he thought, and that tiny gap was enough for Dana, the embroiderer and *espie,* to slip in and tie herself to his heart.

Dana…

Dana who was really Jehanne de Clochard, a young woman who had walked out of her family's home and merchant business one day, to follow the trade routes. Her father died with a cracked heart at her desertion and her mother developed a bitterness to equal Michael's. Later, Jehanne and her mother discussed bitterness with him, as they broke bread in front of the fireplace in Lyon. Jehanne's mother could never understand how her daughter could leave surety, security and love to seek adventure. She saw it as a journey of selfishness, at once facile and ingenuous.

But Jehanne had quickly tied herself to the Gisborne spy network, settling readily in Constantinople. How easy it had been for the apparently docile and deft-fingered embroiderer, ostensibly a Byzantine, to listen as she pinned hems and fitted sleeves for the nobles. Women gossiped readily in Dana's presence and she soaked up the information like a sponge.

She never admitted to her fear that she might be caught and executed. She would say to Michael later that if one acknowledged fear, it had a toe in the door and that is when one made mistakes. She lived a life of lies and the time came for her to leave Constantinople when she realised she had developed feelings for Michael. *That* was the most fearful thing of all. Once there was a second party in one's life, one became vulnerable.

The house was silent except for the sound of birds and the hum of life outside the walls. He assumed the guards had instigated a rotation. Perhaps two rested whilst two guarded. He must talk to Phocus and be the excellent manager he was, but now, he needed to find out what he could from the priest. Everything else would surely fit into place around that.

Noting that Christo's alcove was empty, he headed for the gates, relieved to avoid observation. But as he hauled at the bar, he realised he would be leaving an open and insecure gate behind.

But this pilgrimage, if that is what it is, must surely be accomplished alone...
'*Kýrie* Michael?'

Cursing silently, he turned to face the bulwark of the man from Khorasan.

'It's Michael, Leo,' he said wearily. 'Just Michael...'

Leo huffed and then said, 'You wish to venture out?'

Michael longed to order Leo to a post at the gates, leaving him alone but, 'Yes. I have sensitive business on First Hill.'

'Then I will fetch Julius to bar the gate after we are gone, and I shall accompany you.'

'As you wish...'

'It is not for me to wish, sir. It is for you to express an order and for me to obey. A moment if you please.'

Then I wish I had ordered you to guard the house and leave me alone.

He looked out the now opened gates, at the men and women passing back and forth, and as he scanned face upon face, he knew that he was being unreasonable. Any of them could have malice on their minds.

Presently he paced down Little Mese, heading toward the harbour, wanting to walk along the waterfront – even knowing the tattooed Arab was faraway. He always referred to the man as the Arab, though he knew his name. He found thoughts of revenge so much easier with a level of ambiguity.

Leo paced tactfully somewhere behind Michael. They had come to an understanding. Michael did not want to be seen to be guarded and Leo wanted to watch the crowd. A few steps behind and he could feign nonchalance, giving Michael the space he craved.

The streets glistened in the light, the paving stones clean if worn. He had always found most of this city to be so. As if the citizens wanted to enhance its jewel-like reputation. Of course, there were the inevitable areas with poor drainage and butchering of livestock but the trading quarters were swept and polished as if the merchants wanted nothing to tarnish their goods, or indeed their reputation.

But elsewhere there were gutters that were cracked and broken, arches and columns in precarious states. Green stains like watermarked silk showed where cisterns and gutters leaked and Michael wondered whether the treasury was not healthy, despite the stringent taxation of the citizens. Perhaps border skirmishes and internal politicking had cut into the wealth of the Byzantines. He must ask Christo. If nothing else, was it right to assume the Venetians still hold prime place with the Byzantines? After all, Branco Izzo implied the Genovese houses were prosperous...

Michael felt at home on the waterfront.

The polyphony of bird calls, the eager shouts of vendors, the smell of the sea air and the ripe odour of the weed that clung to the harbour walls. The ragged noise of a dozen languages and the appearances of the crowds – dark skinned and light, red-haired, brown, black or blonde. Clothes from beyond the Speris Zǧua to desert lands near the world's end.

Such exotic variety curried a sense of excitement and anticipation in any merchant and when anticipation began to stretch thinner, so then did nerves tighten. Spontaneous decisions were made, dangerous and ill-thought. Bribery followed because venality and trade were like twins finishing each other's sentences. And when men became venal, nothing was sacrosanct.

Not even life.

Out of the corner of his eye he could see Leo's bulk not far behind. He hadn't thought it would matter and yet the man's presence made him feel more secure. Was it temerity on his own part? If it was, it concerned him. As he set out on this journey, the possibility of any sort of danger had lain dormant in the back of his mind. All he wanted was to find his daughter and to kill the Arab. But now Ariella, a baby, even the house on Basilike Street – all were a responsibility. All were vulnerable to danger.

He began the short incline to the south of Sancta Sophia, up the steps, one by one, trying not to be impressed with the basilica's curves and gloss. One could compare it with the rounded curves of a woman as it glowed in the sun. Around the steps, Judas trees blossomed with pale Tyrian purple-coloured flowers.

Judas...

Was he a Judas? Returning to Mother Church when he had sworn his days were done. Or was it God who was a Judas for failing to protect his family in the moment of their greatest need. Maybe he should ask the priest, this Father Symeon.

The appearance of the crowd had changed. In the streets below, it had been cheeky, brash, colourfully dressed and noisy.

On the elegant south steps of Sancta Sophia, it was measured, softly spoken, and with discretely toned clothing. Even the nobility with their rings and girdles of gold and their exquisitely embroidered silk tunics spoke in deferential tones.

Halfway up the steps, he lowered his gaze, not wishing to see or be seen. He was concerned of what might ensue should anyone recognise him as the merchant. Or worse, the thief. He stopped and turned to look back over the harbour, across the escape to the Sea of Marmara. Further down, incongruous amongst church goers, monks and nuns, Leo climbed slowly, stopping when Michael halted. Tall, broad-shouldered, bald-headed Leo with his plaited tassel hanging from the side of his polished head, around whom, when he began to continue upward, the crowds parted like the Red Sea parting around Moses.

Michael turned to walk on, one step, two, three – each step worn smooth by many feet. He began to count – nervousness at meeting the priest starting to roil his belly. This information might be about his dead daughter…

Four, five, si…

He was knocked heavily from behind, the breath gushing forth. He crashed onto the step in front, catching his kneecap on the edge – a profound bone pain, echoing up and down his leg. Something heavy fell partly on top, a man sliding forward, his head crashing into the steps, a groan and then nothing.

'By the Saints, sir, I am so sorry,' Leo's voice sounded behind him. 'My friend is drunk. He is a disgrace. Here…' he held out his hand to Michael. 'Are you hurt?'

Michael was pulled upright with the force of Leo's tug, pressure on his kneecap as he straightened sending deep-throated pain through his thigh. 'No…' he said.

'Good. I shall take my *friend,*' the emphasis on the word as he slung the unconscious man over his shoulder was deliberate, 'and throw him in the harbour to sober up. You are sure you are not hurt, sir?'

Michael shook his head and Leo turned with his load, the man's arms and head flopping loosely. He could be dead for all anyone knew. A swim in the harbour? More likely drowned. There was something in Leo's voice.

Michael lifted his leg to climb, biting his lip against the pain in his knee, determined now to find the priest, secure the information and plan. As his kneecap clicked and ground, anger rushed from his belly to his head, a rise of blood so fast and furious that he could have cried out with it. A battlecry...

He limped through the south gates, pushing through the crowds, and into the narthex. That damned God light, sunshine in great beams, shone through the windows beneath the cupola – mysterious beams that seemed to sway and move, softening the cavernous interior. He wanted to hate it but the fact that it brought him up short was a sign that even he, a man in pain from his soul to his kneecap, must admire its beauty. After all, when the Emperor Justinian had built the basilica so long ago he said from the depths of his ego, *Solomon, I have outdone thee.*

'Father, father!' He called to a monk walking past. They all look the same, he thought. 'Can you help me?'

'Perhaps.' The man spoke from the depths of thin grey hair and a straggling beard.

'I am looking for Father Symeon.'

'Ah.' The monk's eyes were faded, and he had few teeth in his mouth. His breath smelled of decrepit age. 'He is most popular today. He is there, see? Below the icon of the Theotokis.'

The gilded Virgin's eyes looked down on Michael and beneath the glistening icon, he could see a tall, thin priest with a mass of hair upon which nestled a *skoufos*, talking to someone concealed by one of the porphyry pillars.

'I thank you,' Michael said to the priest.

He moved close to Father Symeon, and within his sightline, so that the monk would know he wished to speak to him. The man looked away from whomever he was talking to, acknowledging Michael.

'Can I help direct you somewhere, my son?'

'I am looking for you, Father Symeon.' *I am looking for news of my daughter and you have information I need.* 'May I speak with you privately, when you are finished?'

'Of course...'

'Michael? Michael!' A small man moved from behind the pillar. 'It is *you*! I thought I recognised that voice. And you are looking for Father Symeon? What a coincidence! This man, Father, is Michael Sarapion, one of the trading family to which I belong.' Toby grinned, as if nothing untoward had

102

happened and that he was thrilled to have Michael meet the priest.

'Michael Sarapion,' the priest's voice was calm and mellow. 'I have heard much of you from my friend, Tobias. And you wish to see me?'

'Um, yes. I do…' *Honesty.* 'I need to talk privately. Toby, I am sorry. I will explain later, back at the house, if you will permit.'

Toby's eyebrows slid forward. 'Is all well?'

'Yes…' *If I ignore the agony of my knee and Leo drowning a man as we speak.* 'I will explain later. Can you spare some time, Father?'

'Yes. As it happens, Tobias and I were just farewelling each other. Tobias, come back on the morrow after you have visited your brother's grave, if you wish, and take heart. I will pray for you and for Tomas. All will be well.'

Tobias tipped his head to the side – curiosity implicit. 'I thank you, Father Symeon, for your guidance. And I shall see you anon. You too, Michael.'

He walked away but then turned to scrutinise both men, walking slowly backward before colliding with a nun, apologising profusely and then hurrying away.

Michael said by way of apology, 'He means well but my business is private for the moment.'

'Of course. Although I expect Tobias has been quite open about *his* business.' It was a mild admonishment as such things went. 'In any case, what can I do for you?'

'I received a letter, Father Symeon, from one of your brother monks,' he reached into his purse and passed the letter over.

Father Symeon unfolded the parchment with care, squinting in the uncertain light of the basilica. Upon reading the words, he folded the letter carefully along its worn creases, handing it back to Michael. 'Come with me. There is a quieter place not far from here. Do you need to hurry away?'

'Father, I have been waiting for many years for anything at all I can glean about a family member. My heart and soul must bide here until you have told me what you know.'

'Hmm,' Father Symeon replied. 'Then come…'

His black robes ebbed and flowed around him as he walked. A slim column of a man who had an air of confidence, a gentle air, as if he was secure in his beliefs. He had such an abundance of beard it was hard to determine if he smiled or frowned. But his eyes were undisguised and his heavy black brows were as filled with expression as Ahmed's finely shaped ones. When he had looked at Michael after reading the letter, those brows had creased – not a frown, but as if he was momentarily unsure how to proceed. His hands though, had found his prayer beads, and in fingering them he stood taller, the air of confidence becoming stronger. Others may not have noticed, but Michael the Merchant had become astute at sizing people.

Did he trust Father Symeon?

Time would tell…

A citrus breeze wafted through a door ahead. The fragrance cleansed the air and they entered a small garden with a ubiquitous Judas tree covered in faded mauve flowers. Lemon-scented vervain girdled the tree, doves swaggered and somewhere water trickled from a spout into a bowl.

'Sit,' said Father Symeon, indicating a stone bench, and folding himself onto it. His robes pooled around his feet, cushioned by the carpet of fallen petals, and his pectoral cross flashed once as it settled. 'I always find this little garden to be conducive to quiet contemplation and the sharing of thoughts.'

Michael sat carefully, sucking his breath audibly as his knee bent and he immediately stretched it out, glancing down and noticing a stain on his tunic.

Father Symeon bent closer. 'You have blood there… may I?' Without waiting for an answer, he folded the hem back and looked at the torn hose, and at the blood seeping through. 'You have an injury. What happened?'

A man tried to kill me…

'I tripped and fell against the steps on the way to the south gates. It is not so bad.'

'Let me see.' The priest peeled the torn hose away from the contusion and a startling pattern of violet and blue flesh with torn skin revealed itself. 'I am going to feel around the edges of your knee. Bear with me, if you will.' He was infinitely gentle and pressed all around, eliciting a grimace from Michael. 'I don't think you have broken anything but see how it swells as we watch? You will be stiff and sore for some time. Will you let me fetch some linen and unguents to bind it?'

Michael nodded. It was easier than saying no and then limping back home under duress. The priest hurried away, leaving Michael to breathe and determine how to move forward with his questions.

He leaned back against the trunk of the Judas tree, looking up through the laced branches and budding leaves, past the soft violet of the blossom to the sky and it seemed ironic that the flowers should be a shade of Tyrian purple. The sky above was an impossible blue – the kind that made one believe there was no sadness in the world, a shade that held hope. A blossom fell to float like a boat on his green tunic and he held his breath, remembering another boat and another sea, as the priest returned with a small woven basket.

'Good.' He knelt at Michael's feet, padding a cloth against a flask from which he had removed the stopper. 'It's just wine. It will cleanse.' It stung but Michael had experienced worse pain when he had been stabbed in the leg by an almost too well-aimed Varangian sword as he ran for his life as a thief. He remembered *that* sword well. As it moved toward him the world had slowed, or so it seemed, and he had noticed the offset fuller along the blade – strange how things made their mark upon one's mind. He had jumped sideways, but not before the tip had gouged his thigh. *That* was painful and so *this* bone ache was nothing. The pain of wondering if Ioulia was alive however, was so much worse.

'And this,' said the priest, dragging two fingers across cream in a terracotta pot, 'is arnica. It will aid the bruising.' He padded a wad of linen and positioned it across Michael's kneecap, beginning to bind. 'I hope you will be more comfortable but finish the wine in the flask. It is un-watered and may help.'

Michael tipped the flask up and sipped as the priest tied off the bandage and placed the supplies back in the basket. 'The letter is true, Michael. I did meet with a young woman some time ago and she told me a story of being held as a slave for almost twelve years. And yes, she was purchased by her master at a slave auction in Agathopolis.'

'Do you know her history? What did she look like?'

'She was pleasant of face with waving dark hair. She was neither thin nor obese and her face was clear of the marks of a troubled life.'

'Did she tell you she had a troubled life?'

'She was a slave…'

'What sort of slave?'

'She was a lady's maid, helping with her mistress's wardrobe, laundry, stitching. She was very good at her stitching…'

Michael's heart ratcheted furiously. 'Her name…'

'Michael, she came to me as a penitent seeking sanctuary. I must respect her anonymity. It is important to her…'

'Then let me tell *you*, Father. I had a daughter. She was lost at sea when the trading galley on which we sailed was sunk near Agathopolis. Does any of this sound familiar? Did this woman tell you? Please! I lost my wife. I lost my child. I even lost my own identity and in many ways, I am still trying to find it. I believed my daughter dead for twelve years until the letter arrived from Father Nicholas. Why would he send me such words if they would lead me to nothing. I beg of you…'

Father Symeon resumed his seat next to Michael and took up his prayer beads. 'Then I will tell you about this woman and you can decide. As for my God, he will judge whether I have broken any rules and I will pay the price. But please, as I talk, finish your wine and allow me to tell you all before you speak.'

Michael nodded and gulped the rest of the wine, feeling it course through his veins, loosening muscles that had seemed knotted beyond help since the mooring lines were cast out in the Nerion Harbour.

'I sat in exactly this spot with a young woman who had entered the basilica dressed as a young man. She was terrified, and I tried to calm her after she had revealed she was a woman, asking her why she was so afraid.'

Chapter Six

×

'I pretended to be a youth and stole some silk…' she said.

'Go on.' Father Symeon passed no judgement.

'I am a servant, Father. A slave. I ran away.'

'Why?'

'My master…' She stopped and Father Symeon's hand patted her kindly. To which a tear crept forth and rolled down her cheek.

He said nothing for a moment and then, 'A nobleman?'

She nodded.

Above them, the tree dropped blossoms, one flower falling into Father Symeon's lap. He picked it up in workman's hands and played with it.

'How long?'

'Since he bought me for a good price in Agathopolis. I was twelve years old.'

'How old are you now?'

'Twenty-three years…'

Father Symeon turned toward her. 'I would prefer not to know your master's name, but I will say this – if your master used you for many years, how is it that you were not…'

'I was. And for almost nine blessed months he left me alone. Thanks be to the Holy Mother.'

'And your babe?'

'It died.'

Father Symeon sketched a cross. 'May God keep the tiny soul. I am so sorry for *you.' He reached into a concealed pocket and pulled out prayer beads – a circlet of deep sea-coloured stones with a black tassel hanging down.*

'I'm not!' She replied with fire but the flames quickly died. Composing herself and with a deep breath, she continued, 'When my mistress was otherwise engaged, he began again. But by the Holy Mother's grace, I never more conceived, and in any case a slave could not complain. I had to bear it. Besides, my mistress liked me, cared for me in her own way, and rewarded my skill.'

Father Symeon's eyebrows rose and in strained tones he asked, 'Rewarded you?'

The young woman smiled but it was empty of soul. 'Not for that. For what I did for her. I'm an embroiderer.' She looked down at her slim fingers. 'An excellent one, and in fact it saved my mind and body to be able to retreat to needle and thread. Can you help me, Father? If they find I have absconded and stolen, I am surely a dead woman…' Her fingers knotted together so tightly that he could see bone beneath the skin.

'Why did you steal the silk?'

She huffed, a hollow sound. 'It was a deep blue colour and reminded me of the sea and I was filled with such anger. Fury at what had befallen my family. It was like battle-lust. I've heard of the rage that fills even a hardy soldier's mind, seeing nothing but mayhem. I wanted to grab it, rip it to shreds, just like my life…'

Father Symeon remained calm and asked only, 'Agathopolis you say?'

'We were sailing by a trading galley from Sozopolis. My father was to become an agent for a Venetian trading house and it was such an opportunity for our family…'

'It's her, Father!' Michael exclaimed. 'It's my daughter!'

'Please, Michael. Let me finish!'

Michael's heart almost burst. He was so overwrought he barely wanted to hear any more and yet, it was his daughter's story. She was alive!

'But we were chased by peirates, hitting rocks, and the vessel sank,' the woman said. 'My parents were drowned but I was plucked from the ocean by the peirates and sold. I wished I had drowned with my mother and father.'

The monk tutted but she seemed to barely notice.

'I had value, you see. Not just because I was a woman, but because I could speak and write Latin and Greek and knew numbers. As well, I could stitch. Value…'

'Why did your father teach you numbers?' he asked.

108

She shrugged her shoulders, 'He was an agent, numbers were an essential part of his trade and he had no sons. Perhaps he thought I might be of use to him one day.'

Michael's heart contracted. That is exactly what he had planned. Like Jehanne or Ariella. Backbones of a business.

'Have you used numbers and writing as a servant?'
'No. Just my embroidery.' She sighed. 'And my body.'

'How could God let this happen to an innocent girl! It's no wonder I left the Church and its values...' Michael stopped. Father Symeon's eyebrows had slid forward to the bridge of his nose. Not anger, but deep hurt. Michael realised the offence he had just spewed forth. 'I am sorry, Father...'

Somewhere Sixth Hour prayers were being sung and Father Symeon's fingers worked at his prayer beads. The harmonies were sublime and Michael thought for one moment that if God gave him his daughter back, then he would return to his Faith. But then one didn't plea-bargain with God.

'We will talk about your angst, Michael and about God. But there is still a story to tell. Do you want me to continue? I can stop and we can each go our way if you want.'

'I apologise again, and if you can forgive me, please...'

Father Symeon's eyebrows relaxed a little and he began again.

'Please Father, in the name of the Theotokis, help me,' she begged.

The priest shook his head and stood. 'I shouldn't. I should take you to the authorities. Theft, absconding from your master. All crimes.' He walked back and forth, his robes agitated and flicking past her feet. 'And yet I find your story and your fortunes sad. I am filled with disgust for your master and I suspect God feels the same because He urges me to protect you. So yes, I will help you. You must wait here – trust in God and in me, please.'

'And so I left her just like I left you a moment before,' Father Symeon said to Michael. 'I thought she would run, not trusting me, escaping from what she believed I might do. But she was there when I returned. A sad bundle of a girl who seemed to have no hope and honestly Michael, God wanted to return hope *to* her. I was merely the conduit for goodness much needed. But quiet now. The story continues.'

'*You trust in God's grace, it seems. Stand if you will…*' She stood and he looped *a worn brown cloak over her shoulders.* '*Now, tie up your hair.*'

She did so, and he gave her the faded skepe *of a novice nun and she tied it over her head.*

'*I will take you to the Lips Monastery on Third Hill where there is a small convent. The* hegoumene, *Abbess Theodora, is known to me and I believe she will shelter you until I can find something more suitable.*'

'*Oh Father, how can I thank you?*'

'*By thinking on your future, my child.*' *His fingers played with his beads.* '*And by thinking how God has intervened to protect you. Now come.*' *He took her arm.* '*I have been neglectful of my duties within the basilica and must make haste.*'

He led her through the garden to a gate and they passed rapidly along the streets of Second Hill and onto Third Hill where the Valens Aqueduct shielded them from the afternoon's spring sunbeams.

The air on top of Third Hill and close to the Lips Monastery which stood before them, smelled of all that made Constantinople a city of religion and trade – olibanum, *spikenard, cinnamon, pepper and more.*

'*There is Lips,*' *Father Symeon pointed at the building which displayed a half cylinder front, elongated arched windows and a dainty Byzantine cupola.* '*And there is the Abbess,*' *he pointed to a small rotund woman emerging from a gate in a side wall.* '*Mother Theodora!*' *He waved his arm about,* olibanum *drifting on the air.*

She walked across to them. '*Father Symeon, you are a long way from Sancta Sophia.*'

'*I have something to ask you,*' *he replied and introducing her to the young woman, briefly alluded to her predicament.*

Mother Theodora listened, studying the would-be thief with intensity. '*I think we may be able to help, child. Come with me now and allow Father Symeon to return to his tasks. But Father, I trust you to find something further for her. If she does not intend to take vows, she cannot remain long in Lips.*'

Promising to do so, Father Symeon patted Ioulia's hand. 'O Theós na eínai mazí sas…'

God be with you indeed, Michael thought. Throughout the telling, he wanted to interject a thousand times. This was his daughter, he knew it like he knew the scar on his leg. It could be no one else. He took a breath to speak but the priest held up a finger.

'You wish to know all I can tell you, do you not?' Father Symeon had the knack of admonishing kindly. 'I can see that your mind and heart are running a race as I pass on all the information I have. At the end, you may ask your questions, but perhaps it is wise to let me finish. There is not much more to tell. The *ecclesiarchissa* at Lips, Sister Euphraxia, was found and on learning that the young woman was a talented embroideress, they set her to work on an *epitrachelion* for the Patriarch. She excelled herself. She worked within Lips until I could find a safer place away from the streets of Constantinople. She is there now.'

'Where?'

'The Xylinites nunnery.'

Michael's heart pounded. Xylinites? What game was God playing. Once, as a thief, he had been close enough to Xylinites to shout to his daughter. At once he felt shattered and let down, but on the other hand, he had just found that she was alive; his daughter was alive!

'Why is she outside the city?'

'My son, she was a slave and is still a slave by law. She is the property of a nobleman who did not choose to free her. I do not know his name as I was quite clear that I did not want to know. But if he managed to find out she was within the city, he would have been able to claim her back readily by law, and she would be disciplined accordingly. You know as well as I that it would not be pretty. I found a place farther away for her security. She is content. And now that I have told you all I know, I will tell you her name.' Father Symeon leaned back, clasping his prayer beads in the palm of one hand. 'She is called...'

'I know her name. She is Ioulia. I am right, am I not, Father Symeon?' Michael was hunched forward, his hands clasped between his knees. He was glad the priest could not see his face as tears dripped to the ground, little damp circles lying on the tiled floor.

Twelve years and I have almost found her.

It was almost too much to bear. The sheer enormity of it.

'For twelve years I have grieved for a wife and for a daughter. I buried my wife, Father. I saw her dead and held her cold body. There is nothing like the feel of someone from whom life has passed to convince one that they are indeed gone from one's own life. But Ioulia disappeared. There was nothing, and so I believed her drowned. But even so, there was a part of my heart and soul that wrung itself thin with insane hope. It was living purgatory and could have driven me to madness. Until Father Nicholas' letter arrived and then I thought perhaps I was not so mad after all. But even *his* letter was a kind of Heaven and Hell…'

'I am filled with sadness for you,' Father Symeon said. 'But you did find joy again, did you not? And it sustained you? Tobias mentioned Jehanne, your second wife.'

'Yes, and Jehanne encouraged me to follow the trail of light lit by Father Nicholas' note which led me to you. Father, is she well?'

'I have not seen her for some time. But yes, she is well. She has settled in her new home and assists the *ecclesiarchissa* greatly because of her literacy. She also stitches and works in the fields.'

'Can you help me see her? The *hegoumene* surely won't let me in if I just bang on the convent's gate.'

'Yes, of course. But Michael, she has had twelve years of life experience and it may have changed her from the young girl you knew. You must be gentle with her and expect a difference.'

'Indeed. We have both changed. And she now has a stepmother…'

'She is an adult, Michael, who is making her own way. Just as Jehanne did when she left her home and joined a group of pilgrims.'

'You know of that?'

Father Symeon smiled. 'Tobias talks. And talks. And he trusts me.'

Michael nodded. He accepted the wisdom of the priest's words. So much time had passed for both he and his daughter. It would be a sensitive meeting.

'And you say she had a child.'

'Yes, but it died within hours of being born. There was just time to christen it so that it could rest peacefully in God's arms, I believe. Michael, Ioulia had some abuse in her time as a slave but her mistress cared for her well.'

'Not well enough,' Michael said with passion. 'If I knew his name, I would kill him for raping my daughter!'

'Then you would be of little use to your daughter. You would be executed. Better to channel your anger elsewhere. To more positive things.'

Oh, I am already doing that, Father. There is an Arab…

'I accept your advice, Father Symeon. I never want to lose her again and I hope in my heart that she will never want to lose me. But it will be a difficult first meeting.'

'Most likely. But God will be with you. And just a small word if I may. Think on this, Michael. It is a small irony is it not, that you were directed by God's servants to find your daughter? God has been kind. Perhaps you may find it in your heart to be more charitable to God, to the Blessed Theotokis and the Saints. They have watched over you for twelve years so that you might find your daughter once more.' He stood and tucked his prayer beads amongst the folds of his robes. 'Now, I must ask your forgiveness and leave you. I have duties, I am afraid. Please come back late tomorrow and I will have an answer from the *hegoumene* of Xylinites. If it is possible for you to see Ioulia, I will give you a letter of introduction then.'

Michael stood, the pressure on his kneecap reminding him that real life stood by his shoulder, that he must make his way back down the steps where he had been attacked. 'Father, I cannot thank you enough…'

'Thank God, my son, not me. He watches over us all.'

They walked back into the basilica together and Michael grasped the priest's hand, unsure if he should bow, kiss the hand he held or simply back away. The priest withdrew his fingers gently.

'*O Theós na eínai mazí sas,* Michael Sarapion. I shall see you anon.' He walked away into the dark depths of the narthex of Sancta Sophia, not looking back.

Michael barely heard the crowd swirling around him as they adored the icons and prayed with enthusiasm. With each aching step past one more porphyry pillar, whilst the dulcet gold leaf and flickering candles lit his way, one word echoed and re-echoed.

Alive…

After twelve years, he would see his daughter. Alive.

How quickly grief changed to joy. The acid ache of sadness that lingered with the death of loved ones softened. When he had married Jehanne, he was positive that Helena would have giving her blessing in the belief that his mourning would be mitigated. That he might even learn to laugh again. A partner in life gave him that second chance.

But the loss of his only child was something that nothing could ease. Not even marriage. Ioulia had been the one remaining child he and Helena had produced. Two sons stillborn and one daughter lost a few days after her birth. Was it any wonder that she was the light of his and Helena's life? Jehanne had understood, pushing him toward Constantinople with a departing kiss.

'Come back to me,' she had said. So that we may give Ioulia brothers and sisters.'

'I will,' he replied. 'I will bring her home.'

He had oft thought of the blame he had lived with in the last twelve years. Guilt that by moving his family from Sozopolis, he had set them up for death. He was, in essence, a murderer.

Then he caught his breath.

What if Ioulia blamed him for her life?

Then like a flood tide, Father Symeon's words came back. *'She has had twelve years of life experience and it may have changed her from the young girl you knew... expect a difference... She is an adult who is making her own way...'*

Her own way without her family. And what terrible life experiences she has had. No love or respect since the moment she was washed off the decks of the sinking galley. Just fear. And anger. Anger enough to steal a piece of blue silk that looked like the sea that had stolen her family away and which she wanted to rip to shreds. Where would her anger be directed when she finally met with her father?

For a moment, he thought of the irony that father and daughter had both turned thief. The apple truly did not fall far from the tree. He barely noticed he was in daylight until a voice said,

'If I didn't know better, Michael, I would say you'd been struck by a Divine revelation.' Tobias sat on a bench outside the doors, swinging his legs. He attracted a modicum of interest from the crowd, but then small entertainers had been gracing the fairs and markets of Constantinople for years. Not only that, freakish types from across the east and through the

Speris Zğua abounded. Tobias would be seen as one such although there was no doubt his ego would be bruised to be included with common folk and not to be recognised as a favoured troubadour of Richard of England and Eleanor, Richard's royal mother. 'And you are limping. Was the fellow *that* heavy when he drove you into the steps?'

'Ah, you have seen Leo.'

'I was almost to the harbour…'

'And?'

'He said you had been attacked again.'

'Possibly.'

'He said definitely, and one does not argue with a man that size.'

'Where is he?'

'Further down with Hilarius. Leo said you and he had an agreement that he not shadow too closely. Are you walking back to Basilike Street now? May I join you or do you wish to be alone?'

Michael wanted solitude. As always. He was desperate to digest the story he had been told, to turn it every way he could to make sense of it. To establish some sort of plan in his mind for meeting his daughter. 'Yes, of course. You seem happier, Tobias. I gather the priest set your mind at rest.'

'He did. He is a very gentle man and in his wise way, told me that God will be with me as I sit by Tomas' grave. He also said he had no doubt Tomas is in Heaven because he repented at the last and was blessed. It makes me feel more comfortable. I didn't tell him I had killed the man who denounced Tomas with a pleasure that damns me to Hell everlasting.' Toby was quite phlegmatic. 'But I dare say he knows. He seems to know everything.'

Michael remained silent, glad of the pain in his knee and the need to concentrate as he walked down the steps.

'Does it hurt?'

'Yes. But your good Father Symeon bound it. It isn't smashed apparently, else I would not be able to walk. So that's rather a good thing.'

'You are a master of understatement, Michael. Does anything fuss you at all?'

Michael had to smile.

If only you knew…

'Many things, Toby. I just try to keep my emotions under control.'

'But you are like Father Symeon. So calm.'

'You have not yet seen me provoked…'

'And *have* you been provoked by life, Michael?'

There was a tone to Toby's question and Michael glanced down. Toby looked up at him, eyes innocently wide.

'You are provoking a response from me, are you not?'

Toby shrugged, grinned and hopped onto the level paving at the foot of the steps.

'Then,' Michael said, 'I will say this. Father Symeon told me something. And I will share it with all of you when we get back to Basilike Street.' He glanced behind them, pleased to see Leo following head and shoulders above the folk that streamed back and forth. 'Do you think Ahmed will have returned?'

'God knows. He's not exactly sweetness and light just now. *There's* a man who's been provoked and who is angry because of it. Would that he would share his distress with us. We are a family, after all.'

'Such a family of misfits, aren't we?'

Toby laughed. 'God's bones but yes! I am writing a grand *chanson* daily!'

If Michael thanked God for anything in that very moment, it was that Toby was in their midst. Toby who had a sense of humour, and whom everyone loved and who could get away with murder and still be accepted by a churchman. He would always lighten the family load with word or song and he would be Ariella's stalwart companion, as he had been Lady Ysabel's. Ah – there was much in Tobias Celho to admire and love and Michael needed him at his side for the delivery of his news.

He ran back and forth over the words he would use for his revelations to the household. The plainer the better. If he wondered at all how things would be received, it was perhaps Ahmed's reaction of which he was most unsure. For the rest, he was sure they would support him.

'Toby, just stop for a moment. I want to tell you what I found out from Father Symeon before we reach the house…'

He led the minstrel to a stone seat on the esplanade. When he looked back, he could see Leo leaning against the wall of a tavern, talking to Hilarius. 'Toby, I have been married before.'

'You have?' Toby sat up as if he had been pricked by a *kontarion*.

'My wife drowned when we were sailing to Constantinople from our home in Sozopolis. The ship hit rocks and sank. I had a daughter as well. To cut a long story short, I thought her dead, but the priest who rescued me and buried my wife, contacted Father Symeon who…' Michael's voice tightened, the words emerging knotted and torn. 'Father Symeon found my daughter. She was a slave but is now in the convent of Xylinites outside the northern walls. I might see her in less than two days.'

'Christ's toenails! Does Jehanne know of this?'

'Jehanne knew I was married before, knew too that I had received a letter from Father Nicholas of Agathopolis – the man who rescued me. Jehanne urged me to find Father Symeon as the letter indicated. That I must do what I could to find my daughter.'

'How old is she?'

'Twenty-four and I have not seen her for twelve years. I thought her dead, Toby. Father Symeon is arranging for me to see her as we speak. Her name is Ioulia.'

Toby sat with his mouth open. Michael could almost see his mind snapping up morsels for his heroic songs, tasting them, chewing on them. But then the minstrel pulled himself together, slapping Michael on the shoulder. 'This is little short of miraculous. How wonderful you must feel. I am delighted for you.'

'I am … happy.'

'Like I said, the master of understatement. Why did you want to tell me this before we reached Basilike Street?'

Michael shrugged. 'I didn't in the beginning, but the more I thought on it, the more I felt I needed a supporter when I bought the news forth. Given that we already have pressures upon the house, I wanted to know someone is… someone feels…' He sighed. 'I think that I am concerned about Ahmed's reaction and to have you there with your lightness of touch – it may help.'

Toby grabbed a strand of his hair as it blew across his face in the seabreeze. 'I can't imagine you are afraid of Ahmed.'

'Not directly, but I am afraid that his tempestuous manner might damage any chance I have of meeting with my daughter.'

'How so?'

'I don't know. He is his own master at the moment. Far more so than normal and he has a tongue about him. Let alone a manner. But then perhaps

I am just overly sensitive just now.'

'Michael,' Toby said. 'Do you not trust Ahmed?'

'I thought I did. But since Gallipolis he has been... different. Does that equate to being untrustworthy? Probably not. I just know that I am heart-deep in an issue of personal importance and he must not and shall not threaten that, nor have it belittled, as is his want lately.'

'You obviously trust Ariella and myself. But what of the rest of the house?'

'I don't know them well enough. Christo yes. Of course. The others? If Christo recommends them, then I must trust in his judgement. Now, I have told you my news. Methinks we must make haste back to the house. There is a lot of ground to cover when we get there.'

Toby jumped up with alacrity as Michael stepped forward with care, testing the ground with his leg and knee.

'A lot of ground indeed,' Toby remarked, 'and methinks we should call for a litter and have you carried home, Michael.'

'I am stiff and sore but I don't need a litter. Let's go.'

With each step to Basilike Street, Michael's kneecap slid back and forth, or so it seemed, the pain sharp and then achingly dull. He supposed the priest's bandaging made things better than they might have been, but he cursed his luck. No one ever won a fight against an enemy standing still, and what if his cursed Arab was close? He was glad of Toby's silence as they progressed up Little Mese, savouring the information about his daughter and undiminished by small talk. He created images in his mind of her face as he remembered it in the good times, her voice, her lithe height and her mother's beauty shining forth from her eyes and her smile. Would there be smiles now? Or admonishment? Or even worse – rejection...

The gates swung wide as they approached the house. Julius and Bonus stood armed with *kontarions*, the tips glinting in the sun – a warning, like a scorpion's tail arching over its back. Michael smiled at them as they passed through. 'Leo and Hilarius are behind. Thank them both for accompanying us and send Phocus to the hall if you will. Is Ahmed returned?'

'He came in just before yourselves,' said Julius, 'and went to the kitchen.'

The two men walked across the yard as Toby muttered, 'Hey ho. Into the lion's den we go.'

'You've both been gone long,' Ahmed lounged in a chair, one leg hooked over the arm, chewing a date and spitting the stone into his palm. 'I trust you've sourced something truly remarkable during your absence.'

Toby poured watered wine into a mug, offering it to Michael. Taking it, Michael was glad that in this Byzantine house, there was a supply of wine as well as syrup. He watched Toby top up a mug for himself as the minstrel answered,

'The same for you. You disappeared without a word or a guard. At least *we* took previous events seriously.' He forestalled any reply by drinking deeply and then added, 'I shall find Ariella.'

Ahmed watched him go before flipping the date stone into a small terracotta pot and turning a lazy eye upon Michael. 'Well?'

'Well what exactly? Both Toby and I had a profitable day at our separate endeavours. You will excuse me. I wish to change and then I would talk with you and the others when I return. Please don't leave.'

As he walked away, Ahmed called after him. 'You are bloody, Michael. Is that a problem?'

But he forbore to answer, limping up the stair and into his chamber. Making fists, he growled, throwing his torn hose across the room. He wanted to like Ahmed but sometimes, it was like sucking lemons or chewing on sand and he didn't remember this about him on the voyage with the Tyrian purple hidden on *Durrah*. Arrogant yes, but fair and an excellent seaman with a loyal crew. Surely loyalty sprang from a perception of courage and clear thought?

He undid the bandage, examining the swollen and brightly coloured flesh, wincing as he palpated around the kneecap. Wrapping it again, he pulled on clean hose, noticing the blood stains on the hem of his tunic and changing that as well; a long tunic that revealed nothing of the bandage and made him look far less as if he had just emerged from some harbourside brawl. He returned to the stair, hand pressing against the wall as he laboured down.

The murmur of voices quieted as he entered, five pairs of eyes turning to watch as he moved to the centre of the room. Toby, brushed and washed, pulled up a stool, saying 'Sit, Michael,' as he grabbed another for himself.

'Michael! You are hurt…' Ariella went to stand.

'Later, Ariella. Other things first.' He deliberately sought Ahmed's face as he spoke. Eye to eye.

Meeting you on my terms, old friend?

'None of you,' he began, 'Except perhaps Christo...' He sat down on the stool. 'None of you will know that I have been married before...'

Ariella gasped, Christo's eyebrows rose and he shook his head in surprise, Phocus sat quietly and Ahmed's eyes slitted – just a fraction.

Michael told the story. If anyone in the room were stunned, or even if they were bored, there was not a sign and so he pushed on, his revelation gathering momentum. He spoke of the twelve years of aching grief, of the letter and finally he talked of the day's outcome.

Ariella's hands rushed to her face. 'Oh Michael...' Her eyes shone. 'You are blessed!'

'I hope so.'

'*Kýrie* Michael,' said Phocus. 'When you go to meet her, I will take you to the convent of Xylinites myself.'

Michael smiled his thanks as Christo said, 'I did not know. Saul said nothing in his communications.'

'For which I am glad. It has been a hard cross to bear and I couldn't abide the pity...'

'Support is different to pity, Michael,' Christo interrupted. 'So is empathy. Any of us might be in the same position.'

Unusually, Ahmed stayed quiet, his arms crossed, and Michael was glad. The sea captain sat in part shadow, the light having drifted from the door as dusk changed places with afternoon. His eyes were hidden, only the lower part of his face showed and a knife edge could have no straighter nor sharper line than his mouth. Something would come forth sooner or later.

'But that's not all,' Toby said. 'Fortunately, Michael took Leo to Sancta Sophia and Leo followed a little behind to give Michael anonymity and to observe if he was followed. Leo saw someone leaping up the steps, moving in too close upon Michael, and readying to attack him!' Toby had jumped up and tracked back and forth, delivering the news with the passion of the entertainer. 'Leo helped him, so to speak, driving into the assailant, knocking him off balance and over the top of Michael. He had a knife drawn which he dropped as he hit his head. Hard.'

'He had a knife?' Michael thought back. He couldn't remember seeing a weapon…

'It fell away in the moment, but Leo has it if you want to see. Anyway,' Toby looked round at his audience, 'Leo made much to the public of his *friend* being drunk and how he needed to cool his head. He threw him over his shoulder and took him to the harbour, tipping him in near some *caiques* that had been pulled onto the slips. No one could see.'

'Unwise,' Ahmed's voice growled from his dark corner and Christo excused himself to fetch candles and tinder. 'Surely it would have been better to secure the idiot and question him.'

'It was too late,' said Toby. 'I asked Leo. The fellow was unconscious and living on borrowed time as happens with a fatal knock to the head. Even if he *had* spoken, chances are he would have made no sense at all.'

'Pity,' was all Ahmed said.

Christo returned and proceeded to light the chamber, the room beginning to glow and Ahmed was no longer able to hide. Perhaps he had had the grace to refine his mood, because he seemed devoid of expression. Not bland, never that. But empty…

Curious…

'I am glad for you, my friend, and I thank Allah that you have found your daughter. To rebuild a family you thought lost to you is surely a blessing. One can ask no more.'

If sincerity could be weighed, then this should have been the measure of Ahmed. Not unnecessarily heavyweight nor as light as a feather but substantial enough to seem real.

Surely…

Michael sat waiting…

'But,' Ahmed continued, and Michael's heart sank. 'What of this latest attack? Did Leo say anything? Something we can use to the advantage?'

Toby touched Michael's arm, an almost invisible nod to being by Michael's side in adversity and indicating that he would take the stand. 'Leo said the fellow was nondescript and had no monies in his purse, no papers, no obvious marks on his person. In fact, nothing to mark him at all. Of course, his accent and some degree of cogency might have helped. But it was too late.'

'Then until we hear otherwise,' Michael said, 'we assume this is the next in a continuing barrage of attacks. Attacks which I believe are designed to fragment us, wear us thin, have us lose faith in each other.'

'I agree,' said Phocus. 'And by this evening in the taverns, it will be noted that Gisborne-ben Simon has a professional guard. By consequence, this house becomes the topic of conversation on two quite negative and powerful fronts. One,' he touched his finger. Michael had not noticed the tip missing until this moment. 'They will think the house is pompous and filled with its own importance. And two, that the house contains or *will* contain something of infinite value.'

'Right on one point,' murmured Ahmed. 'If not the other.'

Michael had a feeling that he had experienced exactly this in Lyon. But then in trade, someone always held something more valuable than the next person. Envy was rife and men stopped at nothing to secure wealth and when one stopped at nothing, it invariably meant revenge would follow. Someone in Constantinople was intent on making the house pay. But whose fault that was and why, was open to debate.

Thus, like dropping a honeypot into a beeskip, Michael asked the question, 'Who amongst us has caused so much angst that vengeance is sought? Ariella?'

Ariella leaned forward, her veil folds slipping over her shoulders. In the late afternoon light, her freckles gleamed against her smooth skin and her eyes became hooded with a measure of dislike. Not at Michael but at life… 'No one likes Jews, Michael. Don't forget that all Jews must live over there,' she gestured with her arm. 'In Pera across the Golden Horn. I shouldn't be here either. Nor is Father's house acceptable, except that it is also Gisborne's and *he* is seen as an integral part of the Venetian community. We Jews are not even allowed to ride horses here, because people would think we are above ourselves. I won't tell you what they *really* think of us, what the common man says because it's disgusting. But you can see, I can offend anyone simply by breathing.'

Michael moved swiftly on, bees in a honeypot and vice versa. 'Phocus, what about you and the men?'

Phocus moved closer to his mother, towering over her. She was his Queen bee perhaps, certainly if aroused and needing to protect the hive.

'I must beg forgiveness from you all,' he said. 'But especially from my mother. In our time in the Balkans, and as we moved around, the men and I offended many and killed more. Even our individual pasts are blemished. I could not give you names or countries. Nothing but numbers. It is the nature of being a mercenary. One does anything for money.'

Phocus had looked down at his mother as he spoke and she had wept, but now she wiped her eyes, grasped his hand tightly and kissed it. Looking at everyone, she said fiercely, 'He is a good boy. They all are. And if anyone says otherwise, they should say it to my face.'

The Queen bee buzzes…

'Toby? What think you?' Michael turned to the minstrel.

Toby shrugged. 'I killed a Genovese Vigia out of the need to avenge my brother whom a Vigia had denounced to the Angelids. The battle for revenge could go onward through history.'

'May Allah protect us from the wrath of fools,' Ahmed murmured.

'Then what about you, oh noble Arab.' Toby stood and bowed with the theatrics of the entertainer. 'How innocent are you?'

'Me?' Ahmed grinned. 'I am like Ariella. An outsider not to be trusted. I am that most feared of people – an Arab. They don't understand our Q'uran and think we are godless. That is enough, I would say. In any case, I am mostly at sea and *if* I offend, it is surely the sea who bears the brunt. May Allah forgive my blasphemy.'

'No grubby deals, secret merchandise, disgruntled crew?' Toby persisted. Only he could get away with such blatant questioning.

'To my knowledge, no.' Ahmed flicked each person in the group a burning glance. 'But I cannot control someone else's envies. And I *have* made men envious. This I do know.'

Michael knew there was little point in questioning him further and he moved on. 'Christo? I apologise for asking…'

The notary shrugged. 'It is only fair. I am not offended, and I confess to you that I can think of nothing at all. I run a trading house for a Venetian company and everything is in a legitimate ledger.'

'Then it is a conundrum,' Michael sighed and rubbed his knee.

'But what about you, Michael from Sozopolis?' Ahmed's voice was as smooth as oil – until a flame is dropped in it. 'Are you blameless, my friend? No one likes a thief.'

'I have gone over my life a hundred times, Ahmed. And like Phocus, there are many who, if they recognised me as Gabriel the thief, would sink a knife deep between my shoulder blades. But I am *not* Gabriel. I am Michael Sarapion of the house of Gisborne-ben Simon. Show me someone who might link me back to the purple because I think I look very different now. At that time, I looked like a nomad from Khorasan. Now I am the trader people remember from the past, only with more grey hair and some lines on my face surely brought on by the pressure of business.'

Ahmed reached for the date stone, palming it back and forth. 'You *do* look different, I will grant that. I recall you on my boat with the purple and you were … travel-stained, shall we say.'

'Then we must accept that amongst us all, one or the other is arousing ire. We must accept a communal blame, tighten our security accordingly and be on guard, eyes in the back of the head.'

'Which means,' Toby pointed a finger at Ahmed, 'That we don't sneak off without telling anyone where we are going and without taking a guard.'

'In the meantime,' Ariella spoke into the charged atmosphere, 'I for one would like to say how excited I am for Michael. To lose a member of one's family is a wound that never heals, an ache that never diminishes. This is the healing of one such wound. I hope that you can bring her to meet us, Michael.'

'I hope so too, Ariella. I would like her to see that she has a family.'

Toby grinned. 'An odd one, but a family all the same.'

As he spoke, there was noise outside as the gates were pulled back and someone entered. Further sound of men's voices drifted on the early dusk air.

'Oh,' Toby jumped up. 'With all the excitement of Michael's glad tidings, I forgot to say that Anwar is coming to see Ariella.'

The house was familiar with Anwar al Din, the reputable Arab physician, known for being excused for his religion and who treated the noble ill. Ariella, however, looked surprised. 'I am quite well, Toby. Well enough for poor Anwar not to have to come as the day winds down…'

'Of course, but your little cargo is very valuable, and your father would expect us to care for you and the babe. This is part of that care. And besides, Ephigenia is preparing a meal to which Anwar is invited.'

The chamber emptied rapidly to wash and tidy, leaving Michael and

Ahmed together, saying nothing to each other. The flames dipped and dived, and Ahmed sighed as if he were tired.

'You are indeed a fortunate man, my friend,' he said finally.

'How so?'

'In respect of your lost family. Many have not been so and would be envious.'

'You think *finding* my daughter might be the cause of the troubles we face? God's breath, Ahmed, I only found out today that she was alive. That doesn't make sense at all!'

'Don't be so sharp,' Ahmed said, and Michael thought it was beyond ironic given the tempestuousness of the man who sat in front of him.

'I was passing comment,' Ahmed continued. 'Aside from which, you thought I would knot your ropes, did you not?'

''Tis true. You have been rude, dismissive, acting on a whim…'

'Oh please, don't stop. It is a veritable cargo of compliment.'

'Ahmed, none of us is stupid. We have noticed a change in you. Do you need to tell me anything?'

'Not at all.' The customary glibness bloomed. 'But let us talk about you. Finding your child. I suspect you have longed for this.

He is so clever, turning the attention when it pinpoints something about which he does not want to speak. What is it, my friend?

'I would be lying if I said no,' Michael replied. 'I lost my life when Helena and Ioulia drowned. Or so it seemed. I was nothing without them. No one knew and I kept it that way. I was a private man in the early days in this city and nothing changed. But to have my child restored to me from the grave? My God above, I can scarce put it into words.'

'You say it well enough…' Ahmed walked to the table and placed the date stone with a pile of others in a small brass bowl.

'Please trust us, Ahmed. If there is anything…'

But as the sea captain turned back, Toby and Ariella entered the chamber, accompanied by the physician.

CHAPTER SEVEN

×

Anwar al Din and his brother, Mehmet, had studied medicine together and worked across the land that Tobias' ilk called Outremer. But Anwar stayed in Constantinople whereas the other had moved on, eventually meeting with Gisborne in the Middle Sea and liking the man, deciding to stay within the merchant house Gisborne was creating. Anwar and Mehmet were brothers who loved and respected each other and to be cared for by one was like being cared for by the other – mirror images. They had a wisdom that set them apart – one that encouraged people to defer to them, to seek them out in times of crisis.

Michael knew Anwar well. The physician had tended Michael's leg when he ran with the Tyrian purple, scraping past a Varangian sword. He had met Mehmet on board *Durrah* as he and Jehanne made their way to Lyon, and he was comfortable now to welcome Anwar into the house on Basilike Street.

'Anwar…' Michael winced as he stood. Limping over to the physician, he enveloped him in a hug, such was his affection for the man who may have saved his life.

'I see you still do not look after your legs, my friend,' Anwar stood back. 'Am I come to see Ariella or you?'

'I would like to think you are here because we have news of your brother and because you are dear to the house,' Michael replied.

'But your leg nevertheless is an issue.' Anwar's pale grey hair could just be seen feathering beneath his dark *keffiyeh* and his black eyes sparkled with intensity.

''Tis so. A small accident.'

'If you say. Perhaps we can adjourn to a more private chamber and I will see to it? Ariella, can you bring me warm water, some wine perhaps, maybe some linen strips if you have them?'

'This is unnecessary...' Michael protested.

'Indulge me,' Anwar said. 'My imperial patients prefer me to pat their hands and feed them poppy. It is the same every day. And because the women are women, if they require somewhat personal care, they are tended by a woman physician or a eunuch. I am allowed to consult with them but it is usually in tandem. In case you are concerned, it will be the same with Ariella. I will always consult with Ephigenia close by. Or you may choose to appoint a woman...'

'I didn't give it any thought, Anwar. Have things changed so much for you in the city lately?'

'Yes and no. I am an Arab. It is what it is. But I am also a man and the Byzantine woman is as precious to the Church family as an Arab woman is to ours by the laws of our Qu'ran. I merely do what is expected of me in such society. It has never been any different. I never consulted without an escort. Usually Fatima who is remarkably well-trained.'

They walked up the stair together, Michael sucking on the occasional breath.

'I see I can walk faster than you even with my advanced years,' Anwar turned humorous eyes upon Michael. 'But if you are walking, there is obviously no fracture.'

''Tis what Father Symeon said...'

'Ah, the good Father. A lovely man.'

'Yes... here, this is my chamber.'

Anwar unwound the bandages and palpated the kneecap, remarking, 'I think you have much bruising, perhaps a little fluid. If it had been fractured, my good teacher, Ibn Sina, would have required me to press the bones together, strapping it firmly and you would have sat quietly for at least six sennights. As it is, I will treat it with arnica for the bruising, bind it – which I want you to remove at night – and elevate it as often as you can. Which,' he grinned at Michael, 'for a man like you may be almost impossible. Now tell me how this *really* happened.'

They sat together, and Michael marvelled at how much it was like sitting with Mehmet. Or sitting with one's father. The voice of reason. He talked too of Ariella and the playact. And of Ioulia.

'Ioulia. A lovely name.'

'Her mother's choice.'

'Michael, have you thought about her likely reaction to you?'

'Every moment. I have faced the Varangians and lived on a knife edge but this concerns me more. She was abused by her master, bore his child at a young age, and has suffered all manner of self-doubt, I am sure. She will want to blame someone for it and I was the one who placed she and her mother on that galley. I am fully aware that our meeting may be anything but joyous.'

'If she is at the Xylinites nunnery, I am sure she will have been well cared for by the infirmarian, but if you think she might need medical support, I can arrange for Fatima…'

'I thank you. But I have no idea what will happen when we meet. She is a woman of twenty-four years and I doubt I can suddenly assume the role of father in her life when she has not had my influence for twelve of those years. I will observe – it is all I can do. Shall we go down?'

'Let me see Ariella first. Would you be so kind to send she and Ephigenia to me?'

Michael nodded and proceeded to the kitchens where he found the two women preparing a fragrant platter of fish. They departed on his request and he returned to the now golden and flickering hall where Ahmed still sat, staring at the flames of the candle trees. Such stillness on the sea captain's part was in itself, a miracle.

'Ahmed. I did not think you would still be here.'

'I am waiting for our feast. It will be pleasant to sit with a fellow Arab.'

Oh, the wincing arrogance never lessens…

'What is the physician's verdict?' Ahmed asked.

'On my knee? Nothing much. Bruised. It will heal.'

'But how fast shall you be in view of attack, my friend?'

Michael sat on a chair and lifted his leg to rest on a stool. 'In truth, I wonder as well. But let us hope I do not need to find out until I am more healed. Do you think we shall be worn down daily?'

'Possibly. Or not, *Insh'Allah!*'

'Whom do you think is most at risk?'

'In all honesty and you may not like my response, but I think Ariella or Tobias. Ariella because she would be a valuable ransom and Tobias because he murdered a Vigia. Not you – no one knows you as Gabriel. Although today's little event puts the lie to that, I suppose.'

'And you?' Michael wanted to keep pushing that point.

'Michael, I do have something to tell you, but it must wait for another day. And we need to be far from the house when I relay my own news.'

'You intrigue me.'

Ahmed turned silky, angry eyes upon Michael. So angry.

But perhaps not with me, he thought.

'Allow yourself to be intrigued,' the sea captain replied, his voice with its deep timbre doing nothing to allay any concerns Michael might have. 'Ah,' Ahmed said more glibly, 'Here is our soon-to-be mother with her physician. Let us celebrate the future...'

Michael chafed at the intrusion. There was something of import to come, he was sure of it, but he stood and welcomed Anwar back into the room as Ariella was pronounced fit and well and perhaps due to give birth earlier than she imagined.

Michael sat in the soft sun, leaning back against the tavern wall, a syrup of average concoction in front of him. He was confident in his forged papers. It merely remained for time to pass so that he might escape to the west with his cargo – cargo hidden outside the city and which he would move close when the time was right. He was Hussein, the nomadic trader from Khorasan, with many wives...

He remembered Dana's soft query, 'They say you trade in ancient essences and lapis...' and his reply, 'It is what my papers say...'

He smiled to himself, amused that a taciturn young Lyonnais woman had wrought hope in him when for so long he had been devoid of such a thing. All he need do now was keep his eye on the harbours and avoid trouble. Dana had said he looked like a native of Khorasan. Perhaps it was the legacy of being born and bred in Trabzon, close to the borders of those remarkable provinces of desert valleys, rocky clefts and snow-capped mountains. He rather liked the idea of reinventing himself. He had never really liked Gabriel after all – always tainted with the smell of the shellfish he had dived for to make the purple. Diving because he had never doubted Saul ben Simon would buy it. Not a shred of doubt.

But the risks haunted him in the dark hours. Not that there was anyone to care if his life ended. But what man amongst men would want to be executed the Byzantine way? Hands, eyes? And what else would they do to him for the theft of a protected imperial commodity? A crime against the empire. There would be nothing left of him but scraps for wild dogs and kites.

He sucked deep on the syrup, wishing for a strong unwatered wine, hearing loud voices coming down the street toward the tavern. Four of the fair Varangian guard walked in, laughing, pushing, off-duty and drunk with it. He had heard them call themselves 'Grikkfari' and the city in which they were domiciled 'Miklagard'. They were big brutes, with hair from white through sand to red and chestnut brown. And they were noisy, walking with a swagger and creaking with multitudinous layers of leather across their bodies.

Discretion, he decided, was called for.

'Hey!' one of the men called out to him as he moved away.

He took another step and a brutal hand yanked him round. 'I said, hey!'

'I am sorry, sir. I thought you called to your friends,' Michael spoke in a suitably deferential way.

'I called to you, arsehole! Let me see your papers.' The fellow towered over Michael, his beard flavoured with red and brown and his sand-coloured hair pulled into a long plait down his back. Michael wished he could match Petrus against him because it would surely be a fair fight. He felt in his purse for the folded documents, fingers grazing the pommel of his curved paramerion as he extracted them. Glancing at the fellow's daneaxe, the broad-shouldered blade just evident at the guard's back, he passed the papers over.

'You're the fellow I saw with the embroiderer.'

Think quick, Michael...

'The embroiderer? The one who works at the palace? Yes. She wished to purchase some lapis powder from me for the dyeing of some of her threads...'

'She seemed to enjoy your company,' the fellow sneered. By the stars his breath stank!

'If you say, but it was business.' Michael shrugged, the epitome of a lowly trader from far offshore. 'I am a married man, I have six wives and many children. I do not need nor want any more complications.' He grinned in the hope it would put the Varangian at ease.

'Then here's a complication...' the Varangian bought a bunched fist up under Michael's ribs. 'Stay away from her...'

The other Grikkfari *laughed, as Michael bent over, coughing up the syrup and the day's food, and gasping for air. The fellows called to their friend to desist. That Dana would surely always have the Varagian's heart.*

'Leave him,' a deeper voice resonant with more authority, possibly the akolouthos, *the commander of the men, called out.*

The man standing over Michael drew a spathion *blade and Michael's hand flew to his own* paramerion.

'I said leave him,' the akolouthos *pulled the man away.*

Michael walked swiftly, coughing and wiping his mouth free of spittle. He turned into an alley that led down to the harbour and lent against the wall. Behind him, he heard the voice of the Varangian calling. 'Here, arsehole! Your papers!'

Damn it to Hell and back!

He had to go back to fetch them, without the papers he was a dead man and seeing just the one man alone at the top of the alley, his heart sank. He let his hand lie lightly on the pommel of the paramerion *and walked toward the guard, sizing up his chances.*

'Thanks to you, sir.' He reached out for the documents, placed them in his purse and turned. There was a faint sound, a whisper of a weapon, and he jumped forward away from the noise. A grunt, a laugh and something sharp slashed across the side of his thigh. He began to run.

'You pig-arsed dust eater! Stay away from the embroiderer!' the guard shouted.

He flipped around a corner and could hear no following footsteps. Perhaps the akolouthos *had called his man back under control. But too late, as blood ran down his leg and into his sandal. He found a dark corner near the Nerion Harbour and dragged up the edge of his robe.*

The wound slashed horizontally, deep along the side of his thigh, peeling back like grinning lips to expose the white inner flesh as blood poured freely. Not death-causing, but bad enough. He had nothing with which to bind it and limped toward Dana's house, the only person he thought might be able to help him. He hoped the Theotokos, just this once, should allow him to enter, unseen by those in the streets. Just once he needed Divine help and he had asked for so very little...

The row of houses close by the imperial palace walls were quiet. Mercifully. Perhaps people dozed, or were at their chosen basilicas, or the markets, the harbour. He walked purposefully as if there were no cares, just a man who must attend to his business.

He knocked at Dana's door and waited.

What if she is not here?

He knocked again.

The door opened and Dana frowned. 'What do you want? I have nothing for you.'

So matter-of-fact, almost dismissive.

He showed the bloody sandals beneath his tunic...

She opened the door wider and he looked up and down the street, and seeing no one, he slipped inside.

'What happened?'

'A jealous Varangian. You have an admirer.' Michael collapsed onto a wooden seat, feeling light-headed. 'He pricked me as a warning.' And so saying, he could feel himself falling and could do nothing to stop it.

How much time had passed, he had no idea. It was dark and he lay on a soft divan. He sniffed – the odour of herbs, oils and essences. He felt down his leg, a thick wad was firmly bound to his thigh under layers of bandage. Then the striking of a tinder, light from a small lamp and a gentle voice. 'Michael, my dear friend, do you feel pain?'

An Arab stood over him, dressed in pale robes and with a dark keffiyeh *folded back. 'I am Anwar al Din and Dana brought you to me. You lie at my house in Water Street, near the Valens Aqueduct. You were very lucky, you know. More of a swing and the wound would have been bigger, perhaps lethal. As it is, he merely filleted your leg like a piece of fish. I have cleaned it and stitched it.'*

'How did I get here?'

'I sent Dana a Persian carpet to repair. During the evening, she and my man rolled you inside. You do not remember? You were loaded onto a cart and brought here. I would say it was more good luck than good management as the cart could have been stopped at any time but it was a risk we needed to take. Your God appears to be on your side, Michael Sarapion.'

Michael lay abed for three days, feverish and vaguely aware of Anwar treating him, as he wandered in his mind through the history of his life. But eventually, as weak as a baby, in some pain and with a large bowl of warmed and fragrantly oiled water he sloughed the odour and sweat of days away. Anwar gave him a robe, girdle and leather slippers, saying 'You cannot go to the baths.'

'You think I would be recognised?'

'Perhaps. Certainly the injury will draw attention to you. But I am more concerned with the wound itself. You contracted an infection, Michael, and I have managed to control it with garlic, frankincense, even apple and other medicaments. But if you place that leg in the pools, I think the wound might fester further as I often wonder just what those baths contain. You might risk losing the limb altogether. No, you will stay here in seclusion until you are well. My Sophia and I will make sure you mend. In the meantime, Sophia has made a camomile tea which I would like you to sip... there... good.'

'You think I am safe here?' Michael asked as he swallowed. Sophia had flavoured the bland camomile with juice of a lemon and a tiny pinch of nutmeg. Even weak, he could name the additives.

'I am physician to the well-born. No one will force their way in.'

Michael slept or discussed trade and the availability of medicinal supplies of which he knew enough to fill Anwar with delight at such conversation. They talked of Ibn Sina's medical Canon and of the plants and spices in the Muslim doctor's pharmacopeia.

'Methinks it is better to be ill where there are Arab doctors, Anwar.'

The two sat under the loggia in the gardens. Above them seabirds from the Harbour of Theodosius wheeled gracefully, reminding Michael that Durrah would eventually anchor, the purple could be loaded and he could escape west, as far as he could possibly sail...

''Tis true,' the physician answered. 'Christian countries to our west are unwilling to accept the notions of Arab medicine.' He shrugged his shoulders. 'It is perhaps their loss.'

He left then to tend the infirm, the ill and those who suffered from hypokhondria at the palace and Michael walked inside, perhaps to sleep. He watched the light dance in colours across the walls as it reflected through a thickly glassed pitcher. Hearing the seabirds and thinking of Durrah, he recalled a conversation with Anwar earlier. He knew he must leave and take shelter beyond the city until news came of the galley. Then, when the time was right, he would bring his goods to the crypt of Saint Theodora's near the Prosphorion Harbour. There was a decrepid gate leading down from what had once been small public gardens. It had been a simple deed to ease the gate open, find the crypt entrance and make sure he would be concealed. It wasn't pleasant inside – there was a stale *ossuary with dust, bones and fallen stones, but it would suit as a hiding place so admirably.*

Thinking on the future he fell into a deep sleep, less riddled with pain and poppy and more natural than it had been for some time.

The days passed and he became stronger, taking to walking along Water Street and down the steps to Saint Basil's. Back up again because the steps helped build his leg muscles. But the wound made him limp and he cursed the Varangian who had hobbled him.

Dana came often now, and they would sit and talk, playing dice, passing time.

'How do you get away without your Varangian spying on you?'

'He is not my Varangian.' She scowled at Michael and he was charmed by the brown hair escaping from her veil and curling round the creamy skin of her face. Her eyes glittered with fire as she continued, 'It seems he has been seconded to the Balkans, his friends said it was punishment for shameful behaviour in the streets. I did not crave his attention, Michael. It was thrust upon me.' She threw the dice into a bag and snapped the strings tight. He loved her strength and sharpness. She was not one to slink behind a man's shoulders.

'I hope he dies there,' he said, quite amicably. 'Meanwhile, I think I will sail toward the Black Sea and try myself as a seaman.'

'Why the Speris Zǧua*?'*

He shrugged. He would not mention the heartache that pulled at him as he lied to her; she had slid under his skin with ease. But the truth was he had no intention of sailing anywhere. Anwar knew that his plans were just to vanish to a place known only to he and the physician until word of the galley's arrival. It was important for Dana to remain uncompromised.

'I leave the city when you leave, Michael,' she said, looking at him from under dark lashes.

'Why?'

So much for being uncompromised.

'The court becomes more insidious by the day and I suspect that my time here is warping like a twisted piece of silk thread. I crave my home and my family and would like to do so in one piece and with my own name of Jehanne de Clochard from Lyon, rather than an assumed name and identity. In addition,' she added with a matter of fact tone to her voice, 'I find I like you, Michael Sarapion, so I will come with your galley when you leave. Gisborne's network will cope when I

am gone. There are others like myself and Anwar.'

'Anwar?'

'Of course. Like myself, he is well-placed to hear idle talk and pass it on.'
She laughed. 'You are *naïve, Michael. How could you not realise?'*

He smiled. 'Too concerned with my own business, I imagine. In any case, are
you sure you want to leave? You were so eager to get here, were you not? You told
me so.'

'One grows and changes. It's a daily thing. Anyway, I have made up my
mind. I will leave on Durrah *when she comes.'*

He smiled at her. 'Then I am blessed,' he said, but still didn't tell her he was
not really sailing to the Speris Zǧua *in between times.*

He left Anwar two days later, making for the hills behind the Charyisia Gate
and despite that he missed Dana, he had no wish to talk with her in case she saw
through his subterfuge. Anwar would tell her he had sailed toward the Speris
Zǧua. It was enough for her to know that when the time was right he would
return. Anwar warned him to be careful as he took his leave, a small sack over his
shoulders – dressed as an Arab, with papers to show he was from Jerusalem and
that he was studying with the physician Anwar Al Din. A slim lie and apt to be
broken like a twig if put to the test, but it might just serve.

No one asked for his papers as he walked along the Mese and out of the city.
Perhaps because at the Charyisia Gate six lepers chose that moment to enter.
Ringing their bells, rattling their bowls and with their eyes downcast beneath
their woven hats, they were given a wide birth and shouted at to hurry through.
What crowds there were pressed back upon themselves and Michael, easing
himself to the rear, passed through the gate with no trouble.

The darker dawn had faded as he passed between the great Byzantine walls.
The day had begun dew-damp, little puffs of mist rising with each step, to dissolve
into a watery sun, the odour of earth and spring crops profound on the air. The
fields had the acid-green glaze of the season upon them and there was the heady
fragrance of likely rain all around. Seabirds swept inland above him, a sure sign
that sea-weather would follow and so he quickened his pace, determined to reach
his hiding place before showers began.

He rested once to ease the throbbing ache of his wound, and to the east of him
he heard chants on the wind from one of the monasteries that made its living in

the arable country beyond the walls. He enjoyed the harmonies because despite his split with God, he was not a Philistine.

No one cared about him as he passed by. He was just another Arab. If they cared about anyone at all, it was a logothetēs *or taxman in his multi-coloured court attire, mounted on a horse of breeding and with two mounted guardsmen behind. Or perhaps they cared about the host of returning pilgrims singing as they entered the city, to board vessels bound for Ancona, or Marseille. Perhaps even Venezia.*

As he pushed off the stone on which he sat, Michael heard hoofbeats behind and a formally clad man rode on past, perhaps a kephale, *the governor of a small province. The man sat astride his beast with confidence, secure in the knowledge that Alexios III Angelos had rewarded him for services rendered. Even though he must provide a sizeable cache of men for the armies of the Byzantine emperor; an acceptable* quid pro quo.

Michael's quid pro quo *was to steal the purple from an empire which over-ruled, spent profligately and ran a shrinking navy that could have cleaned the seas of the* peirates *who killed his wife and daughter. Maybe others would say an eye for an eye, rather than a* quid pro quo. *It was semantics. He stole to make fools of the empire, to make money for Saul ben Simon and himself, and to avenge in part, the death of his family.*

Complete revenge would come later.

He had walked perhaps two mílion, *heading northwest from the gate, when he heard the chuckle of water across stones and knew the Lycus River was close. If he cast a leaf into it, it would flow down into the city, a favourite stream for children who wanted to splash and play before it disappeared underground. This far beyond the walls, it was peaceful, secluded, surrounded by cedars and oaks. The land inclined moderately, boulders here and there.*

As he walked upriver, he heard women from the Xylinites nunnery, their voices raised in prayer, chanting the Sixth Hour liturgy. He zigged and zagged, past bent and gnarled shrubs, dense with sharp twig and fallen branch and eventually he found the small hiding place that he and Petrus had used to secret the jars of olibanum *resin. Big enough for one man to creep into.*

No one had been near. There were cobwebs draped across the rock and a small lizard scuttled away. He had found his hiding place and all else was a waiting game. At some point, word would come from the Arab physician; left beneath a rock near the small and tenuous bridge that crossed the Lycus to the nunnery. Each evening he would check under cover of darkness.

He thanked any of the Saints who might care to listen for giving him a friend like Anwar al Din… he had held the man close when he left, for it had been the nearest to a father he had experienced since he was a child in Trabzon. A good man…

They sat in comfortable companionship, Ephigenia's fine food laid out before them. Shellfish or *kakavia* flavoured with fennel and bayleaf, *moussake* and platters of olives, feta cheese, breads and plump dried dates. Luscious and lightly flavoured *pastfeli* – the orange water giving a hint of angels. There was syrup for the Arabs, wine for the Christians and clear water to mix with the grape for those who wished to. Julius and Hilarius were at their appointed stations, food sent out on a large tray – flat bread and cheeses, dried fruit and syrups. Leo and Phocus slept, ready for the night shift. The household seemed mellow and safe and for once Michael felt comfortable. That he could sit and converse readily with his companions without looking over his shoulder.

'The empire is weakening,' Christo was saying. 'The continued warring in the Balkans and with the German states is reducing the size of our empire and subsequently the income for the treasury. The navy has shrunk to a toy thing and yet, the emperor and his bureaucrats do nothing to suspend expenses, to push diplomacy, to mend what is broken.'

'And trade?' Michael asked.

'They are well aware that trade puts money into their coffers on a steady basis. As you know, the agreement with Venezia to use the city and harbour as a base is ongoing. Favoured nation, and with support from the Venetians for our excuse of a navy. But the bureaucracy is shrewd. Why limit trading rights to just the Venetians when so much more can be gained by treating with others? You will find, Michael and Ahmed, that since you were last here, the Genovese, Pisans and Anconians have built quite a stronghold on the edge of the Golden Horn.'

'That would explain the Vigia's galley then…' muttered Toby.

'You say?' Christo asked.

'The Genovese family I wronged, Christo. The one I spoke of yesterday? They sailed into port in a galley as luxurious as the Doge's.'

'Ah…' Christo nodded his head. 'Yes. The Genovese have the ability to

138

threaten the Venetians. And the Anconians have rather put themselves on the map in the Adriatico, I gather, so they all bear watching. Competition will be tight.'

'We have nothing to fear,' Ahmed's confident voice rumbled from the far end of the table. 'We have secret contacts, we already have goods stored and we are good at what we do. *Aren't* we, Christo?' Such a knowing look pierced poor Christo's composure.

'Um, yes.' Christo looked to Michael for reassurance. 'Yes, we are...'

'On that note,' Michael said, 'Christo has made an exceptional and very rare find...' He went on to tell the story of the *byssus* silk and when he was done, Ahmed sat back.

'I am impressed, Christo. Many have sought that silk for years.'

'Thank you.' Christo's face flushed the colour of a ripe peach.

'And,' Ahmed stood and reached for some bread. 'If ever we needed to keep secrets it is now. Do we all agree?'

'I said so earlier,' Michael replied. 'It doesn't go outside this room. Anwar?'

'Of course. I would say well done, Christo. You have a package in storage that is like to make as much as the purple.'

Ephigenia walked in with a platter in each hand of candied bitter orange slices sprinkled with cinnamon and rose water and Anwar picked one up, holding it like a gold *hyperpiron* between his fingers.

'Did you know a representative of the great Venetian family, Viadro, are here currently? You have heard of Tommaso?'

'Yes,' Michael replied, sitting forward. 'He has rather cornered the trade of the Adriatico for his family. They say he is intrepid beyond reason. I haven't met him.'

'I have...'

All eyes swivelled to Ahmed and an expectant silence followed until finally Toby injected an irritated 'Well?' into the air.

'Well what?' Ahmed replied. 'He is intrepid. It's just been said.' He shrugged his shoulders with the insouciance that so annoyed Michael. 'I admire him because of it. It is good for the Viadro and paves the way for others. If one can't get to the feast before him, there will always be a goodly surfeit after. Besides, he is not a young man. Better still for those of us whose years fall on the other side.'

'He is respected,' Anwar said. 'Despite his success, he is a fair man with morals. And the Venetian quarter is not just honoured…'

'Honour is surely debatable,' Ahmed interjected. 'What merchant is *truly* honourable?'

Michael sighed – more caustic opinion that did Ahmed no favours and raised hackles.

'*I* say honoured, Ahmed,' Anwar replied equably. 'I think I would find him an interesting man to talk to. Such characters are rare in my ambit. But as I was saying, the Venetian Quarter is not just honoured with *his* presence, but with a Contarini as well. It has a diplomatic effect on the Byzantine Court because the latter thrive upon such convoluted discourse and will manipulate it to the fiscal purpose. And if a physician may put an uninformed opinion forward – the presence of such luminaries rather puts the Pisans, Genovese and Anconians in their place.'

'True,' replied Christo. 'The three are making their presence felt. The Byzantines will always turn their heads toward whomever wants to drop money into their palms.'

Michael was surprised to hear this from usually mild mannered and softly spoken Christo. He liked the *volte face*. It made for interesting times.

'Perhaps we should invite Contarini and Viadro to sup with us…' he said.

'Too late.' Christo fiddled in his purse. 'This arrived at the gate as we opened it for Anwar.' He laid a fold of expensive cream parchment on the table. 'They have invited all from Gisborne-ben Simon to a banquet at the Merchant Hall at the waterfront tomorrow.'

'Then,' said Tobias very quietly. 'We had best retire. Ariella, in fact, has beaten us to it.'

She had slumped in her chair, her head lolling against the carved back, eyes closed, hands loose in the folds of her soft green gown.

Ahmed stood. 'I'll carry her to bed if one of you will fetch Ephigenia.'

The party broke up then, Tobias hovering like a hen worried for a chick as Ahmed gently scooped Ariella up. Her eyes opened briefly and she surveyed his face, then the lids slid down again, her head nestling into Ahmed's muscled shoulder.

'Astonishing,' he said. 'Despite that I am carrying she and her babe, she is featherlight.'

'Yes,' said Anwar. 'And despite that the babe is quite big. It is honestly a miracle that she hid her state from you all for so long. I suspect she may go before her time.'

With Ephigenia leading the way, candle held high, Ahmed departed with his load, Tobias, ever loyal, bringing up the rear.

Christo and Michael escorted Anwar to the gates in evening air that was moist and which smelled of sea and salt. No pale moon lit the way, and all was dark, apart from the torches flaring at the gates.

'It's a shadowy evening, Anwar. Would you like a guard to see you back to Water Street?'

Less than a heartbeat passed and the physician replied, 'If you are offering, then thank you. And don't look so perturbed. It is merely night in a big city and I am old and an Arab. We are not the most favoured people within these walls.'

'But you are an imperial physician...'

'Huh, maybe even because of that. Jealousies float on the wind like seedheads in an untended garden. There are some who think I know too much...'

'Then be careful. No secret is worth a life. Hilarius will escort you.'

'Have no fear. I've learned to have eyes and ears wide open. Ah, Michael, it has been good to see you. Good to see you all! My court life is impossibly narrow sometimes.'

'Then come often. And bring Sophia.' Michael clasped the Arab elder's arm and watched him leave with Hilarius lighting the way.

'Times have changed,' Michael said to Christo. 'I find I dislike being under siege.'

'Indeed sir,' was all the notary returned.

So, Michael thought, as he climbed the stair, leaning into the wall for support. The Contarini, the Viadro and the Vigia. As *Durrah* had sailed beyond the Venetian lagoons, he certainly hadn't assumed that Gisborne-ben Simon would be able to go about their interests without competition. It was the very nature of the business in which they worked. But he supposed he had been a touch naïve – not reckoning with the superior competition of someone like Giacomo Contarini or Tommaso Viadro. The Genovese Vigia? Their presence was yet to be calculated – like the value of a pawn in a game of chess. Sometimes the pawn was useless. Othertimes?

Besides, there was the issue of Toby and the possibility of *vindicta*…

But the Contarini erred more to the political side – to negotiating and investment in trade. To arguing Venezia's case. The Viadro though, were different. Tommaso was a seasoned expeditioner, having done his apprenticeship. They said Syria was his sphere of interest.

Tomorrow would be illuminating, Michael thought, as he laid his purse on the table. Although lightweight, it clinked and he pulled the leather buckle undone, tipping out five gold *hyperpirons*. Still lost in thought, he stacked the coins, one on top of the other, and then took one in his hand, to lay it down again, whispering,

'The Contarini…'

He laid another coin next to it.

'And the Viadro…'

Two coins, two powerplays – just like money. The more money, the more power. Below those, he laid another coin.

'The Vigia…'

Surely it was logical they were at the root of the attacks upon Gisborne-ben Simon.

Logical but maybe not feasible. The pieces don't quite fit, remember?

He took another coin and laid it down to make a third row.

'Byzantine bureaucracy…'

Could they grease the wheels, playing off one group against another? Creating tension between merchants above and beyond that which already existed?

Of course they could…

Growling, he scooped up the money, dropped it back into his purse and began to disrobe.

It was important to meet with fellow Venetians on the morrow, but he nevertheless cursed it. He hoped against all hope that the *hegoumene* of Xylinites would allow him time with his daughter. If he was brutally honest, he would say that Gisborne-ben Simon's needs were meaningless compared to that!

He woke suddenly.

As if he should reach under his pillow for the dagger he always kept there. His heart pounded and his forehead was damp with sweat. He hadn't had a nightmare and the light pouring between the shutter slats was golden and mellow. In Basilike Street, he could hear a donkey braying, splitting the dawn air in two with its woebegone calls. As he swung his legs over the side of the bed, Anwar's bandaging pulled and he heaved himself into a standing position. It was painful but not at all like the Varangian injury from the past; that was another thing entirely. He remembered the agony of the bloody former, as he had sat huddled in the rocky shelter near the Xylinites nunnery…

Xylinites!

Now he knew why he'd woken so sharply, why he had sweated. Would he find out this day if he could see Ioulia? By the Saints, if he could pray and if he could fall easily to his knees, he would beg God to allow him this one small favour…

And there was a thing.

Was the fact that Ioulia was settled in the Xylinites Convent a Divine joke? He had sat on cold rock in a small cave, feeling the ache in his heart – the pain of grief that never went away – and surrounded by the stink of *olibanum* resin whilst he waited for word from Anwar and whilst, unknown to him, his daughter lived on the other side of the Lycus. As the harmonies of the liturgies had drifted to him on the bucolic air, his daughter's voice may have been one of those who praised God the Pantocrator and the Divine Mother, the Theotokis. To think that if he had gone to the gate of the convent to ask for sustenance, his daughter may have answered. He shook his head at the unfairness of life.

But I met Dana who then became my wife called Jehanne. I secured an honoured position as a merchant in the house of Gisborne-ben Simon, privy to the most secret facts and figures of the business. News of my daughter found me in its own time.

Life has its own rhythms, he thought, as he dashed water on his face. One can fight those rhythms or accept them. He felt the beard on his chin and knew that the last Ioulia had seen of him, he was clean-shaven, with dark hair without a filament of grey. Now he looked like a man who had opened the door to old age.

Flinging on a robe, he walked to Toby's room.

'Toby, are you there? I need your help.'

Toby pulled the door wide, heavy-eyed and yawning. 'You are up too early,' he muttered, his hair standing on end and his bare toes evident beneath a robe that dragged on the floor.

'I need you to use your skills, Toby. When you prepare yourself for a performance, you appear sleek and groomed. You must shave me and cut my hair to a decent length. Do whatever you must to make me look more like Ioulia would remember.'

Toby rubbed at his eyes, pushing the sleep from them. 'That was twelve years ago, Michael. You don't get those years back with the snip of a scissor blade.'

'I know. But I was beardless when I lost her and my hair was shorter. Is it not feasible that she might see her father more in my face if it is cleanly shaven and the hair cut away?'

Toby screwed up his mouth and sighed. 'Come in, then.'

The morning passed in a plethora of crackling and torn invoices, of spidery signatures, to be aligned with Christo's systematically filed ledgers. The man looked up from his desk as Michael walked in, took in the clipped hairline and the shaved chin, nodded and dipped his quill into the ink-well, tapping it on the side to remove the excess of ink. They worked in silence, Michael sorting invoices, signing off on them, passing them to Christo who marked them in his ledgers and then filed them. Outside, birdsong and Ephigenia's voice echoed round the yard, and a watery sun dropped haphazard beams here and there.

Into the dulcet atmosphere, there was the sound of harmony.

'It sounds like Sixth Hour, Michael. I think you must leave for the Merchant Hall as soon as you can. I will fetch Phocus and Leo to attend you.'

'We should go in a group to make our mark. Christo, you must come as well.'

Christo looked down at his tunic, at his ink-stained fingers.'

'Change if you would prefer, but your ink-stains are a sign of hard work. You are Constantinople's Gisborne-ben Simon far more than us and you need to be presented as such.'

Christo dipped his head. 'Then I will be as quick as I can.'

In time, they gathered. Even Ahmed who wore a breathtaking dark blue robe cinched with a strip of fine damask and with a *kilij* and purse buckled over the top. Michael thanked the stars that the sun wasn't shining because the reflection from the gleaming bald pate would blind anyone. Tobias of course, was polished like a small gem, as always when he appeared in public. He grinned at Michael, flicking his hair away from his own collar in recognition of his work on Michael's appearance. He too had an ornamental dagger sheathed at his side, the leather tooled, the metal trims glinting.

'Perhaps I should become a barber,' the little man said, 'And leave singing behind. In truth, there is probably more money to be made.'

But the crowning glory of Gisborne-ben Simon glided down the stair, the folds of a richly black gown held in her hand, her veil snowy and soft against her face.

'Truly, she's a Madonna,' Toby whispered. 'She glows. Look at her…'

Folds of ebony griffin-woven damask draped against Ariella's pregnant belly and Michael noticed how the 'wedding ring' glistened against the ivory skin of her fingers. She wore tear-drop pearl earrings – Byzantine jewelry that was finely wrought and expensive and enhanced the bloom of her appearance.

'We need to find a jeweler who can provide us with such work,' Ahmed said in Michael's ear. 'They will sell well in Paris.'

'Perhaps that is tomorrow's task, Ahmed. Not today's.'

Christo rushed in, a clean black tunic brushing his finely shod toes, his face rubbed so that his cheeks shone like apples. Michael thought an impression would be made when they entered the hall. But then, of course, he had no idea how the other houses would be represented.

They left through gates held open by Julius and Hilarius, Michael assured of the house's security. Giant-sized Leo bought up their rear, Phocus taking the lead and looking round, Michael noticed Ahmed and Toby with hands on hilts. They were not fools.

Street people stared and children dressed in rags begged for coins. Ariella reached for her purse and Ahmed spoke sharply. 'Do not. Keep walking. It is best, Ariella.'

'But…'

'No. Trust no one.'

She grimaced, angry with him, but Toby reached for her hand and squeezed and she walked on. They entered the waterfront where the waters of the Golden Horn glittered and where the moderate slopes of Pera climbed across the way. Ahead of them, well-dressed individuals entered the elegantly crafted Merchant Hall – another sign of the trading success of Venezia.

'*Kýrie* Michael, we will wait in the street for you.' Phocus said.

'Thank you. And when we are done, we will return the others to Basilike Street and if I have heard from the monk, you and I will go to Sancta Sophia. Yes?'

'As you say, sir.'

CHAPTER EIGHT

×

As Michael climbed the steps to the hall, he hoped this banquet would be short and to the point.

'*Messere* Michael Sarapion?' A tall man, well-appointed in eastern damasks and silk and with a handsome tooled girdle, bowed his head. 'Welcome. I am Giacomo Contarini.' The man's smile was honest, his eyes engaging and there seemed to be an openness about him that surprised Michael. He had been expecting a diplomat hiding behind compliment and obfuscation. 'I think I knew this was the representative group from Gisborne-ben Simon,' Contarini said. 'You made an impression as you all walked along the street. There is a freshness. Venezia will benefit.'

'A pleasure to make your acquaintance, *Messere* Contarini. And may I thank you on behalf of my partners for inviting us to your assembly today. May I introduce you to them?'

They were the last group to arrive and Contarini took pleasure in greeting everyone and passing comment, even with Ahmed whom he chided for being the sea captain of whom all merchants were afraid, because they knew *he* was afraid of nothing. 'I think you will enjoy chatting with my good friend, Tommaso Viadro, Ahmed. I believe you have both crossed paths before.'

But then his eyes settled on Ariella and his astute expression softened. An older man, it was obvious that he appreciated a pretty woman, but this was something else. Michael would say there was a carefully controlled admiration. '*Madonna* di Gisborne, this is an honour. I know your father well and whilst I have never had the good fortune to meet *you*, may I say I have heard of the way you stepped in to support *Madonna* di Clochard in Lyon, in her time of need. Might I also say that you have cornered Venezia's notice in the way you have come abroad to pursue mercantile interests. Some say you should have perhaps stayed and plied silken thread in a frame, rather than to seek the commodity itself. I applaud you!'

Ariella dipped her head as Contarini kissed her hand and then she gave a light laugh. '*Messere*, I have always been unconventional. Every grey hair on my father's head attests to that.' But then her expression became more serious. 'In truth, I have the world's best teacher in my father, and I am his only child. He marks no difference between a man's abilities and a woman's. My lately departed husband was the same…'

No one from the Gisborne-ben Simon group looked at her as she underlined the seed of her lie, but Michael examined Contarini's face. It showed subtle condolence – nothing overt as the diplomat came to the fore. 'I heard, my dear, of your sadness. But I see that you carry a memory of him and I'm sure the babe will be a child of which Guillaume de Gisborne would have been proud. Now, may I escort you inside? I have sat you and *Messere* Michael near myself and *Messere* Viadro for the festivity. You must pardon the noise, but I am sure it will quieten.'

They followed him in, a wave of men's voices rising and falling within the cavernous marble interior. The cool stone reverberated with talk of markets and men but when it became obvious that Contarini had entered with a woman on his arm, and a beautiful pregnant woman at that, the noise quieted and then died. A quick glance around the room indicated many men of all ages. From Venezia, from Genova, Pisa and Ancona. And yes, there were Byzantines looking like plush peacocks; crowning the room with their silks and jewels and primped hair and beards. But there was a dearth of women.

Except…

There was Branco. And his Vigia wife. Michael's heart sank. He had hoped to avoid Tobias and Izzo Branco meeting, at least for today. At least until he himself had met with his own daughter. He wanted nothing to damage that possibility. He hoped Tobias had a sixth sense and that he would seat himself far from the Genovese merchant.

Contarini was like a Venetian galley in full sail, gliding across the chamber to his position at the head of the long table, whereupon he pulled a chair for Ariella, and she subsided almost gratefully. Michael sat on Contarini's other side as the man called out, 'Gentlemen … please take your seats. And remember, we have two very honoured women in our midst. I rely on your manners and discretion.'

A robust man with thick peppered hair flying from his forehead like a lion's mane, pulled back the chair next to Michael and lowered himself into it. His clothing was unremarkable beyond being excellent quality – black velvet and fine hose, and he wore a handsome gold ring.

'So, Michael Sarapion. I meet you at last. I have heard of you, although you went missing in action, I believe. It was said you were in Venezia but none saw you and then you were rumoured to be in Lyon. A phantom, no less.' His weathered hand reached for a flagon and he poured the ruby wine into Michael's goblet and then his own.

Michael had always expected some sort of inquisition at some point in his life and he had practised for it, the lies rolling easily off his tongue. 'I travelled. Saul ben Simon expects value for money, *messere*. But tell me, whom do I have the pleasure of addressing?'

The man had the deep creases of a seasoned traveller cut into his face and rather than being intimidating, the wrinkles, especially at his eyes, made him appear jovial and pleasant.

'Then you must have travelled very wisely,' he replied, 'judging by the success of Gisborne-ben Simon. There are some who can't believe the cheek of Gisborne, to come from nowhere and invade the marketplace. He challenges Venetian family names, you know. And in answer to your question, I am Tommaso Viadro and I am heartily pleased to make your acquaintance. I see a fellow survivor sitting next to me.'

Viadro's manner might have been patronising in anyone else, but the way his words were delivered held an honest depth that Michael liked. 'A survivor?'

Viadro laughed. 'Of life, of course.'

Whilst you jest, you have no idea of the truth of it!

'*Messere* Viadro, your fame precedes you. I've heard much of your activities in the Adriatico and there is part of our company here present who holds you in great esteem.'

'You say? Do I know them?' Sharp eyes sparkled with zest and energy.

149

'It is our shipmaster, Ahmed, who speaks highly of you. You see him further down the table. There is also Christo, our notary and manager, the one in black with the harassed face of a man of law. In truth, I think our unannounced arrival has aged him in a short space of time because we are rather unconventional. Oh, and further, the smaller man? That is Tobias Celho, a troubadour of note, a valued family member and loved by us all.'

'I will delight in meeting each one of you. I like unconventional sorts. Unconventional usually means that risks are taken with a good end-result. And Ahmed you say. Ah…' Viadro drew the word out. 'Redoubtable, I think. His reputation precedes him.'

'Good or bad?' Michael asked.

Viadro seemed to search for the right word – perhaps the least offensive word. 'Intriguing, shall we say, maybe even enigmatic…'

It could have been worse.

'*Messere* Michael…'

'Please, I am just Michael.'

'Michael,' Viadro lowered his voice. 'Is it true that you were attacked yesterday? And that your headquarters in Basilike Street are under duress?'

Michael was surprised that the gossip had spread so fast. But then, had not Phocus warned that once guards were spotted at Basilike Street, two and two would be put together? Besides, merchants liked to gossip and if it was likely to bring trouble to the name of the competition, it would spread like fire, and, like Greek fire, be impossible to dowse.

'God's teeth, *Messere* Tommaso, word spreads fast! And here I was thinking Constantinople a large enough city for our house to be immune from the gossip mongers. In answer to you, yes, I was attacked by some felons and no, Basilike Street is not under threat.'

Viadro studied Michael and Michael felt like an insect under the curious scrutiny of a child and yet, there was nothing childlike about the man.

Lowering his voice further, Viadro said, 'You are calm, Michael. But if I may offer advice – beware. There has been curiosity…'

Michael's blood began to rise as heaped platters of food were laid before them. He took his dagger and pierced a *keftede* with force. 'Curiosity from whom?'

Viadro shrugged his shoulders. 'From whom I do not know, but word drifts on the streets. Ripples along the waterfront. Always remember that

Enrico Dandolo lost an eye here as an attack was made upon Venetian property. Venetian success comes with a price.'

A bray of laughter echoed from further along the table, close by Tobias. It cut a swathe through the salt-cellars and platters, past the piled dried fruits and breads, to arrive in front of Michael and cast shivers down his spine. He noted the other woman to whom Contarini had referred, presumably Pieta Izzo of the Vigia House. That she was with child was obvious to a blind man, her stomach full as soft silks cascaded over it. A pretty woman, her face seemed sad, and next to her loud husband, she appeared diminished.

Worse, they both sat near Tobias.

'You see there,' Viadro nodded, 'the Genovese, Branco Izzo. A lust for name and success. So much so that he married Pieta from the Vigia house. He sits close by your famed troubadour. You are surprised I know about *him*? I am a music lover, my friend, and am well aware of the respect Tobias Celho holds as a minstrel. But back to the Vigia; Izzo in particular. He bursts with self-importance and the need to best we Venetians at every turn. Not to be trusted, I think.'

'I heed your warning,' Michael said. Of course, Viadro told him nothing of which he wasn't aware, but to have it confirmed was valuable, *and* from a fellow Venetian.

He tried to catch Toby's eye, but the minstrel's attention was on his food and he was not engaging with the woman to his right. Unusually for Tobias because it was the very nature of his profession: women were nectar to him. His face had set into a mask of indifference and his shoulders were pike-shaft stiff. Michael cursed that his friend had been forced to sit near his enemies.

'I know a little of the Vigia house,' he said carefully, wanting to test the waters. 'Did they not lose their only son in the Adriatico?'

Viadro chewed on a piece of lamb and washed it down with a swig of fine Greek wine. 'They did. He apparently stole an icon or some such. But then you know that, don't you? Our esteemed minstrel is the brother of the thief Pietro Vigia aided, abetted and some say finally denounced.'

Michael shook his head in defeat. 'Most everyone knows of Tobias' brother, *messere*. I do not deny it. Tobias and Tommaso are not easily forgotten for their shape and their twinship. My fear is the potential outcome of past history.'

'You mean that gossip says Tobias killed Pietro in revenge?'

Michael didn't answer.

Viadro sighed and shifted in his seat. 'As you say, *Messere* Michael, people gossip. If *I* heard, then I have no doubt Izzo has also and will have a plan of some sort or other. If I liked him and enjoyed his company, I would say that Tobias and your house has nothing to fear, but having met him, I would say you need eyes in the back of your head.'

Michael's worst fears were now well-rooted and beginning to grow. Further along the table, Izzo was holding forth. The Anconians and Pisans sat observing. If they were sensible, Michael thought, they would just let the Genovese merchants and the Venetians confront each other and implode. That said, this was neither the time nor the place for any confrontations at all.

'*Messere* Tommaso, I need to be able to trust you,' Michael whispered with urgency. 'I need your help.' He knew the risks of trusting a man he had barely met. 'I need to remove Tobias from the ambit of the Vigia. Can you convince *Messere* Contarini to invite him to sing immediately?'

Apart from a slight downward shift in the corners of his lips, Viadro showed no animation – as if he knew everything and would swear to nothing.

'We are merchants, Michael,' he said. 'We trade for a price and if I do this for you, you must pay me in some way, at a time of my choosing. Is your minstrel worth that?'

'A thousand times yes, *messere*. But let me ask you, how much do you like the Genovese Vigia house?'

'A pig's turd upon them.' Viadro's response was swift.

'Then, as we are agreed on the absence of quality of the Vigia, shall we set a low price on the exchange?'

'How low?'

'A meal at my expense?'

Viadro laughed, a discrete splutter that drew no attention. Mopping his mouth with a plain linen square, he replied, 'Done! I like you, *Messere* Michael. I think we could be good friends.' He shook Michael's hand and drank off a mouthful of wine before speaking across the table to Contarini, lifting his voice so that others might hear. 'Giacomo, we have a famous troubadour in our midst – Tobias Celho. Honoured by Richard of England, they say. Loved too by Eleanor of Aquitaine and a staunch friend of the great

Blondel. Can we prevail upon him for a song?'

There had been no doubt that naming Toby's royal benefactors had been deliberate. Something to shake up Branco Izzo perhaps. But which way? That was surely the question. The chamber echoed with a cascade of interested applause and excited whispering.

'If *Messere* Celho agrees,' Contarini said, looking directly at Toby. 'We would be most fortunate.'

Toby flicked a subtle glance at Michael who nodded imperceptibly, and pushing himself down off his chair, he walked to the head of the table. To any who didn't know him, he was confident – shoulders squared, head held high, walking with ease; almost a swagger. And yet, as he passed Michael, it was possible to see a glint of animal fury in his eyes. And to those who knew him, it was not because he had been prevailed upon to perform. Performing was his lifeblood. No, this was something different…

'*Messere*,' the small minstrel said, bowing low, as if Contarini were a potentate. He held his palm over his heart and placed his finely shod foot forward in a most courtly style. 'You do me a great honour.' Standing straight and half turning toward the rest of the chamber, he continued, 'As you can see, I have no instrument, so if you allow, I shall sing *a capella*. The song praises His Illustrious Majesty, King Richard, who, as you all may know, has been freed from his reprehensible prison. As my dear friend, Blondel, was instrumental in finding his liege, I choose to sing a song which he and His Majesty have no doubt often sung together since.' Tobias cleared his throat, apparently relaxed, and continued, 'The song is poignant. Essentially it tells of Richard's sadness and despair at being so long imprisoned and it is a gentle rebuke and a call to arms of all his men through England, Normandy, Poitou and Gascony – all the Angevin lands. If you will allow, I shall sing it in the *langue d'oïl*.'

The chamber fell silent – a silence filled with the comforting and intimate texture of velvet and the shivering excitement of silk. Michael dared glance at Branco Izzo as the man whispered to his wife who smoothed a hand over her pregnant bulge, closing her eyes and then crossing herself. The young Genovese merchant then lifted his own scrutiny to Tobias and rampant dislike illuminated the swarthy corners of his face. Was it because of Tobias' freakish shape or because he had been targeted, Michael wondered?

Tobias began:

Ja nus hons pris ne dira sa raison, Adroitement, se dolantement non;
Mais par effort puet il faire chançon.
out ai amis, mais povre sont li don;
Honte i avront se por ma reançon
Sui ça deus yvers pris.

Ce sevent bien mi home et mi baron
Ynglois, Normant, Poitevin et Gascon
Que je n'ai nul si povre compaignon
Que je lessaisse por avoir en prison;
Je nou di mie por nule retraçon,
Mais encor sui je pris...

Michael knew the translation. Anyone who lived with Toby could barely do otherwise because the little minstrel was nothing if not forthcoming.

No man in prison can tell his tale true
Lest he himself has known what I've been through
In writing song he may comfort renew
I've many friends but their gifts are few
They'll bring dishonor for my ransom's due
These two long winters past

My noble barons and men surely knew
England and Normandy, Gascon and Poitou
Ne're would I forsake or be untrue
To any friend; noble, commoner too.
I do not mean to reproach what they do,
Yet I remain held fast...

Tobias held onto the last note of the second verse – there were eight – and Michael guessed he was concluding what was essentially a long and mournful ballad. The audience applauded appreciatively, asking for more and the minstrel looked to Contarini for approval.

'Please,' the Venetian gestured with a sweep of his hand. '*Messere* Tobias, it's not often we merchants have such excellent performers in our midst. Your voice is a gift for us to take away today. More valuable perhaps than the commodities we strive to trade.'

Michael wondered if a price had just been placed on Toby's head and he looked down at his hands.

'You think he has just become a commodity, don't you?' Viadro said, an observation, a statement, most definitely not a question.

Michael's eyebrows lifted in surprise. 'I was unaware you were a mind-reader, *messere*.'

'We think alike, 'tis all. And yes, I think he might just have become valuable to someone who has something to gain. Ironic given he just sang a song about a ransomed king. In any case, time will tell, my friend. Remember, eyes in the back of the head. Now, about our dinner. Tomorrow, later in the day?'

I have so much more to deal with than dinner debts...

Michael surveyed the room. Everyone's attention was pinpointed upon Tobias. Even Izzo's, whose face was still and eyes slitted. His wife however, the true Vigia, sat lost in the cloud upon which Toby had elevated everyone. Her face had softened, she had closed her eyes on the world, and her lips curved. Obviously, she had no knowledge of the *langue d'oil* or she would not be smiling at the words of a king admonishing those whom he felt no longer loved him.

'If it suits, then yes,' he replied to Viadro.

'Good. Ah...' he turned slightly. 'It appears you have a message, *messere*.'

Michael turned to find a servant badged with Contarini's crest, holding out a small piece of parchment. 'From Father Symeon, *messere*,' the smooth-faced young lad said. 'A monk has just delivered it.'

Michael's mouth dried in an instant and he was sure Viadro would see how his heart quaked. 'I thank you.'

The servant nodded and as Tobias began to sing a song from the famous troubaritz, Beatriz di Dia, Viadro tactfully turned away and Michael flipped the message open.

To Michael Sarapion from your friend in God, Symeon of Sancta Sophia, greetings.

I would like to see you tomorrow between Sixth and Ninth Hour at Sancta Sophia, if it is convenient.

I leave you, my son, with blessings from God in your endeavours. Σε ειρήνη. Se eiríni.

Tobias had begun to sing in a higher-pitched tone – unusual and haunting, like the gelded men's voices one heard throughout the east. The song, *A Chantar M'er de So*, spoke of love and wanting and Michael wondered at that irony as well.

I must sing of what I do not want,
I am so angry with the one whom I love,
Because I love him more than anything…

'You have bad news?' Viadro whispered.

'I'm not sure,' Michael folded the parchment and slipped it into his purse. 'It's the way of business, is it not? But I will not be free till after Ninth Hour tomorrow. Does that suit?'

'Of course. I shall come to Basilike Street. If you're busy until we can leave, I'm sure someone will entertain me. I'm an easy man to please. Besides, I confess I would like to see your headquarters.'

Michael nodded, thinking that if Viadro sought to examine their potential cargo, he would be sorely disappointed. Nothing would be obvious.

He sat back then and allowed Toby's voice to fill the air. Most everyone sat transfixed and at any other time, Michael would have been thrilled for Tobias but there was so much at stake here. He ached to find out what Father Symeon had to tell him. Surely it could only be good news – that his daughter was eager to see her father, to be held in his arms, to laugh and to cry and to share the love that had been taken from them twelve years before.

As Toby's melody filled the hall, he found his gaze had settled on Branco Izzo and he wondered if a reckoning of sorts would come sooner rather than later. Something crept down his spine as if a ghost had walked across Helena's grave – a realisation. It *was* the Genovese who had organised the mob outside Basilike Street when they arrived. It was the Genovese who had Tobias and Michael followed from the baths. But that was mere benign stuff, like a cat playing with a mouse. Michael wondered if Branco Izzo would attempt a mercantile coup against Gisborne-ben Simon, or whether something would occur that was far more lethal and aimed specifically at Tobias. His heart quailed for the minstrel, simply because Toby was such an honourable and loving man.

Mais aitan plus vuoilh li digas, messatges,
Qu'en trop d'orguoilh o ant gran dan maintas gens…

Tobias dipped his head as the applause ebbed and flowed around the room, some even whistling and slapping their palms on the table. He turned to Contarini and bowed. 'I thank you, *Messere* Contarini, for the honour you have shown me.'

'Ah, *Messere* Tobias,' Giacomo Contarini replied. 'It is we who are honoured. Your voice is sublime, and I feel *I* owe *you* for agreeing to entertain my guests. A Contarini always honours his debts, never forget.' The consummate diplomat lifted his voice further. 'I think we must let *Messere* Tobias eat, drink and enjoy our banquet now. Please, there is more food and wine for everyone. My greatest wish is that we leave here today, familiar with each other and with a cordial sense of collegiality.' He pushed back his chair and excusing himself from the head of the table, began to walk around, speaking to people easily and elegantly.

'He is a spectacular diplomat, isn't he? But then the Contarini legacy is larger than life,' Viadro said, *sotto voce*. 'Ah, but looking at you, I would say your mind is not on Contarini, is it?'

'I am that obvious?' Michael replied as he took bread and cheese onto his platter. He found he couldn't stomach anything stronger.

'We've talked about quite a few things, Michael. May I call you that? And I think if I had a member of my family with Tobias' background, then I would worry for him, for everyone in the house in fact.'

'What you say is true and perhaps let us not talk of it here – maybe tomorrow. Tell me, what have you heard about the state of Byzantium. You head onto Syria, but we are staying here for a three month at least and there seem to be noises in the streets. So they say…'

'Then I suspect *they* are right. The territorial *archons* are filled with their own power, the Balkan uprisings continue to deplete what is left of an insubstantial martial force and treasury and within the city here, already I have noticed surreptitious groups chattering intently. As is usual with the empire, it doesn't appear to have a dedicated hold on its emperors. They seem to come and go swiftly with horrendous injuries, and rather like the Rome of old, it is familial and always factional. Somehow, we merchants have to steer a course through and maintain our privileges. I think that just like the times when the Venetian Quarter was attacked and Dandalo lost his eye, so will times turn and the Venetians will be hanging on by their fingernails. If nothing else, the Genovese and Pisans will make it so. Isn't trading fun?' Viadro laughed, deep in his belly and Michael couldn't help but smile.

In truth though, and even if the three-month wasn't up, his plan had solidified in that one succinct comment from his dining companion. He, Michael, would collect his daughter, load *Durrah* with all they could lay their hands on, and with Ahmed's agreement, spirit everyone out of the city without loss of life or limb.

The dinner wound smoothly on and Viadro turned his attention to Ariella who chatted amicably with him. He was an engaging man and Michael found he liked him, this from someone who didn't trust easily. At one point, Ariella burst into laughter, a musical chime that soared above the mostly bass tones around the hall. Men lifted their heads and as with most men, lust floated on the air. Michael was glad she was apparently a widow, it made things easier.

Merchants were standing, moving from one group to another, introducing themselves, chatting, and Michael moved to place his arm under Ariella's, with Viadro thoughtfully on her other side in the absence of Contarini who still circled amongst his guests. Ahmed drifted over and hand to his heart, he bowed his head in front of Viadro.

'*Messere* Viadro. This is an honour.'

'Ahmed, I have looked forward to this day. It's been long in coming.'

'You jest, of course,' Ahmed said and preened a little, whereupon Michael sighed. 'Are you not the intrepid explorer and trader who has effectively chained the Adriatico to Venezia's waterways?'

'Maybe. Maybe not. I know you are a merchantman with a sharp eye, loyal crew, a good boat and that Gisborne-ben Simon are lucky to have you. Can I persuade you over to my side?'

Ahmed laughed. 'Maybe one day when I have worn out my welcome with my friends.'

Michael squirmed at that, thinking of the times when Ahmed had riled him to hair-tearing in the last few days.

'I hear you have bought another boat,' Viadro said to Ahmed and Michael's attention sharpened. He looked at Ariella and noticed her eyebrows had risen.

'I have,' said Ahmed smoothly, not a shred of guilt evident at not sharing this news with the house. '*Durrah* is my queen, my daughter, my wife. But she is small, and I find I need another vessel to run in partnership with her.'

'You will sail in convoy?'

'For the journey home, yes. In between times and after, the new vessel will travel to new places. Maybe, *Messere* Viadro, she will sail to Syria…' The look in Ahmed's eyes was ambivalent. He might have been joking – or not.

There was quiet conversation as the groups ebbed and flowed. It was believed that Alexios III must surely look to his safety since usurping his brother in March of the year. Whilst the Venetians talked and posited, so Isaac II sat in his prison cell beneath the palace, blinded and emasculated. It was a common enough usurpation within the empire and the Venetian traders were used to the currents changing and the need to push the tiller this way and that.

'It all works in our favour,' said Contarini. 'Alexios III has almost emptied the treasury and so we are able to discretely bribe him with money and favours. For example, we still provide crews and galleys for the imperial navy. They know they cannot do without that support. We just have to help them believe in their own unmitigated importance.'

'Do you mean that Venezia would walk away at a moment's notice from its interests in Byzantium if things did not go in our favour?' Ahmed asked. 'I find that hard to believe.'

'I am interested in your reply, *Messere* Contarini,' Ariella added. 'Many of the merchants here,' she indicated the room at large, 'have longstanding trading ties within this city. To walk away would be…expensive.'

Contarini glanced around the circle of Venetians who surrounded him. His reply might not have pleased Pisans, Genovese or Anconian ears and thus he was careful. 'The art of diplomacy is always making another believe willingly that their way is theirs alone and not actually yours, my dear. It is my job whilst I'm here, to tactfully persuade Alexios III that we have listened to what he says and we will only ever act according to his imperial wish.'

'And you think the Genovese and others will allow us to dominate?' Ariella replied. 'I find it hard to believe.'

So did Michael, given what Gisborne-ben Simon had already been through since arriving. There was a plethora of bowing and scraping in this city and whilst it irked Ahmed, Michael had done enough of it through the years to know that Contarini spoke the truth.

Michael took Ariella to a seat. The banquet had begun to wind down and people were taking their leave. Viadro approached, took Ariella's hand and kissed it, the noble forehead and lion's mane hair so striking as he bent down.

'My dear *Madonna* di Gisborne. I do hope I see you again before I leave for Syria. I am having dinner tomorrow with Michael so perhaps I may see you when I call for him?'

'I would enjoy that, *messere*. It has been such an honour to make the acquaintance of someone so substantial within Venetian trading circles.'

Viadro replied with inoffensive and charming comments and then took his leave and Michael decided to gather his friends together and follow whilst there were convivial people in the streets with whom they could mingle. Safety in numbers.

Tobias glowered into their midst, complaining about being put upon, and annoyed at the company with which he was forced to mix. But Ahmed spoke sharply to him and he shut up, bottom lip protruding. Ariella ruffled his hair and kissed the top of his head. 'My dearest Toby. I think this is the first time I've seen you in a bad mood.'

'There was one other time, Ariella, but you didn't know me then. The common denominator was a member of the Vigia house.' He pushed past her to the door and Ahmed said that he would go after him and they would wait with Leo and Phocus in the street.

Ariella stood, shaking out her crisply whispering black folds and they made their way to Contarini to thank him for his hospitality. He kissed Ariella's hand and wished her well, hoping they would meet again before he returned to Venezia. To Michael, as farewells were made, he whispered, 'Viadro is right. Watch your back – the Genovese intend to take no prisoners with we Venetians.'

Outside, the late afternoon sun cast a long golden gleam across the street to the water. The Horn glittered like precious metal, living up to its name, and voices were amplified, vessels plying to and fro, from here to Galata and back and from one harbour to another. Michael never tired of the scene and he took Ariella's arm to help her descend the steps. As they started across the road to their companions, a voice called to Michael.

'*Messere* Sarapion, wait. *Messere!*'

Michael's heart sank. He knew the voice and had wished to conclude the day without speaking to the man.

He and Ariella turned, and Branco Izzo and his wife walked down the steps, Pieta grasping her husband's arm as if it were a lifeline. Her draped folds showed that she was far further advanced toward childbirth than Ariella and there were shadows under her eyes.

'*Messere* Michael,' the man's whip-thin face creased into what passed for a smile. Slash after slash, as if he had been scored by a *misericorde* blade.

'I'm sorry to have missed you,' the Genovese continued. 'But it was crowded, and I needed to talk to so many. However, I see I am not too late. Fortuitous as I would be remiss not to greet you and to introduce my lovely Pieta. My dearest wife, this is the man of whom I spoke and if I am not mistaken, the woman by his side is *Madonna* di Gisborne, nominal head of Gisborne-ben Simon here, in the absence of her father and their English business partner.'

The comment held a patronising edge but Izzo bowed and Michael and Ariella could take no umbrage.

'*Madonna* di Izzo, how lovely it is to meet another woman from a trading house in this city,' Ariella spoke with genuine kindness. She bent forward and kissed the woman on each cheek. 'And not only that, another who is in somewhat the same situation as myself.' She patted her belly and Michael suspected she gauged the tension with Izzo and sought to defuse it with the diplomacy that Contarini had mentioned.

But he dared not turn to look at Toby's face.

Pieta opened her mouth to speak but her husband replied before she could take a breath. 'Indeed. Our little heir will be born any time soon. My Pieta is very tired. But perhaps you can visit her, some company will help her with her lethargy.'

Patronising, unsympathetic…

'I should be delighted…'

This is something we must discuss, Michael thought. It might be fraught with all manner of problems…

'And you, *Messere* Michael. Did you enjoy this afternoon's little festivity? Did you find the great Contarini reassuring?'

'I assume you mean about our position here in Constantinople,' said Michael smoothly. 'Of course. *Messere* Contarini is highly respected in imperial circles. It is good to have that reinforced.'

A shadow passed behind Izzo's eyes, as if he had hoped to curry nervousness in his competitor. Hoped but failed, thought Michael. What next, my friend?

'We must go,' Izzo said. 'Pieta needs to rest and our litter is come. We go to the Palace of Botaneites. I'm sure you know that in the Treaty of 1192, the palace was given to the Genovese to use as they saw fit. I have been fortunate enough to secure one of the villas within the grounds for the duration of our stay. We have been highly honoured.'

'Indeed,' Ariella replied, as if in awe. 'I look forward to seeing it. For ourselves, we live above the business so to speak. Nothing at all grand.'

Pieta managed to utter a few words as her husband summoned the litter closer. 'I find as my time approaches that I have little interest in venturing out. I will be very grateful if you could come.' She turned her head toward the west, sighing. 'I find I am homesick and not a little lonely…'

Ariella reached for her hand and squeezed and Izzo guided his bulky wife into the litter, closing the curtains around her. 'I am pleased to have seen you before we leave. I look forward to meeting again soon. *Messere. Madonna.*' He bowed and walked off with the litter, a lift of the head and a slight shake of the shoulders indicating what he obviously considered distasteful duty now done.

CHAPTER NINE

×

'Jesus' teeth and bones, Michael!' Toby rushed to their sides. 'How could you? And you Ariella…'

'Toby, hush,' Ariella caught his hand. 'It is called manners. Nothing more. If we had shunned he and his wife, what would that say about *our* name? It was not done by us to hurt you, but I wonder if Michael agrees that it was done by them to stir *us*?'

'I do.'

'Well yes then,' Toby said. 'Consider me stirred. That son of a bitch!'

'That is as may be, Toby,' said Ariella. 'But I feel sorrow for his wife. I'm surrounded by those that I love and admire. Even here, in a city where I could be so lost, I feel safe and I'm never lonely. She, poor woman, is married to a man who is blind to everything but ambition and rides rough-shod over all to see it through.'

'Exactly so. Now listen…' Michael drew his friends and the guards in close. 'I believe it is the Vigia house that seeks to sour us…'

'Sour? You put too nice a point on it, Michael,' Toby growled. 'He doesn't so much as want to sour us, as shred and bury us! Be honest.'

Michael shifted, looking after the fast-disappearing litter. 'Alright, I *shall* be honest. I think he wishes to avenge the Vigia by killing Toby…' Ariella sucked in her breath, but he continued. 'He could easily murder Toby and have the weight of law on his side, arousing Toby, making him so frustrated and angry that he attacks Izzo first and Izzo then claims he was merely protecting himself against an insane man.'

'And I *would* attack him! Mark me when I say the thought of him makes me boil with fury,' Toby hissed. It was like watching a flame grow as the air fed it. 'He would then so blacken our name through the house's association with me, that as a merchant business, we will lose the trust of traders and of purchasers,' he added.

'No one would believe him,' Ariella said.

'They would, Ariella,' said Ahmed. 'Murder is murder and revenge can be couched in no other term. Tobias knows this, don't you, little man?'

Toby said nothing, merely continued to stare after the long-departed litter.

'Putting murder and revenge to the side just for a moment,' Michael said, 'I believe he wants to break our house commercially, simply because like the Vigia House we are relatively new. It galls him and the only way he could best us is to steal the *byssus* about which, I hope, he knows nothing as yet. Add revenge to all of this and it's a seriously potent problem.'

'Then what shall we do?' Ariella's joy in the day had patently dissolved and like Pieta Izzo, her face had dark shadows beneath the eyes and some auburn hair escaped from beneath her veil.

'Take you home to rest, I think.' Michael said. 'Leo and Phocus, will you return Ariella to Basilike Street, please? Ahmed, Tobias and I have business on the dock. We won't be long at all.'

Phocus began to argue but Michael pointed out that each was armed, that they were now fully alert to their dangers and Basilike Street was merely a moment away from where they stood. 'Take Ariella home and if you are concerned, send Bonus to meet us on *Durrah*. He has had his rest.'

Phocus' mouth flattened in disagreement, but he stood straight, 'As you wish, sir.' And directing Leo to Ariella's other side, they began the walk to Basilike Street.

'So,' Michael turned to Ahmed. 'A new boat?'

'Yes. I planned to tell you…'

'Eventually…' growled Toby.

'Although,' Ahmed spoke over the minstrel, consigning his mood to the air, 'the business only owns a small portion of it. I will charge Gisborne-ben Simon for the use of my share.'

'Of course, you will,' Toby responded. 'When have you ever done something for love?'

'Many times, little music-man. Cast your mind back to your last time here and you will remember. Would you like to see her, both of you?'

'A boat is a boat,' said Toby with a slight softening of his manner. 'But I need to wear off my mood so a walk along the docks might help.'

They approached *Durrah*, moored by the Nerion Harbour wall. Faisal coiled ropes as they stood above him, looking down and he smiled warmly. 'You come to see the new boat? She's nice,' he said. A man of few words.

Ahmed nodded to a vessel moored astern of *Durrah*. 'There. There isn't a lot of difference apart from a sharper bow.'

'She's brand new,' Toby uttered as he walked to her stern. 'How...'

'Gisborne agreed we needed more vessels if we were to expand our capability. He was happy to partner me and invest if I found the right craft. This is she. What think you, Michael?'

The galley was sleek and lean, a fine line against the wharf. Her oars were stacked starboard and larboard and she glistened with newly oiled timbers. She had six seats either side, the same as *Durrah*, but her lines would make her swifter. 'I can see she will have speed if she is loaded evenly,' Michael said carefully. 'I like her. What's her name?'

'*Sada*. Good fortune. *Durrah* is my pearl.'

Michael looked back at the weathered timbers of *Durrah*. She was still a beautiful boat and in the few days she had been in port had been oiled and polished, with new ropes and a new canvas tightly furled. She was majestically aged, and eye-catching with it, but *Sada*'s newer timbers glistened like the gold of the Horn and as the sun sank, it looked as if she were blushing under the men's scrutiny.

'The house is fortunate to have such good vessels, Ahmed...' Michael replied.

'The house is fortunate to have Ahmed,' the Arab responded. 'But then I am not telling you anything you don't know.'

'Then tell me, you arrogant windbag,' Toby added. 'When we are ready to go, can your boats outrun the Genovese galleys?'

'You mean the Vigia galley? Of course.'

'Good,' Toby replied.

They began to walk back to Basilike Street – three men in a row, Tobias in the middle. The pace was slow to adjust to Michael's limp but they didn't speak to each other, each lost in the progressions of the day, it seemed.

Michael had a thought that if Ioulia did not wish to see him – ever – then he wished he'd never located her and had gone on through life in the belief that she was dead. It would hurt less than the thought of rejection and the associated guilt. He was a parent and surely it was natural that he should blame himself for all that she had suffered in the last twelve years. But try as he might, he would never understand why she might inevitably choose convent life over freedom.

Jehanne would remind him that Ioulia in fact might choose convent life for its security and familiarity. An almost closed community that was regulated by the Church, and that was run by a group of women. Maybe, Jehanne might say, Ioulia sees the *hegoumene* as the mother she lost. Maybe the Church succours her.

And as always, he would see that Jehanne was right. Confronting as it might be to admit such a thing.

On the edge of his consciousness, as they wound through the waterfront alleys toward little Mese, he heard the decorative rings rattling on the *kilij* strap and scabbard that sat atop Ahmed's sash. They sounded a warning, each little metallic jingle like a tripwire, tossing him out of his head and into the real world. In the corner of his eye, he saw Ahmed's *kilij* being drawn.

'We have company…' the sea captain said. 'Don't turn. There are two behind and I think when we turn the corner ahead into the next alley, you will find there will be more.'

'Christ Jesus!' Toby spat. 'I swear I am done with this…'

'Shut up, music-man. Be calm and arm yourself. Michael?'

'I have my *paramerion*.' His hand rested upon it and he waited until the shadow of one of the alley's houses crept across them, then with speed he withdrew the weapon and gripped it.

'Do they seek to kill *me*, think you?' Tobias was quite matter of fact. 'Because they will have to catch me first…' He began to run, zigzagging along the alley and behind them was a shout, a warning…

'Damn the idiot! Go after him, Michael. I'll deal with those behind.'

Tobias had already reached the end of the alley when two men appeared in front of him, one dragging a longblade sideways to catch the minstrel. But

Toby was always an acrobat, part of the training he had learned at the College of Minstrels. He somersaulted past the two men, rolling like a sewn leather ball, doing what he and Tomas had always done well, their size confusing their enemies. These felons turned swiftly to attack again, one to each side of the alley, but Toby ran toward them with speed – a skip and bending double, somersaulting past them, taunting them before they even had time to swing.

Ahmed backed up against Michael. 'He does seem to apply himself, does he not,' he commented. 'It's you and I now. *Insh'Allah…*' Ahmed swung his *kilij*, no grunt nor sigh, not a sound. But as the curved weapon caught on cloth and one of the attackers cried out, Ahmed smiled.

Michael waited until the other was a mere blade length away and then stepped forward swinging backhand, confusing his opponent who would have noted the weapon in the right hand, expecting the swing to come from the right. The fellow jumped back with a rat's whisker between him and a strike, but Michael stepped in again, this time swinging backhand, leaving no time for the attacker to re-gird. Angry, the man came at him, and weapons collided, blades sliding, foul breath puffing across Michael's face. He had no idea of the attacker's appearance, focused only on brown bloodshot eyes.

He pushed the man back, crosspiece against cross piece, a harsh jerk, then swiftly lowered his weapon, bringing it up between the man's moving legs. There was such a scream, an unearthly sound as the *paramerion* found its mark and ground on upward. Michael twisted the blade sideways and pierced the man's thigh in the process and the felon slumped to his knees, blood pouring from between his legs as he grabbed at his groin, trying to hold it together and crying, '*Theé mou, Theé mou.* Oh God, oh God!'

Ahmed had his opponent on the wall, holding him with calm deliberation, the *kilij* at the cartilaginous lump that bobbed up and down. Already a fine line of blood trickled into the fellow's clothes. As Tobias yelled from further along the alley, Ahmed sliced a deep line across the man's neck, withdrawing the *kilij* and swinging round, running to assist Tobias. The man slid down the wall, his life's blood spurting as his eyes glazed.

As Michael limped after Ahmed, Bonus flew into the alley from Tobias' end, a *kontarion* held in front like a pig-stick, scooping up one of Toby's attackers on the end and continuing to run forward, the man screaming.

'I want the last one!' yelled Toby. 'Let me have him!'

But Ahmed had swung his *kilij*, first one way then the other, a graceful move like a figure of eight, a barely contrived move from a weapon that could slice through fine hair. The final man fell, holding a desperate hand against his middle.

'You bastard!' Toby screamed at Ahmed. 'I wanted him…'

'You have only a dagger, little man. I think you might still be fighting if I had not.'

'Go f…'

'Enough, Tobias!' Michael shouted. 'Enough. It's all done. Bonus, you arrived just in time.'

Bonus had pulled his *kontarion* clear and was wiping the point on the folds of bloody robes that lay on the bodies in the alley. When they all took a breath, they noticed a pale and intent group standing at the exit to the lane, whispering to each other.

Michael walked forward, slipping his unwiped blade into his belt. He wouldn't do the scabbard the dishonour of soiling it with bad blood. 'My friends,' he held out his hands, palms up. 'We were attacked, and I am so sorry you should be witness to what we have had to endure. Could someone call the guards, please?'

'Michael!' Ahmed grabbed his sleeve.

'I have to do this to protect the house, maybe even protect Tobias. Izzo will hear soon enough.'

'You think he organised this?'

'Don't you?'

In moments, guards had arrived, four of them with an officer. The guards held the curious watchers away whilst the officer spoke to the companions. Michael was honest. 'We are four men from the trading house of Gisborne-ben Simon in Basilike Street. We were set upon.'

'You say? And why do you think that would be?'

'Look at us,' Toby burst out. 'We are dressed in expensive attire. What do you think?'

Michael frowned at Tobias, wishing he'd be quiet to allow him to handle the situation. 'We had been to a feast at the Merchant Hall with foreign traders and diplomats, indeed some of your own. We were no doubt marked on our departure and they thought to steal from us and leave us for the street dogs. It happens.'

Plausible...

'And that is all, think you?' The officer took their names.

'What else would you suggest, sir?' Michael replied. 'We are newly arrived in the town and have seen and done little since settling in Basilike Street. We were walking back to the house after inspecting a new boat on our way home. These felons were opportunists, surely. If you think they weren't, would *you* care to explain?'

The officer looked down at Tobias by Michael's side, the minstrel bristling with an excess of anger and blood lust. The man examined his height, his odd conformation. He knew who Toby was, of course he knew. Brother and twin to a misshapen imp who had stolen a sacred icon and who had been executed. How could he not know? But finally the officer said very carefully,

'There is nothing to explain. As you say, opportunists, but just not their day. I apologise on behalf of the citizens of Constantinople. This is normally a safe city...' Tobias snorted and the officer pinioned him with more scrutiny. 'Please move on to your home. This will be dealt with.'

Michael gathered his companions and they squeezed through the crowd, eyes straight ahead, speaking to no one until they had almost reached Basilike Street. Then Toby, still filled with battle lust, muttered,

'Opportunists, my arse.'

The gates rolled behind them, the bars sliding across.

'You are covered in blood,' Phocus noted.

'We were attacked,' Michael replied. 'It was unprovoked. The guards were called and a report made.'

'And?'

Michael rubbed at his bloody hands. 'If we had wanted to slip unnoticed around the city, that has now changed. But I felt it was necessary to report the assaults to the authorities – to get in first. There were, unfortunately, witnesses to the event and so word would have spread quickly if I hadn't. Further, I think they were paid assassins and that Izzo organised it, but we will never be able to prove it.'

Phocus nodded his head. 'Perhaps you should clean up in our quarters. I would hate my mother or Ariella to see the way you look. Hurry, and I will make sure Ephigenia is in the kitchen when you go to change. Leave your weapons and we will clean them.'

Toby ripped off his girdle and flung it and the dagger scabbard down on the trestle in front of the guards' quarters. 'Ariella?'

'She sleeps.'

The three companions scrubbed their hands and faces and then beat a swift retreat up the stair to their chambers.

'We will have to tell Ariella,' Toby said.

'Yes, but not till the morrow, after she is rested,' Michael said. 'And if nothing else, we now know irrevocably that we need guards wherever we go.

The family met later in the hall and all sat quietly, occasional words, a little laugh from Ariella if she bested Tobias in a chess move. She sat in ignorance of the late afternoon's events because Michael would not have her distressed until she had a night's sleep. He had tasked Toby to make the revelation next day when he thought she may be rested enough to know. Ahmed sat at the table, with a map and a list stretched in front of him.

'Are you planning something, Ahmed?'

'In a manner of speaking. I thought to trial *Sada* tomorrow, with part of *Durrah*'s crew. A little voyage into the basin if the winds allow. I want to see how she handles. What think you?'

'About safety?' Michael replied. 'I suspect if Izzo is unaware that you plan to sail away, then you'll be safe. Your crew are as silent as the dead most times anyway, Ahmed. If you have faith in them, then I don't think you need worry.'

'I'm not worried about our safety, more about yours. With me away you shall be one man down, so the guards will be doubly vital. I'll leave Faisal and another to guard *Durrah*, but just to be safe, I'm thinking to take her from her moorings and have her anchor in the middle of the harbour.'

'That's your decision,' Michael replied. 'It seems sensible. I don't trust Izzo on any account now. Tell me, do you think to look for any likely merchandise whilst you are out?'

Ahmed shook his head, saying no, it was a run to test the ship, purely and simply. 'But on my return, I believe you and I should seek out jewellers. Those earrings of Ariella's were spectacular. A treasure chest to take back to Venezia, Michael. Think of the gems and goldwork...'

He agreed. One didn't ever second guess Ahmed.

He was glad to drag his damaged knee to bed that night. It had been an almost fatal day and he needed to revive himself for the meeting with Father Symeon on the morrow. There was always that vague thought in the back of his mind…

His *paramerion* had been returned and he wrapped it in linen and placed it in the chest as it was surely unwise to go to Sancta Sophia armed to the teeth. He would take a dagger in his belt, it was enough. He undressed, draping his tunic and hose on the chest, feeling every part of his body aching with the effort of the fight and with tension. He lifted his leg, balancing it on a stool, running a hand over the bandage, feeling the tightness, wondering if the linen strips should be removed to allow his leg to breathe, to let the blood flow. He couldn't remember what Anwar had said and cursed that his head was always elsewhere than where it should be, doubly cursing the injury. Deciding to leave it alone, he lifted the covers, slid onto the mattress and stretched his naked, stiff body out, feeling the throbbing, the flow of pain, closing his eyes and seeing nothing but dead men and blood.

'Christ dammit,' he hissed, throwing back the rugs to limp to the window, pushing it open to stare down toward the Nerion Harbour where the moon cast a trail over the water. Was this what it would be like every day whilst they were here? Blood and bodies all around? It made no sense.

Iisoús Christós! He wanted a half a day to visit the priest, just a half a day without the problems of Gisborne-ben Simon intruding on a very private quest.

Signing deeply, but yet one that still did not reach the inner edges of his chest, he slipped back into the bed and drifted at last into an agitated and unrefreshing sleep.

He broke his fast next morning in haste. He had slept later than he wanted and knew that Third Hour would almost have passed by the time he had dressed, eaten and made his way to the guards' quarters.

He found Phocus laying out weapons on his cot.

'I must go to Sancta Sophia immediately, Phocus. Will you come?'

'As you wish, *Kýrie* Michael. You are armed?'

'I have a knife.'

'No long blade? A *paramerion*?'

'No. Not for the Church. I must show respect.

'I have my *spathion*,' Phocus said. 'We shall keep our wits and our lives,' he added pointedly.

As they wove between the waterside folk near the gate of Saint John de Cornibus, Phocus wanted to know if it was good news that they went to collect.

'I don't know. I received a summons only.'

But a summons for what? He wondered why Father Symeon should want to relay the *hegoumene*'s decision personally.

It was a day that could only have been ordered by the Saints. The sky was lapis blue, unmarked by cloud stain, and the sun glittered with a promise of summer heat to come. The harbours sparkled, a vacillating sheen of silver and gold, and the cupolas of each basilica glowed like molten copper. Accordingly, the street crowds were happy, bright, stepping along with decision, as if a new energy was filling their bones after the cooler winter months.

Such a day must *surely* promise a good outcome. God would not be so unkind – despite that this penitent, Michael Sarapion, had foresworn Him a dozen years before.

His damned knee was on fire by the time they had climbed the steps to the great South Gates and made their way into the narthex. Almost as if he had been waiting, Father Symeon glided across the marble floors, nothing so much as an elongated black streak with his long hair and beard flowing around him and his *skoufos* always precariously balanced.

'Father...'

'Come with me, Michael, to the garden. Your man may wait at the gates.'

Phocus touched his heart and bowed, backing away, obviously at peace with Michael in the care of a priest. Like Ephigenia, it seemed Phocus has great faith in his Church.

The Judas tree was even thicker with purple blossom than before, and fallen petals carpeted the ground. The tiny garden was such a light and comforting space compared to the shadowy golden largesse of the icon-strewn basilica. Michael wished it impressed him, the great artwork, the gold *thymiateria* swinging from heavens' heights above, the heady odour of *olibanum*, but it galled him. Not the harmonies of the liturgies, never those, but the vast richness. Then to enter this tiny simple space with its singular tree and the shrubs of vervain, with its solitary remove from the rest of the basilica, and everything almost seemed right.

'Please sit…' Father Symeon said. 'How is your knee?'

'It will do. Father…'

Father Symeon held up his hand with its long fingers. 'Let me speak, Michael. As you know you are here because a reply has arrived from Xylinites. The *hegoumene* has spoken to your daughter and Ioulia was vastly shocked, even distraught. The *hegoumene* gave her time to digest what she had heard and then asked her if you might visit with her.'

Michael's heart stopped. Every sound around him diminished as his attention sharpened on the priest, on his expression, on the words to come, almost as if he was in a tunnel. Father Symeon's face was kind but no more nor less than normal. A shield perhaps when one has often to deliver bad news? Fatalism had invaded his thoughts for days in respect of Ioulia. Maybe it was because deep within, he didn't, couldn't, believe that either of them was due happiness at last. Grief did that to a person…

'Michael?'

Michael jerked himself back to reality. He was afraid…

'The *hegoumene* asks that Ioulia be given time,' the priest said. 'She appears to be greatly distressed and they are afraid for her. I did mention, I think, that this was a possibility.'

'I know, but I'm her father, I mean her no harm. She must be told that.'

'I don't think there is any doubt of that, my son. But to explain – the *hegoumene* said that at first, your daughter sat speechless. Then she paled significantly, stood, walked a few steps and collapsed. They tended to her, but she spends much time…'

Michael had closed his eyes. He could see his beautiful daughter, his lost only child and all he wanted was to hold her, tell her he was so very sorry, and to wipe her tears.

'…much time weeping,' the priest was saying. 'This is why the *hegoumene* thinks she needs time within the convent, to come to terms with such news. Michael, are you listening?'

Michael flicked his head up. 'Yes, Father, I am listening.' What more could he say?

'I understand this may not be what you wanted to hear…'

'No. It is not.'

'But think of Ioulia.'

'You think I don't?' Michael scoffed. A flush burned up his neck. 'If you had said that *Ioulia* wished for time, that she herself had demanded it, then perhaps I could understand. Hard,' his fists crunched into tense balls. 'Nevertheless, I would have understood. But to have the *hegoumene,* a woman I have never met and who doesn't know me, tell me I can't see my daughter and that she needs time! After twelve years?' He laughed, the sound cracked and angry. 'How *much* time?'

Father Symeon retrieved his prayer beads from some secret pocket in his religious folds, and his thumbs began to work over the sea-coloured stones. Round and over. 'Two days.'

'Two? So it will take only two days for my daughter to digest the news that her father is alive?' The cracked laugh came again, like an old bell swinging back on its arc. 'Such an arbitrary figure! I think the *hegoumene* has plucked it from the air! If she'd said seven days, I might have understood. Even five. But two days might as well have been one or none. Thank you, Father…' He stood. 'For your help.'

'Michael, I am so sorry. Would you like me to try and intercede?'

Michael shook his head and walked off his frustration, hobbling around the Judas tree. As he drew level with Father Symeon, he said, 'Please inform the *hegoumene* that I love my daughter, that I only wish to talk to her briefly in the first instance and that I shall come at Ninth Hour tomorrow. That surely is nearly two days from when she heard the news.'

Damn Gisborne-ben Simon and company demands. He could have gone first thing in the morning, perhaps even this evening, but he had responsibilities and how it rubbed at him – pebbles in his boots, sand in his clothes.

The priest opened his mouth to speak but Michael merely moved to the entrance of the garden, saying over his shoulder, 'It is my wish, Father. I have only my daughter's happiness and security in mind.'

He hurried down the hall and into the basilica, weaving between the porphyry pillars and people to the South Gates. He knew Jehanne would agree with what he had decided. Helena even more so. Mothers especially knew what was right. A short initial visit with his daughter and then time for them both to digest the meeting. It was surely his right as a father, and her right as his daughter for this to happen.

The *hegoumene,* damn her, had nothing to do with it.

'*Iisoús Christós!*' he swore as he trailed Phocus in his wake, down the steps away from Sancta Sophia. Phocus grabbed him by the arm and hauled him to a limping halt.

'Stop! Explain, please.' He stood in front, one step down, blocking Michael's progress.

'The *hegoumene* says it is best not to see my daughter immediately. *She* says, not my daughter! Some old religieuse who hasn't seen life since she wedded herself to the Church and who is no doubt a wrinkled, unused virgin with no idea of what it is like to *have* children let alone lose them, dares to say to me that I can't see my daughter.'

'Can't?'

Blood roared in Michael's ears, making it hard for him to think, but he sucked in a deep breath. 'No, not can't. She said two days. But it's *none* of her business. I've ordered Father Symeon to tell her I come tomorrow at Ninth Hour, like it or leave it.'

'You *ordered* Father Symeon? A senior priest within Sancta Sophia?'

'I did. Say no more please, it's done.'

Phocus stepped aside, Michael moved stiffly down and the two walked side by side in silence as the sun shone, the gulls cried and people laughed and shouted around them. As his heart rate settled, Michael realised that life went on – death and loss notwithstanding. It was a salient lesson and he abhorred what he had become in the last few days.

'Phocus, I apologise.'

Phocus shrugged. '*Kýrie* Michael, it is no matter. Whilst I have never lost my family, I have lost good friends in terrible circumstances. It changes one, sometimes in the short-term, sometimes forever, so I can understand.'

'You're younger than me, and yet you show a remarkable grasp of life.'

They turned back along the contoured lanes and streets of First Hill toward the Nerion Harbour, the sun had moved directly above them and gold beams flashed from every cupola in the city. It was a sight Michael never got used to.

'Age has nothing to do with it,' said Phocus. 'But I suspect a mercenary sees the best and worst of life. The best and worst of men. In the Balkans, we fought alongside those who were as apt to slit *our* throats at night as the enemy's.

When mercenaries are employed, they aren't employed for their sanity.'

It was such a throw-away comment but one that illuminated Phocus' experience and wisdom.

Bonus opened the groaning gates for them at Basilike Street. It was a comforting sound, the sound of heavy impregnable timbers.

'All is well?' Phocus asked.

'Of course,' Bonus said cheerfully. 'Ahmed has gone to the docks and Julius walked with him, he will be back in a moment. Christos is in his pigeonhole, Ephigenia is in the kitchens. Listen, you can hear.'

Her tuneless singing wound through the loggia and across the yard and Phocus grimaced. 'I'm sorry. She gets no better with age.'

Even Michael had to smile as he sank onto a hogshead and rested his leg. 'Tobias and Ariella?'

'They received an invitation to visit and left with Julius.'

Thinking Contarini may have sent for them, Michael asked 'Where?' with no real worry.

'The Genovese house – Izzo's. Madonna Pieta sent her servant with the invitation. And before you go off like Greek fire, we all counselled them, told them it was unwise, but Ariella said she felt Madonna Pieta was in need. Leo went with them. Hilarius and I guard the house.'

Damn Pieta Izzo, damn Ariella's soft heart, thought Michael. But at least ours are guarded well. 'We'll go to the Izzo house immediately. Phocus, I need my blade…'

Phocus nodded, and Michael hurried off as fast as his knee would allow. He could kill for some poppy. Just so that he could run, move anywhere without pain. Truly, what possessed Ariella? She knew the danger.

Unless…

Perhaps Tobias had not yet informed her of yesterday's attack. Or maybe Toby *had* informed her, and she thought to investigate the lion's den herself. She wasn't named daughter of a lion for nothing. He grabbed his *paramerion* from the chest, leaving the swaddling linen lying on the floor, buckling the weapon around his hips over his dark green tunic.

He met Phocus at the gates and as they were swung open, a voice called out.

'*Messere* Sarapion, Michael!' Tommaso Viadro waved from across the street and then loped toward them. 'You go somewhere? Have you forgotten we were to eat together?'

Michael shook his head. 'No, but we have somewhat of an emergency…'

'You do?' Viadro was energised at the revelation. 'Can I help?'

Phocus bowed, '*Messere*, we go to the Genovese quarter. Perhaps we need to go alone.'

'The Genovese? Ah,' Viadro's face lit up. 'You go to Izzo's, do you not? Oh, please let me join you. I would enjoy seeing that upstart put back in his box. I am proficient with a blade and an extra hand would surely be of use. Besides, I met Ahmed on the dock and I know he is gone for today at least. I will fill his spot amply!'

Viadro vibrated with excitement and Michael was unable to take umbrage. 'Tobias and Ariella were invited there this morning by Madonna Pieta, but there are any number of reasons why they shouldn't be there. Besting the Venetians at trade is only one.'

'Of course,' Viadro said. 'They have rather entered the lion's den, have they not?'

Phocus and Michael exchanged a glance and Michael said. ''Tis what I thought.'

Viadro was a good man and what would be the problem with letting him join them? For sure there was safety in numbers. So he welcomed Viadro's company and Viadro punched his arm playfully. 'See? We will be an excellent team. So young man,' he said to Phocus, 'and you are?'

Phocus explained and Viadro stepped along with them, waving to anyone he knew and even those he did not. If they had thought to make their progress quiet, he foiled the idea until he suddenly turned to them.

'May I make a suggestion?' he queried.

Michael nodded.

'If we approach the Genovese quarter from the other direction,' Viadro said, 'it may look less as if we march as an army direct from Basilike Street and more as if we met up at the markets at say, the Prosphorion Harbour, and that we thought to collect young Toby and sweet Ariella to take them to eat with us. Perhaps I insisted, especially as I fell in love with the lovely widow yesterday.' He grinned. 'I can be exceedingly charming and disarming.'

Better than I can be right now, Michael thought, shoving everything of this morning and Father Symeon to the back shelves of his mind. They walked up to the Tower of Eirene and then to a gate in the Severan Wall, on to the Wall of Byzantium, and all the while the routine of the city shouted around them. Housewives and whores, butchers and bakers, with coins clinking, dogs barking and children yelling. No city was any different – not Venezia, not Lyon, not Paris, London or Roma. The rhythm of life beat by the hour in each city. Sleep, eat, do business, procreate and sleep again. Nothing changed.

By the time they reached the slopes of First Hill, the sun had arced past midday and Michael could barely walk, Phocus noticing and putting a hand on his employer's arm.

'*Messere* Viadro, Michael is in great pain…'

'It is nothing,' Michael gritted his teeth. 'There are more important things.'

'I hadn't realised you were injured. Is this from the rumoured attacks upon the house?' Viadro asked.

'Another time, *messere*. I will manage. I have no wish to look hopeless. That would give Izzo everything he wants – the infirm co-head of a merchant house he wants to drive into the ground. No, let's go. They are staying in a villa within the grounds of the Palace of Botaneites. You can see the cupolas of the two churches from here.'

With both Phocus and Viadro slowing their steps to match Michael's own, they reached the gates of Botaneides. A guard stood either side, a rather enlightening and indeed shocking sight because the guards were Byzantium's own, not just mercenary guards employed by a Genovese trading house.

'Interesting,' Viadro said. 'I wonder if Contarini knows. It rather puts a cat amongst the pigeons, I think, to see that the empire is so supportive of Genova. I wonder why…'

Michael wondered the same, a point to remember. That Venezia was not perhaps the favoured nation they supposed and this despite the fact Venetian crews and galleys armed the Byzantine navy. What did the Genovese provide beyond money?

He climbed the steps to the gates and in his most authoritative and least pain-filled voice, he said, 'I wish to see Madonna Pieta Izzo, if you will.' He gave his name and the name of Gisborne-ben Simon and watched as his words were relayed to a passing servant. The fellow disappeared behind one of the churches and they waited in the hot sun. Michael wished he could sit on a harbour wall, maybe dangle his leg in the cool water of the Propontis, where it would hang weightless and where the sea temperature might reduce the blazing heat that had spread from his knee as far as his thigh and below to his calf.

'*Messere*,' the servant had returned. '*Madonna* Izzo wishes you to follow me.'

The guards shifted their *kontarions* to allow all three men to enter, not once looking at their faces, eyes fixed on some mythical horizon across the street.

'Well,' said Viadro in Greek. 'This is more than I expected for a meal today, Michael. Methinks we may have just stumbled upon an uneasy diplomatic situation. Add *that* to the mixture you play with today.'

Michael didn't need to be told. If he handled this next badly, all of them could end up beneath the Great Palace in the cells. And Gisborne-ben Simon might well be banished from Constantinople.

'Then maybe Gisborne-ben Simon shall come to Syria,' he replied, trying half-hearted levity.

Viadro humphed. 'You could do worse.'

The servant led them past the two little basilicas, dainty half curved and arched buildings in flesh and scarlet bricks. Trees littered the green space – oaks, firs and cedars providing welcome shade. It was a pretty place, well-grassed and with tubs of young peach trees, of olives and lemons. Leo stood well back from a group of three people who sat under an oak, watchful of them but keeping a discrete distance. He nodded at the men as they approached but betrayed no surprise. The oak's lime green buds rattled in the breeze that soughed from the water, a peaceful sound to accompany the least sinister sight one could find, especially as the *alto* tones of a Byzantine *lyra* drifted across the sward.

'Hello there,' Toby said, as his fingers plucked notes. 'I've always wanted to own a crafted *lyra*. I've never played one, you see. This is superb.'

Ariella looked up and smiled, but there was a shadow in the smile, as if she had things to say later.

'My friends,' the heavily pregnant Pieta said from a cross-legged folding chair, 'I have been lonely for days and now I have five people to keep me company. Do sit. There is refreshment on the tray. Help yourselves. I have dismissed the servants back to the villa.'

'*Madonna*, it is a pleasure to see you again,' Michael bowed, swallowing on the grinding slide of his kneecap. 'We were on our way to eat with my friend here and he insisted we collect *Madonna* Ariella and *Messere* Tobias to eat with us. May I introduce you to Venezia's famed explorer and merchant, *Messere* Tommaso Viadro?'

Tommaso took the woman's hand and bent over it. 'An honour, *madonna,* and please excuse my brashness, but I did rather fall a little in love with *Madonna* Ariella yesterday and I am only in the city for another day and would relish her presence at my table before I leave.' He looked around. 'May I compliment on your beautiful home?'

Pieta gazed across the gardens, almost surprised. 'I suppose it is lovely. But in Genova we lived next to the water and I find I miss it. All I can see from my chamber window are the walls of the basilicas. Meanwhile, Ariella said her own chamber hangs out over the street with a view straight to the water. I envy her.' The plaintive tone in her voice and the way she arched her back against the chair in pregnant discomfort made one feel sorry for her. Michael tried hard not to.

'We have a very small compound,' he said. 'And no garden to speak of, *madonna.* You must visit one day, you and your husband. Is he here?'

She waved a hand. 'I have no idea. He is not often here at all. Bartering I would say, for commodities to take home.' She sounded ill-impressed with her husband. 'The sooner we fill the galley, the sooner we may leave. Although I suspect my child will be born in the city.'

'How soon, *madonna*? May I ask?' Viadro sat beside her. 'My own wife gave birth to a son before I left.'

'Any moment, *messere.* I find I am done with lumbering around the villa like an oliphant.'

'Your first?' Michael asked.

'Ariella and I have been swapping notes, *messere.* Yes, my first, and perhaps the only, for who would want this more than once.'

Viadro laughed. 'My wife has been through it many times. She enjoys being with child. Says it's the only time I spoil her.'

Pieta's voice almost whispered, 'Then she is lucky, *messere.* My husband seems to forget that I am about to birth the heir to the Vigia house. It would serve him right if it was a girl child.'

Michael swooped on the apparent lack between husband and wife and stored it away. Toby began to play a song that none of them knew but it was sweet and pleasant and they chatted of many things until Toby washed a waterfall of sound from the *lyra* and laid it aside.

'*Madonna*,' Michael levered himself off the low wall on which he sat. 'We must all leave. *Messere* Viadro has only a short time with us before he must tie up his official ends. He leaves tomorrow for Syria. You have been most kind…'

'Syria!' she gasped. 'Oh *messere*, I wish I had known. I should love to talk to you of it. Branco never talks of such things to me. Perhaps if you are ever in Genova in the future…'

'I would be greatly honoured, *madonna*,' Viadro bowed and gave her a smouldering look. One could be forgiven for thinking he flirted with her, but it served their purpose to keep the day so well-oiled.

Michael and Toby helped Ariella to rise and then Michael put his hand under Madonna Izzo's arm and assisted her to ease from the chair. She held a hand to the small of her back.

'I will walk with you to the gates and thank you for visiting with me. I find I am quite revived for whatever tomorrow might bring. Ariella, will you come another day? Please?'

'Ah…' Ariella looked at Michael and he lifted his eyebrows. 'Of course, if I am free,' she replied.

'Free?' asked Pieta.

'I work with my companions, *madonna*.'

'You do? I am impressed and so envious. My husband would never allow me to do anything in trade.'

Viadro patted her hand. 'Madonna, both you and Ariella will soon be far too busy raising little merchants to be involved with mercantile endeavour. Do you both not know that the roof of the world is held up by mothers' endeavours?'

Pieta laughed. 'I wish you would stay in the city longer, *messere,* for I think you would be good for me.'

They had reached the gates, and each took their farewells.

As Michael reached for her hand to kiss it, Pieta said, 'Methinks, *messere*, that perhaps you came because you were worried for your friends. I am fully aware of what Tobias may have done, but then you did not know my brother as I did. He was… not a son of whom my father would have been proud. My father sent my brother on the voyage as much to make him grow up as to make Vigia great. It failed, and I would bet my life it failed dishonourably.' It was a long statement and Michael held her hand the whole time. 'Besides, *I* like Tobias. It is what matters. And I do not mourn my brother.'

'And your husband?' asked Michael.

Pieta's face stilled, and she withdrew her hand and folded it with the other upon her belly. 'He was my brother's closest friend, *messere*. Be warned.'

CHAPTER TEN

×

'Christ Jesus, Mary and Joseph, begging your pardons,' said Toby. 'But when you three came storming in, I thought the worst. By the Saints, I'm hungry. Honeyed figs and herbals only go so far. What about that inn over there?'

He pointed to a small inn where trestle seats were shaded by a budding grapevine and where people were shouting farewells and slapping backs as they prepared to walk back to warehouses, carpenters' and boat builders' yards, butcher's stalls and baker's ovens.

'Phocus,' the imp continued. 'You were very quiet, which I assume means you were very observant. What think you? You too, Leo.'

Phocus shrugged. 'We think the same, Leo and myself. Your Genovese friends live under the auspices of the empire. They seem wealthy. She seems jaded.'

Viadro laughed. 'Succinct, except I wouldn't call them friends. For myself, I wonder what went on before we arrived, young Tobias. That is what is most important. But let's order some food. Roasted goat? Some breads?'

They all agreed and after Ariella had been seated, they placed themselves beside and opposite her.

'If I may say, *Messere* Tobias,' Viadro continued, 'You were a courageous fool back there.' Viadro had a way of delivering thoughts from which one could draw no insult. There was no barb – it was merely an observation.

'You may say so, *Messere* Tommaso. I will of course disagree with the fact that I was a fool. Courageous yes. Of course.'

'Why?' Michael could contain himself no longer. 'Why would you put yourselves and the house at such risk?'

'Risk?' Toby replied. 'That's exactly why I went. Ariella was determined to go, and despite that she had Leo to guard her, I felt she needed a companion. It seemed right. No one else was available, because you, Michael, were tending to your business and Ahmed to his. I don't argue with the needs of either of you, but I did feel it was beholden to me,' he patted Ariella's hand, 'to tend to the daughter of our house.'

She had the grace, and humour, to meet Michael's frown and shrug and he couldn't argue; Tobias was right. Someone had to accompany Ariella, but… 'Ariella, why did you *need* to go? You know we suspect Izzo of foul play, do you not?'

The shade dappled Ariella in coin-spots of sun, alighting on her white veil and on her sombre widow's clothes. 'Toby told me. But when the message came, Pieta sounded…' she grimaced, '…so bereft and sad that she almost begged for my company out of the mouth of her servant. You saw for yourself what she is like.'

Indeed, Michael had. A woman who he suspected suffered from an arranged marriage with her brother's friend. A woman who carried the future of the Vigia house on her slim shoulders. A woman who was insecure and far from everything she held dear. If ever a woman required her family and friends, it was surely as she approached childbirth. Michael remembered Helena whose mother assisted her daughter to birth Ioulia. It was the way of it. Pieta Izzo would not be so fortunate.

Neither would Ariella.

But then Ariella had a household to protect and succour her.

'She is vulnerable in her condition, I accept that,' Michael replied. 'What concerns me is what she said to me as we left.' He told them of her feelings toward her deceased brother and to Toby but added, 'Branco was her brother's closest friend and ally. She warned us. Toby?'

The minstrel sat rolling his thumbs over each other. 'What?' he said without looking up. 'Nothing changes.' He stopped twiddling and cast a ferocious glance at his friends. 'I knew where we stood even before her warning. As did you. It is war between Izzo and us, but especially between Izzo and myself. I'm under no illusions, despite her kindness toward me today.' He stood, swigging down the last of his wine. 'I find I'm no longer hungry. May I be excused if I take Leo with me? Do you mind, Leo?'

Leo stood as Toby apologised to Ariella and Viadro and then the two walked toward Basilike Street – an odd sight, tall and small, the kind of sight that drew attention, unwarranted or not.

Ariella sighed. 'This is not how I imagined our time here.' She rubbed her protruding belly. 'My babe senses the distress, I think.'

Viadro leaned forward, taking her hand in his. 'Come now, *madonna*. You are named for the strength of lions. I'm convinced yours and Guillaume's child has the fire of courage flaming through its veins.' He kissed her knuckles, let her hand go and sat back. 'I'm sure Phocus would agree with me when I say the house must just control its emotional excesses. If you keep cool heads, all will be well. If you allow battle fever to overrule, then…' he lifted his palms as if to say, *On your head be it.*

He was right. So was Toby. Nothing had changed beyond Pieta Izzo removing herself from the board. But Michael lived with a household of hot-headed egos and therein lay the problem, as Viadro intimated. Tobias was a performing minstrel with all the élan that clothed such characters. And Ahmed? By all the Saints! The world passed through day and night because he willed it so, *Insh'Allah*! In addition, and aware of his own failings, Michael had to place himself at the head of the list. Everything that he thought he had diluted to nothing had risen from the murky depths of his soul.

'*Messere* Tommaso,' he said as a platter of aromatic roast goat and fresh flatbreads was laid on the trestle. 'A not altogether easy task, methinks.'

They ate the goat and talked about trade venality, of secrets and lies. The goat was flavoured with honey and well-cooked so that it fell apart, but it might as well have been ashes in Michael's mouth. Every second beat of his heart, he thought of Ioulia, so close to him and he unable to hold her. He made an inhuman effort to push it away, to be the manager of a successful trading house and he thought he had succeeded in not disturbing the others with his private issues, until, as they prepared to leave and as Phocus escorted Ariella into the street and as Viadro placed money on the trestle, the explorer said in almost a whisper, 'You wear two masks, Michael. I see it and I barely know you, so you must assume your friends see it as well. Trust me when I say you must lead this house from the front in these exceptional times. Only then will the house be the winner and you by association.' He gripped

Michael's forearm in a gesture of farewell. 'I like you, Michael Sarapion. You are honest and your friends value you. I wish I was staying in Constantinople longer. I would support you in whatever trying times head your way. But Syria calls me and my boat like a sea siren, so I wish you well. I hope we meet again somewhere along the trade routes. I would consider myself fortunate.' He smiled and threw back his lion's mane of hair, walked to Ariella and kissed her hand before bowing and the last they saw of him was a tall, well-set man walking away whistling.

'Such a wonderful individual,' said Ariella. 'So astute. I wish he wasn't leaving.'

'He said the same thing,' Michael replied. 'He would have been a good addition to our circle, if only to balance Ahmed. But he has his plans, as we have ours. Come, it is getting late and you need to rest. I need to talk to Christo about some visits to traders on the morrow and it must surely be time for Phocus to sleep, ready for his next turn of the watch.'

Phocus laughed. 'If only it was as easy as following a routine, Michael. But the house being what it is, and especially now with imminent danger, we must take sleep when we can. It's as well my companions and myself are used to living on the edge. Shall we go along the waterfront? It is more level for Ariella and for your knee.'

Basilike Street held a heaviness that evening, as if the day's revelations had far more weight than they expected. Tobias was not in evidence although they could hear him singing in his chamber – dark ballads that struck sad chords in those who cared to listen. Ariella stitched for a little, but then complained of a backache and Ephigenia assisted her up the stair, leaving Christo and Michael alone amongst the bend and gyre of candle flame. The guards were in the forecourt or asleep. Phocus managed the men well and it was one aspect of life in Basilike Street that Michael was able to pass to others. A relief.

'Ahmed feels we should visit jewellers to look for unique and valuable work that may catch the western eye,' said Michael. 'What think you, Christo?'

The notary looked up from his papers, which lay sea-like around him. 'There are excellent jewellers in Pera and some in the tradesmen's quarter behind the Grand Palace. Do you think to buy gems or crafted work?'

'Both…'

'And when would you want to go?'

'On the morrow. And whilst we can talk in peace, I should say what is in my mind at the moment. I haven't talked with the others but I am of a mind to leave before the three month is done. I am concerned that Ariella will be unable to return to her father with the babe because the sea lanes will be closed due to encroaching winter. Perhaps it is best for us to leave before she gives birth. But mostly I'm conscious that the house is treading a fine line between security and danger. If we can work like the Devil possessed over the next few days and source enough to fill both boats, then I would have no hesitation in leaving the house in your admirable care.'

'But...'

'No buts. You sourced the most valuable part of this shipment yourself, using innate good sense. I think you can keep us supplied in Venezia and thereby Lyon, without us hanging on every invoice. It also removes Toby, Ahmed and Ariella from escalating trouble.'

'I thank you for your compliment, Michael, and am infinitely sad that so much trouble threatens the house at the moment.'

'I feel we must apologise to *you*. It followed us to the gates of Basilike Street – because of Tobias, one can't deny that, but perhaps also because of the swift rise to prominence of Gisborne-ben Simon. Jealousies abound.'

'In which case, whether you were here or not, the house would have been under threat anyway.'

Michael's mouth tightened. 'Perhaps. We will never know.'

The two lapsed into silence and Michael rubbed his knee with a cupped palm, pushing at the inhuman ache that shouted at him no matter where he was or what he did. No relief from the constancy.

'But what about your daughter, Michael?' Christo gathered up his papers, the parchment crackling, one sheet over another.

'I have no reason not to believe she will want to come with me when I leave.'

'Then my heart is glad, and I will be happy to do whatever I can to assist you and the house to move forward in business.'

They discussed who they would visit and what commodities, what precious metals, what gems would likely suit the marketplace.

'It's a pity Ahmed is not returned,' Christo mused. 'I suspect he would know intrinsically what we need to look for.'

But Michael had guessed *Sada* would stay out overnight. These were sea-trials after all.

The next day hung like a bad mood over the city, with a damp fog and the coolness of a winter that had supposedly left days since, almost as if it refused to let go. Ariella wrapped a shawl around and asked if she could remain behind. She was tired and heavy of leg. Ephigenia said that the physician was calling to see Ariella and that she would handle everything should Michael have business outside the gates. Toby asked where Michael was going and on hearing, said, 'A treasure-hunt! May I come?'

Michael's heart sank, thinking that they might as well pin targets to their backs. Just once, innocence and absence of concern would have been nice and later, as the sky lightened from the colour of a steel blade to that of an oystered pearl, and with Hilarius the Chaldian in attendance, he, Christo and Tobias left for Pera.

The slopes of Pera, across the dark, choppy waters of the Horn, brooded with evergreen pines and myrtles. If there were blossoming Judas trees, the proud colour was concealed. Only the cupolas glistened damply, always beckoning the believer. Toby stood at the prow of the little *caique* that transported them across the strait. His cloak billowed and flapped and small beads of moisture sat on the weave. Not rain, merely the sea fog that wafted in thready skeins along the foreshore.

The fragrance of Constantinople hung on the heavy air. As the four men walked along the waterfront, the odour of the catch was nothing like the spiced bowls of *kakavia* that would be consumed at the taverns. But as they progressed to the streets, smells drifted from perfumers' stalls. Toby remarked again on the exotic nature of the air and the way the Byzantines used perfumes to great effect – in the churches, and distillers' stalls. Even on the food stalls. Nobility and commoners used scents to drive away bad humors and as Tobias noted, who could stay angry or gloomy with the fragrance of *cassia, olibanum,* myrrh, pepper, balsam and much more? By contrast, they passed the premises of a dyer's, the galling taint almost making them gag.

'Odd how cloth can be dyed to wonderful shades, but it needs piss to make it so,' Toby muttered, taking a breath and hurrying on past.

Michael saw a baker's stall, the smell of bread drifting forth, a unique air, the fragrance of mastic through the bread. It wasn't cheap, but he bought a loaf and they shared it as they walked further up the slope to the place Christo called Stone Street. It implied nothing precious nor beautiful and little doorways lay open to the streets as if no one could steal the contents. But then, at the head of the small thoroughfare stood two Byzantine guards with *paramerions* and *lamellar* breast plates – big men, muscular of leg and arm and bruising expressions upon their faces.

'This is the workshop,' said Christo. 'I'm unsure what you seek, but I know this man's reputation. He has premises on the other side nearer the Grand Palace for his finished work. But this is where he creates the fine pieces and where he has raw gems with which to work. I thought this would be the better place to visit.' He moved into the interior which was lit by lantern flame, and by fire for warming metals. '*Kyrie* Ignatios Trafines, good morning.'

An old man looked up from a table where he sat bending gold wire into a perfect spiral. Beside him sat a small bowl of round pearls. Michael could have sighed deeply and blown the man away, so thin and frail did he look. But his eyes were clear and sharp, and his knotted fingers moved the thin rods about which the gold looped, with dexterous care.

Christo introduced himself, Michael and Tobias, explaining what they were looking for – some unique raw stones and some finished work with garnets and pearls, maybe even amber or chalcedony.

Kyrie Ignatios laid down his tools and stood, a small man, shrunken with age, hunched with being seated over his table for a multitude of years. 'Of course, sirs. A moment please...'

He disappeared to the back of the shop behind a latticed screen, then returned with small rattling leather bags in his hands. He cleared a space on the table and then worked at the lacing of the first bag, tipping it to allow iridescent pearls to roll out, sliding around his palms like a sea of froth. Each was unique, with bumps and indents but all were oval, and he allowed them to clink into a small bowl before taking two that looked as if hatched from the same shell.

'These are as close to a perfect pair as you could find. Colour and shape and indeed weight. I would have made them into earrings for one of the noble ladies, perhaps with a small circle suspended beneath. I have some very pale chalcedony that is the colour of the sky when the sea-mist begins to drift in. It has a harmony with the pearls…'

Michael knew little of gems. Cloth was his strong point. Neither it seemed, did Christo. But Tobias, always the minstrel and aware of women's tastes, began talking with the master craftsman. He looked back at Michael for approval and Michael nodded, trusting Toby to make elegant choices from which they could recoup good money.

They settled on a number of pairs of earrings and some necklets and amulets, some bags of raw gems – pearls, *amethystus*, chalcedony. He retrieved a green mineral stone that he claimed came with silks from the east. 'It is rare and it is expensive.'

Michael declined, although he was sure Ahmed may have closed the deal. He laid down part payment for the work and as golden Byzantine *hyperpirons* spilled from a leather bag not unlike the jeweller's own, he said, '*Kýrie* Ignatios, before we sign off on this agreement, I would ask you two very important questions. Do you do business with any other merchants?'

'Not on a commission basis like this…'

'Can you explain?'

The old jeweller humphed, patently disturbed at having to explain his manner of business to someone he hardly knew. 'I sell to any and everyone from my shop near the Grand Palace. I would not know whether my customers are merchants or curious travellers from around the empire. That said, I know my noble patrons well and they make up most of my clientele.'

'So, to your knowledge,' Tobias butted in, 'no western merchants have come here to commission from you or buy gems direct in the last few days.'

'No… although…' He scratched his chin. 'There was a man a day ago. Is it really relevant? He bought such a small amount from me.'

Michael signalled Toby to be quiet and responded, '*Kýrie* Ignatios, we have hopes for our trading house. Already we do significant business with the royal houses of the west. If your work is exclusive to us, then you stand to make a great reputation and a great deal of money. Can you describe this man?'

'He was tall, well-built, plainly but expensively dressed, large of voice and he said he was a Venetian. Wait, I have his name as he said he may return to me on his way back to Venezia…' he scrabbled in a box and finally found a wax tablet and pulled it out. 'Here, his name is *Kýrie* Tommaso Viadro…'

190

The exhalation of air in the room was palpable, prompting Michael again to wonder how the little man didn't blow away. Christo and Toby laughed – relief therein.

'He is a good friend, *Kýrie* Ignatios. And a fellow Venetian who is on his way to Syria, not to the markets of the west. My point is this – are you prepared to deal with us exclusively, along with your noble clients?'

The jeweller's eyes slitted, becoming wary. 'You mean no Genoveses, no Pisans or Anconians, do you not?'

'Exactly so.' Michael knew the crunch approached.

'Make it worth my while, sir, for I'm an old man and I want comfort and surety…'

'Our notary is Christo, here. He lives in Basilike Street in the house of Gisborne-ben Simon. He will pay you a retainer and help you in any way you need. Secure premises, guards – you have only to name it.' Michael smiled at Christo, who like any good money-man, had paled to the colour of chalk.

Kýrie Ignatios sat rolling the gold wire spiral, thinking. He tapped his bronze jeweller's scales and they tinkled in the silence. Then, 'It is agreed on one condition.'

'Yes?'

'Find me a room in Basilike Street where I can be fed and watered and where I am secure. Then I am yours.'

'Christo?' Michael asked.

'Done,' the notary's colour had not improved, and his throat croaked as if someone clutched fingers round it. 'There are two small rooms on the first floor at the back of the house. One for a workshop for *Kýrie* Ignatios and one for sleeping.'

Michael looked back at the old man. 'Deal?'

'Deal,' *Kýrie* Ignatios replied, slapping his hand on the table so that tools, wires and precious gems jumped and rolled. 'I am old with no family and I deal in precious gems. If I can be moved today or on the morrow, I should be happy.'

Christo and Michael assured him they would send guards and handcarts that afternoon, if *Kýrie* Ignatios could be packed. Michael cinched the leather bag of *hyperpirons* and placed it in the jeweller's hands, saying, '*Kýrie*

Ignatios, it is truly an honour to have you as part of the Gisborne-ben Simon house. Thank you.'

They left with small bags of raw gems secreted under Hilarius' leather vest and as they walked down the street, there was a lightness on the air, that of a great business deal and the sun trying to break through the sea-mist. Michael for once felt he had achieved something of which Ahmed might approve because the Arab loved shining things...

They turned a corner, heading back to the waterfront and Tobias, who had been lightly stepping ahead, as he often did, walked straight into the over-perfumed, silken-clothed Branco Izzo.

Here? In Pera? Why?

'My good friends,' he smiled, thin lips stretching to nothing as he grabbed Tobias' shoulders to stop him from falling. 'How good it is to see you. And here – in the lanes of Pera. What a coincidence! I am so glad, because I want to thank you for visiting my Pieta yesterday. She was much cheered when I returned to the villa. Do you not think it is a charming place? I consider we are fortunate to have the imperial family's notice and support, enough that they should devolve a Botaneides Palace villa upon us. What think you, Michael Sarapion?'

'It is indeed a perfect headquarters for the Vigia House, *messere*. And yes, you are fortunate to have imperial notice. It was a pleasure to wait upon *Madonna* Pieta. I hope she is well. You must excuse our haste, however. We have a *caique* waiting to ferry us back to the Nerion Harbour.'

'Then do not let me keep you. I have business in the Jewish quarter and am late. I hope to see you in less rushed circumstances.' He bowed his thin body and signalling with finger to forehead, he hurried onward through the archway that separated the Jewish quarter from the rest of Pera.

'You think he told the truth?' Hilarius asked.

'It is a risk we must take,' said Michael. 'I need to get back to Basilike Street quickly because I want to organise for *Kýrie* Ignatios to move this afternoon. My head and heart tell me we need guards with him immediately.'

Hilarius said he had a friend who lived on Pera and if they could wait, he would organise for him to keep the jeweller secure until this afternoon.

'Go,' said Michael. 'Quickly. We will wait at the *caique*.'

'You will be safe?'

'We are armed, and you will be a short while only. But Hilarius, we must be quick on two counts. I am worried for *Kyrie* Ignatios and I must be at the Xylinites Convent by Ninth Hour. Go swiftly!'

Hilarius set off at a jog and the others continued to walk toward the water, Toby shuddering.

'I hate the man. Hate him!'

'Leave it, Toby,' Michael replied. 'He was innocuous. We can do nothing but be wary. Christo, you are very quiet. I assume you're concerned I employed Ignatios without consultation. I am sorry if I offended you. It's probably too late to ask if you think we can afford it.'

Christo scrabbled at his hair. 'Money is tight, Michael. Until we begin to sell some of our commodities it will remain so. But I can secure some sort of cash-flow from the Jewish moneylenders.'

'Would you likely be concerned that Izzo goes to the quarter to muddy our name?' asked Toby hopping around as if on coals. 'It's the kind of thing an oily bastard like him would do.'

'Christo?' asked Michael.

'Yes and no,' Christo replied, his face creased with thought. 'It's a possibility but we have a reputation there, as I said. Ariella is Jewish and her family have been connected with the quarter for many years. The Jews are tightknit around our world and I doubt they will listen to a Gentile they don't know. Ariella and I can visit this afternoon, if you think it might be politic.'

'Do it,' Michael said as they walked down onto the waterfront. The *caique* that had ferried them across from the Nerion Harbour swung idly at its moorings on the jetty, the waters glassy, the mist lifting and Pera displayed for all to see. Above them, the sun gained more strength and cloaks were removed and held over the crooks of arms. The *caique* was empty as they threw in their cloaks and Michael looked around for the helmsman. A thin string of a man approached, asking if they wished to be ferried to the other shore. 'Are you *Kyrie* Christo?' he asked the notary.

'I am. Where is Menas? He said he would wait here.'

'Menas has been called back to the other shore, *Kyrie* Christo. I am Pavlos, his friend. He asked me to return you when you are ready.'

Michael tried to pick holes in the man's story – always on the lookout for some untruth, some calculation. But Pavlos had jumped into the boat and was piling their cloaks under his seat amidships, coiling a rope and rolling the oars in their locks. In time, he called up to them to step aboard.

'Thank you, but we must wait for our friend. A moment only,' Michael replied, looking back up the hill to see if Hilarius approached.

The vessel was small and whilst it had a mast and square sail, the canvas was furled. When Menas had ferried them earlier, he had rowed them across and Pavlos looked to do the same, as the breeze of earlier had died away and the waters were flat and burnished.

Tobias called out and waved and they turned to see the athletic frame of their guard loping toward them. He leaped aboard with the ease and confidence of a man used to the sea.

'All done,' he said. 'My friend goes immediately and will return with our new man later today.' He scrutinised Pavlos and the man grinned innocently back.

'Good,' Michael's relief that one problem had been solved with ease was replaced then by thoughts of his daughter and chafing to get things moving, he said to Pavlos. 'Let's go.' He stepped to the stern and sat with Hilarius, Christo and Toby in the bow.

Turning to look back at departing Petra, Hilarius lowered his voice and murmured, 'Do you trust him?' he indicated back to Pavlos with a flick of his thumb.

Michael breathed deeply. 'God knows.'

Hilarius said nothing more, but his hand drifted to a knife and hairs stood on Michael's neck in consequence.

They made swift passage beyond Pera, Pavlos calling for clearway from other vessels. He sang a little song in Greek, Toby tilting his head, but at the off-key notes, the minstrel frowned and turned back to face the Nerion Harbour. They had almost reached the middle of the Horn when Pavlos' song stopped in a shriek as he shoved the oars away from him, dragging at the cloaks. 'O Theós na mas sósei! We have a leak! God save us!'

Hilarius swiftly knelt down. 'The plank is cracked, and water is coming in fast. All of you, call for help. Can you swim?'

There was no reply as they all yelled and Pavlos squeaked and jumped to the larboard wale, the boat listing

'Sit still, man!' Hilarius ordered. 'You'll sink us sooner. Listen,' he stood and began to remove his leather vest, a creased linen tunic lying underneath

194

with the bags strapped across his chest. He manoeuvred his tunic out from under the bagged gems and pulled it off, revealing a scarred but muscular torso. As he bent to take off his boots, he looked up. 'I suggest you all do the same. We must swim till someone comes.'

Christo was even paler as he dragged off his long notary's gown and pulled at his wet boots. 'Hilarius,' he said. 'I can't swim…'

'Then hold onto me. You Toby?'

'I can swim.' Toby had stripped to his hose.

Michael followed and as he stripped to his bare legs and thin under-tunic, he recalled his days diving for the purple mollusc.

'I can swim,' he said to Hilarius.

By now the boat was knee deep in chilled water and wallowing. Hilarios pulled at an oar so that it slipped from its lock. 'Christo, hold onto this. It will help. Don't let go. I will stay with you. And everyone, keep yelling!'

Pavlos' voice shook as he held to the wale, knuckles bleached white. 'I can paddle sir, but I'm not a good swimmer.'

'Then float on your back,' ordered Hilarius. 'See? A *caique* has turned toward us. They will pick us up. Go now, one after another and swim toward it.'

Toby went first, striking out with confidence, an acrobat, able to do anything, despite his size and conformation. Michael thanked God, not thinking twice about deity and gratitude as he turned toward Hilarius who was endeavouring to ease Christo into the water.

'Hold tight, Christo,' the guard said. 'Come now. I have the oar and I'm at your side…' He took Christo's arm as the man gripped the paddle and the two drifted out of the boat's wallow, into the deep dark water of the Horn. Michael followed, his knee screaming and he cursed, pulling harder with his arms. He could hear the panic is the notary's voice as the man coughed a mouthful and so he turned back to help.

'Keep up with Toby,' Hilarius ordered calmly. 'We'll manage, won't we, Christo?' The notary said nothing, spluttering, clinging to the oar with the guard taking the weight of it. 'Where's Pavlos?'

But Michael could see the man; a man who apparently couldn't swim well and yet he powered toward Tobias. Gorge in his throat, Michael struck out for the pair with one thought raging in his head.

Izzo…

Bloodlust thrilled through his body and the pain of his knee vanished in the surge. Five body lengths away, Michael saw the man's arm swing and Toby vanished beneath the water.

Michael dragged at the knife he had left around his waist as they disrobed, water slowing the pull, the weight of his impotent bandaged knee dragging at him as Toby appeared again, coughing.

'Toby! Toby!' Michael yelled. 'Watch out!'

Pavlos raised a piece of wood and Toby ducked under again, the wood coming down hard with all the strength Pavlos had. As it cleaved into the water, splashes shooting into the air, the ferryman screamed with the effort, his teeth bared in a grimace. Michael swam fast toward them, knife held tight, coming up behind Pavlos, ready to stab. But too late, as the man floated in a stain of red, the offending wood drifting from his grasp.

Michael grabbed him from behind and turned the limp form round. Pavlos' eyes were wide and empty, water splashing into and out of his open mouth. Michael pushed him away and he floated aimlessly, lifelessly.

'God, Toby! Toby!' Michael dived under the water, saw the little man drifting below the surface and grabbed his hair. He pulled him up, rolled him onto his back, holding his head clear of the water, thumping his chest, seeing a lump the size of an egg on his head and blood oozing. Toby's eyes were closed and Michael needed all his strength and concentration to keep both their heads clear of the water. 'Tobias! Damn you! Breathe!'

He glanced around, saw the *caique* closing in and prayed like he had never prayed before. 'Here! Come here!' And in moments, hands reached down and grabbed Tobias, hauling him over the wale. Crew members' hands then reached for him but he pointed them toward Hilarius and Christo. 'No, pick them up. I can wait! One man can't swim!'

As the crew rowed the *caique* toward Hilarius, Michael heard a wet cough come from the decks of the vessel. 'Toby, breathe,' he called out. 'Breathe, you little bastard!'

He lay on his back, letting the water cushion him until the *caique* returned. Holding his arms up to the crew they pulled at him, and he flopped onto the decks. But he needed to see...

'Tobias!' he called, then coughed, realising he was bitterly cold and that his skin was blue and white. Someone kindly wrapped a cloak around his shoulders and said, 'Your little friend breathes but he sleeps long. We can't wake him.'

'*Iisoús Christós!*' He tried to push onto his knees but Hilarius, who was sitting beside him and also wrapped in a cloak, held him back with icy hands.

'Leave it, Michael. There is nothing to be done. When we get to shore, we will call for a litter and send for your physician. You need to breathe and warm yourself in between times.'

'I'm warm,' Michael replied bitterly. 'I'm burning with hate as we speak, Hilarius. Izzo tried to kill Tobias.'

'Of course. We know this and we knew he would try. Tobias fought the felon well. We can only pray now.'

How phlegmatic was the guard, Michael thought. His own emotions ran hard and hot and it was all he could do not to spew venom. His instinct was to send word to Branco Izzo, to call him out somewhere discrete, to make him pay. Vaguely he heard a harmony on the air from the basilicas of the city and a thought pierced the anger. 'Is that Sixth Hour?'

'It is.' Hilarius rubbed his scarred hands together, pushing body warmth into them as if he were lighting the fire of life. 'You worry about going to Xylinites by Ninth Hour, do you not?'

'I do. Christo is exhausted, I cannot leave him to deal with this. I must see what the physician says…'

'*Kýrie* Michael, Phocus is a good commander. He will handle things for you whilst you do what you must. And besides, Ahmed will be back. See? *Durrah* and her sister ship are there, look!'

The two ships sat glowing in the sun, the light bold and brazen after flirting through veils of sea-mist earlier. For the first time on this venture, Michael was glad to know that Ahmed might be relied upon and he sat back, his eyes never leaving the swaddled form of Tobias.

'He is awake, although he drifts.' Anwar washed his hands in a basin provided by Ephigenia. 'He is warmer now and I have stitched his head. He will have an ache for a few days, but I don't believe his skull is broken. He seems lucid. You can see him briefly but then let him rest. Ariella has said she will sit with him.'

Michael breathed out. Was his whole life to one of breath-holding? 'And Christo?'

'He is fine. But swears he never wants to go to sea again. A difficulty for a notary in this house, I said and suggested he learn to swim. He agreed reluctantly.' Anwar al Din wiped his hands dry on linen. 'And you Michael?'

'I'm better now that I have had some wine and dressed in dry clothes.'

'I meant your knee.'

'Anwar, I don't have time to worry about it. I have to be at the Xylinites Convent by Ninth Hour.' Michael stood. 'I hate to be so rude as to leave you, but I would like a quick word with Toby and then I must make haste.'

'Michael,' Anwar's gentle voice called him back. 'Take care, my son. Nothing is worth pushing yourself to the limits of your emotions.'

The physician's words hovered and then sank in and Michael stood silent for a moment. Then, 'I thank you, Anwar. I heed your words.' And then he climbed the stair, trying to conceal the agony of the grating kneecap.

Toby lay piled on pillows, his hair awry, his chest bare, the covers pulled to his armpits. Ariella looked up as Michael entered.

'He is asleep?' Michael asked.

'No. I'm not. My head thumps like an ill-used tabor. Michael, I'm going to kill Branco Izzo.'

'Tobias, I suggest you sleep on the idea for the moment. I thought Pavlos would kill you and I have no wish to lose you twice over.'

'Pavlos! He found my knife buried in his guts. Pity he didn't ask how well I could swim and dive before he tried to hammer the life from me. I got him after his first effort which missed me as I dived beneath him, but damn it, he tried again as the life drained around him and he got me. I suspect *I* might be dead if he had his strength. I don't mourn him at all! Nor will I mourn Izzo. Although I will feel some grief for *Madonna* Pieta. Christ but my head aches.'

'It aches because you need to rest,' Ariella said and passed him a wine goblet. 'Drink that, it's relief for your injury mixed with wine.'

Toby sipped and a look of bliss passed across his face. 'I do love Anwar. He has magical drugs at his disposal…' The minstrel lay his head back and closed his eyes and in a breath, he was asleep, his chest rising with reassuring regularity.

'Ariella, Ephigenia will sit with Toby. I need for you to go to your Jewish friends in Pera and tell them what is happening. I suspect Izzo will try and destroy any line of credit we might have and destroy our reputation in the process. Leo and Bonus are going to Pera to collect Ignatio, our new company jeweller, and you can go with them, if you are well enough.'

'I am fighting fit, Michael, and intrigued. A jeweller? Can you explain?'

'I haven't time. I must head to the convent. Later, when I return. Take care, do what the men say, and I will see you anon.'

He hurried back down the stair, noting that Anwar had departed, seeing that Phocus had briefed Leo and Bonus. The house never stopped heaving, he thought. Entering the courtyard, he informed the guards that Ariella would only be a moment and then he asked Phocus if they could leave now, immediately.

Michael and Phocus climbed Little Mese, Michael's knee dragging and he wished he had a staff or a swift donkey.

'If we are to reach Xylinites by Ninth Hour,' said Phocus, 'then we shall have to hire horses. You are lame and slow.'

'Not to put too finer a point on it,' Michael cursed his leg. 'Where do we find them?'

'Just off the Mese near St. Ephemia's on Third Hill, there is a small livery. Can you make it that far with as much speed as possible?'

'Yes…'

Phocus began a slow jog-trot and Michael limped and skipped beside him, telling himself over and over again that pain was nothing, that Ioulia was all. They turned up Makros Embolus to Third Hill and the sweat began to form on his forehead. In time, albeit slower than either would want, they could see the wrought gold cross at the top of Saint Ephemia's, the fragrance of horse drifting toward them. They hurried under an arch through the walls of porphyry-coloured brick as a horse neighed deep and long.

'Rest, Michael. I will deal with this.' Phocus said.

'Here,' Michael opened his purse, holding out money and pushing the old note from Father Symeon deeper inside the leather. The note meant nothing more than identity but he was glad to have it and grateful too that Phocus took control, just for a moment. The guard disappeared into a low brick building, a barn where shifting hooves and men's voices could be heard. Michael rubbed his knee carefully – the swelling had grown substantially with the run up the hill and he knew it could only get worse. Even in the saddle, maybe even because of it.

In less than a breath, Phocus reappeared with a saddled mount, another man leading a further horse behind. 'There is a block you can use to climb, *Kýrie* Michael. Here...' He passed the reins over and Michael stood, ignoring the knife-like shaft of pain as he placed his weight on the damaged leg. Taking the reins, he climbed a block of stone and eased himself into the saddle, bending his legs to slip them into stirrups. The bay horse stood quietly as he adjusted his seat, the animal's ears flicking back and forth. Phocus' black horse was smaller, but just as bright, as if they both relished a ride in the country.

They left the livery with a wave to the ostler, turning north, heading onto the Mese at a fast trot, toward Fourth Hill and the Constantinian Wall. Breaking into a canter, keeping clear of folk walking, past empty carts heading back to the countryside. There were others on horseback as well – officials with shining horses and clinking metalware on their trappings and who looked at the men cantering past with curiosity. Michael hoped he garnered nothing more than vague interest as his kneecap rubbed back and forth.

They reached the Charyisia Gate with speed, slowing the horses as they approached, the animals blowing down their noses and dancing excitedly on hoof-point. Phocas' animal shook itself to a carillon of bits and buckles as each man pulled out their papers and passed them to the guards.

'Business?' asked one of the official gatekeeper guards.

'We go to the Xylinites Convent. I have a relative there who is in dire need.' *Not such a lie...*

'And you will return through the gate before it is shut?'

'It is my hope.'

'You may pass.'

They left the gate at a ground-covering gallop, Michael's horse bucking with glee, ears back and snorting as the pace lifted. Under other circumstances, Michael might have enjoyed the spirited ride. He had loved horses all his life and learned to ride early. If he had not become a merchant, he always wondered if he would breed horses for the wealthy of Byzantium. With the tension of riding to a new fate, and despite the furious bone pain, he shouted as his mount lifted its hindquarters in a joyful kickback. Like his mount, he was filled with hope and anticipation. Phocus' horse was no less energetic. Catching up, it snaked its head toward the other horse's neck to bite.

'Good horses, Michael,' Phocus shouted.

'They are...'

They thundered over new planks on the bridge that crossed the Lycus River. Its handrails had also been repaired, and at the clatter of the hooves, waterfowl flew up with clacking wings and mournful honking, the horses startling at the sight and sound. Michael's shied and he gripped hard with both knees, calling 'Steady, whoa!' The two men wheeled sharply around a corner in the track, slowing the horses to a lumpy trot, the animals snorting and shaking their heads with fury at curtailment of their fun.

The Xylinites Convent rested in a glade of heavy cedars, its gilded cross gleaming atop the globe-like cupola. Michael felt as if he had been dragged back through time as voices lifted in praise – the Ninth Hour liturgy. He pushed memories of his hiding place away and as they reached that gate, he flung himself from the saddle, ignoring the ache, hammering on the wood in the wall and begging, *begging,* God to grant him this moment.

The heavenly voices of the nuns soared above the common battering he gave the gate and in moments, the grille had flipped back, and a gravelly voice said, 'Eh?'

'Please, Sister, I must see the *hegoumene*, Mother Irene.'

'You cannot. It is Ninth Hour. If you cleaned your ears out, you would hear the liturgy being sung. The *hegoumene* leads the service.' The raw-voiced woman slammed the grille shut.

He hammered the gate again. 'Please, it is urgent.'

The grille snapped open again. 'I said Mother Irene is in chapel, leading the sisters in prayer.' She went to slide the grille shut again, but Michael flipped his dagger blade between the bars, jamming it so that the nun growled.

'Sister, in the name of all that is holy, I beg you. Let me see Mother Irene. It is a matter of great personal import to myself and to Xylinites.' Michael ached with desperation. 'I have had the assurance of Patriarch George that your *hegoumene* will see me.' If he was going to be damned for anything, he might as well damn himself completely as he furthered the lie. 'Patriarch George II Xipphillinus has given my meeting with the *hegoumene* his blessing. If you do not fetch her immediately, the Xylinites Convent will lose valuable support from the Holy Office.'

The woman's eyes skewered him – sickly green ones that were cobwebbed with blood vessels. She was well-chosen to guard the gate with a ferocious scowl embedded into her face like some holy stigmata. Perhaps she knew he lied, but she gave her *skepe* a tug, pulling it further down her forehead. With a vicious, 'Wait here…' she hurried away as body odour lifted upward to the grille.

Michael looked back at Phocus, who held the impatient horses. Their sides were no longer blowing like a blacksmith's bellows but were lathered with sweat and they no doubt itched uncomfortably. Michael paced back and forth, trying to ease his knee pain and his nerves. And then presently there were voices, and he quickly grabbed his dagger blade, sliding it from the grille and replacing it at his girdle.

The bolts of the gate grated as they were moved back – one… two… three – and in time, the gate was hauled open. The gatekeeper stood like some malevolent angel from Hell and next to her stood an ascetic, elderly woman, draped in black, her face clear and guileless. Michael knew there would be no falsehoods told with Mother Irene.

'Mother Irene, I beg your forgiveness. I have a note from Father Symeon of Sancta Sophia…' he scrabbled in his purse and withdrew the folded paper.

She opened it, read it, pressed her lips together in reproof and handed it back, adding, 'You lie.'

'I beg your pardon?'

'You are not Michael Sarapion.'

'I am…'

'You are not and this paper is false.' Mother Irene turned to walk away, the gatekeeper beginning to heave the gate shut.

'He is, Mother,' Phocus cried out. 'He is Michael Sarapion, lately of Venezia and Lyon, from the house of Gisborne-ben Simon in Basilike Street in the city. He is my employer.'

'And why should I believe you?' Around them the harmonies flew, the antithesis of the mood and manner at the gate.

'Send a message to Father Symeon. We shall wait here until an answer comes.'

Mother Irene took a further step toward Michael. 'Tell me why you want to see me.'

'My daughter…

She sighed then and held up a white hand. The palm was lined and near the wrist, as her sleeve fell back, there were delicate blue vessels close to the surface. He swore he could almost see the blood beating through them, so defined was everything at that moment – the nuns' voices, the smell of juniper close by, the rank body odour of the gatekeeper nun mixing with the horses' sweat. 'Your daughter, Ioulia, whom we see as our daughter and who has been in Xylinites' keeping since Father Symeon brought her to us.'

'Yes!' The affirmation gushed forth, mingled with relief and an easing of the tension in his body so that he almost began to smile. He felt the tears in his eyes but would not acknowledge them. 'Yes...'

Mother Irene said. 'Walk with me.'

Michael looked back at Phocus, signalling him to wait, and pushing past the odious gatekeeper, he walked to Irene's side as she led him toward a small wooden gate and a garden of herbs. Birds twittered, and he welcomed their sound, a counterpoint to the voices in the chapel. The *hegoumene* sat on a bench and patted the space next to her. Her face was perhaps more serious than he wished and for one tiny moment, his burgeoning joy stopped in its tracks.

'*Kýrie* Michael, I could see how much this means to you when I saw the tears in your eyes. Which makes this next...' She pushed at the *skepe* around her forehead and then fumbled for her prayer beads. 'I am unsure how to say this.'

'Say what? That my daughter does not want to see me? I think, Mother Irene, that you made that decision, not my daughter.'

'I did. For her own good. She needed time. But in any case, she can't see you, *Kýrie* Michael.'

'Why? Is she in seclusion?'

'No. She can't see you because she isn't here.'

Michael's breath stopped. 'Not here? I don't understand...'

'She left between Sixth and Ninth Hour prayers. We received your note delivered by your men's own hands.'

Michael could barely force the words between his teeth. 'I sent no note.'

'But two men came with a letter...'

'Someone has taken her...' He wanted to shake the divinity out of the *hegoumene*'s soul. 'I sent no men!' He shouted this last, the words bursting forth like so much poison.

'But...' the *hegoumene* had the grace to look rattled. 'Your name...'

'I said, Mother Irene, that I sent no letter in my name or anyone else's. This...' he waved Father Symeon's note in front of her, the parchment snapping back and forth, 'This is the only letter that matters. This identifies me as the man Father Symeon wrote to you about previously. You sent a message back saying my daughter needed time to assimilate the news that her father still lived. I gave her time and you gave her away!'

The *hegoumene* shook her head. 'I am so sorry, my son...' she reached out to touch his arm, but he stepped back.

'I am *not* your son. Nor God's. You have forsaken me, and you have especially forsaken my daughter. Tell me what these men looked like?'

Mother Irene's face had paled to alabaster. 'One was younger than yourself and stood a little back from the other man. The leader was older, grey hair cut hard against his scalp. Both spoke perfect Greek and were solicitous of Ioulia, providing her with a horse. They were dressed in good Byzantine tunics, well presented and I had no reason to doubt them. But I thought they might be Arabic.'

'Arabs?'

'Yes. And the older one had a mark on his hand like...'

Michael knew. God, he knew. He drew in the dust at the *hegoumene*'s feet. A sharp half-moon.

She nodded, her thumbs rolling her prayer beads back and forth.

'So help me, Mother Irene,' Michael's words were filled with bile. 'If anything happens to Ioulia, you shall know of it. Father Symeon shall know of it and the Patriarch and your imperial patrons shall know. Pray, Mother Irene. You need to.'

He left the *hegoumene* sitting where she was, damning her to perdition. Thrusting past the odoriferous gatekeeper, he grabbed his horse from Phocus, and kneecap crunching, he flung himself in the saddle, whipping the reins on either side of the surprised animal's neck, and shouting to Phocus. 'Arabs took her. We must get to the Theodosian Harbour!'

They slid to a dust-filled halt at the Charyisia Gate and the same, small-minded officious guard looked up at them.

'You were swift. You have a problem?'

'No.' said Michael beginning to push his horse through.

The guard stood in front of the beast's nose. 'But you are in haste.'

Phocus' fingers slid to the pommel of his *paramerion* as Michael replied, 'Time is precious in business and I dine at the Imperial Palace shortly. Give me your name and I shall be sure to commend your service.'

The man tilted his head back, saying nothing for a moment. Then, 'Isaac Eugenoides,' as he bowed.

'Thank you.' Michael kicked his horse on, urging it to a gallop so that the gate was left behind. 'Phocus,' he shouted. 'Show me the quickest way to the harbour!'

The wider lands of Sixth Hill gave way to the more densely populated areas of Fifth and Fourth Hills and the horses had to slow to avoid people and carts and presently even a trot was useless. Never had people moved so slowly and so lacking in goddamned purpose.

Michael hauled on his reins and went to dismount. 'Christ Jesus! We might as well walk, this is pointless.'

'No.' Phocus said. 'Save your leg for when you need it.'

The blood coursed through Michael's veins, carrying such black hatred that if any defied him, he would have aimed a knife blow at their heart and thought later. Anyone at all. Except Phocus, so he subsided in the saddle as Phocus continued.

'Am I right that you know this Arab thief?'

Michael didn't answer immediately.

Know him? I have slept with the man every night for the last twelve years...

'You need to tell me, sir. I need to know who is the enemy.'

Michael grimaced. 'He is the *peirate* who captured our boat twelve years ago. He is the cause of my wife's death. Of Hell for my daughter and myself. I will kill him.'

The horses clipped along at a fast pace, the waters of the close-by Theodosian Harbour glistening in the last light of the day. How vivid were the memories of this harbour – where Michael had sourced the Tyrian purple, where he had spirited it aboard *Durrah* with the *olibanum* resin. It was the start of his re-made existence. Another irony surely, that the Arab should die here.

'Michael, the bloodlust rules your head. Think. How do you know the Arab is actually at the Theodosian Harbour? He could be anywhere. The Prosphorion, the Nerion, or any number of a dozen other moorings.

Or maybe not even in the city at all. He is no fool and you must not be either.'

Michael shook his head – this was his moment, by God it was.

'*Listen* to me,' Phocus grabbed Michael's reins and held tight so that the horse snorted and pulled back. 'Listen,' the guard lowered his voice. 'Let *us* find him. You wait for that moment.'

'If I agree, Phocus, it *must* be soon. My daughter…'

'Which brings me to a question. Why would he steal your daughter? What has he to gain? What does he know? Think on it.'

The bloodlust was receding like a murky ebb tide. Everything Phocus had said made such sense, and if he, Michael, thought on it, he knew the reason behind this went deeper than anything he could have imagined. Proof that there was a traitor amongst them. For how else would the Arab know of the connection between Michael, Ioulia and the Xylinites Convent.

'Yes,' said Phocus, nodding his head. 'I see you think as I think. We may have a traitor.' He pulled Michael's reins, turning the horse and Michael sat, compliant. 'We should return the horses to the livery and go back to Basilike Street. I would that we sat with my men to talk this through.'

'You don't think one of them might be the traitor?'

'No. It galls me to say this but look to your own.'

My own? How so?

He felt sick with sadness, on a knife-edge of anxiety for his daughter. 'Phocus, I must resolve this as soon as I can. Tomorrow. No later. There is a life at stake.'

Phocus rode on, looking straight ahead. 'Then I am sorry to distress you further when I say there is likely more than one life at risk.'

CHAPTER ELEVEN

╳

They returned the horses, apologising for the sweat and tiredness of the animals and offering more for the trouble and which the ostler palmed before turning his back on them. At the gate to the house, Phocus held Michael's arm in a bruising grip.

'I will talk to the men, Michael. Go inside. Do what you must to be calm.'

Be calm?

What did women do to keep calm when their families were threatened? Did they pick up an embroidery frame, thread a bone needle and take a stitch? When what they really wanted was to fling the frame hard against a wall, watching the wood splinter, the cloth tear and the thread to knot? A perfect reflection of what life could become in an instant.

Iisoús Christós!

Bloody Christ!

He swept into his chamber and slammed the door so hard that dust drifted down from above and then he limped to the chest across the room to sweep Ephigenia's cushions off, his voice a rising howl. He imagined Viadro chiding him with a wry expression upon his leonine face, 'Well, *messere,* if anyone was in doubt about Basilike Street being under duress, they know differently now.' His window was open and even the heron on the roof opposite looked toward him in alarm. He didn't dare rip the window shut for fear he would break the valuable glass.

Instead, he stood breathing the sea air, pulling it in so deeply that his shoulders lifted halfway to his ears. Three or four times and his heart began to slow, the blood-lust draining to lesser parts of his body, so that his thinking became more rational. The anger still bubbled, but there was a cold clarity now. A focus that had never been this sharp in the past because he hadn't known where the Arab was. Now, he had news that the man had sailed into the vicinity and had abducted his daughter. Again. He needed to plan the final resolution. Because it would happen, there was a surety now that had never been so real before.

He looked at his hands, holding them out to see if they shook. Not a tremor. Nor marks and scars.

No tattoos…

He walked back to the chest and heaved the squeaking lid, reaching for the *paramerion* wrapped in its linen. Deeper in the corner of the trunk was another smaller bundle and he grabbed that, pulling the lid down, barely noticing Ephigenia's cushions scattered to the four corners of the room.

He descended the stair to the yard, to sit under the arbor in the last of the light, his back turned to the men near the gates.

He pulled the *paramerion* from its scabbard, the weapon sighing forth, glistening wantonly in the failing light and he shook the linen out across the table to place the *paramerion* upon it. Then he took the smaller bundle, unfolding it with care. A small worn whetstone fell onto the table, colliding with the blade so that a bell-like sound rang under the arbor. Not loud enough for the men to hear, but enough for Michael to grab the linen and muffle it. He wanted solitude.

Thus, he began.

With each rhythmic sweep of the whetstone, he uttered a pledge that death would come to he who deserved it, that it would not be swift. That there would be twelve thrusts for the twelve years. He closed his eyes, moving the whetstone by feel and then pressing the edge of the weapon with his forefinger.

'You must have the eyes of an angel, *Kýrie* Michael.' Michael's eyes flew open as Ephigenia placed an oil lamp on the table. 'You play with weapons in the dark and you can see? Ah, but there! You have cut your finger. Maybe the angels didn't guide you this night.' She bustled off, her sandals slapping on the tiles as the lamplight flickered in the dusk and a moth danced with death around its flame.

A bead of blood sat on his forefinger. The weapon was honed then. *Good.*

And making a blood oath with himself, he sucked his finger and then re-wrapped the whetstone. The *paramerion* slid with less than a whisper into its scabbard – a whisper that held death in its promise, and this time he left the linen swaddling off, folding the cloth into a pedantic square, then carrying everything to his chamber.

Below, he could hear voices as the companions began to move about the villa. It felt intrusive. He had set a path and their presence would only impede him on that pathway. The more so, he thought angrily, because one of them was a traitor.

'Michael!' Toby's voice sharpened as he raced up the stairs, boot-soles tapping urgently. 'Michael!' He threw open the door and Michael, closing his eyes and sighing, turned around.

Not Toby. Please not Toby…

'Michael,' Toby held out his hands, palms up, his hair stuck together with the blood from the harbour. 'I don't know what to…'

'To say? Nothing. I have been sorely used, Toby, and trust me in this. I shall take revenge of the worst kind. What are you doing up? You should be resting.'

'Meh,' Tobias shrugged and sat on the edge of Michael's bed. 'My head is thick. It will mend. Besides, I know what it feels like to want to avenge yourself and your family.'

'Yes. You do.' Michael wished he could believe Toby wasn't acting but he was so very good at it. It was his life's profession after all.

'Michael, do you think it's the *peirate*?'

Michael swung a knife-edged glance over Toby.

'Phocus told us,' the small minstrel explained.

'Then yes. I do. Unless he belongs to a band of *peirates* who all share the same mark.'

'But why? What do you have that he wants?'

'*I* have nothing. But Gisborne-ben Simon has the *byssus.*'

'He trades your daughter for *that*?'

'I have no idea. It is but a guess.'

'But how would he know about the *byssus*? Unless he spoke to the old weaver.'

'He may have. But Phocus thinks we have a whisperer of secrets.'

'The guards…'

'Phocus says no.'

'Ephigenia then. In idle gossip.'

'Perhaps…'

'Christo?'

'No.'

Tobias was silent as he stood up and began to walk around the room, straightening the icons on the wall, closing the window through which moths fluttered, and picking up the scattered cushions, replacing them on the chest. 'Then what you are saying is that it is one of your close friends. It is either Ariella, myself or Ahmed. Jesus, Michael!' His tone was one of sheer horror. 'Christ's bloody balls!'

'Exactly so.'

Toby hurried to Michael, grabbed his arm, shook him. 'It's not me, Michael. If you believe it is, then…'

Michael gritted his teeth and looked down at Toby. 'In truth, I don't know what I believe. But tell me this. Did Phocus imply that any of you might be the traitor?'

Toby's hand fell away from Michael's arm. 'No…'

'Then if it isn't you and you want me to believe you, say nothing to anyone. Not even to Ariella.'

'But…'

'No, Tobias! Do as I say.'

Tobias looked as if he were being drawn and quartered. Finally, he nodded his head. 'I can say nothing to convince you?'

'No.'

Tobias' expressions could be masterfully cloaked when he wanted. He had learned the art of invisibility and it was ingrained in his nature. The only time Michael had seen beyond the veil was when they had sailed away from Constantinople with the purple. Tobias' brother had died because of a traitorous action and Toby's face had held such pain. Such hatred.

He turned back from the door. 'Michael, if I may say, you look just as I felt when we sailed away from the Theodosian Harbour with the dye. I recognise what you feel. Take care, my friend.' He shut the door quietly.

It is not Toby. I know it is not. It can't be...

'Phocus?' he whispered. 'Phocus?'

A cot creaked in the dark and Leo's deep voice replied softly. 'He is not here, Michael. You want him urgently?'

'You know then.' Michael replied.

'Yes. Phocus informed us. He and Julius are investigating the waterfront people whilst I sleep and Hilarius and Bonus guard the gate after returning with Ariella and the jeweller. I am too obvious it seems, to do the surreptitious search and the others are good at obfuscation.'

Obfuscation?

'Leo, what *were* you before you became a mercenary?'

'A well-educated nomad chieftain.'

Michael had no idea if he was joking, unable to read his face in the shadows. But his voice held a faint upward lilt. 'And why did you not remain a *well-educated* chieftain?'

'Huh,' Leo replied. 'Tribal infighting. My brother drugged me almost to death, stole my wife and moved my tribe whilst I struggled for life. When I was strong enough to plan, I decided to leave Khorasan for the west where money could be made. In time, I had made enough from my fighting skills to buy property in Trabzon. If a nomad can cease being nomadic, then I shall be comfortable.'

'You have no children?'

Leo chuckled, a sound that gurgled up from the subterranean deeps of his belly. 'Probably. In Bulgaria or anywhere in the Balkans that I rested my loins for a moment. But I have no wish to claim them. *Kýrie* Michael, you are here for a reason. How can I help?' The cot creaked as the guard sat his broad height on the mattress.

'I want to find him, Leo.'

'That is what Julius and Phocus are doing.'

'No. *I* want to find him.'

Leo shifted on the cot. 'So what you are saying is that you don't want anyone else to approach him.'

'Exactly so. It's my right to confront him. I want the element of surprise.'

'Well, if *I* were you, that's exactly what *I* would want. But what of the traitor amongst you? Do you not think that he or she might forewarn the Arab?'

'Not if they are told something different from whatever facts we might have. Perhaps that he has disappeared.'

'I see.' There was a spark as he took a tinder and lit a candle. Long shadows flew across the walls, gyrating as a small breeze crept into the sleeping quarters. 'That assumes you can act to save your life. Because if your traitor has even the smallest clue that the Arab has been found, everything will be for nothing.' Leo's face appeared demonic in the candle light, planes shifting and changing, his eye-sockets just that – empty craters as expressionless as an angel from Hell.

'I know the risks, Leo. And despite being overwrought with grief at my daughter's plight, I am trying to think this through as best I can. It is why I sit here, talking to you. I trust you and I believe you think similarly to me. The most outstanding risk is the risk to my daughter's life. If anything will make me tread carefully, it is that. All I am asking is the element of surprise and to secure that, I will do what must be done. Also, you may forget – in my time, I have been a respected merchant, a shell-fisher, a trader from your own Khorasan and a thief, and each time, my life was at stake. It all required acting of a kind.'

The silence that followed was profound, to the point where Michael wondered if Leo had fallen asleep. 'Leo? Well?'

'Well what?' the bodyguard replied. 'There's nothing more to be said.'

Michael frowned. Was Leo backing away, was Michael's faith in him misplaced? 'Except that I would like to know if you agree.'

The big man sighed. There was so much about him that reminded Michael of Petrus, as if his very size meant he should never have to explain himself. 'Whether I agree or not is immaterial. It is what you wish. It is my job to protect you and make sure that happens.'

'But?'

Another sigh and a further creak of the long-suffering cot as Leo moved, leaning forward, moving into the light of the candle flame, clasping big scarred hands between his knees. 'If it were me, I would seek that son of a bitch out, tie his limbs to four horses and whip the horses off in four different directions.' He shrugged. 'Old tribal punishment in Khorasan. And then,' he held up a forefinger and tapped the air as if it were a solid piece of wood,

'I would retrieve his limbs, remove his head from his torso, chop everything into pieces and leave them for the kites to feed upon.' He sat back, the demonic features settling into a rictus of a grin. 'That's what I would do.'

'So you will help me?'

'You mean me alone, don't you.' It was a statement, not a question. 'You are asking me to go against the bonds I have with my comrades. It is quite a price to pay.'

'You wish me to pay you extra? Then I will...'

'No. I do not. But I will say this – you are, as you say, distraught. Perhaps you are not thinking quite as clearly as you could. My advice is to treat we guards as one. If you do that, then including yourself, you have six for the price of one and thus a six in one chance of finding the man whose life is forfeit.'

Michael pushed hard at the blood-haze that had plagued him since he left the Xylinites Convent. Leo was right, of course, and he could do no better than have seasoned mercenaries at his back.

He left Leo to sleep. Part of him was satisfied with the outcome. The mercenaries' lives had hardened them to the point where they saw life less through a prism of colours than in uncompromising black and white. Kill or be killed. Simple.

But the biggest part of Michael ached for Ioulia. She would be so afraid. Would the Arab have used her?

He wanted to weep with fear and frustration but there was no time. He pushed on into the hall and two faces looked up as he entered. Surprised, concerned.

'We thought you were in your chamber,' Tobias said.

'Michael,' Ariella laid her embroidery frame by the side of her chair. Even with tension on the air, the flamboyance of her stitching shone from the work she had laid aside – another of her assets to the merchant house. She had eschewed her widow's black around the house and the wine-tinted gown became her, complementing her autumnal colouring so that it was as if she and she alone were in that room, lit by sun, moon and stars. She glistened like a ruby or a garnet and he had seen every man at Contarini's banquet fall over themselves to be by the side of the Widow de Gisborne. By God, her pregnancy suited her, Michael thought, and her stomach seemed to expand as they lived and breathed.

'Michael,' she repeated. 'Can I help? There must be something…'

'I take it you know? Then no, there is nothing you can do. Unless you can find my daughter and return her to me unscathed. And in your condition, that would surely be a miracle.'

His bitterness rang round the hall like an off-key bell. But why not? Show me any parent, he thought, who would not be as passionately bitter if they had their daughter resurrected from the dead, only to lose that same child again before even holding her. Not to be able to beg forgiveness for what had befallen her. To be denied *that* surely accounted for everything. No apologies.

'But there must be things we can do. Contacts we can use…' Perhaps Ariella saw his pain and he knew in his heart he should respond gently and in kind. Instead,

'Arabs and Jews barely ever consort together to my knowledge. Unless there is money to be made.'

Unkind.

Ariella's face betrayed nothing of the hurt of his words. But then she had also schooled herself to invisibility. That was the trouble. His companions were accomplished forgers of life…

Tobias thrust his stool back, his face flushed with fury, no invisibility evident at all and Michael armed himself. 'That was uncalled for and rude,' Toby's voice was like the worst ice-storm as his hand gripped the pommel of the dagger in his belt. 'Mind your manners, *messere*.'

'Then I apologise, Ariella,' Michael said, but there was another part that wondered if he truly was as abject as he sounded. He was a traitor to himself, surely. 'I'm anguished because my daughter has been betrayed so often in life, and as her father I seem unable to prevent it. If this pig's bladder of an Arab wants money in exchange for her life, then I shall probably need to use your contacts to raise the ransom and I thank you for your offer. But the Arab must be found first. He is adept at hiding and therein lies the problem.'

'You don't think he will make contact with you or that we can find him?' Ah, sweet Ariella, forgiveness incarnate.

'To your first question, he might. To your second question – he is an Arab *peirate*, Ariella, and you and I both know he will be like a rat hiding in a rabbit warren. This city is rich with such hiding places. And besides, who is to say he isn't at sea already? He is no fool. Which reminds me. Where is our own Arab? Where *is* the redoubtable Ahmed?'

Toby's reply dripped with poison. 'He said Arabs find Arabs. Perhaps you don't believe him. Come, Ariella. I shall play dice with you in your chamber until Ephigenia helps you to bed.' He held out a hand and she took it, frowning and saying nothing, and without either of them looking back, they began to climb the stair, Michael left to stand in a pool of self-loathing.

He had no doubt there would be discussion over the dice – impassioned from Tobias and quite calmly rational from Ariella. Thus is a man reduced to a dark shadow of himself, he thought, and yet in truth, it is as it must be until I find my daughter.

He threw his head back and sucked air greedily through his nose. He wished he were alone simply *because* of his emotions and because he wanted *not* to have his friends involved at all. Not to have any of them proved to have sold him to the Devil.

There was only one person whose discretion he could count on and he wished he had removed himself there earlier. He turned and walked swiftly back to the guards' quarters.

'Leo! Leo, wake up!'

'What has happened?' The big man jumped from his cot, fully dressed and alert, a dagger in his grasp, gaze flying over Michael's shoulder to the door.

'Nothing yet. But I need to go to Water Street immediately, and I want you to accompany me.'

At the gate, he spoke softly to Hilarius and Bonus, sure that a whisper was a shout in the silence of evening. He asked that when Phocus returned, they should tell him where they had gone, and that they would be there overnight. For the rest of the house, nothing was to be said at all. Hilarius had saluted and closed the gate behind them.

They walked along Basilike Street, beginning the gentle incline to Third Hill, keeping to the shadows, both men adept at moving like phantoms, albeit one with a limp. Not a word was spoken as they progressed along the grand sweep of the Mese, the large thoroughfare that proved daily that it was the land-based lifeblood of the city – always noisy, crammed with folk of all classes and bursting with the colour of Byzantine life.

Now it was empty.

Close to the basilica of Saint Basil's and the stair up to the top of Third Hill and the Valens Aqueduct, they heard booted feet and voices and they squeezed into a narrow gap between the basilica and the ruins of old Roman baths. Four guards walked past, their *klivanion* cuirasses creaking, *spathions* rattling at their sides. They walked in unison, the tattoo of their booted soles sending a message that this was a city with laws and that no over-reach would be tolerated. Criminals' and law-breakers' remains hung on walls as a reminder of what laws were for. The lives of men meant little as Emperor Alexios III Angelus defended himself and his empire.

'Serious...' Leo whispered so that Michael could barely hear. The feet marched on and Leo muttered more loudly. 'The devil to wear in battle, too hot. Rather them than me.'

The feet had moved on out of hearing and they eased out of the space and on up the stairs, Michael touching the bricks for support as his kneecap slid and clicked back and forth with each step.

'Your knee?' Leo asked.

'I will survive. Besides, I am to see a physician...'

At the top of the stair they were confronted with the two massive levels of the Valens Aqueduct. A long thin street passed via an archway beneath the span and as they looked out over the top of Saint Basil's and across to the pallidly lit Theodosian Harbour, water raced along the stone channels, heading down to the cisterns of the city. Michael recalled the story of Tobias and Tommaso fleeing across the top of the huge structure to escape to Ahmed's boat. He also recalled that it was Ahmed who came to their aid as they were ambushed atop. A good friend to his peers surely – a man to be trusted. Tobias would no doubt think so.

He and Leo turned in the direction of the Hippodrome and Sancta Sophia and soon, the well-remembered iron gate that led into Anwar's property faced them. 'We have no choice but to make noise, Leo.' He rapped the gate. 'Maybe the residents of Water Street are used to night time calls.'

The ornamental grille slid open.

'Abdul, *Salaam Alaykum*. It's me, Michael. I need the doctor's care.'

'Michael!' The gate was unchained and opened by an elderly man. 'It is good to see you, sir. Are you ill?'

'I have damaged the bone in my knee…'

'Then I shall wake the doctor,' Abdul answered, looking up at Leo with awe.

'This is Leo, my personal guard. Can you give him a sleeping space for the time I am here?'

'You will stay?'

'I may have to…'

Leo had propped himself under Michael's shoulder, adding life to the serious image Michael was spinning for the old gatekeeper.

'Then come to the house. Are you able to walk?'

'Not well. But Leo helps me.'

'Tuh,' Abdul clicked his tongue against his teeth. 'I remember the last time you were with us, wasn't it leg trouble then? You must be more careful.' The old man closed and chained the gate and lit their way through gardens to the cool space of the house. They entered the front chamber where divans lined the walls and cushions of colour and texture were stacked on each other, a gentle space, designed to relieve pain and tension.

Michael remembered it well. For a long time, he'd reclined upon those cushions, watching light move in ever-shifting patterns across the walls and until he was well enough to escape to the cavern close by the convent. Tended by the physician and his wife, or Abdul – always with respect and affection.

'Michael!' Sophia rushed into the room, her head covered untidily, her eyes glazed from deep sleep. Her voice was throaty as she hugged him to her frame, gold bracelets jingling. 'What has happened? Are you hurt? Oh, and you have a friend with you…' She stared up at the guard, a diminutive woman with an air of confidence. '*Salaam Alaykum*, I am Sophia, wife of Anwar al Din, the physician, and you are very much welcome in my home.' She could not disguise her awe as he towered over her.

Leo bowed his head, returning the greeting and as Michael began to explain their late presence, Abdul returned with Anwar on his heel. The physician had dressed hastily and still had bare feet and an uncovered head, his steel grey hair brushing his shoulders. So like Mehmet that Michael's western life passed before his eyes.

In moments he had been seated, with his leg supported on a tooled leather stool, Leo had been taken away for refreshment by Abdul and Sophia and the physician had sat himself on another stool by Michael's knee. A faint rumble of voices drifted from the far reaches of the house and then there was silence.

Anwar folded up the length of Michael's tunic, and then began to unroll the grubby linen from around the knee. As the cloth fell away, Michael's eyes widened at the amount of sweaty swelling indents creased into the skin where the bruised flesh had strained at the bandage.

'Methinks,' said Anwar, palpating the kneecap and tutting as he pushed gently at the swelling. 'You have probably done permanent injury to what might have been remedied if you had taken my suggestions to heart. You will be forever lame, I suspect. This,' he said, pushing his fingertips into the swollen flesh, 'shows me that you have put the joint under great strain.'

Michael didn't try to hide the pain. It was what it was.

'But in any case, this is not why you are here, is it?' Anwar's eyes were as dark as oakgall ink. He had deeply incised wrinkles at the corners and a chiselled face that softened as it further examined the knee.

Michael began to talk as the candles flickered in the brass lamps. Anwar listened. That was the beauty of this visit. He allowed Michael to spill every detail without interjecting and even then, when Michael had run dry, he sat without comment, letting the stillness of the night soothe.

Eventually he removed his hands from Michael's knee, saying, 'The joint is over-heated. We must ease it and you must rest till the morning. And *then,* I will tell you how I can help you. Be assured that as an Arab amongst Arabs in this city, I *can* help.'

Exactly what Ahmed had said…

Later, with a mug in his hands and the smell of aromatic spices and camomile drifting to his nose, he watched Anwar rub an unguent into his knee. Willow, he had said, combined with garlic, cinnamon, camphor and frankincense.

As Michael swallowed the last of the tea, the physician began to bind the joint and Michael said, 'Phocus believes I may have been betrayed but I cannot imagine why. Worse, he says it may have been my own friends who betrayed me – Tobias, in God's name! Maybe Ahmed. Even Ariella…'

Anwar looked up at him, frowning, but then continued rolling meticulous folds round and round and Michael's limbs loosened, his eyelids drooping as the gentle doctoring continued. His tongue wouldn't work as he tried to articulate words. He knew what he wanted to say, but nothing emerged.

Instead, they echoed in his mind as he drifted.

You drugged me. Are you also my enemy?

He woke to the familiar light patterns shifting across the white painted walls. But they were weaker, end-of-day flitterings. He allowed the somnolent heaviness of his limbs to anchor him to the divan on which he lay. Someone had placed a cushion beneath his head and a soft rug draped across him. He fingered the lapis-coloured weave. From Khorasan, he thought, the idea sparking in his mind and then dying.

Someone shuffled around the room and he became aware of Sophia placing lamps here and there. She passed by him and looked down.

'Ah,' she murmured and knelt to take his hand.

'He drugged me...'

'Anwar never does anything to hurt people, Michael. You and your knee needed rest. He gave it to you.' She pushed herself to stand and sighed. 'It has been a long and ... interesting day in this house.'

'Day?' Michael pulled himself to sit up, brushing his hair back, feeling the grittiness of sleep in his eyes, his mouth stale where he had slept with it open.

'I will get you some peppermint tea,' Sophia turned away.

'Don't drug me, Sophia. Please. I must find my daughter...'

But Sophia had gone, and Michael stood, the rug falling to his toes, his wrinkled tunic folds following. He limped to the door, vague pain on the edges of his senses and for that, if nothing else, he was grateful. He pulled the door open to see late afternoon cloud drifting high above the Propontis, the ubiquitous gulls swooping and calling.

A busy day...

And he had missed it.

Sophia came back with a rattling enamelled tray, a mug, a flask and some nuts and dates but he made no move to accept the refreshment.

'It is not drugged,' she said. 'Eat, drink and you will feel better. Abdul is fetching washing cloths and a bowl and when you are ready, Anwar waits for you under the arbor. You remember where it is? He has news that will interest you.' She left on the wings of her prophetic words, passing down the hall to the nether quarters.

Interest me, he thought? There is only one thing I want to know right now.

Arabs find Arabs…

He threw back the peppermint tea, chewed on a date and was drinking the last of the tea when Abdul walked in with his supplies. 'Shall I help you?' he asked.

Michael shook his head. 'Thank you but no. If you could tell Anwar I won't be long, I would be grateful.'

As the old factotum left, he dipped his hands in the cold water and scrubbed at his eyes and mouth, feeling rough stubble on his chin. Abdul had thoughtfully left a comb, a beautifully wrought piece of ivory and probably Sophia's, so Michael dragged it through his hair. Adjusting his tunic and girdle, fruitlessly searching for his boots, he took a breath, not daring to hope that Anwar had discovered anything. And where was Leo? He had not been mentioned at all. He padded barefoot out the door and along the path past shrubs of rosemary and tubs of mint and tarragon. Doves bobbed their heads at him, burbling their discontent at being disturbed.

The arbor had a view of the Propontis – clear and unsullied, and the sea sparkled in the last of the day's light. Down on the Harbour of Theodosius, galleys and *caiques* swung at their moorings and below Water Street, on the slope of Third Hill, men's voices drifted up toward the physician's gardens. Anwar sat at the table, *keffiyeh* draped over his head and robes pale and neat. Even Michael, angry and hungover, had to admit to the man's dignity. Another man sat with his back to Michael dressed in a worn cloak, head covered by a dirty *keffiyeh*. He turned as Michael bent beneath the budding grape vines.

'So, Michael Sarapion,' his tones lifted the hair on Michael's neck. 'At last! You sleep while we do all the hard work.' Only Ahmed could be so insouciant.

'I slept because I was drugged.' Michael turned to the physician. 'I don't thank you for that, Anwar.'

'You needed to rest your mind and your knee,' Anwar replied placidly. 'You will thank me. I would say get over your misplaced anger and listen, but if you do not want to, then I shall call Abdul and he can unlock the gate for you. But remember I am here if you need me.'

Chastened, Michael sat, his eyes on Anwar who nodded.

'Good,' the physician said. 'Short story? We have found him.'

'In truth, Ahmed found him and came straight here,' he continued as Michael's attention became blade sharp. He could bare believe that it had been so easy. A day only.

Arabs finding Arabs.

He turned his attention to the harbour view. Somewhere down there…

'Not at the Harbour of Theodosius, my friend,' Ahmed said. 'He's in Galata.'

'The Jewish quarter?' Incredulity crept into Michael's voice.

'No, there is a small enclave of Arab traders on the waterfront.' Michael levered himself up to go but Ahmed grabbed his wrist. 'Sit. He is going nowhere immediately. He is sick. And as Anwar said, Phocus watches the house.'

Michael subsided momentarily.

'He has the flux,' Anwar explained. 'I have examined him and given him something to help. Eventually. In the meantime, he is too ill to move off his pallet. Perhaps he ate bad food.'

'Ioulia?'

'We do not know yet,' Anwar replied, carefully. 'But we do not foresee an issue in finding out where she is.'

It must have been obvious to both men that Michael's heart shattered just a little bit more because Anwar reached over and clasped his hand. 'You need to hear what Ahmed has to say, before you go racing away. Please trust me on this. I went to see this man you hate and I tended him. He was feverish and making little sense but I will return to him later today. In the meantime…'

'In the meantime, you want me to sit and wait? I can't!'

'Yes, you can,' the Arab sea captain interrupted. 'Things are playing out now, Michael. The piece of scum is sick, he is forced to lie low. No one but a physician will go near him because people are suspicious of the flux. I would suggest you go with Anwar later and see for yourself.'

'God Almighty, I will kill him!'

'Eventually yes, I have no doubt you will. But not yet.' Ahmed's reply was serious, grave, its tone one with which Michael was unfamiliar in the man. Odd…

'Let me tell you how I found him.' Ahmed leaned back against his chair. 'I did not intend to sit whilst my friend's daughter was bartered for like a piece of meat. I slipped out of Basilike Street, which in itself wasn't easy. Hilarius was all for pulling me back and tying me down, but I told him he would be dispensed with if he did not let me go. That I had your ear and he needed to remember that.'

CHAPTER TWELVE

'I have no use of men who are not obedient and whom I cannot trust,' Ahmed said.

Hilarius flicked two fingers against his forehead, unbarring the gates and stepping back, merely asking if Ahmed was armed. As Ahmed walked away, he thought that the guards were good men, the kind of men he would like in his galley crews.

He kept to the shadows of the houses, aware that guards crawled over the city at night like spiders. Alexios III Angelus must expect rebellion against his rule at every turn, he thought, as he crept into an alley, allowing a quadrum *of guards to pass by. They looked like Varangians – even in the dark, one was aware of the height and breadth of the men, and the moonlight caught on that remarkable fair and russet hair.*

But Ahmed shifted quietly, like a rat or a scorpion, not a pebble or a scrap of dirt moved as he passed by. It was an art-form learned early in his life. One didn't reach the lofty heights of a galleymaster and ship owner otherwise. He had risen from the gutters and he knew how to navigate them.

He reached the Harbour of Theodosius without incident, grabbing a keffiyeh *that hung on a rope between two tawdry dwellings. It was damp, as if some caring woman had washed it for her man and hung it out to dry and he hurried well beyond the house where he could change his appearance without being seen.*

He found a pile of empty barrels stacked on the dockside and sat, folding the keffiyeh *into a triangle and laying it over his head. He folded back a band on his forehead, something any Arab could do in his sleep as he took one of the points,* twisting it, draping it across the forehead band to tuck into the back. Then taking the other point, twisting it and draping it under his chin before tucking it firmly at the back on the other side. His bald, distinctive head was concealed and by sitting on the ground, he dirtied his robes, patting the length with dusty hands.

As he worked, he thought of Michael's evident pain, of how the father had lost his daughter again, just as he had found her. He knew what loss was like. He had lost his own family and the grief always sat in the soul, eroding corners. He knew what Michael felt, of course he did, and he liked the man from Sozopolis and trusted him. It was enough to encourage him to help. Besides, as he had said, *Arabs find Arabs.*

He guessed Michael had been betrayed, but unlike Phocus, he thought it had perhaps only been accidentally from within. And in the meantime, he would find the man with the tattoo.

Insh'Allah…

He found the house of a man he knew, an Arab craftsman, a builder and repairer of boats, a man called Rasheed who knew all the gossip along the foreshore.

Rasheed barely opened the door to a slit after Ahmed's light tap.

'Rasheed, it is I,' Ahmed said and slid his toe in the crack. 'Let me in.'

The man opened the door enough for the shipmaster to slip through and then shut it and barred it.

'Salaam Alaykum. *Why are you afraid?*' Ahmed asked.

'Alaykum as Salaam, *Ahmed. We aren't loved, you know this. It goes back through time. Too many wars between us and the Byzantines. We are tolerated, that is all. Just like the Jews.*' The scruffy shipbuilder walked to his little kitchen in the back of the house. He had no wife nor children, but the space was tidy and clean and his tools lay on a trestle where he had been sharpening and oiling them. The smell of oils and timber drifted through the house, a heady odour that made Ahmed long to cast off and sail away from Constantinople. It was the fragrance of vessels, seas, trading and freedom.

But he had things to do…

Rasheed poured two mugs of pomegranate syrup and led Ahmed back to the main room. 'What do you want, Ahmed? I have already found your second boat. On top of your first. And they are both the essence of seaworthiness.'

'You know who comes and goes, Rasheed. I am looking for a newly arrived Arab. He came yesterday. He has a tattoo on his hand.'

'Ah…'

It was all Ahmed needed as confirmation that the man who had abducted Ioulia was here, in the city somewhere.

'Where?'

'He docked briefly in the harbour and then just before dusk yesterday, after loading goods…'

'What goods?'

'Pitch, food, water, oils, rugs.' Rasheed shrugged. 'An ordinary loading for someone who doesn't intend to go far and would perhaps be working on his vessel somewhere close.'

'Rugs?'

'He's a trader like you, isn't he? Maybe they are a good buy.'

'Not like me Rasheed. Never like me, Insh'Allah. So, where is he?'

'Galata. There is a small dry-dock there.'

Ahmed threw back the last of the syrup in his mug and stood. 'Thank you, my friend.' He pulled some silver from his purse and laid it on the man's table. 'We are good friends, Rasheed. Keep quiet about this and I will make it even more worth your while. If you do not keep silent, then be warned. Salaam Alaykum.'

He unbarred Rasheed's door, but before he could leave, Rasheed asked, 'What has he done that is so bad?'

'Stolen my friend's daughter.' Ahmed slipped out, heading back the way he had come to Basilike Street.

Phocus stood in the shadows of Basilike Street when Ahmed arrived. 'You look different,' he said indicating the worn keffiyeh on Ahmed's head. 'A good enough disguise, but not enough, I think. Did you know that Michael and Leo have gone to Water Street?'

'No. But it does not surprise me. Michael trusts Anwar. You think I need to change my appearance even more?'

Phocus nodded, adding that rougher clothing would effect a complete transformation and to use his own battle-worn tunic and cloak.

Dawn had just begun to lighten the edge of the eastern sky, a faint running stitch of gold sitting low on the dark grey velvet of the horizon as Ahmed and Phocus arrived at the Nerion Harbour. Slipping quietly along the waterfront, Phocus found a flat-bottomed boat with a stern oar.

'It'll do,' said Ahmed. 'And we can be thankful it is calm.'

The Horn was like burnished gold as the sky lightened a fraction more. But there were no reflections of the hills behind, nor of the lights which were beginning to flicker and die.

'You are happy to steal it?' Phocas said as he slipped into the boat, beginning to undo the rope that was knotted to a ring in the slimy wall.

'Our needs are greater than whomever left this here to rot. We will be lucky to make it to Galata without springing a plank.' He slid into the bow seat as Phocus took up the stern-oar which squeaked at its post. They began to exit the harbour across the still waters and he watched the hills of the city drift away behind Phocus' back, turning then to glance at Galata and wanting to beat that arse-hole peirate into a strip of fine shoe leather.

'How shall we find him?' Phocus asked as he poled the craft. They were early enough in the morning to observe the infamously secure chains being lowered between the promontory of Galata and the promontory at the base of First Hill. Now vessels could readily come and go in daylight and others could lie protectively at their moorings in the various harbours.

'He's at a house in Saint Paul Street, close by Saint Paul's Basilica which in itself is amusing. You would think he would be deep on the slopes of Galata amongst the dense housing, and not immediately behind the walls. But then he is wily...' He pursed his bottom lip as he thought on it. The peirate was slimy and had enemies in all quarters, but perhaps less over in Galata than any of the harbours of the city, which was of course why he had sailed there yesterday before the chains were raised. It's what Ahmed would have done and ugly as the thought was, he knew it took one to know one.

Phocus remarked on Ahmed's luck that his shipbuilder friend was so astute and aware of people coming and going. Ahmed just grinned. Serendipitous for sure. But then life was always about being in the right place at the right time and if the man was going to abduct someone from the Xylinites Convent, it was a given he would have docked at the closest harbour – the Harbour of Theodosius. He would have re-entered the city from the gate of Saint Romanus and wound his way straight down Seventh Hill. In addition, Ahmed would bet his life on the fact that one of the rolled rugs was wrapped round Ioulia.

Michael frowned. 'All those enclaves – Arab, Jew, Christian and you find him like that!' He snapped his fingers. 'A man I have not seen a hair of nor heard a word of for twelve years. Such serendipity.'

'That is exactly the word I thought to use,' said Ahmed. 'Look, my friend, the boat-builder Rasheed, is at the Theodosian docks every day. He attends the harbour markets, lives by the harbour, buys his timber from suppliers at the harbour. If a rat so much as farts he knows. Lucky for you.'

Indeed, thought Michael, lucky for me and by the Saints and the Theotokis, I am glad! 'So what happened when you found him?'

Ahmed leaped ashore, rope in hand, dragging the punt onto the shingle close by the dry-dock. There was a lightweight dromon *pulled up and men were beginning to climb ladders to the decks and to work around the hull from the shore, hammering, repairing. He recognised the boat. Oh yes...*

'Recognised it? How?' Michael broke in.

'You described it well, Michael.'

Had he? He couldn't remember...

'Follow me,' Ahmed ordered Phocus. 'And don't speak. Let me do all the talking.'

They walked up to the vessel and Ahmed waylaid a flea-bitten boy who could have done with a good feed and a bath. 'You work on the boat?'

'Yes sir.' The boy showed rotten teeth. 'Just on repairs.'

'Do you know the owner?'

'Mmm,' the boy mumbled, eyeing off Phocus' spathion.

'Is he still at Saint Paul Street?'

'Yes sir...'

Ahmed began to walk toward a gate in the wall with Phocus close behind.

'But sir,' the boy called out. 'He is sick. He has the shits real bad.'

Ahmed tossed a coin to the boy and kept walking.

'Sick,' Phocus said. 'The flux. You will still see him?'

'Yes. Are you afraid?'

Phocus replied that everyone got the flux in the Balkans, that raging bellies and filthy arses were a fact of war. 'But can I ask a question? How did you know this man would be at Saint Paul Street?'

'I would ask the same,' said Michael, his guts rolling this way and that. One moment he thought he could trust Ahmed. The next? 'What do you hide, Ahmed?'

'Nothing, my friend. It's just that Saint Paul Street is the place where I know some Arabs live and I just decided to try the waters with the boy. As you see, it worked.'

'Long story, Phocus. I will just have to ask you to trust me.'

Ahmed didn't turn around to see Phocus' reaction. There was a story to tell but a time and place was needed and preferably with Michael, above and beyond everyone. He had tried to tell him prior to the banquet, but luck hadn't been on his side which was odd, as that happened so rarely...

They walked along the wide road between the defensive walls and the hill. Houses were crammed cheek by jowl and so different from the grand buildings of the city. Here in Galata and Pera, they were half-timbered with overhanging balconies, perhaps not unlike Basilike Street but the Venetian Quarter had expense and style, and stone. These reminded one of the Balkans, of Trabzon — worn timbers and matchstick extrusions.

'Galata's almost an after-thought, isn't it?' said Phocas.

Ahmed said nothing. Buildings were buildings. He preferred living on a boat, so it made little difference what houses looked like.

The sun had risen well above the roof lines and the pocked and paved streets of Galata gleamed dully. But even to the most cynical, and Ahmed was one of those, it had an aged charm that was missing in the ordered streets of Constantinople. The two men passed under a stone arch in a wall and at the north east end of a terraced street, a small brick basilica stood proud. Trees graced the hill behind and there was a sense of remove from the city across the water. So near yet so far.

'Saint Paul's,' said Ahmed. 'This is the street.' He stalked along, examining doorways. Blood began to hammer through his veins as he spotted the place he sought, and his hand crept to the kilij *he wore tucked in a sash under the cloak. If he could, he would have slammed into the house, surprising the sick man and removing him from his torso. It would surely help his flux. But there was so very much at stake, and he needed to curb his excesses. Just for a while longer. He owed it to Michael...*

'How so?' Michael asked. 'I would appear to owe *you* for finding him...'

Christ Jesus. He just wanted to find his daughter…

'I owed it to you, Michael, so that Ioulia could be found and returned to safety.'

'This is it,' he said, stopping, Phocus standing by his side. 'Let me go in. You wait.'

'You are sure?'

'He is a man bedevilled right now, Phocus. I doubt he can do anything.'

Except that he will have a man watching the house and at the first sign of real trouble, there will be standing orders involving lives of hostages. It is what men like this peirate *did.*

'We will be watched,' he added, 'so we must be careful. See if you can spot the watcher whilst I am inside. If I'm too long, come inside quietly but without a drawn weapon. It's best to be careful with Ioulia's safety at stake.'

'As you say. I'm yours to command.'

Ahmed climbed the steps to rap on the door and with no response, he tried the latch. It was unlocked, and he pushed the ill-fitting timber wide. The stench that wound outside nearly knocked him sideways and he turned his head and took a breath. He had come across this before, but it didn't make things any better. The illness could spread rapidly – that much he knew. But there was a life – lives – at stake.

He walked in.

The peirate *lay on a pallet, the mattress and his clothes stained. A bucket overflowed in the corner of the room and a pitcher of Allah knew what lay upended. The man was pale and in the quiet of the room, his stomach roared like a caged lion.*

'Nāsir! Nāsir! Wake up!'

Michael slammed the table with his fist. 'How do you know his name? You bloody traitor!' He moved to grab Ahmed but the Arab held his arm as if he would break it.

'I am no traitor. Before the banquet, I said I had something I wished to talk to you about, do you remember? This man was the man I wanted to tell you of. I wanted to warn you. I had heard he was approaching the city.'

'You bastard!'

'Michael!' Anwar shouted, fury sending the doves clacking skywards. 'Let him finish! Remember your daughter! You have cause to thank Ahmed, so sit or I shall throw you out.'

Michael subsided but he could feel his hackles had risen too high to ward off the bloodlust that had begun to rush around his head again. Christ Jesus, if Jehanne had known this was the outcome of a journey to the past, would she have been so approving of him coming back to the east? He was nothing like the man he used to be.

'Nāsir! Nāsir!' Ahmed wanted to shake him until his brains fell out his nose – this man who had destroyed so many lives.

The deathly ill man on the bed opened crusty eyes and blinked to focus on the intruder who had turned to close the door. As Ahmed turned back, he awoke more fully and gave a weak grin, grabbing at his belly as the foul wind and liquid escaped to the mattress. 'Salaam Alaykum, brother. If I had known you would visit me, I would have made an effort.' He grunted. 'As you see...'

'Brother be damned. You stopped being my brother a long time ago. I won't honour you with a blessing by return. You are not worth it.'

'Brother? Brother!' Michael shrilled, slamming the table with a palm.
'Michael!' Anwar said. 'I will not ask you again.'

'Maybe not. But I have something you want, don't I? Or you would not have come.'

Ahmed ignored him. 'Who cares for you in this state?'

'No one. They are too scared. Anyway, this is a passing illness. I ate something – bad goat maybe, who knows? It will get better.'

'Methinks you could possibly die before it does,' Ahmed walked to the bucket and fabricating an untruth, he said, 'Did you know you have blood in your shit?'

For a moment Nāsir's eyes widened but then he shrugged. 'And what do you care?'

'I don't overmuch. But I can help you. If you want. Insh'Allah.'

'Ahmed, I am your brother. I know what you are like. You do nothing without reward. What do you want by return? Humour me. If there is blood, I need humouring. Be kind...'

Ahmed hated Nās.

Nāsir. Had hated him for many months, for years. Had avoided him since he was young, disowned him, begged Allah to remake he, Ahmed, in any other image but his brother's. It seemed to have worked. And then...

230

'You have abducted a young woman.'

'Ah,' the word was sighed out with pain. 'The young woman. You bargain my life for hers when there is...'

'I will get an Arab physician here and you will tell us where she is.'

'Will I?'

'You want to live? To use all the treasure you've stolen in your misbegotten life?'

Nāsir moved his head from side to side on the pillow, mouth turned down. ''Tis a good bargain, I must admit. I do have rather a lot... But then there is that byssus.'

'You know of the byssus?' Ahmed tried to keep the surprise from his voice.

'Oh yes.'

'How?'

Nāsir farted again and groaned. 'Allah save me, please! I have nothing left inside...' He grasped his belly. Then, in a slightly stronger voice he replied. 'There was an old woman in Limnos.'

'And there it was, Michael. The old woman who sold the *byssus* to Christo. She was on the waterfront when Nāsir sailed into Limnos and one thing led to another. Like all of us, my brother knew the value of such cloth and as the old woman said it would be many months, maybe a year or more, before more became available, he just sailed ever closer to Constantinople on his misbegotten way. May Allah curse him to the fires of al-Nar, he swore he would get the cloth somehow. Sadly, too, he knew of my connection with Gisborne-ben Simon so it suited him to follow us.'

'But how did he find out about *me*, about Ioulia?'

'Pure serendipity. But then isn't that what we just said? Isn't that life?'

Ahmed described how Ephigenia had been talking with Christo at the corner of Basilike Street after Michael's revelations to the household. The two had quietly commiserated over Michael's pain. What they didn't know was that squatting against the corner like some street beggar was a filthy-hearted Arab who knew Nāsir well and sold the information for money. Whereupon his throat was cut and the money re-pocketed.

'Nāsir might pretend to pay for something he wants, but he invariably gets his coin back. And now he had potential for a high ransom,' Ahmed said. 'I think he had thought merely to steal the *byssus*. But when he had Ioulia's name...' he shrugged. 'I tell you, this is the kind of game Allah plays

231

when he is unhappy with something we have done. I am yet to work out what that might be. What have *you* done, Michael, that would make *your* God treat you in such an underhand way?'

'I don't give a curse in Hell for my God. He let this happen to Ioulia in the first place, an innocent woman in a convent!' Michael was as cold as ice with rage. It was a clear-thinking feeling, with none of the confusion of red battle lust. With this he was calm. He had a list in his head and now Christo and Ephigenia were added to it because they chatted mindlessly on the street and his daughter became a pawn.

Unaware of the frost settling in Michael's heart and head, Ahmed continued, 'It was a simple case then of Nāsir waiting and watching. He is like oil, my brother – he slides like a snake and finds out things people try to hide. You have seen how an *espie* works for Gisborne, you even married one. It is only necessary to be diligent and sift everything you see and hear. He went to Xylinites, posed as one of the men from our house with a well-crafted note to the *hegoumene*. It actually became very simple. The ransom was to exchange the *byssus* for Ioulia.'

'And I would have done that. Gisborne-ben Simon be damned.'

'No one would blame you, Michael,' said Ahmed. 'But now we will have Ioulia *and* the *byssus*.' He stopped for a moment and looked down at his hands and then continued. 'Nāsir has nothing to bargain with but his own life and I believe you want to take it. So be it. *Insh'Allah*.'

Michael wondered at the ease with which Ahmed was throwing his brother's life away. 'I owe you,' he said.

Ahmed's face stilled, perhaps he too was burned with the winter frost. 'Kill him, Michael,' he said, his voice uncompromising. 'For I cannot.'

Anwar looked away, out over the beauty of the harbour as if it would mitigate the baldness of Ahmed's words. Around them, the seabirds swooped and cried, and the doves returned and cooed and pecked at their feet.

'Then,' Michael replied, 'tell me the last, Ahmed.'

'Anwar came to Nāsir's house,' Ahmed continued. 'By this time, my brother knew that he had little left to bargain with on any account, not even with Allah, his God. For the first time in my life, I saw him not care, he was so weak. And trust me, Nāsir always makes sure he bargains to win. It is why he took Ioulia after all. I needed Anwar to keep him alive until we knew where she was. After that, he could die. I didn't care, still don't.' Ahmed looked down at his hands, rubbed the palms together as if he wiped dirt from them and pulled his leg across his knee, his foot tapping the air with an urgency that defied his normally composed arrogance. 'Anwar treated him like the consummate physician he is,' he continued. 'With pleasant things like apple, garlic, coriander and more besides. And water, a lot of water. Nāsir just did as he was told. I have never seen him so compliant. But then I have never seen him look like a dirty rag either.'

'*Iisoús Christós!*' Michael swore, gripping the edge of the trestle, a stray splinter of sundried wood driving into his palm. 'I don't care how he was treated, I care only that Ioulia can be retrieved unmolested.'

Ahmed's eyes rested on Michael's hand. 'Which is why I came here as soon as I could. You do realise you have driven a splinter into yourself?'

'You think I care?' Michael thumped the table again and Anwar stood, taking Michael's hand in his own and using the tip of his knife to ease the hefty splinter out. The sounds of the city drifted up the hill and attempted ingress into the gardens. But the foliage of cedar and budding oak, of olive and oleander all conspired to veil the men from the sounds.

'Please,' Michael begged. 'Do you know where she is? Have you an idea?' How often had he begged in his life he wondered. Perhaps it had been constant since receiving that fateful message in Lyon from Father Nicholas. When was that? A lifetime ago and yet only a three month. Had he become plaintive? Did the Saints turn their backs at his whining? And what about God, the great Pantokrator?

Anwar tamped his finger down on the beads of blood oozing from Michael's palm where the splinter had been. 'Come with me now and you can ask your questions.'

'He will not die before we get there?' Michael never trusted the games God played.

'I think not. Unless he has taken his own life and I suspect he has no plans to do that just yet. And we have Phocus watching that his men do not spirit him away.'

Ahmed stood. 'The man has a king's ransom stored across the seas in various boltholes. It calls to him the way the sea calls to me. He has every reason to try to live yet. I will attend you both.'

'Ahmed, go ahead to the harbour of Nerion,' said Anwar, 'and find us a ferryman, and find a litter to carry Michael and myself from Water Street to the harbour. I am old, and Michael is lame. He has subjected his knee to enough for the moment.'

Ahmed left, touching his forehead and heart and the air appeared empty, as it always did when he vacated a space. He was such a large personality and Michael would have bet his life that he may have been the traitor. There was so much one didn't know about him, dark corners in an otherwise bright façade. And yet without him, Michael would not be that much closer to finding Ioulia. He owed the man more than his life…

'Does Ahmed accompany us because he fears for us? Or for his brother?' he said softly, not directing the thought anywhere, but Anwar replied.

'You will not harm Nāsir yet, Michael.'

'You think?' Michael began to walk along the path with the physician. His knee ached but he would not say. He wanted his head to be blindingly clear.

'I do. You will allow him a fair fight.'

'You condone my desire to kill him? I am surprised.'

'I condone nothing, my friend. I just pick up the pieces afterward and hope that those I value will not be hurt.'

'Where is Leo?'

Anwar explained that the guard was ordered back to Basilike Street where the need was greater. 'You will excuse me, I have supplies to collect before the litters arrive. And you must get your cloak and your footwear. As to your knee – shall we check it now or later?'

'Later. Ioulia's needs are greater.'

Anwar touched Michael's shoulder with understanding and left him standing at the entrance to the front room. He began searching for his boots, finding them under the fallen blanket, half-shoved beneath the divan. He needed time to think, quiet time, and so he folded Sophia's blankets, tidying the cushions, placing his mug neatly on the enamelled tray along with the comb.

The physician was right. He wanted a fair fight with Nāsir, which surprised him because nothing Nāsir had done was fair. But Michael wanted the man to be able to stand and hold a weapon and he wanted him to fight back. For what is the point of revenge if one can't look one's enemy in the eye, watching them pant for air, watching the thoughts shifting through their minds, the pattern of fear in their eyes.

But all that was when Anwar declared Nāsir able to stand. In the meantime, he would tell them where was Ioulia. Only when she was freed and declared safe and whole – then and only then would he avenge his family.

'Michael! The litters are here. Are you done?' Anwar called from the gates and strapping on his knife, he hurried to join the doctor.

Each litter was curtained, which suited Michael. He laid his head back and tried to settle his mind. But if not brooding on Ioulia, he thought of Helena, of how she would be so gladdened to know their daughter lived. And he thought of Jehanne – strong willed, outspoken Jehanne whom he wished was right by his side at this moment. Would she bless his desire for revenge or would she condemn him as no better than Nāsir? Worse, what would his daughter think? She who had been in sanctuary in a convent and whose hours had been filled with prayer.

He must not think on that. Nāsir's life was forfeit. It was no one else's business. But he did think on the *byssus* and how easy it had been for Nāsir to find out about it. Who else knew? What value was there on the old woman's secrets now? To obtain more of the cloth in the future would be a battle of price advantage and nothing more. And suddenly Michael had an image of a thin Genovese in his mind and he knew without doubt that Branco Izzo knew of the cloth. He sat up, the litter tipping slightly and the bearers calling for him to hold still. Somewhere amongst the emotional turmoil of his mind, a thought was forming. He just didn't have the time to articulate it yet…

The sounds around him changed. Soft light pierced the rough weave of the linen curtains and the sound of seabirds became shriller. The cloying odour of the harbour became stronger and he took comfort from it as the bearers held the litter firmly and he slid out. Ahmed was helping Anwar with his linen bags and in time the three had walked to a small *caique* tied to the side of one of the wharves.

'It is a *caique* that now belongs to Gisborne-ben Simon and this is one of my crew. Michael, you remember Faisal, of course. Anwar, this man is my second and I trust him with my boats which is the same as trusting him with my life.' He settled Anwar's bags in the bow, helped the physician to sit and then sat himself next to Michael in the stern. Faisal slid out the oars and began to pull them past the walls of the harbour toward the busy Golden Horn.

'It is good to see you, Faisal,' Michael said but Faisal merely smiled and kept pulling, the boat cutting cleanly through the water, a moist breeze hitting them as they entered the open water and Michael breathed it in.

'A good smell, eh?' Ahmed said. 'Reminds one of freedom.'

'Indeed,' was all Michael replied. He wanted no idle chat. Not now.

Ahmed kept up a line of rapid Arabic with Faisal and Faisal answered in his monosyllabic way. The two were a good pair – completely loyal to each other. Like brothers…

Or maybe not.

Nāsir was Ahmed's brother. But then not by choice. So often Michael had heard people say how one was always at liberty to choose one's friends but with family, one more often got lemon juice than loyalty.

Soon they were within Galata's harbour walls and Ahmed clambered to the bow and flicked a line to a scruff who stood on the dock. Anwar climbed ashore with assistance, shouldering his two linen bags and whilst he and Michael waited for Ahmed to leave orders with Faisal, Anwar spoke quietly.

'Michael, I suspect you will see your daughter very soon. I have taken the liberty of sending a message to Fatima. She is impeccably trained and used to working with women on many private issues. I thought Ioulia may like to speak with her and it may reassure you if you know that she is unharmed. *Insh'Allah.*'

God willing, indeed…

'I assumed that you will bring her back to Basilike Street,' Anwar continued, 'and so I arranged for Fatima to meet us there.'

'Thank you. I appreciate your forethought.'

Anwar said nothing, merely touched Michael's shoulder once again, affirming, strengthening.

They wound their way through the lately gilded streets of Pera, the lowering sun flicking gold leaf across the ancient paving stones. Dusk approached with speed, a fact that galled Michael who wanted daylight to shine upon his daughter, not the shadows of night.

They passed the archway which led to the Jewish Quarter and Michael wondered where was the house of Saul's friend, the moneylender. *Iisoús*

Christós! If the moneylender knew of the secrets and lies running through the household, it was hardly likely he'd loan a bull's nose-ring to Gisborne-ben Simon, let alone bags of gold and silver. And what kind of merchant's house was it whose senior representative, visiting from the west, hadn't even bothered to introduce himself?

Michael didn't even know the moneylender's name and yet a simple question to Ariella or Christo and it would have been revealed.

'You are very quiet,' Ahmed said. 'Have you nothing at all to say?'

'Beyond who gave you the approval and money required to buy a *caique* for the business?'

'It is my gift to the house. Christo, Ariella, the guards, any of us might need to travel to Galata or Pera. It's best the house has its own boat and crew and we are then less likely to have near-drownings or worse, methinks. Besides, it makes the house look even more prosperous.' He looked sideways at Michael and Michael knew he was right, embarrassed at his own lack.

'Indeed. I should have thought…'

Ahmed didn't disagree, at which Anwar asked how Michael's knee travelled. To which Michael replied that it would serve.

Shadows littered Saint Paul Street and rubbish blew toward them as the breeze which had flirted with them on the water now snarked. An involuntary shiver rippled down Michael's body beneath the heaviness of his cloak. A warning or just the weather?

He could be stretched no tighter. Even stealing the purple, the tension had been different. That was his own life at stake and he had known the risks. *This* was his daughter's life, her freedom and the resurrection of a family. Blood ties ran deep.

'This is the house.' Anwar nodded to a plain home wedged next to identical others. Aged timbers, blackened and cracked with the weathering of centuries. The door was solid though, with a caste-iron latch. Anwar pushed and as the door moaned open, Phocus met them on the other side.

'All is well,' he said. 'No one has come or gone, and he has mostly slept.'

'It smells marginally better…' Ahmed sniffed.

'Money moves mountains of shit when you want it to,' Phocus said in a matter of fact way. 'You know where he is. I will watch the door.'

Ahmed led the way, walking to a room at the back where a man lay on a pallet. The mattress was clean, the rug that covered him new. The floor was still damp from scrubbing and there was a tray with a flask and mug beside the bed.

'Wake up, brother!' Ahmed shook the man's shoulder and he groaned.

'Ahmed!' Anwar shouldered him aside. 'That's enough. I will deal with this. Stand back.'

Michael studied Nāsir and found him little changed. A few wrinkles and thinner, but the eyes, though sick and tired, were as hard as twelve years ago and the tattooed hand lay across the blanket. His hitherto bald head was stubbled and there was a perverse joy to be had in seeing the man brought so low by illness. Not enough joy though – that must surely come when the reckoning was made.

Michael felt as if he stood outside himself, gazing at the man who had wreaked a ruined life upon the Sarapions. Forgiveness might have hovered, momentarily. The man was ill, frail. Barely able to lift his head as he looked at Ahmed and said,

'Brother,' in a croaky voice. 'You came back. Me and my soul are so honoured.'

And there it was. The insouciance, the boldness, the posturing. So like Ahmed. And yet not. Michael shrank back into himself, looking at Nāsir as nothing redeemable. He was glad. He wanted to plunge a knife into the man's heart and sweat broke out on his forehead, his hands clammy. But he didn't move, allowing Anwar to do what he must.

The physician asked Nāsir questions. Had he moved his bowels at all? Had he voided his bladder, was there blood, did he wish to vomit? Had he slept, drunk water? He palpated Nāsir's belly, asking if it hurt and the man never took his eyes off his brother, challenging Ahmed as he replied without much care to the doctor,

'Some pain. No shit, a little piss, and yes, I have had a mug of water. Mostly I slept and dreamed of heaven and virgins. But perhaps that was the old women who came in a scrubbed me and the room and laid me out as if I was dying.' He grinned at Ahmed then, maliciousness at its best, ignoring Anwar whose hands still lay on his belly. 'Sorry to disappoint you, my brother.'

Michael kept in the shadows at the back of the room. He didn't trust himself – to the point where his fists had crunched so tightly they cramped.

'I can you give you pain relief for a few more hours and by tomorrow, you may be able to eat dry flatbread,' said Anwar.

Nāsir's black eyes never left their scrutiny of his brother, ignoring the doctor as he replied, 'More poppy? How can I decline? It is such a journey into the mind.' Again he grinned, a sickle of a smile and as sharp. 'So many memories…'

Ahmed's fist moved forward with speed, but Anwar pushed it aside and then took out a small stoppered bottle, counting out drops into the mug. 'It will be bitter as we have no wine or tea to disguise it.'

Nāsir shrugged, 'No pain, no gain.' He gave a little laugh and then coughed and turned his head to the wall. Michael shifted, fury incarnate, wanting to throttle the life from the man's throat.

'Tell me, Nāsir,' Anwar said as he held the mug of medication, 'you have brought a woman into the town from a convent. The *hegoumene* wishes her to return. Can you tell me where she is?'

Nāsir's eyes widened and he replied with false innocence. 'Have I? A woman from a convent? A vestal virgin?'

Ahmed grabbed Michael with speed and pushed him out the door, strong-arming him to Phocus. 'We need to keep him here. I can feel murder in every breath he takes.'

'And none in yours?' Michael spat back. 'Hypocrite!'

Phocus levered Michael's arm up his back, pushing it harder as he struggled. 'Say nothing, Michael. Let the good doctor and Ahmed handle this. If you show a man like Nāsir that you are desperate for what he has, then he will play you like a fish on a line.'

Michael pushed against the two men holding him. 'What makes you think Anwar can get what I want?'

'He has ways,' said Ahmed enigmatically.

Michael sagged. It seemed to him as if he was ever a watcher in his own life's drama, never a player.

'That's better,' Phocus relaxed his hold. 'Michael, if you trust Anwar more than anyone, believe in him now. We must wait.'

They heard a chant from Saint Paul's – a liturgy. Ninth Hour? Time was racing, and they were still no further advanced. But in moments, Anwar had joined them, folding the linen bags, shouldering them, the small boxes of pots and bottles rattling.

'He dozes. In moments he will be asleep. I gave him a strong dose which will see him sleep into the morrow. Phocus, he may be a little delirious this evening. But do not worry. He will not get off the cot. We need to go.'

Phocus nodded and Anwar shepherded Michael and Ahmed to the door.

'And? In God's name, Anwar,' Michael said, turning back to the physician.

'She is on the waterfront. There is a whorehouse there…'

'A whorehouse! I'll kill him!' But the others grabbed him and held tight.

'He asked who you were with, Ahmed,' said Anwar, 'that you walked arm in arm with him from the room. I said Michael was one of your guards. And perhaps because he was still weak and hazy, he accepted that. But then he asked me what I could give him that would make her location worthwhile and I said his life.'

Nāsir laughed. 'Good doctor, I have my life back and I thank you for it.'

'Not precisely,' Anwar replied. 'The drops I have just given you will kill you by Third Hour tomorrow.'

Nāsir's eyes widened and he coughed, grabbing at his throat, pushing his finger to the back of his mouth and retching.

'It is no good. They are absorbed quickly. But,' Anwar said quietly. 'I have here…' he held up another small bottle. '… the remedy. You take this, and you will be well. In fact, by tomorrow night, you may well be back on board your vessel.'

'Give it to me…' Nāsir tried to sit up, reaching for Anwar's arm.

'Not until you tell me where is Sister Ioulia.'

'Damn you to the unending pain of Al Nar and Hatamah!'

'You waste time, my friend…' Anwar held up the insignificant bottle and Nāsir shook his head as if it were full of goosedown.

'I can't think…'

'Exactly so. You will drift and then you will sink…'

'She…' he stopped, slitting his eyes and rubbing a thumb furiously against his forehead.

'Yes?'

'She's at the house in Waterfront Street that they call Paradise.'

'You have sold her as a whore?' Anwar began to lift the linen bag as if to place the bottle inside, unused.

'No. Allah help me…' Nāsir rubbed at his eyes. 'No! She is merely there until *a business arrangement is concluded.'*

'Good. Then I will find her well, and able to return to her convent, shall I?'

'Yes! Have pity…'

'Then here, drink the lot and by dawn tomorrow, you will feel much better.'

Nāsir grabbed for the bottle but Anwar held it to his mouth, the man sobbing as he swallowed.

Ahmed slow-clapped. 'Ah, my good friend, you have made my day. What exactly did you give to him?'

'Initially he did indeed have poppy. But the second time I just gave him water with a drop of aniseed. It makes it cloying and bitter. It was all in the play act and the fact that he was drugged just enough for his mind to alter what I was saying. I could have told him I'd turned him into a woman and the poppy would have him believing me.'

Michael shook his head, unable to speak, as they approached Waterfront Street, looking for signs of the place they sought. But through the bustle of men on the street there was nothing and in desperation, Michael grabbed a Jewish man, bedecked in his long robes.

'Please, Paradise. Do you know it?'

The Jew looked as if Michael had emerged from Be'er Shachat, stepping back and holding his folds away from evident soiling.

'Please. I am searching for my daughter…'

Always pleading…

The Jew's face softened, and his eyes held pity as he pointed back the way they had come. 'Third house from the corner. I wish you good fortune, my friend.'

Michael called thanks over his shoulder as he ran back the way they had come, Anwar and Ahmed hurrying behind him. They would have had to use chains to hold him back as he turned into the dimly lit door of the place called Paradise, where a thug of a man leaned against the lintel, cleaning his teeth with the tip of his knife.

'I need to enter,' Michael said.

'Show me your money.'

Michael grabbed at his purse, realising how little was inside but Ahmed shoved his own across Michael's shoulder and it clinked heavily with coins. The thug pulled the drawstrings apart and looked inside, then at the companions.

'Three?'

'Three,' said Michael, assuming authority.

The Byzantine pushed aside the door and an odour of perfume, sex and stale bodies wound passed the stained timbers.

'*Iisoús Christós…*' Michael swore.

'Courage, my friend…' Ahmed whispered in his ear.

Girls of all ages lay around in various states of undress, all eyeing him hazily, all drugged for compliance. An older woman drifted across, dressed in tawdry silk and pulling at her veil, eyes alight with greed. 'Can I help you, sirs?'

'I come from the Arab, Nāsir,' said Michael, 'to collect the woman he left in your care.'

The woman's hazel eyes half closed. 'How do I know?'

'He sent you this…' Michael tipped up his purse. Three silver *hyperpirons* slipped out, along with a pearl that he had palmed whilst with the jeweller. Deliberately? Probably… he was a thief after all and was glad.

The woman bowed as her stained hands closed over the purse. 'Of course, sirs. A moment…' She backed away to a curtained door and the men waited, Michael's guts twisting violently with nerves, his heartbeat a tattoo that all in Galata must surely hear.

The curtain pulled back, a creased drape of linen held in the hands of the whore-mistress and a young woman walked into the room, dressed in the sombre robes and *skepe* of the Xylinites Convent. She stood there like a street cur trapped in the light of flame, staring at the three men, her mouth trembling slightly. But she stood tall, her dead mother's calm beauty evident and Michael's eyes filled. He moved to go to her, but Anwar held him.

'Softly, my friend. Softly…'

Ioulia recoiled, colliding with the whore-mistress who pushed her back into the room. She stumbled, and Michael reached for her arm, steadying her as she stared up at him.

'It is I, Ioulia. I am here.' Michael said it gently, afraid to frighten her.

Ioulia's forehead creased and she frowned. 'Papa?' She shook her head and put a hand to her mouth. 'My papa?'

'Yes,' Michael held out his hands. 'I am here.'

It seemed an age as she stared at his palms, and he wondered if like him, she too was trying to reconcile twelve years of loss with the reality of what was now.

She reached a tentative hand forward and his fingers closed over it. Intermittent tears trickled down her cheeks, but she said nothing, made no sound.

'I am here, Ioulia.' He moved closer and took her in his clasp, smoothing her head beneath the common linen of her *skepe* and he thought he would melt into the ground, such warmth had not been his for twelve years. His daughter...

'Let's go,' Ahmed whispered. 'Get her away.'

'Ioulia,' Michael held her away from him, but keeping her within the protective circle of his grasp. 'Will you come with me to my home for the moment? To where you can be safe, and we can talk?'

There was a heartbeat of time and more and Michael knew then how much her life had been reshaped by distrust and abuse. Eventually she nodded, and he took her hand once more, leading her to the door, led by Ahmed and followed by Anwar. The thug blocked their way as they attempted to step down into Waterfront Street but Ahmed told him the whore had been paid for and to desist. The whore-mistress had followed them, and she nodded grudging acquiescence so he stood back ungraciously, the flame light catching on the edge of his knife blade.

Closer to the dock, Michael stopped and wrapped a shivering Ioulia in his cloak. 'Daughter, these are my friends and therefore yours. This is Ahmed, the man who sailed me here to find you and this is our honoured physician, Anwar al Din. You can trust them.'

Each man bowed, and Anwar said with doctorly kindness, 'Ioulia, you have had a shock. We will get you home to Basilike Street and you will be warm. When you are rested, then you can talk with your father.'

She was as compliant as a feeble ancient and in time, they had placed her in the *caique* and Faisal rowed them across the now still waters of the Horn, a delicate flamelight hanging in a lantern from the bow. Ioulia fixed her gaze on the lamp, saying nothing, but she held her father's hand in a grip of iron and for that, Michael was thankful. Without his cloak, he should have frozen, but he was lit from inside by a fire that was stronger than *naphtha*. His protective instinct was honed to blade sharpness and whilst his heart beat with love, his mind plotted with a deeply incised hatred.

Chapter Thirteen

✕

Basilike Street basked in golden lamp light, every window glowing with a friendly flame, as if Ephigenia and Ariella knew that it must welcome to those in distress. But it was obvious to a blind man that Ioulia saw none of it. She walked with her head down, her hand deep inside Michael's own. They were met by Leo, who pushed the gates open.

'There have been no problems, *Kýrie* Michael. Except that you have had a message from the Contarini house. I left the parchment on the table.'

'Thank you, Leo. Are Ariella and Tobias inside?'

'Yes, with the physician sent by Anwar.'

Michael needed to introduce Ioulia to the household, but it must be done gently and to have his daughter confront so many curious faces at once may be too much. He looked to Anwar for help.

'Perhaps if you wait here whilst Ahmed lets the house know we have arrived,' Anwar said. The galley master nodded and went on inside, whilst Anwar continued, taking Ioulia's hand from her father's. 'My dear, you have had some deep shocks in the past few days. This is a big and sometimes noisy household. Would you prefer to retire to a chamber until you are ready to meet everyone?'

She looked to Michael for reassurance and he merely smiled, encouraging her to make the decision herself. He did not want to swallow her up. For someone who had lived a slave's life for so long, she deserved freedom now, to think and to do the way she wanted. 'If that will not offend anyone, then thank you,' she replied.

Her voice was quiet, melodious, with a tone Michael was sure Tobias would like. She had matured into such a beautiful woman. When he had wondered what she would be like, he had never thought of her voice. He could only remember her wavy hair which was the colour of Helena's and her eyes which were the colour of Helena's. And the shape of her fingers, long and elegant, the kind that could hold a needle and stitch fine embroidery, were always like Helena's.

But her voice lent something else to her presence. Another dimension and something he held close, wanting her to say Papa, over and over again.

Ahmed returned, stuffing a date in his mouth as he said, 'The hall is empty, it seems everyone's in the kitchens. And I took this from the table, Michael.' He held out the rolled parchment, sealed with the shield and broad bends of the Contarini coat of arms impressed deep in the black wax.

Taking the message, Michael said he would show Ioulia her chamber and then he would see the household anon. He shepherded his daughter up the stair and into his own chamber, he would sleep with Toby if necessary, and found that the room was warm, the window closed and a lamp lit, the candle's flame gently welcoming. 'This is your room for as long as you wish, Ioulia. Can I have anything sent to you?'

'No thank you, Papa. I just need to sit for the moment. Can you stay?'

He gestured for her to enter and she walked to the bed and ran her hand along the covers. 'Papa, may I sit?

'Of course. Do you wish for some syrup, some wine...'

'No,' she interrupted. She undid the *skepe*, revealing her hair. Her beautiful hair cut brutally short and blunt and through which she scrabbled fingers, as if she tried to chase tension away. 'Please, I need nothing. Tell me...' She couldn't finish, shrugging her shoulders, pleading with her eyes, her hands.

Pleading. Like her father...

He dragged a stool over in front of her, sat and began to tell her the story of that fateful day.

Her face paled and she broke in. 'Papa, the man who collected me from Xylinites – I recognised his voice too late. I tried to hit the man who held me on his horse, a younger man. He bound me, bound my mouth,' she became agitated and a tear rolled, but with astonishing self-control, she took a breath, stilling her demeanor and continuing. 'The older man just watched, and I relived that day on the galley...'

Michael could say nothing. He just reached forward and stroked her rigid hands and took up the story again. Telling her that he was still a merchant, but that he had left the city and gone to the west, unaware that any of his family still lived. He told her of the good woman he had met who was a merchant's daughter, and whom he had a married a year ago. 'When the message came from Father Nicholas of Agathopolis, Jehanne, for that is her name, and myself were living in Lyon.'

'So far away, Papa.'

'I had to leave, Ioulia. I had almost twelve years of grief and it was a chance for a new life. I hope you will, in time, understand why I did it.'

'I understand now...' she replied softly, and he wondered if she had a similar awakening as she had stolen that square of silk. That it was possible to escape boundaries and be free. He told her nothing of the purple. Not yet.

'Is Jehanne like Mama?'

A difficult question, hard to answer, but he tried. 'Stalwart and strong like your mother and I believe she cares for me like your mother did. But she looks nothing like your mother, although she is striking, but your mother? Helena was...' he looked down at his hands. '... a goddess. In truth, Ioulia, they cannot be compared. But it was Jehanne who sent me back here to search for you.'

'You would not have come otherwise?'

He recalled Anwar's words – *Softly, softly* – and shook his head. 'Wrong choice of words. Jehanne said I had to come. That she would support me in what I needed to do.'

Ioulia nodded, 'Then she is wise.'

'I believe you would like her.'

He asked her then about her own life and she talked of the slave market in Agathopolis, of being in the same house in Constantinople for almost twelve years. Of running away and of Father Symeon and the Xylinites Convent. She did not mention being raped, nor of the lost babe or of stealing a piece of blue silk. Nor did she once hint at the loss of herself.

By the time her words rolled to a stop, she seemed shattered. Shadowed rings cushioned her lower lids and there were lines strung tense and taut from nose to mouth. She clasped her hands tightly together and Michael called a gentle halt.

'We have time to talk another day, my daughter.' He reached forward and kissed her forehead. 'But you must rest, and I will send a message to the *hegoumene* to tell her where you are. I will have a tray sent up and perhaps some washing things.' He remembered Fatima, waiting patiently down the stair to consult his daughter. 'Ioulia, we are fortunate to have two physicians with us. One is an Arab woman who treats some of the nobles at court. She also treats Ariella, whom you will meet.'

Small lies amongst truths…

'May I send her to you?' he asked.

'Why?'

He shrugged. 'To make sure you have no injury, nor aches and pains from your abduction. She is a fount of wisdom and like everyone's grandmother.' He spoke lightly, having no idea of the woman's age and making things seem normal and natural, from which she seemed to take heart.

'My head feels as if it is cleft into two halves,' she said.

'In which case, I shall send her up.' As he walked to the door he added, 'Ephigenia, our housekeeper and the real grandmother of the house will bustle in with a tray, call you her daughter for evermore and smother you with love and much food.' He grinned at his daughter and winked, keeping the moment as light as a dove's feather. 'You could do worse. I shall be in the chamber along the corridor on the right if you need me.'

'You have a house of many women,' Ioulia said.

'Not really. We are rather unbalanced in that respect. Many men and only two women to control us. Fatima comes and goes.'

'Your merchant house is successful, Papa.'

'It is not mine, Ioulia. I am merely a senior representative of the Venetian house of Gisborne-ben Simon. But more of that on the morrow. Sleep well, my child. I am content to have found you.' He touched his heart.

She managed a smile, the tension lines dissipating and Helena's face looking back at him. He turned away, awash with sadness and relief in one.

He found Fatima with everyone else in the hall and after a quick talk, she went upstairs. Michael watched her go, her *hijab* floating behind with her quick step. She was indeed grandmotherly, and Anwar nodded reassurance in his direction. The group sat quietly until Toby could sit still no longer, jumping up and touching Michael's arm.

'Well?'

Michael looked up, shocked to see that he sat with a room full of people, so deep in memories was he. He gazed at them all, wondering at how he managed to believe they were traitors. Even Christo, who sat in shadow as if he had already been found guilty of idle chatter – Michael wanted to tell him that all was well, that there was nothing to be guilty for. Not now.

'I think she is well. She seems to be strong for all that she has been through. And there is a deep tranquility there that surprises me.'

'Perhaps she has found God.' Tobias said it lightly.

'More likely she found her father,' Ahmed said unusually.

'Does she need clothing, Michael?' Ariella asked. 'I can find things...'

'She would appreciate a clean tunic.' Michael hadn't thought of the mundanity of a woman's life. 'In truth, I think she needs to sleep, and so do I. Toby, can I sleep with you this night? She has my chamber.'

'Of course. And do you know, I have never heard myself snore...'

Ariella laughed out loud at this, obviously remembering the voyage from Venezia. To which Toby lifted just lifted his voice above her and continued, '*So*, you will sleep deep and long, my friend. I won't even ask questions.'

'I thank you, Toby, and will retire now if you all forgive me. Ahmed, Anwar – I owe you more than you can imagine.' He clasped the shoulder of each of the men and climbed the stair, only then realising that his knee was on fire, that the pain was angry, and that good news and anticipated happiness had dulled his aches in the meantime.

In Toby's smaller chamber, he pulled at his girdle, ready to rip his long tunic off, and found the wad of Contarini parchment. He moved to the lamp flame, cracking the seal, brushing the flakes of wax away as he unrolled the missive.

The writing was darkly forthright, a strong hand. Michael was of the opinion that Contarini had penned it himself, rather than using his notary.

To Michael Sarapion from your friend, Giacomo Contarini, greetings.

I write to invite you to meet with me on the morrow, as soon as you are able.
For the sake of Gisborne-ben Simon, I must speak with you. I have lately had
tidings that affect us all.
   By the Grace of our God sir,
   Valete.

Michael had hoped to fall immediately to sleep, but now he thought back over the banquet, puzzling at what might be wrong as he pulled off his boots and clothes and scrabbled cold water across his face. He climbed into the bed to breathe in time to his heartbeat which seemed to crash with painful regularity somewhere around his kneecap. But in moments, he felt himself slipping away from all that was of concern, and he let go, knowing his daughter, his beautiful only child, slept safe, only one room away.

He was woken next morning by a hard kick to the buttocks.

'Wake up! It's dawn and I need to sleep!' Toby growled, pushing him with his feet. There was one small moment where Michael wondered why he slept with Toby, but then he stretched out his knee and yelped and the last few days flooded back to his memory, his stomach contracting.

He lowered his legs to the floor, taking a step, holding his breath, heading for the door as Toby called after him. 'She's fine. Not a sound. I should know because you snored like a pig in its cups, so I walked the house all night. And Jesus Christ, Michael! Put some clothes on before you leave the room.'

To which Michael dived into his crushed clothing. But as he flung his girdle round his hips and attached his dagger scabbard, Toby grumbled again from the depths of the bedding. 'Get your damned knee sorted, Michael! You're no good to anyone.'

Michael shut Toby's door, half his mind asleep, the other thinking on Ioulia and Contarini. Seeing his chamber door shut and needing clean clothes, he thought to find Ephigenia who perhaps had some of his laundry, but as he limped closer to the smell of baking, he heard singing. Ephigenia's voice murmured '*Téleios…*perfect…' and he stopped at the door, listening, watching. Ephigenia mixed the doughs for their breads, closing her eyes in beatific reverence as Ioulia sang a soft liturgy. She sat at the table with a woven basket of tumbled silken threads, taking each hank out and carefully winding it onto a piece of whittled wood.

It was an age-old scene, one that had no doubt happened for centuries among Byzantine women and would continue for centuries yet and Michael took such comfort from the placid nature of it, loathe to interrupt. He had no idea that his daughter's voice was so beautiful and he could have stood listening for an age. But Contarini waited…

He rapped on the doorframe and the melody stopped, Ioulia looking up. 'Papa,' the word was mouthed with quiet joy. Everything about his daughter was restrained and he tried hard to remember if it had always been so. But there was such a chasm in his memories – half a lifetime.

'Did you sleep well, my daughter?'

'Fatima gave me something to ease my headache and I suspect it helped me sleep. I don't think I moved the entire night. The birds woke me and when I opened the window, there was the most beautiful heron on the roof across the street. Have you seen him?'

'I have. Is Fatima returning?'

'She and Anwar will come later. Anwar wishes to check your injured knee which Fatima assures me will heal. Is that so?'

Michael grinned. 'Of course. Ioulia, I must pay a visit to one of our Venetian dignitaries urgently. Will you be alright?'

'Ephigenia will make sure I am,' she looked across at the housekeeper who patted her on the arm. 'But may I ask if you sent a message to the convent?'

'The message leaves this morning with one of our guards.' In truth he had forgotten and had no wish to engage with the *hegoumene* anyway, but it seemed to matter to Ioulia. 'I will see you anon, my dear.' He took her by the shoulders and kissed her forehead. It was then he noticed that she had once again covered her butchered hair with the *skepe*, but that she wore a soft green gown that he had oft seen Ariella wear. He was sure Ariella would have offered a white linen veil, so why the soiled and faded *skepe* from the convent?

He grabbed a staff from under the arbor and hobbled to the gates, picking up Leo on the way, climbing the slope with the pace of the infirm and cursing the way he had been reduced to the status of the aged, one who needed someone by his side to help him walk. So it seemed, and he cursed Izzo afresh. Izzo, Nāsir – such cursing greased the axle of his day as they approached the handsome villa of the Contarini which looked across the Venetian quarter. The marbled façade glistened in the morning sun, for the

251

day promised its azure best. There was a dryness to the air which presaged summer and crackling heat. Days when one would rather sit by a bubbling fountain or drag one's hands through the public water cisterns. He hated summer in the city.

He and Leo entered the residence by the heavy main gates, armed guards standing with pikes upright, their clothing rich blue and with the Contarini crest emblazoned upon their hearts.

A notary in the ubiquitous black gown of such men from Bologna and Paris, saw them and politely asked their purpose. On hearing Michael's name, the man sharpened and became even more business-like.

'Come this way, sir. *Messere* Giacomo has been waiting for you.'

The notary tapped on a door and led Michael into a sparse room, almost monastic in its simplicity, and Michael was surprised. He had expected Contarini to be surrounded by largesse, but the only largesse were the piles of parchment, maps, an over-full box of wax tapers and a bowl of seals, all spread across a massive table over which Contarini now leaned, his back to the door.

'Excuse me, sir,' the notary said. '*Messere* Michael Sarapion…'

Contarini turned around swiftly. 'Michael! Come in, come in. And your man. Be seated. Some wine perhaps? Giorgio, get some wine for us, if you will.'

The notary left, and Michael and Leo sat on chairs on the other side of the table. Contarini stood, filled with a taut energy that hadn't been evident at the banquet. Whatever news he had received, it obviously agitated him.

'What I expected is coming to pass, Michael. It seems the Emperor is being beguiled by Genovese whispers in his ears and it seems they are to have many more privileges than we could have thought possible. They may well be on a par with us with little to no taxes and much more freedom.'

'How do you know?'

'I was at the palace yester-morn. And I confess, I was treated to some second-rate behaviour. Most unusual. I was left sitting in an ante-chamber for too long and then met with an administrative subordinate who informed me that Venetian rights were to be curtailed and potentially taxes might be put in place. I demanded to see senior representatives or even the Emperor Alexios and eventually, after bashing my head against imperial protocol,

I saw the *logothetēs tou dromou*, the head of foreign representatives in the city. But he merely underlined the fact that the Genovese privileges would be on a par with our own.' Contarini began to walk, his robes whisking the air as he swung round to walk back again. 'Since the usurpation of the imperial throne by Alexios III, and the blinding and house arrest of his brother Isaac II a few months before you arrived, he has bled the treasury dry. Nothing good will come of this. We have arrived at a watershed moment in Venezia's position here.' He hit knuckle against palm, the slap sharp in the quiet of the chamber. 'We have worked hard to solidify our position here after Manuel I. I don't want a repeat of that.'

'How and when does all this come into effect?'

'Almost immediately. They tell me they think to reduce the size of our Quarter which they say is overlarge and overwealthy for a mere trading community, hinting that we have ulterior motives. Huh, the Genovese are good at dripping poison, I'll say that!'

'So, the Genovese traders are now on a par. Who do you think has been instrumental in this?' Michael knew of course. The smooth serpent's tongue of Branco Izzo flicked in and out.

'Izzo. He has been granted a villa within Botaneides but then I am sure you knew this. I suspect he has been given freedom by the Genovese trading community both in Genova and here, to make an exceptionally large donation to the imperial treasury. I also suspect that they have made other promises. Like the Venetians, perhaps they donate ships to bolster the navy, maybe even mercenaries. I have also heard vague rumours that strong Genovese interest lies in the Black Sea, a place we have only flirted with, and the Byzantines seem happy to let it happen.'

Michael was Byzantine and whatever else, he knew the way Byzantines thought. Monies in the imperial treasury would be welcomed warmly, along with increased defensive capability. But there would also be a significant portion of Byzantine traders both in Constantinople and along the Black Sea who had long felt Venezia's merchants were too powerful. They were the families who had attacked the Venetians twenty years before, imprisoning thousands of Venetians within the city. No wonder Contarini was concerned. He would be held to account by Venezia and the Doge for the safety and surety of those Venetians who continued to live and trade through the great city.

'Then what would you have us do, *messere?*'

'In truth, there is little we can do. But I am forewarning our merchants. Personally, I think there is something in the air in the west that will catch fire here in time and Venetians will suffer. They talk of another crusade, you know.'

'I had heard vague rumours. You think it might come to pass?'

There was a knock at the door and Giorgio, the notary, backed into the room with a tray of wine and wafers. Michael wondered at the godly symbolism. Giorgio poured three mugs from a damascened pewter flask and passed one each to Michael, Leo and Contarini. He bowed then and excused himself, the door closing quietly behind him.

'They rattle swords in scabbards, those in the west who itch in the name of God. And here is as good a place as any on which to launch an attack. This city is the centre of so much wealth and magnificence, coming from all quarters of the known and indeed unknown worlds. And it is a pivotal position between here and Outremer. The city arouses all manner of jealousies. Emperor Alexios needs to keep his empire defended and the Genovese bribes might help.'

'May I ask what some other of the Venetian merchants plan to do?'

'Solidify their contacts throughout the region, remove as much merchandise as they can from their warehouses and form an armed flotilla to sail back to the west while they can and before we lose what beneficial privileges we have.'

'And you are advising me to do the same? You don't think this is a precipitate reaction, to turn tail and flee? You don't think the Genovese want us to do exactly this?'

Contarini frowned lightly and then shook his head. 'I am thinking that you have the lovely Ariella in your midst. Heavily pregnant. She will be safer back in Venezia at this time of flux. I understand you have also, God be thanked, discovered your daughter whom you thought dead. Surely she too would be safer in Venezia. Vague whispers reach me that you have acquired such a cargo that will have customers in the west at war with each other to have access and I would hate you to lose the benefits of such a cargo. If what I hear is right, the arrival of your cargo in the west will make waves the like of which we haven't seen for some time. In many ways, your cargo may actually solidify our strength and our reputation here.'

Anxiety began to grow, a shadow thrown over what should be one of the most wonderful days of Michael's life. 'Where did you hear such rumours about Gisborne-ben Simon?'

'Sailors talk, Michael. But ostensibly from Izzo. He diminishes you by saying your house is nothing but bluff, that you deceive your way through marketplaces and that often the quality is lacking.'

Michael snorted and shook his head. 'He's a son of a bitch in so many ways.'

'He is the friend of questionable people as well.'

'What say you?' This conversation had taken turn after turn and now Michael's belly burned with acid. He sucked back some wine and chewed on an almond wafer.

'He was seen in Pera,' said Contarini, flinging himself into a creaking leather slung chair. 'Nothing new of course, as the Genovese are more at home in the quarter they are expanding there, than amongst us. But what *was* disturbing was his companion. The man he spoke with was an Arab *peirate* called...'

'Nāsir.' Michael closed his eyes. Everything about the day had become rank. 'You know of him?'

'Yes.' He dared not look at Leo who sat as still as a statue.

'Then you now know everything I know, my friend. And you can make plans. What do you think to do?'

Michael's eyebrows lifted, and he breathed in a chestful of air. 'Coincidentally, a day or two ago, I had almost decided to take our cargo and leave in the next few days with Ariella, Tobias and assuming I found my daughter, her as well. Our trading house is being pressured from a source we can't identify but in truth, the pieces now come together.'

Contarini nodded. 'Keep clear of him, Michael. He is poisonous, is Izzo, and to be a friend of the imperial house gives him a licence we may not have. In fact, quite the reverse.'

Michael stood. 'What surprises me, *messere*, is that the Contarini name is so strong, and so honourable and yet, the Byzantine Court can't see sense for snakes.'

'Michael, they blind their own. They are a jealous, insecure, pathetically self-indulgent and maybe even insane court. They will be the death of their own empire. Mark my words...'

Michael held out his hand. '*Messere* Giacomo, I am in your debt. If you

255

need Gisborne-ben Simon to stand by your side at any time…'

Contarini grasped Michael's hand and arm, rapport and respect obvious. 'You are a good man, Michael. Gisborne-ben Simon and indeed Venezia are lucky to have you amongst us.'

Leo and Michael walked down the hill, Michael leaning heavily on the staff. Leo said nothing, just shortened his pace to match Michael's and finally, Michael broke the silence.

'You're very quiet, Leo.'

'There isn't really much to say, is there? I think we were all quite aware that there might be a link between one man and the other. As to the political situation? That is for you to manage, in the house's interest.'

Michael looked down the slope of Little Mese toward the harbour where the Horn sparkled like steel armour. The analogy worried him – armour, battles, fighting. Another crusade? He saw a need to keep Basilike Street safe and yet, within the bounds of trade, he wondered if they should withdraw to the Adriatic for the foreseeable future. He must talk with Ahmed and Christo.

And Ariella?

And Ariella. She had as much say as anyone.

'Leo, would you come with us when we return to Venezia? You heard what I said to *Messere* Contarini about an imminent departure.'

'Ah. Do you mean myself solely? Or the others as well?'

Michael shrugged. 'All, if you wanted. We could easily find places for you in Ve… Leo?'

Leo had shoved closer to Michael and had his hand on his *spathion*. 'Arm yourself! We have compa…'

He didn't finish, swinging round and slashing with his blade. People in the street yelled, jumped to the side and someone called for the guard. Michael had no time to pull his own blade, hampered by the staff he held. Instead, he turned on the agonising bone of his kneecap, swinging the strong wood with all the anger and fury he had stored. As he flung round, all he saw was a dark shape and so he whirled blindly but with enormous power, yelling with an exultant shout as the wooden staff hit something hard, bones crunched and someone screamed with pain and fell against him. He threw the staff aside, assured that Leo kept the other assailant busy and grabbed for his dagger, stabbing down into the chest of the oily figure who lay underneath his feet. No thought, no care, just one blow, a grunt, a spreading stain and eyes staring lifeless beyond him. He turned then, but Leo had despatched his attacker, a massive gash in the side of the neck, as blood pulsed onto the paving stones of Little Mese. Leo stood over the man, breathing hard, wiping his blade on the man's tunic.

In moments, a crowd had closed around them and a moment more and Varangians in their leathered glory had shouldered through, grabbing Michael and Leo by the arms and pinioning them.

But a voice called from the crowd, a gentle voice that Michael recognised. 'Let them go. They were defending themselves…' A tall darkly-robed figure pushed through the interested onlookers, some dipping their heads politely. Father Symeon's presence in front of the Varangians was like water on fire but whilst the fire went out, it hissed and steamed in the process.

'You say, Father,' said one of the guards, his fair hair sitting as wildly on his shoulders as Father Symeon's own.

'I was following them down the hill, trying to catch their attention and the two felons moved in from the side and attacked with no warning.' He spoke smoothly and with such honesty that Michael thought he was probably telling the truth and was glad. 'I am sure there are those here who will agree?' The priest turned to the crowd and there was a chorus of acknowledgement.

'Why did you wish to gain their attention?'

'I am a priest,' Father Symeon swept his hand over his robes, 'as you can see. I know these men through my ministering within the church and have been summoned to their house to offer prayers for one of the women at the house. I wanted to walk with them.'

The Varangian spokesman said nothing, just stared with cold Northern eyes and Father Symeon added, 'Could you please let them go, my son?'

'There will be a report,' said the officer. 'Tell us where you live as you will be called to account. You have killed two men.'

'Two *felons*,' said Michael and the crowd murmured, adding fuel to his fire. 'These good people saw. We did not provoke this…'

The Varangians were tall men, but no taller than Father Symeon, and Leo towered over them all. He moved now, removing a hand gripping his arm and standing to the full extent of his height. 'Thank you, sirs, for your swift arrival,' he said as he stowed the stained *spathion*. 'And thank you,' he called to the onlookers, 'for defending us and getting help.'

Michael took his lead and offered his thanks as well. 'May we leave?' he asked the Varangian officer. 'We are of the house of Gisborne-ben Simon in Basilike Street should you need any more detail.'

The officer nodded to the others and they stepped back, allowing Michael, Leo and Father Symeon to move on. Father Symeon bent to retrieve Michael's staff from the side of the street and passed it over, Michael conscious of many eyes on the priest, the giant from Khorasan and himself. Looking back over his shoulder, he saw four men had been coerced to lift the bodies, and with the Varangians on either side, the maudlin cavalcade left via a sidestreet, someone throwing a bucket of water over the blood stains.

The stained water accompanied them down the street, trickling apace, but it continued on past them to the harbour as they stopped at the corner of the house, no one speaking until Bonus had slammed the gates shut behind them and lowered the bar.

'Goddamn it!' Michael growled.

Father Symeon looked pained but said gently, 'You are not hurt? Either of you?'

'No, Father,' Leo said. 'Always safe. It's a gift I have.' He grinned and added, 'Michael? Father? Excuse me, if you will?'

Michael nodded, and he and the priest made their way inside. 'You come to pray with Ariella or Ioulia, Father?'

'Neither. It was mere happenstance that I walked down the hill behind you. I thought a little help in the face of the bloodlusty Varangians wouldn't hurt.'

Michael's eyebrows rose. 'Then we thank you and owe you.'

The priest touched Michael's shoulder. 'You owe me nothing. Call it an effort to pay a debt. I was concerned you might blame the Church for much over the last few days.'

'There's been a lot to blame the Church for...' Michael began. But then he thought of his daughter within the house, and of the news from Contarini and he realised that nothing mattered beyond getting people and cargo out of the city. 'But perhaps we bring trouble on ourselves, Father. Would you like to talk to Ioulia?' He did not mention the notion of revenge. He was sure it would have no place in the priest's lexicon.

'I would, my son. It has been some time since I have seen her.'

Laughter and singing drifted down the stair and Michael twitched his hand, 'Follow the noise, and it sounds as if you will find her with Toby and Ariella. If you will excuse me, I will rejoin you shortly. It's good to hear laughter…'

The priest moved on up the stair, his athletic stride taking two steps at once and Michael envied him his suppleness. He rubbed at his knee as he turned away, wanting a quick word with Phocus, assuming he had now returned from Nāsir and Pera.

As he walked under the arbor to the guards' quarters, Ahmed's voice wound out of the shadows. 'Living here is like living in a marketplace – merchants, minstrels and monks to which we must add guards, cooks and jewellers. There is a jeweller up the stair who is making the stuff of dreams, did you know? Do you realise this house has swollen from two to twelve in less than seven days? What would Saul and Sir Guy say?'

'Damned if I know or care, Ahmed. It has been necessary, and we called it so at the time.'

Ahmed sat up, clasping his hands on the table. 'You are testy today…'

Michael sat, shoving his leg out in front and grimacing at the pain.

'Your knee?'

'No.'

'Then what? My brother?' Ahmed minced no words. 'You want to kill him? I won't stop you.'

'So sanguine, Ahmed.'

'He is a boil on the backside of Allah's world, Michael. There are many reasons I want him dead, but sadly, I find I cannot kill my own brother.'

'So instead, you urge me to do your dirty work.'

'Don't pretend it is not what you want.'

Michael played with the hilt of his dagger. Of course he wouldn't deny it. This was twelve years in the making. And Nāsir was not *his* brother, he had no familial guilt to worry on. 'What has he done to you, Ahmed?'

Ahmed laughed, that empty sound that chilled men when it was armed with a *kilij*. 'He cuckolded me, and my wife carried his child. We were newly married, but she was soiled with another man's seed. She died in childbirth and my mother reared the boy, until Nāsir came and took him to sea when he was six. The child was treated like a galley slave – I heard because word spreads on the sea like oil, as you know. Eventually the child died from a fever in one of the many harbours that Nāsir infected with his presence. I have no idea where my nephew is buried. Suffice to say when my mother found out, she died of shock as she loved the child as her own.'

Ahmed knew loss then, Michael thought. He understood revenge and he didn't suffer fools. 'Why did you never marry again, Ahmed?'

'I was never in port long enough.'

Which of course was a lie because Ahmed had spent an age anchored off Venezia. But Michael let the untruth sink and die. The man's face had shuttered as sure as if he had slammed wood over it and barred it. No more answers from the deep soul.

'But you want me to take his life for the life of your wife, your nephew and your mother.'

'Of course.'

Iisoús Christós, but the man was terrifying in his delivery. Not a speck of emotion showed in his eyes, his mouth or his body as he sat relaxed, with hands loosely clasped. Even Michael, who would happily strike the death blow, had the grace to feel a shiver down his spine.

'Surely it helps to add that to Ioulia's and Helena's fates, does it not?' Ahmed continued. 'Nāsir is weighted down with boulders of guilt. He just doesn't recognise it. But for sure with a sword through his middle, misdeeds will flash through his mind like *naphtha*. Now tell me, why were you hurrying, and I use that word with some doubt, to the guards' quarters?'

Michael relayed the information from Contarini's meeting. Short and succinct. But left out the kernel of Nāsir's connection with Izzo, to plant later.

'It is not surprising. Men talk on the docks. It just takes some time to reach the minds of men who matter.'

'Like Contarini, you mean?'

'Like him. Like you…'

'Perhaps you could have shared what you knew.'

'You mean like you not sharing the fact that Izzo met with Nāsir?'

Michael sat up. 'How do *you* know of that?

'I know men who know men…' Ahmed's gaze held Michael's. It burned with fire and only then did Michael realise how Ahmed curbed his emotions, chained them down and how truly astute he was – way beyond the incipient greed of a trader. There were lessons to be learned from the Arab. It was no wonder the man never made mistakes. Everything was thought through and managed with a cool clarity that defied belief, and suddenly Michael knew why Gisborne had chosen Ahmed to be his galley master. The man was the very personification of professionalism and innate subtlety.

'Ahmed, will you leave me to handle Nāsir in my own way?'

Time passed. The perennial doves of Basilike Street burbled, and the heron could be seen through a gap in the budding grapevine, gracefully sweeping across the sky to land on the opposite roof. Ahmed rubbed his jaw and then flicked a hand across his polished and domed head. 'I am inclined not to...'

'Please.'

Ahmed sighed. 'If you wish. Does your daughter know?'

Michael shook his head. 'Nor will she.'

'I am the model of discretion, my friend. Now tell me, in the light of Contarini's divulgences, what do you plan?'

Michael told Ahmed of his plan to leave the house strong and most likely with honest and respected Christo at its head. Nothing would change there. But he would fill the boats with whatever cargo they had and leave in a few days, weather permitting. 'If you are happy for us to use both of your boats.'

Ahmed shrugged. 'They are underwritten by Gisborne-ben Simon, Michael, and in any case, Faisal has been reprovisioning for a day or two. If the men,' he cocked his head to the guards' quarters, 'intend on coming, then I would have a formidable second crew with their bulk.'

A hint that the guards would be more than welcome and no arguments about a turnaround in a sennight. Almost as if Ahmed had already thought of the idea himself but let Michael think it was his own. All that was left was for Michael to inform the house. Ariella might be a stumbling block but the others not so much. He had confidence that Ioulia would want to accompany her father to Venezia and then Lyon. Judging from the happy sounds he had heard, bonding with Tobias and Ariella had already occurred.

Michael levered himself up. 'You must excuse me. I would find Phocus...'

'Michael...' Ahmed called him back.

'A word of warning. My brother is slick with a blade and he is dishonourable.

You are not fit or swift. Worse, Nāsir has allied himself with Izzo, who wants to see the end of you. Do not expect a fair fight.'

Michael nodded. There was nothing more to be said.

Phocus had returned and was forthcoming about Nāsir. The Arab had been collected by two of his men and was helped to walk back to his boat. He was weak, but that was expected. But colour had returned to his face and his manner was as self-assured as ever. Indeed, the physician had predicted the recovery would be swift, had he not?

'By tomorrow morn he will be more himself, Michael. Food in the belly, a good sleep.' Phocus had said.

It was all Michael needed to know. Tomorrow then and it was good to see the end approaching. He moved back to the hall, pleased to see all gathered round the table with piles of food thereon. Such an eclectic group and people with hearts and souls. Voices were happy, people laughed and Tobias, as always, sang. Even Ahmed grinned at the bawdy song Toby dared to sing in front of Father Symeon. But Father Symeon was as worldly as he was wise. He replaced his mug on the table and said he must return to Sancta Sophia, that too much festivity would not sit well with his serious duties of prayer and more of the same. His soul might become used to the levity! He said it lightly and no one took umbrage, a chorus of farewells following him out the door. Michael noticed a small nod pass between Ioulia and the priest but thought nothing much of it.

He stood with Father Symeon at the gates, thanking him again for his support. The Father demurred but offered words as he passed through the entrance into the street. 'She is brave, your Ioulia, Michael. Courageous and mature in her thinking. She has made great decisions in her life and whilst we might think they are wrong, they are what she has chosen, and we must respect that. I will offer prayers for her.' He bowed his head, the *skoufos* hanging atop by the grace of God, and took his leave. Michael's last sight was a dark column of waving hair and robes striding up Little Mese and the words, '*what she has chosen,*' flying in his slipstream.

But as with every moment of Michael's life since he took a step off Durrah onto the city docks, he had no time to think of anything profound as Bonus handed him a parchment roll.

'From the physician, *Kýrie* Michael. It arrived just before you and the priest came to the gates...'

Michael took it, walked a few steps as the gates were closed behind him and in the relative quiet of the forecourt, he flipped Anwar's wax seal off and unrolled the note. He read the words and his heart contracted, stopped, he held his breath and then his heart beat again, only this time it wreaked furious, black blood round his body and somehow, God help him, he had to contain it in front of the house to whom he must speak at any moment.

Everyone except the guards sat around the long table, even Ignatios the jeweller, who fitted into the family as if he had been born to the house. He and Ephigenia sat gossiping together – the oldest people present – having old people in the house was surely a sign of longevity. At any other time, it would have given Michael feelings of warmth and happiness. So too should the presence of his daughter who now sang a soft Byzantine song with Tobias. *Iisoús Christós,* but her voice was beautiful! With pus and murder in his heart and news to impart to the household, his memory slipped back to when he hid with the purple near the Xylinites Convent. Back to the sound of womens' voices singing the liturgies. Her own voice had been amongst them, he was sure of it.

She glanced over her shoulder, caught his eye and called out. 'Papa! Tobias and I have found common ground!'

'I am glad. Toby is nothing if not experienced in many things. But then I dare say you have also found common things with Ariella. I did see you tidying threads after all!' At which, Ariella held up neatly tidied basket.

When Michael had spoken, he expressed himself with lightness of heart, completely at odds with the darkness that burned holes in his soul. He was amazed at how easy it was to operate on two planes when someone was so very dear to one's heart. But even so, he had still to deliver Contarini's news and his own decision in response; Ahmed sat back, slightly removed from everyone, watching with interest. Michael almost wanted to ask him for help but in this instance, he knew he must speak as the head of the house. And speak convincingly. He reached for a mug and the wine jug, poured, swallowed a goodly amount and then tapped the edge of the mug with his dagger. The idle gossip, the singing, all continued until a sharp whistle emerged from where Ahmed sat with a leg lying across his knee. Everyone turned to him.

'Did you not hear Michael calling for your attention?' He wafted his hand toward Michael as if he swept them up like kitchen crumbs.

'I thank you, Ahmed, and apologise to you all for breaking into a happy meal. I have just returned from *Messere* Contarini and without putting too finer point on things, the news I bring is not good. Firstly, the Genovese have acquired equal trading rights in the city. Maybe even more than equal trading rights. Our friend Izzo would say so...'

Tobias growled and stamped his foot, 'That son of a ...'

'Thank you, Toby. Let me finish, if you will. You may all remember that twenty years ago, Venetian merchants were attacked by the Byzantines and many were imprisoned on the orders of the emperor. Are we moving toward that again? I hope not. But we must be forewarned and forearmed. Thanks to the way in which Christo has managed the trading house here in Constantinople, we are very successful. In fact, our return cargo may well be one of the best yet. This is why I am proposing that we load what we have acquired and leave in the next few days. Ariella, I know what you might think, but I implore you to hear me out.'

Ariella sat back on her stool, her expression perturbed.

'This is the way of it. The new concessions to the Genovese begin immediately. We suspect they offer money and men to the empire in a time of flux. Being the Emperor's new best friends and with the Emperor aware that the general populace are still concerned at the way in which Alexios III usurped Isaac II, I suspect that the Genovese will grease their wheels with the oil of slander and innuendo against the Venetians. In order to avoid any further nastiness for ourselves, I think it is time to leave. We have an excellent cargo and Ahmed agrees to make both boats ready for imminent departure for any who might want to come.'

'But I have only just arrived. I wished to have my child here...' Ariella seemed nonplussed. 'There is so much I want to do...'

'Ariella,' Michael spoke with calm kindness. 'Leo and I were attacked again – moments ago.'

The table erupted, Tobias becoming even more warlike and Christo holding his mother's hand.

'This is becoming too frequent,' Michael continued, and the household hung off his words. 'There has been barely a day since we arrived that we haven't been under duress. Ariella, you must make your decision for yourself, but I beg you to think of your child.'

'Do you mean for us all to come? To leave Basilike Street empty?' Christo asked. He looked at his mother and the concern on her face was writ large as new wrinkles etched into her skin. 'Because, speaking for myself and my mother, this is our home, the city too. And Gisborne-ben Simon is all I have known for years.' The notary had never seemed so worried, as if all the doors of his life might shut in his face.

'Christo, we would not shut the business down. Far from it. I am proposing that we just take what we have, you know how exceptionally valuable is our cargo, and get it away from the city as soon as possible. I hope that with us gone, the Genovese may leave the house alone. That you can get on with business quietly, as you have always done. I also suspect that ultimately, the Genovese and Venetians will learn to operate alongside each other. But at this time, and if we stay, I foresee trouble for our house.' He knew then that he must throw out the last line, or else he could never bring those who sat before him alongside. 'It appears that the Genovese merchant, Branco Izzo, has pinpointed us and has most lately been consorting with the Arab called Nāsir who was responsible for Ioulia's capture. This is more than just Genovese jealousy and I would not see any here in this room hurt because of personal rivalries. Sadly, I can't say that Izzo and Nāsir feel the same. We could report them to the imperial officers but Izzo has the Emperor's delicate ear. It is doubtful we would receive any assistance.'

When he had mentioned the alliance between Izzo and Nāsir, Tobias had jumped up, ripping his dagger from its scabbard, his face puce with fury. But Ariella took his arm and pulled him back, frowning. Ioulia had paled to the colour of her *skepe*, the obvious happiness of the previous hour swirling away like water down a drain.

'To be frank – all of you must make up your own minds. The guards will be given the same option. Can I ask you one by one?'

There was a nodding, if cautious assent.

'Ariella?'

She rubbed her belly, her expression sad. 'I owe it to my child, to Guillaume and to Father. I will return home. By doing so, I hope that Basilike Street will be left alone to prosper quietly.'

'Toby?'

'Whither Ariella goes, so do I. But I have things I need to do…'

Michael knew exactly what was in Toby's mind and thought, *Not before I get there first, my friend.* 'Christo?'

'We stay. It is our home. But thank you for asking.'

Ephigenia agreed clasping her hands tightly on her knee. 'Phocus will also stay here. I know he will,' she said. 'When he returned to us from the Balkans, he said he was home and would never leave again.'

'Ephigenia, if he stays, I am confident you and Christo will be well looked after. What about you, Ignatios?'

The jeweller played with silver and lapis prayer beads on which a sunbeam caught and flashed. 'I am old, *Kýrie* Michael. And I find I like Basilike Street. If we are well guarded, would I not be as safe here as on the high seas? I have never sailed on a boat and would not wish to die on one.' His fingers moved back and forth across the stones with ill-concealed agitation.

'I understand. You will still be a member of this house, a valued artisan, and you would still be employed to make jewelry for us to sell. If it is your choice to stay here, then I accept that. We will surely thank you for what you have created for us already and we anticipate great things into the future.' He took another long sip of the wine, his throat dry and tacky. 'Well, it seems that apart from those guards who may accompany us, it is only your recent arrivals who leave again, Christo. We will talk more about plans anon, but in the meantime, I would speak with the guards. Will you excuse me?'

He turned toward the door and as he moved away, felt a hand in the crook of his arm, and his daughter's voice behind him. 'Papa, I will go with you.'

Thinking she meant to Venezia, he grinned. 'Of course you will, and I am glad of it.'

They had reached the arbor and she stopped. 'Papa, you did not ask me what I wished to do.' Her expression was complex, and he could read nothing in it and wished he could. The breeze had begun to blow and the cool air off the harbour curled round his neck, tightening fingers. Ioulia shivered and pulled her shawl tighter round her shoulders.

'No,' Michael said. 'I didn't...'

'I have my own mind, Papa.'

'Of course...' he had thought fear and beating hearts were done with for today but it was a fool's thought.'

'Can we sit, Papa? I have barely had a chance to speak with you at all.'

He sat, collapsing onto the trestle under the arbor. 'I am sorry, Ioulia. Business never stops and as you heard, we have been under attack...'

'Yes. I am concerned for you.'

Michael reached for his daughter's hands and held them as if they were wrens' eggs. 'You are safe here, Ioulia.'

'Exactly so, Papa. And if a letter purporting to be from you had not arrived at the convent, I would still be safe there too.'

'I can only apologise...'

'Papa, you don't have to apologise. It is obvious that someone seeks to destroy you and yours. But what I need you to know is that what you are asking me to do, effectively to move to a new world and a new life, is something you once asked my mother and I to do many years ago.'

'Yes, but it won't be like that.'

'It may. It may not. There are never any guarantees in life.' Ioulia spoke with the wisdom of a person many years older and Michael felt as if roles had been reversed – that he was the child and she the adult. 'In any case, Papa, I wish to make my own mind up and before you say anything, I ask that you give me time.'

'There is little time, Ioulia, and besides, I have just found you. I would not lose you again.'

'No matter what, Papa, you will never lose me again. But all I ask is for that little speck of time.' She removed a hand and measured the amorphous moments with her fingers.

What could he say? He was her father and by rights he should be ordering her to do what he wished, not what she wanted. It was the way of it in the wide world. But he closed his fist over hers and nodded. 'I would be a poor father to you if I said no, wouldn't I?'

'Papa, you will never ever be a poor father. I am the most fortunate of daughters.'

He kissed her forehead. 'Go back to the others and I will speak with the guards and then join you.'

She walked away, Ariella's gown folds swinging around her and he watched her go. She had been damaged beyond belief and yet still managed to be calm, even self-assured. He was so proud of her strength, but he would never let her tribulations go unavenged. Never... the black blood of hate began to flow faster.

CHAPTER FOURTEEN

✕

Phocus sat tending his armour and weapons, metal and leather bits scattered across the table in the guards' quarters. The quarters were cramped but functional, and there were never the full complement of men inside anyway, as they completed their rotations guarding the house. Phocus rubbed hard at the leather and metal *klivanion*, buffing it, despite the dents, stains and scratches. 'It's precious to me,' he said. 'Although it looks as if it has had better days. Can I help you?'

'Leo has not told you what passed between Contarini and myself?'

'Some thereof, yes…'

'But not that I intended to ask all the guards if they wanted to leave the city and come to Venezia when we leave in a few days?'

'No. He is nothing if not discreet.'

'Then I ask you, and all the others. Would you wish to come?'

Phocus folded the cloths and began buckling straps and sheathing weapons. 'For me it is easy. I have family here. I will stay. Do you wish to keep the house in business and guarded?'

Michael responded, telling Phocus that he would still be the head of Basilike Street's security. 'Shall we ask the others, then?'

Hilarius and Leo sat in the sun, cleaning their own weapons. It gave Michael confidence that they took their employment seriously enough to do what all militia did in spare moments – keeping that which mattered to theirs and others' lives up to the mark. He asked them what he had asked Phocus.

Hilarius spoke first. 'For myself, I will stay. I like Basilike Street and always enjoy working with Phocus. I would miss him in Venezia.'

'Leo?' Michael enquired.

'If my friends do not see this as turning my back on them, I would come to Venezia. I have not seen the city and besides, methinks you need me at your back, Michael.' He winked and Michael was relieved. He liked the big nomad from Khorasan and thought he could only be an asset on their travels. He knew Ahmed would be delighted.

Bonus said he would stay at Basilike Street, if his presence was required, but Julius declared a hankering to sail the Adriatic again and to seeing his home of Cyprus. Would Michael allow him to sail with the great Ahmed? It was said with a grin and Michael agreed. So, two of their steadfast guards to accompany them – he was glad. And relieved too that Basilike Street would have a strong compliment to care for the house and for Christo and the elderly Ephigenia and Ignatios. A good outcome surely, in difficult times.

For once he felt that things were being administered the way he had once hoped, the way he used to work before he had stepped foot on Constantinople's shores and his life had fallen about his ears. He took a breath and thanked the men for their time.

He limped back to the hall to sit with the others over the remains of the meal, praying for peace and quiet afterward, a moment to plan. Until he had his ulterior motive laid out in his head, he had no space to talk administration with Christo. Revenge required unmitigated and scrupulous attention.

People with full stomachs and news to digest often drift away to quiet corners. Perhaps to pick up a needle and thread, or to play softly with a tired old lute. Maybe to play chess or just daydream. Michael watched the household go their separate ways, Ariella and Ioulia walking up the stair, discussing some embroidery that Ariella wished to try. He thanked God for the way Ioulia had fitted in – like fingers in the most perfectly stitched doeskin gloves, and then caught himself up short.

Thank God?

Was that all it took to make him believe in God's goodness again? For Ioulia to be returned to him? He tried to rationalise it and soon realised that some things couldn't bear the unpicking. So be it. He thanked God.

But he couldn't thank God for what had happened to Ioulia between the convent and Basilike Street. Walking to the arbor which was blessedly empty of any of the household, he pulled Anwar's letter from his purse, unfolding it and reading, longing to puke away the midday meal.

To Michael Sarapion from your friend and physician Anwar al Din, greetings.

What I am to tell you are not the kind of facts a father wishes to hear and I must beg your pardon to be the one who must make you heartsore. I wished to tell you personally, but I am called to the Palace imminently which makes the writing of this message even harder.

Fatima examined Ioulia and talked with her. It seems she was ill-used both by Nāsir *and by the man accompanying him.*

You should know that Ioulia is unable to conceive since the birth of her only child many years previous. A blessing, I believe.

She is a strong woman, healthy of body and sound of mind and otherwise shows no marks of her travail. Fatima believes her commitment to her faith is part of her strength and that she will rise above this travesty.

I tell you of this because it is your right to know and I ask that you trust in your God, Michael. Ioulia is in the safest hands.

Bismillah Arrahman Arraheem

Trust in my God? Really, he thought? My daughter was raped for years as a slave and has once again been raped, not once but twice as she was abducted. And yet there she was today – sweet and as sparkling and pure as water from the mountains. How can that be?

He wished he could be so accepting of what life throws at one, but he knew he never could. Never would either, until wrongs had been righted. Had his daughter had the moral fibre to forgive her attackers and put their fate in God's hands? Is that what God intended? For the punishment to come from the hands of the attacked woman's father? What Divine irony. Perhaps God saw things his way after all. Maybe God wanted to share in his plan.

He sat cossetting his knee, pedantically folding Anwar's note into smaller and smaller pieces. Opening it up again and tearing it in half and tearing the halves in half and half again until a pile of tiny pieces lay before him. The rub of it all and the Divine irony indeed was that he had no plan.

271

Twelve years of dreaming of revenge and it had always been coloured merely by the act of plunging a sword into Nāsir's belly, drawing it down and allowing the coils of his gut to splay forth in a pool of blood. Watching the horror on the man's face as his sword was withdrawn and then turning his back and walking away and knowing the man had little time to live, and all those moments filled with raging fear.

But there had never been a plan. Just the thought that one day he would find Nāsir and kill him and now that day was here. Only this time he must find the second man and kill him as well. In the back of his mind was a thought about Branco Izzo but he shifted it to the side, where it cast no shadows. Just for the moment.

'Michael! Michael!' Ariella hurried from the hall to where he sat, her veil flying out behind her, Ioulia on her heel. 'Michael, I have had terrible news!'

Ariella sat, Ioulia by her side, both women white and shaken as she laid a message on the table. 'It is from Fatima…'

Michael's heart stopped as he waited for what he thought was the inevitable.

'Pieta Izzo is at Death's door.' Ariella said, her words rushing out, breathless and concerned. 'She has lost her babe, a boy, and she is bleeding as we speak. Michael, you know what bleeding means. There is no hope. Should I go…'

Relief? Yes, relief!

'No! No, you must not. You are with child. A child that has not been granted to Pieta and her husband. To someone like Izzo it will be bitter salt in the wound. It is kindness to offer but you must leave this to Fatima and stay well away.'

'Michael, she was so lonely…'

'I understand. But in truth, my dear, you must look to your own.' He watched her hand rubbing her belly. 'Trust me in this.'

Ioulia slipped her hand through the crook of her arm. 'Ariella, let us go to Ephigenia. I would guarantee she has just the kind of thing to revive us after such a shock. We might perhaps pray for God to intercede for Pieta. There is nothing else to be done but believe she is in His safe hands.'

The two women left his presence and he found he could not sit still, anxious for Ariella, afraid for her babe, filled with hate for Izzo, thinking it served him right after daring to abduct Ioulia, and distraught with rage at

Nāsir, everything stretching every fibre of his being to pure bloodlust.

The gates were open, he could hear Bonus shouting to someone on the corner and he found he could slip through unseen, no one calling after him. He walked away from the direction of Little Mese, relying on the pedestrians to shield him from observation, amazed that he had managed to get away without so much as a blink from a guard, feeling at his side for his sword, aghast that he had nothing but a dagger and walking on, knowing that he couldn't go back.

He wound his way back across the hill behind the Contarini villa, down to the Prosphorion Harbour and hailed a *caique* to take him across to Galata. Everything happened so easily, almost as if God smoothed his way. He looked around and could see nothing that he should fear, just the sun gilding the Horn and the perennial call of men on the water. He cursed the lack of blade and asked the boatsman if there was somewhere he could buy weapons and was directed to a maker one street back from Waterfront Street at Galata.

God guides me, surely...

The weapon-maker was mediocre but the *paramerion* would do. It was new, sharp and not too badly balanced. He slipped it through his girdle, having no scabbard, and walked back to Waterfront Street, passed Paradise and where he felt vomit fill his mouth as visions of Ioulia gathered in his mind. He pushed the visions down, setting them as kindling amongst the bloodlusty pit of his soul, walking right to the harbour where boats slid back and forth in the wash from arriving and departing vessels. Men mingled on the docks with purpose – selling, buying, carting, talking. A little further to the edge of the harbour, a small stretch of shingle foreshore flowed into the water, allowing craft to pull up for repairs, propped with great slabs of wood, rolled on logs in and out of the Horn. Across from the dry dock, a small tavern sold wines and syrups and a questionable supply of food, and he sat there now, taking a wine from the tavernkeeper, and sipping, coughing on the bitter acid of badly pressed wines. But glad of the blaze it ignited as it burned into his gut. It might stoke the fires of anticipation even more. Just enough for clarity of vision so that he could examine each and every face close by the *dromon* which was pulled ashore and which he knew was Nāsir's.

Time passed. From the basilica of Saint Paul on the foothill of Galata, he heard the Ninth Hour liturgy sung by resonant voices and knowing the words, he mouthed them. As he studied each and every man, the chant gave him a certain pleasure, anchoring him to his task.

O Christ God, at the ninth hour You tasted death in the flesh for our sake: mortify the rebellion of our flesh and save us!

In the midst of two thieves, Your Cross was revealed as the balance-beam of righteousness.

For while the one was led down to Hell by the burden of his blaspheming, the other was lightened of his sins to the knowledge of things Divine. O Christ our God, glory to You!

Hooked noses and snub, light skin and dark, turbaned and bare-headed, bald and hirsute – none were Nāsir. He threw back the last of his wine, lay down some coins and slipped away. If he acknowledged anything, it was that the long shadows and deep dark of night approached with speed, too fast for his liking but he trusted in Fate – just this once.

He walked up a lane leading away from the harbour, finding more shadow than he wanted but pleased to see many of the seamen and carpenters using this way as a shortcut. He eased himself into a deeply incised doorway where the door was locked, barred and sheathed in cobwebs. It suited his purpose and he watched men track back and forth, listening to their voices because in voice there was dimension and he would never forget Nāsir's.

His attention was rewarded in a heartbeat as two men walked along the alley carrying a plank each. Both were thin, with plain *keffiyehs* covering their heads and even as they passed, their body odour filled the alley – rank with sweat, even piss. Michael's lip curled.

'Nāsir will whip us to shreds…' one whined.

'Not our fault that the planks were not ready,' the other replied.

'He waits on the boat and his temper is as foul as his shits.'

The whining one spat, the gob of sputum landing close to Michael's toes, and they hurried on, the planks swaying on their shoulders.

Michael pulled away from the door, walking back to the tavern, this time sitting turned toward the *dromon*, trying to see the man he hated.

There…

Nāsir shouted at the two men, swearing, ordering others to grab the planks and start work, lashing the men with his tongue, tearing strips off.

His abuse travelled far and wide and Michael gloried in it.

More honorable than the cherubim and beyond compare more glorious than the seraphim; who without corruption gavest birth to God the Word, the very Theotokos, thee do we magnify.

And then Nāsir looked up, across the shore, over Waterfront Street to the tavern, his eyes meeting with Michael's. Michael's hand slipped to the hilt of the *paramerion*, but he kept his seat, his gaze fixed on the Arab. Daring him.

Nāsir broke first, his shoulders stiff, his face cut through with malicious intent as he spoke to a man who might have been his second, pointing to the shore and then beginning to climb down off the vessel. Michael slipped up the alley, unafraid now that the moment approached. The alley emptied into a small square which had an exit toward Saint Paul Street and he walked to the Saint Paul's end, turned and waited, leaning against a faded timber wall, hearing nothing but women's voices within the properties surrounding him.

He scanned his body and it hummed with burning anticipation. Even his knee which must surely be as lame as ever, had not noticeably pained him. The power of vengeful ambitions, he thought.

Footsteps echoed up the lane, one man only.

When Nāsir appeared, Michael took his cue, turned his back on him and walked swiftly along the exit, hearing the Arab following. In Saint Paul Street, there were more people, the usual hubbub of folk moving through the routines of the day – men and women, even of the cloth, moving this way and that and Michael wove through them, knowing that Nāsir followed behind as sure as night followed day. The connection between them was now recognised and there was only one way for it to be severed...

Michael passed the house in which Nāsir had lain so ill the day before, walking on until he reached the small basilica of Saint Paul, turning up the side to the slope above Galata, where there lay a small church precinct – a cemetery and a small orchard filled with Armenian apricot trees, almond and hazelnut trees. The blossoms filled the air with a spicy aroma, petals fluttering like the finest white and flesh-coloured silks in the light breeze off the water. Swallows swooped under the eaves of the basilica and doves paraded along the paths between the graves. Tranquillity was foremost, the noise of Saint Paul Street hovering below. At the top of the orchard, Michael turned. Nāsir had opened the gate and stood watching him, but there was another with him and Michael's heart lurched.

He drew his *paramerion* and called out. 'Go home, Izzo, to your ailing wife where you are sorely needed. This does not involve you.'

'My wife needs me less now than she ever did. I leave her in the hands of priests and God. You on the other hand...' Izzo snarled.

'Then my heart goes to your wife who is dying as we speak, after trying to birth your son. I honour her. You and Nāsir on the other hand...' Michael replied in a flat, almost bored voice.

It was like throwing a flame on oil and the two men growled and began to walk steadily up the hill, one on one side of the dainty cemetery, one on the other. Michael refused to countenance the odds, all he could do was fight like the Devil possessed and if nothing else, take down Nāsir in the doing. He realised that he was in a blind spot to the two oncoming men owing to a turn in the path, and he used that to an advantage, bending low behind a headstone and moving far to the right, where he would stand concealed as Nāsir rounded the corner. Izzo would still not be able to see Michael until he had ventured closer to where Michael actually stood.

Perhaps the two men had miscalculated, not realising the after almost twelve years in Constantinople, Michael knew every kink in the landscape like the wrinkles on the palm of his hand. Saint Paul's was no idle choice.

Petals fell and still the swallows chittered around him, unaware of the murder that was about to take place. Nāsir's feet moved softly but in a mere muted heartbeat, he emerged at the bend and Michael lifted the *paramerion* in a dark two-handed stroke, cutting down hard. He hit Nāsir in the shoulder joint, cutting deep into the leather and metal of his *klivanion*. But not enough, damn it! Nāsir yelled, spinning around, his blade clashing against Michael's, he repeated the strike but Michael was quick, following through with his own edge, down into Nāsir's leg, feeling the weapon slow as it hit substance and hearing Nāsir's scream of fury.

Blood began to flow, to lie on the path in the sun, and the birds fell quiet as Michael listened for Izzo's approach. Nāsir panted, re-engaging, coming at Michael with two swift left and right parries, despite his ugly shoulder wound, but Michael fended them off, moving back off the path and up the hill, with the purpose of keeping clear of Izzo who must surely be near. His knee buckled slightly as he stepped backward but he commanded the joint not to fold, to allow him to climb the incline. Sweat had gathered on his forehead and began to trickle down his temples, down the side of his face. He longed to wipe it away but was eager to get higher in order to defend himself.

Nāsir was bleeding heavily, but there had been no cursed and fatal blow, only enough to slow him and give him pause for thought, leaving Michael to deal only with the Genovese whose footsteps could be heard running from the left, across the hill contour. He raised his *paramerion,* fury incarnate, and Michael began to feed the fury, keeping the man's mind busy. If he needed to think to speak, he would think less about duelling.

'Does Gisborne-ben Simon concern you, Izzo?' Michael chided. 'Are we too successful? Do we outdo you? Do you crave our cargoes?'

'Crave your cargoes? Some spice and oils? Why so?' Izzo moved in closer, slashing in a downward sweep to Michael's arm. Michael jumped back, and the Genovese's blade sparked on the top of a headstone. The discordant harmony of blade and stone filled the pathway and more petals fell, landing on the Genovese's short velvet tunic.

'You covet our success,' Michael goaded. 'Why else do you pursue us? You attack us, over and over, and then you try to abduct my daughter.' Strike, parry strike! Izzo whirled his blade toward Michael, Michael surprised at the weapon skill.

Not just a trader then and where is Nāsir?

'Covet you? You son of a bitch. Led by a Jew woman!' Another strike, this time blade grazing the skin of Michael's wrist leaving a red trail behind. Michael reached for the insignificant dagger by his side.

'A Jew with child,' Michael replied, gauging his attacker's skill. 'A healthy widow. It seems unfair does it not, that her house has the interest of all the west. You covet that, do you not?'

Izzo's face had flushed, bloodlust and hate spreading across the thin planes. His lip curled and he stood still for a moment, gathering his breath. 'This isn't covetousness,' he snarled. 'This is revenge. I will kill you because the house of Gisborne-ben Simon killed my brother in arms, my family – brother of my wife.' Izzo came on then, sword swinging like a dervish and Michael parried every stroke, wondering where the greasy Arab had slid to.

Nāsir may be bleeding but the serpent wouldn't leave the fight.

He lifted his sword and it met the edge of Izzo's, metal screeching as the men breathed in each other's faces and then Michael bought the dagger in from the other hand, pushing through velvet into Izzo's side. Izzo grunted and looked down as Michael pulled the dagger free so that he could leap higher still, hearing Nāsir shuffling from the right, knowing that bloodlust alone was propelling the Arab forward.

Michael spun to meet him, catching his blade on the edge of Nāsir's and thinking for the first time, that whilst he had sustained only a scratch and whilst he had scored two meaningful wounds on his enemies, that he was in fact outnumbered and that time was not on his side. They had only to keep him busy, to bait him until he was exhausted and then deliver the final blow. Or blows.

He looked above, a quick glance as he hauled his wretched knee after him, feeling the joint slide dangerously. All that lay between he and Death was a stone wall and so he edged to the fence, dagger held firmly in the left, *paramerion* in his right. Izzo reached forward with a hard strike, catching him on the side, tearing through the damask of his tunic and he sucked in a breath and pulled himself out of the way, parrying – a downward chop that deflected the blade.

Nāsir dragged himself up the hill with difficulty. The wound in his thigh was white fleshed, turned out upon itself and bleeding freely. Michael cursed that he hadn't pierced the son of a bitch deeper to penetrate the vessel through which the Arab's life would have drained. He lifted his *paramerion* again, jabbing forward and puncturing the man's chest, again, not enough, damn it, not enough. His back was now pressed into the stone but he refused to despair.

'We excel when you two cannot. Doesn't that rile you? Think of the money…'

Nāsir now stood next to Izzo, the two sucking in breaths, blood dripping, as Michael stood above them like some towering Angel of Death, rolling the *paramerion* in his grip, dropping the dagger. The blossoms continued to fall delicately amongst them and for one brief moment, Michael caught a subtle movement behind a tree. He stood straight, believing that one of Nāsir's crew, maybe even more than one, had followed. That even now they would storm forward and that he would die on the end of their blades, Ioulia's name on his lips and Jehanne's face in his mind.

'The money?' Izzo sneered. 'We will get everything of Gisborne-ben Simon's, even your *byssus,* when you lie at our feet. We will say you attacked us and that we defended ourselves, that you dared mock me at the death of my wife. I have imperial friends, Sarapion. You are done for and your house with you. Even your daughter.' He laughed then, a chilling, gut-wrenching laugh that raised Michael's hackles wolfskin-high. 'Who I might add, tasted like eastern spices. Nāsir would agree.'

Black blood hurtled through Michael's heart and he leaped forward off the slope onto Izzo, holding his sword in front with two hands, the better to impale the Genovese. He thought he saw Nāsir raise his own blade to slice into Michael as he landed on top of Izzo, heard the Arab yell.

Izzo grunted as Michael's blade entered his chest and the two fell together in a lovers' knot. He grinned at Michael, a sickly smile filled with loathing and blood poured from his mouth, fountaining out as Michael rolled to the side, waiting for Nāsir's strike, trying to turn to defend himself with nothing but bare hands.

Nāsir was crouched, his blade gripped in a bleeding fist.

'You would kill me, brother?' he whined.

Ahmed stood as bold as life, not a speck of dirt or blood on his robes, his bald head gleaming in the soft spring late afternoon light. 'You dare to ask?' was his reply.

'But is blood not thicker than water? Have a care…' Nāsir's tone had lost a little of its edge.

Michael pushed himself up, wrenched his sword from Izzo's chest, blind to the damage, not even looking at the face of the man who had raped his daughter. It was enough that he was dead. Revenge was sickly sweet.

He stood behind Nāsir, listening to the two brothers bait each other and then breathless as Ahmed's glistening *kilij* swooped forth, waiting for the upward gouge from which no man would survive. But Ahmed let the edge kiss his brother's side, a deep kiss to be sure, but not fatal. Not yet.

'That was for my mother,' Ahmed said calmly. He flicked the *kilij* over itself and then swooped in again. 'And that is for my wife and for your son.' Deep cuts to be sure, but still not enough.

279

Nāsir tried to parry, ineffectual moves filled with sweating urgency, a smell of fear drifting from him. Each time, Ahmed would move a fraction, lifting or lowering his blade so that Nāsir missed and swiped empty air. The cockiness had gone and he almost begged. 'But brother, we are family…'

'I think not,' Ahmed said with the chill that Michael remembered. The freeze that made men shiver on the hottest day. 'Tell me, Nāsir, is it true that not many days since, you raped a woman from a convent?'

Nāsir stood silent, his hand trembling as it held his blade.

'That you and your pinned friend on the ground there, abducted her, raped her and then intended to barter some cloth for her life?'

Nāsir dropped to his knees. 'Ahmed, in the name of Allah…'

'You dare to invoke the name of Allah? You who have broken every pillar of our Faith?'

'I beg of you…'

Ahmed began to turn away. 'Michael, he is yours.'

As the mention of rape hung on the air, a winter frost had flooded through Michael with the speed and tumultuousness of a snow slide in the mountains, demolishing all in its path.

He saw the two men taking their turns with his precious daughter, had seen the way she removed her soul from her experience as she was subjected to such fear and pain. Briefly he wondered if her calm in the face of everyone at Basilike Street was a defence against life. He remembered a young girl who had stood on the pier in Sozopolis, laughing at her father's *paramerion*, the one with which he had girded himself as they left for the journey into the rest of their lives. He felt the hilt of the newly acquired weapon in his hands, his grip tightening, and as Nāsir began to scrabble on his knees to stand, Michael approached him from behind and with little care, reached over and slit the man's throat.

He let Nāsir fall, walking down the path after Ahmed, stopping only to puke his guts dry next to a tombstone. At the bottom of the hill, where swallows dipped and blossoms fell, Ahmed waited, wiping his *kilij* back and forth on tufts of spring grass.

'You are covered in blood. How much of it is yours?' he asked.

'Some…'

'You are hurt?'

'Am I? I don't know…'

Twelve years of hate, all gone. He wondered what God thought.

'Anwar waits inside the basilica.'

But he was numb, could barely feel Ahmed take his arm to lead him inside.

'An Arab in a Christian church,' he said inconsequentially as he saw Anwar sitting to the side of the basilica in the light of candles, and as he spoke he folded, aware only of Ahmed catching him and then nothing more.

He woke to a sharp sensation in his side, hands holding him still.

'Don't move,' Anwar's voice pierced his consciousness. 'I am stitching. Stay still.'

He sank back, letting the physician do what he must.

'I don't approve of what you have done,' Anwar offered into the deeply shadowed silence of the basilica.

'I don't seek your approval, Anwar.' His throat was dry and the words cracked.

'Indeed. Perhaps only your God's.'

'Perhaps.'

Anwar knotted the thread and cut it, placing a clean wad of folded linen over the wound and then swaddling Michael in linen strips. 'I have heard from Ariella that Guillaume died of such a wound. You are lucky, Michael, that yours is not as deep. Even so, you will need to watch how you move. As to your knee – I hold out little hope, you will always be lame and I can claim without argument that you have not been my most successful patient. Shall you tell Father Symeon what has transpired?'

'No. He will guess when the bodies are found. We will not be identified, Ahmed?'

'No. Michael, the boats are loaded. I want to be in Gallipolis before dark tomorrow.'

'I see no issue,' Michael pushed himself up. 'I apologise to you both for fainting.'

'You are injured,' Anwar said as he packed his supplies away. 'Men faint, it happens. Frankly, I think you are lucky on two counts. One that Ahmed had the sense to even follow you this day and the other, that he sent a message for my attendance. May I ask – do you plan to tell Ioulia what has transpired today?'

'No.'

'And she leaves tomorrow?'

Michael looked at Anwar, surprised at the baldness of the question. 'Of course...' he replied.

Τέλος
(END)

×

He sensed Ariella behind him as he stood at the wale. They had left Gallipolis behind, loaded with the spices and pigments that Yusuf Al Fayaad had stored for them, sailing toward the straits where the Propontis joined the Adriatico. They sailed in their own personal convoy, *Durrah* and *Sada*, with Ahmed helming the vessel on which Michael stood, Tobias by his side and Faisal helming the other, Leo and some newly acquired crew providing the muscle. Beneath *Durrah,* the sea creamed, split asunder by the polished bow. The sea was calm, a blessing he felt, but here and there was an odd wave break as the water churned in small whirlpools from the outward flowing current between the twin points of land.

The vessel broached slightly, Ariella stumbling against him and he reached around to steady her. The action pulled at his wound and he unwittingly hissed at the pain.

'Do you hurt?' she asked, thanking him and standing beside him, gripping the wale, her veil tossing back behind her, annoying her so that she ripped it off and crunched it in one hand.

'Yes.' He looked down at the water. 'I hurt everywhere in truth.'

'Do you remember standing with me not far from here, as you warned me about the sea giving and taking?'

'I do,' he replied.

'Do you still feel the same?'

It was a personal question and dug deep into the wounds in his heart.

He didn't want to answer, wanted to tell her to leave him alone, to let him dwell on what had transpired. But he was never a rude man and she had been so kind to Ioulia. In any case, he admired her. There she was, heavily pregnant, sailing back and forth on the trade routes with no fear or worry. He had no doubt Gisborne-ben Simon would survive and move forward under her eventual stewardship.

'The sea took my family from me, Ariella. And I don't see that the sea has given me Ioulia back...'

'But she is not dead,' Ariella replied. She was nothing, if not forthright.

'No...'

'Would you rather not speak of it, Michael? I would leave you if it is the way of it.'

He thought he never wanted to talk of it again, but then he was surrounded by what was as near to family as he could have, and it was only right they should know why his daughter had not left the city with them. Why would he not share that?

'She decided to stay, Ariella. Against everything I believed, she rejected me and what remained of our family for something else.'

'Tell me,' Ariella touched his arm and he looked down at her elegant embroiderer's fingers. Just like Ioulia's.

'When we returned from Galata, you and she had gone with Julius to Xylinites. That surprised me and did not sit well...'

'Iisoús Christós! You are so bloody, Kýrie Michael!' Ephigenia exclaimed. 'Have you been in another fight?'

He dared not tell her that he had killed two men, that he had been wounded, that he ached with exhaustion and pain and that all that had kept him whole was the thought his daughter was waiting for him.

'Where is Ioulia?' He needed to know she was with those who paved her way with familial love and care. Especially now.

'She and Ariella left earlier with Julius,' the old housekeeper replied. 'They thought to pray for the soul of that poor Izzo woman, and where better than with the nuns of the convent?'

Not right, thought Michael. Not right at all. For a start, Ariella was a Jew. She would hardly be likely to pray in a Christian church. And it was late. Dusk was almost done. 'I see,' he replied, although he did not.

'And dear little Ioulia wanted to show Ariella the exceptional embroideries they do at Xylinites. Something about the Patriarch's vestments and many others.' Ephigenia grinned from her sparsely toothed mouth and moved on with her arms full of laundry, leaving Michael bloodstained and concerned. 'I suspect the three will stay overnight. Xylinites has travellers' quarters. No doubt a message will arrive any moment, so don't look so worried. Go clean yourself. And then give me your washing. You look like a butcher!'

He went to his room, Ioulia's room, looking at how neat she had left it. Not a sign that she had even been there, and his heart turned over. A lamp glowed, welcoming any who entered the room, Ephigenia's doing no doubt. The jug was filled with cool water and he poured it into the bowl, stripping off his clothes, folding them into a bundle. He took a plain linen square and began to wash his face first, then his hands and arms. There wasn't much blood, it was mostly over his clothes but when he ran the cloth over his body, he came to the wound in his side which Anwar had stitched and bound. There was a faint stain on the new dressing and he knew he would have to be careful not to open up the deep slash.

He pulled on clean under garments, a sparkling chemise, a deep green ankle-length tunic which he belted with a leather and damascened silver girdle. Sucking in a breath, he bent against the pull of the stitches and dragged on soft leather boots. No weapons. No need. His enemies were done.

It was dark now, stars beginning to fill a pristine night sky with a new moon standing upright and clear in the cloudless heavens. He needed to ride to Xylinites this night because he needed the women back and packed. He needed to be gone from this city.

He needed to introduce Ioulia to her new home and a safe and gentle life.

And he desperately needed Jehanne.

When he walked to the gates, Leo stood armed and formidable. A good sign.

'Michael?' he turned, surprised to see his employer cleaned and presentable so quickly after allowing a bloodier version through the gates earlier. Michael spoke quickly and to the point.

'Now?' Leo queried. 'In the dark? In curfew? The city gates will be locked.'

'Leave that to me. Hopefully God might be on our side.'

And now I speak with God in mind as though he is my ally. How times have changed…

'I need horses, Leo.'

'I can arrange,' Leo replied. 'Give me a short while. I will fetch Bonus to take over my watch and you will wait here. You can tell me about the blood and injury as we ride.'

One never argued with the implacable Leo, Michael knew that. Better to just do as one was told. There was so much about the man that reminded him of Petrus, of home. It was like an ache that would not go away.

They wound their way noisily, clip-clop, over the hills of the city to the Charyisia Gate. Soldiers leaned against the walls, yawning and surprised to see men on horseback requesting exit. They looked at each other in the light of the torches and one ran inside the gatehouse to fetch a senior officer.

The man came out, tetchy, grumbling and Michael breathed. So far so good…

I thank you, Lord, my God, that you have not rejected me, a sinner, but have made me worthy to partake of your holy Mysteries.

The man was the officer of previously, when he had sped to Xylinites with Phocus, searching for Ioulia.

'Ah…' the officer said tiredly.

'I beg your ear and your leniency, sir,' Michael said. 'I have had news that my relative, who you may remember was in the Convent of Xylinites, is worse and like to die. I seek leave to hurry to her bedside before it is too late.' To add to the charade, the horse obligingly stepped quickly sideways, jerking Michael in the saddle so that his voice tightened with pain. The very sound of a man who is upset.

'But you have no paperwork.'

'I do not. I was so shocked, because she was well the last we heard, able to move from her bed. All I did was grab my man and our horses as we left my house in Basilike Street. It mattered only that we get to Xylinites as swiftly as we are able. Please, sir, if you have a heart, allow us through. Think of your own family…'

Pleading. I thought I was done with that. Help us now, Oh Lord.

The officer rubbed at his eyes, longing to return to his cot, signalling his men to allow Leo and Michael through. 'I wish you and your family member well. Goodnight.' He turned away, caring nothing it seemed, for Michael's family or his own, or maybe remembering that Michael claimed connection in the imperial court. Either way, they were through and Michael whipped his reins either side of his surprised mount's neck and launched into a dust-eating gallop, Leo at his shoulder.

'You lie well, Michael,' he shouted. 'Perhaps it is your ability to dissemble that allowed you to vanquish your enemies today.'

Michael said nothing, just rode grimly on to the Lycus river, thundering over the bridge and dragging his horse to a sliding halt outside the gates. He threw his reins to Leo and hammered on the studded wood until the grille slid open and the ugly gatekeeper stared back at him.

'You are not welcome here,' she said sourly.

'I must see the hegoumene.' *Perfunctory at best. He made no allowances for nuns, offering no etiquette. He needed entry.*

'She has retired for contemplation.'

'Get her now. Or I will hammer this gate until the whole convent is disturbed.'

The gatekeeper knew enough of Michael from the last occasion to realise he spoke as he meant, and slammed the grille shut. They heard her slip-slop in her sandals, across the paved forecourt. It seemed an age before she sloped back, but this time she had a companion and the gate was opened.

'Kýrie Michael Sarapion…'

'I need to see my daughter.'

The hegoumene *sighed. 'Your timing is always a little out, sir. Sister Ioulia…'*

Sister? Michael's brow creased.

'…has retired to her dormitory. Her friend, the Jewess, is in our travellers' quarters and their guard sleeps in the stables. Perhaps come back tomorrow…'

'It is true, Michael,' Ariella broke in. We met with the *hegoumene*, and she kindly allowed Ioulia to show me the embroideries which were beautiful. Ioulia should be very proud of her work. And then we had a small repast with the Sisters who although restrained in their welcome, showed immense affection for Ioulia. And she them. It was time for Ninth Hour prayers and Ioulia asked me to excuse her. I thought nothing of it and she went to the basilica with the other Sisters. I was of course, prevented from following because of my faith, which I accepted. But then it was dark, one could hear the convent going through its nightly motions and I didn't see Ioulia again. Not even a message from the *hegoumene*. I couldn't seek out Phocus and had no choice but to wait until the morning. But of course, you arrived, *which*

I heard I might add and … well, I know nothing more. That journey with you, back to Basilike Street was rather wracked with questions.' Ariella spoke softly. 'But Leo and Phocus said it was best to leave you alone.' Her hand touched his arm and she added, 'Which is why I appreciate you speaking with me now.'

He gave a small half laugh, an empty sound, filled with the heart ache that consumed him. Thank God for being at sea! He was glad for the tangy fragrance of sea air that stripped one's insides clear of murk when one breathed deep. He was grateful for the beauty of the seabirds as they dipped and dived with infinite grace around the vessel. And he was glad to be in another world entirely because the world of Constantinople had almost consumed him, and he a man who had lived on the edge for almost his whole lifetime and survived. He returned to his words and Ariella stood quietly by his side.

'I am unable,' he answered the hegoumene. *'Our ships leave in the early afternoon and I need everyone ready to depart. I apologise for interfering with the convent's schedule, but I have my own. Now if you will fetch Ioulia.'*

The hegoumene's *mouth flattened but she ordered the gatekeeper to take Leo to the stables. 'Walk with me, Kýrie Michael,' she said and led the way across the torchlit forecourt to a door. They entered the cool basilica, the interior of which flickered and danced in the light of many lamps, rich colours and slashes of gold flaring off the icons and then disappearing as they moved to a further door, entering a whitewashed chamber. The air of monasticism lived and breathed with the paucity of furnishing, the floor covered in two goatskins, one each lying in front of two long wooden seats facing each other. On the wall was an icon of the Theotokis and Her child, looking down upon whomever sat on the seats, a compassionate gaze, holding them in an eternal blessing.*

'Mother Irene, I realise that every time you see me, I am distraught and offensive and thus I ask for your forgiveness. But it is so very important that I speak with my child. Have pity on a father and his daughter, in the name of She who watches us now.' He indicated the icon and then let his hands drop to the sides, fists balled with nerves. Everything seemed wrong when it should have felt so very right. Vaguely, he wondered if his misdeeds were being tallied and he closed his eyes momentarily. He was surprised to feel dampness in the corners and blinked swiftly. He would not have the hegoumene *see his weakness.*

She waved her hand. 'It is no matter. You love your child. That I see. Sit Kýrie Michael and I will call Ioulia. You both need to heed each other.'

Heed? What do you mean?

But he sank onto the bench seat without protest, glad to rest his leg, his side, his whole damned body. His mind though? That was another thing. The hegoumene left and he closed his eyes; he had no wish to engage with the icon of the Theotokis. If She had any compassion at all, She would know what was in his heart. He listened to his breath, to the quiet of the convent, just resting…

'Papa? Papa, wake. It is I…'

He woke with a start, astonished to even think he had fallen asleep sitting on that hard bench. Like some old man, frail and lost. The hegoumene sat opposite and Ioulia subsided next to him. He blinked, rubbed at his eyes and apologised.

'There is no need to apologise, you are very tired, I can see.' She reached forward and traced under his eyes. 'You have shadows here and lines here,' her fingers ran from his nose to his mouth.

He realised that she had changed. Her clothing was not the soft folds of Ariella's gowns but the faded black of a nun's robe, and on her butchered hair, she had tied a skepe.

He began to speak but she interrupted. 'Papa, it is I who must speak first. Please allow me this time.' She took a big breath, looked briefly at Mother Irene who nodded, and began.

'Papa, I am not departing to the west with you. I plan to stay here at the Xylinites Convent. No, do not speak – let me say what I must. When I was brought here by Father Symeon, after my initial time at the Lips Convent, I truly felt the closest thing to a homecoming since I left Sozopolis. It was soul-deep, as if God, the Theotokis and the Christ Child, even the Saints and Angels welcomed me into their embrace. It was enlightening. With each passing day, as a lay worker, I felt my load diminish. I was able to give to this place with my stitching skill and slowly, as I took part in prayer, I realised that I wanted something more. I wanted to become a part of God's life.'

She looked between the hegoumene and Michael, never once faltering. He sat silent and hopeless, knowing that almost everything he had experienced in the last few days had been for nothing.

'It was discovered that I could sing and when I partook of the liturgies, I was transported to a place that even now, I cannot describe, and I knew from *the first that I was to become a nun. When you arrived, I had almost completed my novitiate. Papa, I beg you to understand.' She took his hand and something cool and moist dripped onto it and he was surprised to see tears washing his skin. Were they hers or his? Perhaps both. But he nodded for her to continue. He owed her that.*

'When the false note came, Mother Irene gave me leave to go to you, to see you, to explain what I was. Sadly, it did not transpire as any of us might have hoped...' Her fingers gripped Michael's hand and he immediately responded, holding her wet and trembling face in both his hands.

'Ioulia, I am so very sorry...'

'It is not your fault,' she said. 'They are evil men and they will be judged. But Papa, you need to know that it was my beliefs that sustained me at that time and it is my beliefs that sustain me now. I am making the right decision to remain here to finish my novitiate and move on into the convent.'

Michael cleared his throat, holding her hands in his own, trying hard to hold back a flood of words. Instead he picked carefully through the rocks and boulders of his emotions, looking for small shining gems that would only ever illuminate this immense moment. 'I accept your choice, Ioulia. Who am I to forbid it? You are a grown woman with a lifetime of experience. Only you know what is right for your future. I could sweep you up, take you back to Lyon by force, place you in a convent there. To what purpose? You and I have a loving bond. And whilst I am jealous of the Divine hold upon you, I can't gainsay it...'

Ioulia began to cry, big shaking breaths and the hegoumene *reached forward with a linen square. 'Do not upset yourself, my dear,' she said. 'You are safe and your father and I are with you.'*

Michael turned to Ariella. 'And I cannot understand if the *hegoumene* meant I was Ioulia's father or that God was. In any case,' he said quietly. 'It matters little.'

'You will always be her father, Michael. No one can take that away.' Ariella folded her creased veil with difficulty in the breeze and then turned her back on the water, leaning against the wale but holding on with the unencumbered hand.

'It is true...'

Ioulia's weeping subsided and she leaned against Michael, resting her head on his shoulder. He knew he would carry the warmth of her for the rest of his life.

'Papa, you have been in my heart since we were parted so long ago. You and Mama, and that won't change. But now, as a grown woman, I choose to work for the love of God. You and Jehanne and Ariella and the whole wonderfully joyous and buoyant house of Gisborne-ben Simon work for trade. And that is your choice. Your right.'

This was his time, he knew. What he said next would break or make any further connection with his daughter.

'Ioulia, you deserve to make a choice that sings for you. If you wish to remain here at Xylinites, I support you with my heart and soul and will make a dowry payment on your behalf. I will miss you...' he stopped and cleared his throat again. 'I will miss you, but I will live in the knowledge that you are happy and complete.'

He turned to her then, Mother Irene not withstanding and enfolded his daughter in such an embrace, knowing all the while that it would come to an end.

Presently they stood, and he kissed her hand, before the hegoumene *guided her to the door...*

'My last sight of my daughter was her back, tall and straight with a veil across her shoulders, as she walked away.' Michael finished.

'Did the *hegoumene* say nothing more?'

'Strangely she did. I had thought she would leave me and send the wretched gatekeeper to collect us and that we would all leave without another word. But she was quite kind.'

'You are a brave and insightful man, Michael Sarapion. I know that your heart bleeds. Can I reassure you that she will live well amongst us? She is committed to service to the Lord and I see her fulfilled at the end of every day. It serves to mollify the pain she has experienced in her life and gives her gentleness when there was none. That is not your fault. It is the perils of the world outside our gates. I thank you and I am sure our Lord thanks you for allowing your daughter to follow her chosen path. Come, I will take you to the stables where your men and your friend, Kyria Ariella wait.'

'I am permitted to write to Ioulia, Ariella. Which gives me great joy. And she is permitted to write to me perhaps once or twice in a year. Messages will be sent through Christo. It is something.'

'It is. But perhaps not enough?'

He sighed. 'I cherished a dream this last year. It didn't transpire and now I must return to my wife and to our business. I have duties...'

'I speak self-evident facts when I say this, Michael, and forgive me for being forthcoming, but you have reassured yourself that Ioulia is safe and well, you have a loving wife and a thriving business to which to return...' She stopped as Tobias shouted, pointing at dolphins looping between *Durrah* and *Sada*. There was something about the creatures that instilled joy in one's heart and she laughed as one leaped out of the water, Toby shrieking with delight. 'And not to belay the finer point, you are surrounded by those who love and admire you, even if they are noisy and opinionated. Can you make it enough?'

He looked down at the radiant woman who had lost the love of her life and he realised that she knew his pain and that she knew also that one can make the best of things in the right circumstances and with the right people.

'Perhaps,' he replied as Toby laughed and shouted again.

Thank you for reading *Michael*. Please consider posting a short review on Amazon and/or Goodreads and social media if you have time.

OTHER BOOKS

The Triptych Chronicle
Tobias – Book One
Guillaume – Book Two

The Gisborne Saga
Book of Pawns
Book of Knights
Book of Kings

The Chronicles of Eirie
The Stumpwork Robe
The Last Stitch
A Thousand Glass Flowers
The Shifu Cloth

Childrens' Books
Nugget the Black Wombat

Short stories
(free via www.pruebatten.com)
The Orchard of Chance
The Moonlady

Anthologies
Historical Tales
Tales from a Carboot Sale
Winter's Edge

You can find purchase points on www.pruebatten.com

Please feel free to connect with me via my email list sign up
and my blog at www.pruebatten.com

You can also connect via Facebook at
www.facebook.com/prue.batten.writer

And for a visual treat that will inspire your journey through my books,
go to www.pinterest.com/pruebatten

AUTHOR'S NOTE

×

When I first began writing Michael's story, it was always planned that he would travel to Constantinople to source rare goods to trade in the west. Of course, I knew his main purpose in making this journey was to find the truth in the rumour that his now adult daughter may still be alive, but the mask of concealment was his role as a merchant. Michael's persona had always been gentlemanly, quiet and well-balanced despite the dreadful losses in his life and I knew if I took up his story that he would change as men do in the grip of trade and vengeful acts.

Within trade there is a shocking undercurrent, as men's self-interest and greed enter the game. Revenge would indeed feature in Michael's story because revenge is a theme in *The Triptych Chronicle* and people/characters lose their lives. Sadly in trade, it is not unlike war – may the best or even the most insidious man win.

And thus, I began my reading…

On rare goods and the extent of the markets. The commodities traded in the twelfth century were so beautiful and perfect that they took my breath away. With each discovery, I felt if I were dipping my fingers into treasure chests. There are images I have saved to a board on Pinterest, should you wish to sink yourself into the visual delights of twelfth century trade in Constantinople: https://www.pinterest.dk/pruebatten/michael/

On the Eastern Church. There is something incredibly tranquil and beautiful about the Orthodox church – its icons, its music and its rituals.

On politics. It seems nothing changes. The use and abuse within the Byzantine court can even to this day, be mirrored in contemporary governments across the globe.

And on human nature. Again, nothing changes. It's all there – greed, hate, love, fear and joy. Grief plays its part in this novel and there is always much conjecture that because medieval/Byzantine folk lived in hard times, they would never experience grief as we know it. But for me, human emotion ranges across the centuries. I was pleased to read this – http://www.medievalists.net/2016/05/grief-and-spiritual-crisis-in-the-middle-ages/

It provides the perfect argument as to why grief would be as strong then as now.

As the framework of the story began to build, the part that was most frustrating was the lack of a commodity so rare, so perfect, that it could almost be Divine. That divinity had to arouse huge jealousies across the trading quarters of Constantinople.

One day, on Facebook, and knowing my love of textiles and embroidery, a writer friend, Australian historical fiction writer, Kathryn Gauci, tagged me on a link she had found about a rare fabric called byssus. https://www.inquisitr.com/4487211/the-delicate-science-of-working-with-coveted-sea-silk-chiara-vigo-is-reportedly-the-last-seamstress-left/

I had never heard of it and was fascinated with its enigmatic nature. Wondering if I had found the rare commodity I needed for this book, I began to research *byssus* and found that its history goes back to Christ, even to the Pharaohs, maybe even earlier still. Trading of the fabric began to be a distinct possibility. I searched for twelfth century references but there was little to be had and so I made the call to use it in this fiction regardless. I personally believe it is entirely within the realms of possibility that *byssus* was traded in my timeframe. Not in great quantities because of its supreme rarity and the refined skill needed to source it, process it and then weave it. But that would surely have only increased its value amongst traders. Thus, I must thank Kathryn for sharing that fateful link.

It is also important to mention that Ariella, the Jew's daughter, and Jehanne, Michael's second wife, even Michael's daughter, Ioulia, together represent the kind of women who are considered very rare in medieval times. Academic theory shows us two types of women – those that stayed wedged in their lives by the strictures of society and those few (eg: Heloise, Hildegarde von Bingen and Anna Komemna to name just three that have always interested me) who stood apart from society and wove their own cloth. My story is fictitious, and within the scope of the fiction I have chosen to make Jehanne and Ariella self-directed, even ambitious, breaking free from the societal cords that bound them. In fact, Sharon Bennett Connolly's recent released monograph 'Heroines of the Medieval World' is most definitely fuel for my fire. There is also primary evidence that women did indeed hold significant places in the world of trade. Many will disagree with me for giving Ariella and Jehanne such independent roles but I can only reiterate that this *is* a work of fiction and I mirrored their journey upon the journeys of other female traders at the time, of which there is evidence.

In addition, as I studied the detail on Arab medicine, I was fascinated to see that woman physicians existed, something that arose from the requirements of Islam. Islam precluded intimate examination of women by male doctors. It is how Fatima emerged in the novel. Arab physicians like Ibn Sina (Avicenna) had established the depth and ground rules of medicine and thus Arabs were well-recognised as the foremost doctors of the time. If one was ill, whether Christian, Arab or Jew, one would most likely have tried to secure treatment from an Arab doctor, knowing that one had the most skilled available.

As I have mentioned in previous novels that have used Constantinople as a setting, finding one's way around the twelfth century city is not easy. Much was wantonly destroyed in the Fourth Crusade and the Ottoman Conquest, and so I have taken what remains and turned the facts to my advantage where possible. The formerly Byzantine Christian churches in Istanbul were converted to mosques after the Ottoman conquest and it requires a new mindset to imagine a city without graceful minarets punctuating the skyline. There has however, been wonderful three-dimensional modelling done of the city on the cusp of the twelfth and thirteenth centuries (http://www.byzantium1200.com) and it remains my go-to reference on a daily basis.

The Palace of Botaneiates was mentioned in the Trade Treaties of 1192 as a gift to the Genovese delegation. Whilst it may most likely have been found close to the gardens of Topkapi Sarayi, I have placed it a little closer to the Venetian Quarter to suit the purpose of my story. My street names are also fictitious, because street names changed through millennia. The actual settings of Galata and Pera were even more difficult, requiring a leap of fictional faith. I hope my readers will accept it.

Judith Herrin's various books (*The Formation of Christendom; Byzantium – The Surprising Life of a Medieval Empire; Women in Purple; Unrivalled Influence*) have been go-to references regularly. In finding a suitable convent outside Constantinople for Ioulia, I was concerned by Herrin's prophetic words *'many others are noted for a single reference and remain unidentified'*. Once again, it seemed I was entering unchartered waters. This is the dilemma that historical fiction writers most often love because it gives them free licence and so I chose to once again make another fiction call, placing one of the 'single reference' nunneries, Xylinites, outside the city in a location of my choosing –west of the River Lycus that flows down into the city. The book ends with Ioulia deciding to return to the lifelong security of Xylinites and I cannot find any reference as to whether the convent survived the Fourth Crusade. Being a 'single reference' convent, my guess is that it did not, which therefore makes Ioulia's final decision an exceedingly tragic one…

The Contarini family had a huge political, diplomatic and religious presence within Venice throughout its medieval and Renaissance history. Whilst there is evidence that they had dealings with Byzantium, there is no evidence of *which* of the family members might have travelled there in 1195. I 'created' a fictitious Contarini – Giacomo – as it suited my storyline. But the Viadro are different altogether. There is evidence that Tommaso Viadro did spend time in Constantinople. He was an intrepid explorer of new trade routes and having conquered the Adriatic, making the Baltic coast his own, he was in fact known to be investigating markets in Syria. It suited my plot to have he, 'Giacomo' and Michael in the same room at the same time. It was one of Dorothy Dunnett's greatest techniques and I enjoyed playing with the dice in such a way and hope it works in this novel.

In addition, the rise of the Genovese influence in Constantinople is well documented. The change began to speed up when Alexios III Angelos usurped the imperial crown by blinding and imprisoning his brother, Isaac II Angelos, in March of the year that Michael arrives back in the city. Historians tell us that the treasury was almost bankrupted as Alexios III bribed his way to acceptance. The court and the Emperor were susceptible to influence from any who offered it. The Genovese thus began their rise to trading eminence.

It should also be noted that I have used the quotation *'The apple doesn't fall far from the tree'*, that we use readily today. According to the 3rd edition of the Concise Oxford Dictionary of Proverbs, 1998, it is 'apparently of Eastern origin' and used 'to assert the continuity of family characteristics.' I cannot date the expression precisely but feel its eastern origins settle it comfortably in the polyglot society of twelfth century Constantinople.

I should also mention that Tobias sings for polite company at one point and I have taken the legend of Blondel's search for Richard Lionheart as a truth. In researching Blondel's life and times for previous novels, I used *Blondel's Song*, by David Boyle as my reference point. Toby goes on to sing one of Richard Lionheart's own songs at the merchants' banquet. It's reputed to be what Blondel sang in his search for Richard.

In essence, this is a book about Byzantine and medieval trade and the way it impacted the human experience. I have loved writing it and hope that you take away interest and joy from reading it.

Prue Batten

*A*CKNOWLEDGEMENTS

To Simon – always an absolute inspiration and a tremendous friend.

To Libby and to Brian for being my beta-readers.

To Clare Batten, graphic designer, for another atmospheric cover to close the trilogy. Always empathic with her covers.

To my editor John Hudspith, thank you for keeping me in line with such iron fists in velvet gloves.

To JD Smith for formatting so swiftly.

To friends at The Review and to other global friends on Facebook. A veritable fount of information and camaraderie amongst writers and readers.

To my family for being my most loved friends as I scribbled away.

To my Jack Russell who is jealous of all the time spent writing and has a way of curving claws, not so carefully, into the top of my hand and pulling my fingers off the keyboard when he is bored. Often…

And finally, to my husband, who was facing a serious cancer operation when I began this novel in late December of 2016. It usually takes me 12 months to write and release a novel, but 2017 was a convoluted year for us both. I'm in awe of his courage and thank him for finding that ultimate treasure of remission.

Lightning Source UK Ltd.
Milton Keynes UK
UKHW011812250220
359313UK00001B/70